"Laymon always takes ⟨…⟩ m and you're going to have a good time with anything he writes."

—Dean Koontz

"If you've missed Laymon, you've missed a treat."

—Stephen King

"Laymon is Stephen King without a conscience."

—Dan J. Marlowe

"Laymon's writing's super-tight and characters well detailed and believable, which makes the savage termination of so many of them all the more shocking! The unbridled joy of a delightfully fertile and *wicked* imagination at work."

—*Terrorzone*

"Laymon is an American writer of the highest caliber."

—*Time Out* (London)

"Laymon is unique. A phenomenon. A genius of the grisly and the grotesque."

—Joe Citro, *The Blood Review*

B!TE

RICHARD LAYMON

LEISURE BOOKS
NEW YORK CITY

A LEISURE BOOK®

June 1999

Published by

Dorchester Publishing Co., Inc.
276 Fifth Avenue
New York, NY 10001

ISBN 0-8439-4550-8

The name "Leisure Books" and the stylized "L" with design are
trademarks of Dorchester Publishing Co., Inc.

Printed in the United States of America.

This book is dedicated
to
Marshall P. Oliphant

Friend, matchmaker, writer
"Go for it, buddy"

1

Somebody knocked on my door. I opened it, and there stood Cat.

I hadn't seen her in ten years, not since we were both sixteen. But this was Cat, all right. In the flesh. In the flesh and a blue silk bathrobe and apparently nothing else. Her feet were bare. She didn't even carry a purse.

'Cat?' I said.

A corner of her mouth tipped up. 'How are you doing, Sammy?'

I was barely able to stay on my feet. That's how I was doing.

'Come on in,' I told her, and staggered out of the way.

She stepped into my apartment, swung the door shut, then leaned back and rested a hand on the knob. 'It's been a long time,' she said.

I responded with, 'It's great to see you.' Which may have been the understatement of all time. I was *shocked*. I'd loved Cat Lorimer. Though I hadn't seen her since she'd gone off to live in Seattle with her parents all those years ago, I'd dreamed about her plenty. I'd *day*dreamed about her plenty. I'd even toyed with fantasies of looking her up – going on a Cat Lorimer hunt – a pilgrimage in quest of my one-and-only true love.

And here she was.

Right in front of me, appearing out of nowhere in the middle of the night, wearing a royal blue silk robe that matched her eyes.

'You're lookin' good,' she said.

'You, too. You look great.' She also looked tired and a little too thin.

'My God,' she said, 'we were just a couple of kids . . .' Eyes fixed on me, she did her half-smile again and shook her head. 'You recognized me right away, didn't you?'

'Of course.'

'Amazing.'

'You haven't changed much.' She'd changed a *lot*, but not in ways that made her difficult to recognize. She still had hair like sunlight, the same blue eyes, and the pale slit of a scar like a nick on her right cheekbone. Her face was more defined, more mature – in some ways more beautiful – but it was still the face that had haunted my life for the past decade. I would've known it anywhere. And cherished it. 'You look better than ever,' I said.

'You, too,' she said. 'You turned into a man.'

'Yeah?'

'Yeah.' One of her shoulders hopped up and down, sliding the silk against her breast. 'What've you been doing with yourself?' she asked.

'Not much,' I said.

'Married?'

'Nope. You?'

'Not anymore.'

So she *had* been married. I'd suspected as much. Every guy wants a girl like Cat, so it only made sense that one had gotten her. I despised him.

But apparently he was no longer in the picture, which pleased me.

'Divorced?' I asked.

'He was killed about a year ago.'

'Oh.' I scowled as if troubled by the news. 'I'm so sorry.'

'Thanks.' She raised her eyebrows. 'You haven't been married at all?'

'Not yet.'

'Never found the right girl?'

The question slugged me. She seemed to know it, too. Some answers popped into my head. Things like, 'I found her, but she got away.' And, 'I've never wanted anyone but you, Cat.'

Only a guy doesn't say stuff like that. Not unless he wants to look like a jerk.

All I said was, 'Nope. Guess not.'

She made her shoulder hop again. 'So you're basically unattached at the moment?'

2

'Basically.'

'So you could . . . come with me?'

'Come with you?'

'Over to my house.'

'When?'

'Now.'

'Now?'

'Are you all right?' she asked.

'Sure. I think so.'

'I think you're in shock.'

'Maybe a little.'

'I'll drive,' she said. 'My car's out front. Maybe you should get your toothbrush and whatever else you might need for the night.'

'I'm staying overnight?'

'Is that all right?'

'Sure,' I said.

'Do you have a job, or anything?'

'No. Yeah. But it's summer vacation. I teach. So I'm off till September.'

'Great. This'll work out great. If you'd like, you could pack some things and maybe stay for a few days.'

I nodded.

And just stood there, gaping at her.

Nothing seemed quite real.

But real enough. Even though the past three or four minutes seemed like a wish-fulfillment fantasy, I wasn't dreaming. I was awake. Only a lunatic can't tell the difference.

'What's going on?' I asked, surprising myself that I was able to come up, at last, with a sensible question.

'I need your help,' Cat said.

All I needed to hear.

Hell, I didn't *need* to hear that. I would've gone with her, no matter what her answer had been.

'You aren't in some sort of danger, are you?' I asked.

'You might say that. I'll tell you about it on the way over.'

'Okay. I'll go get a few things.'

When I left the living room, Cat was still leaning back against my door. My first stop was the bathroom. Instead of just grabbing my toothbrush, I used it. I couldn't avoid the

3

mirror; it was straight in front of my face while I scrubbed my teeth. My hair was shaggy and mussed. I had a two-day growth of whiskers. My T-shirt was coming apart at the seam in front of my left shoulder, and its faded front showed a turkey vulture looking dour. The caption under the vulture read, 'Patience, my ass. I'm gonna kill something.'

I looked like a bum.

The last thing I had expected, that night, was a surprise visit from the only girl I'd ever loved.

Sprucing myself up would've taken too long, so I only brushed my teeth. Then I took my toilet kit into my bedroom, dragged an overnight bag out of my closet, and started to throw things in.

'Don't bother to change,' Cat called from the living room. 'You're fine the way you are.'

I wasn't so sure about that. But maybe a nasty old vulture T-shirt and ragged blue jeans were appropriate attire for whatever brand of 'help' she required. Socks were not, so I put sneakers on over them. Then I pocketed my wallet and keys, and hauled my bag into the living room.

Cat was standing in front of my bookshelves, her back to me. She didn't look around. 'I see you're still a reader,' she said.

'Yeah.'

'I remember that. You never went anywhere without a paperback.' Turning her head, she smiled and gave her right buttock a smack through the clinging robe. 'Here in your pocket. Even when you took me out. You wrote such beautiful poetry.'

'I've mostly switched to prose.'

She turned around. 'Do you still have that old copy of *Dracula*?'

'Sure. Somewhere. I never get rid of a book.'

'It got all wrecked by the rain.'

'I still have it,' I said. There was a tightness in my throat. Because she remembered.

'We got soaked, too,' she said. She tilted her head to one side. 'Remember?' she asked.

'Sure. The Santa Monica Pier.'

'We ate fried clams.'

4

'And got caught in a downpour.'

'Drenched.' Head still tilted, she smiled a little sadly. 'And then we went under the pier to get out of the rain. Do you remember that?'

'Yeah. I do.'

'It was the first time we ever kissed,' she said. 'Standing in the sand under the Santa Monica Pier. It was cold under there. And scary.' Her smile suddenly lost its sadness, and she laughed softly. 'You kept telling me the trolls were gonna get us.'

I had to smile, too. 'Did I?'

'I guess that's why I'm here.'

'Huh? Trolls?'

Shaking her head slightly from side to side, she walked toward me. 'Because I felt safe with you. I always felt safe with you, Sam. But especially that night under the pier when we were drenched and the rain was coming down and . . . the trolls were all around us. And we kissed.'

Stopping just inches in front of me, she stared up into my eyes. She smelled the same as when she was a teenager: like cotton candy and Wrigley's Spearmint Chewing Gum.

'And you had *Dracula* in your back pocket,' she whispered.

'Yeah,' I said. My heart was thundering. I put my bag down on the floor.

'I want to feel safe again,' she told me.

By the look in her eyes, I thought she wanted me to kiss her. I wondered if her lips would feel the way I remembered them.

They were slightly parted, the lower lip full and pursed out a little.

I was about to kiss them.

But she said, 'Take a look at this, okay?'

And fingered open the front of her robe, sliding the glossy blue silk sideways to the left, exposing a sliver of bare skin all the way down to the sash around her waist. Just as her left breast started to show, she cupped it with her right hand to hold the robe in place. Her other hand slid the fabric almost to her shoulder.

She tilted her head to the right, giving me a good, clear view of the left side of her neck.

5

She had a pair of holes down low where the curve was. As if she'd been stabbed there a day or two ago with an ice pick or a freshly sharpened pencil. Neat little punctures, an inch or so apart. Tiny craters plugged by dark, dried fluids.

'What do you think?' she asked.

'You're not going to tell me a vampire did this,' I said.

'Think again.'

'A *vampire*?'

Gazing into my eyes, she said, 'He comes into my bedroom at night, bites me and sucks my blood. What would *you* call him?'

Lucky, I answered in my mind. And felt like a jerk for thinking it.

'Let me feel,' I said.

She hoisted an eyebrow. 'Go ahead.'

I used the tip of my forefinger. Her skin was slightly puffy around the edges of each hole. I really couldn't feel the punctures; they were too small.

'They're real,' Cat said.

'Yeah. They are.'

Real, but possibly self-inflicted.

A decade had gone by.

At thirteen, fourteen, fifteen and for the small part of her sixteenth year before I'd lost her – Cat had been impish, tender-hearted, innocent, full of dreams and game for anything.

How much of the old – the young – Cat remained?

Had she turned strange, gone mad?

Though her sudden arrival in the middle of the night dressed in nothing but a robe was very odd, she didn't strike me as nuts.

Drawing her robe shut, she said, 'I want you to stop him, Sammy. I just can't stand it anymore. I've tried to kill him myself, but he's too strong. I thought maybe you could hide and take him by surprise the next time he comes.'

'You want me to kill him?'

'Would you?'

'I don't know,' I said.

'Just come over and be with me, okay? Can you do that?'

'Sure.'

2

Cat's car was parked on the street in front of my apartment building. On the way out to it, we didn't run into anyone. I walked behind her, carrying my bag.

It was a warm July night. A breeze was blowing softly. It came from the ocean, about eight miles away. If you wanted to be wandering outside in nothing but your robe, this was a good night for it.

At the rear of her car, Cat took the keys out of her pocket. She unlocked the trunk. I swung my bag in. The trunk lid made a good, solid thunk when I shut it.

We split up. I walked to the passenger door, and she went around to the driver's side.

'It isn't locked,' she said.

When I opened it, the overhead light came on. We both climbed in. Cat had a difficult time keeping her robe closed. I looked away to avoid embarrassing either of us. We shut our doors and the light went out.

After taking a couple of seconds to straighten her robe, she started the engine. 'I should've gotten dressed,' she said.

'It's a nice robe,' I told her.

She put on the headlights and swung away from the curb. 'I just wanted to get away as fast as I could. Didn't even know where I was going. I threw on my robe, grabbed my keys and ran. And ended up at your place.'

'You knew where to find me?'

'Sure. I've known for a while.'

'For a *while*?'

She turned her head. I looked over at her. 'Actually,' she said, 'I've always known. I've never lost track of you.'

Her words stunned me.

She faced forward again to watch the road.

'You're . . . like my safety hatch,' she said. 'The one person I figured I could count on, no matter what. So I always had to know where you were living. Just in case.'

'That must've been a pretty good trick.'

'I've stayed in touch with Lynn.'

7

'My *sister* Lynn? You're kidding. She's never mentioned anything about...'

'It's our secret.'

'I can't believe she didn't *tell* me.'

'She didn't want to get your hopes up. It would've driven you crazy. I mean, I only wanted to know where you *were*, not marry you.'

I grimaced.

And took it without a complaint.

One thing I'd learned – mostly from my early experiences with Cat – is not to whine or beg. Acting like a baby never improves your situation with a girl. And it makes you feel like a jerk. You've got to keep your dignity.

'So, why tonight?' I asked. 'This vampire ... he's been at you for a while, apparently. But you waited until tonight to ... come and see me about it.' *Make a run to your safety hatch.*

She glanced at me, then faced the road again. 'I don't know why,' she said. 'I was starting to get ready for him tonight, and...'

'Ready for him?'

'He likes me to do certain things before he shows up. Take a bath ... a few other things. Light candles.'

'And you *do* this stuff for him? The *vampire* you're asking me to kill?'

'It's complicated.'

'I guess *so.*'

She gave me another glance. I couldn't see the expression on her face, and she couldn't see mine. That was probably a good thing.

'We ... came to an understanding,' she said. 'Elliot and I.'

'*Elliot*? Your vampire's name is *Elliot*? What's his last name?'

'I don't know. He's never said. But even Elliot might not be his real name.'

'Why would anyone make up a name like that?'

'I don't know. But I'm pretty sure he lies about a lot of things.'

'What was this "understanding"?' I asked.

8

'Like an agreement to get along. I used to fight him. I mean, he came at me in the middle of the night like a rapist, so I tried to fight him off. I would've killed him if I could. But it was never any use. He was always either too strong for me or too clever. No matter what I tried, he'd end up winning. And then he'd ... punish me.' She sighed, glanced at me, and said, 'So we finally called a truce. I'd be nice to him, and he'd stop ... doing certain things to me.'

'How long has this been going on?' I heard myself ask. It seemed like someone else's voice. Someone pretending to be me, and rational. While the real me was half crazy, laughing and screaming at the monstrous absurdity of what Cat was saying.

'He started coming about a year ago,' she said.

'A *year* ago?'

'He doesn't come every night. He gives me some time to recover between visits.'

'My God,' I said.

'Tonight, I finally just couldn't face going through it all again. It's like ... being his whore. I feel so filthy afterward. Soiled. Ashamed of myself. I *like* how it feels when he has me. That's what makes it so awful. I *love* it. But then I hate myself.'

When she said that about hating herself, her voice trembled and she started to cry. Weeping quietly, she leaned forward so her face almost touched the steering wheel. We passed under a streetlight, and I saw silvery trails of tears on her cheek.

I hate it when women cry.

Cat crying almost broke my heart.

Reaching over, I put my hand on her shoulder and said, 'It's all right.'

'No, it's not.'

Her shoulder was jerking as she sobbed. It felt small and warm and smooth. I didn't try to say anything else. She continued to cry, hunched over the steering wheel. After a while, I slid my hand off her shoulder and rubbed her back.

Comforting her. Comforting myself.

Her back sure felt good through the silk.

At last, she settled down. She sniffed a few times and wiped her eyes with her hands. Then she eased herself away from the

9

steering wheel. My hand almost got trapped against the seatback, but I moved it out of the way in time. She took a deep breath. On the way in and out, it made trembling sounds as if her lungs were shaking.

'Anyway,' she said. 'I was getting ready for him. I took my bath for him, the same as usual. But then when I climbed out of the tub and looked at the mirror...' She shook her head. She was silent for a few moments. Then she said, 'I see myself in the mirror all the time, but tonight was different.'

'You couldn't see yourself in it?'

'What?' She let out a small, quick laugh – a very good thing to hear after the crying. 'No. I could see myself just fine. That was the problem. I hadn't *really* seen myself in a long time. Tonight, it just hit me. How I'd changed. I saw my wounds. I saw how thin I'd gotten to be. How tired I looked. I saw that I'd turned into his ... his slut, his midnight snack. And it hit me that this was my *fate*, this was it, this was how I'd be spending the rest of my life. As his slave. I *had* no life anymore. I was *his*, and he was destroying me. So I didn't wait around for him. I just threw on my robe and grabbed my keys and ran.' She glanced over at me. 'I should've done it a long time ago. But ... I don't know, you go along to a certain point, even with something you know is awful. Then all of a sudden you just have to make it end ... even if it kills you.'

'Do you think he'll want to kill you?' I asked.

'If he can't have me, he'll kill me. But I don't think he wants to *lose* me. I mean, he's been at me for a year. This is a guy who could have almost anyone, but he keeps coming back to me.'

'I can understand that,' I told her.

'Yeah, I'm such a prize.'

'Do you think he *loves* you?'

'No. Are you kidding? If what he does to me is *love*, I'd hate to see the way he hates.'

'But he keeps coming back,' I said.

'I don't know what he sees in me. Maybe I remind him of someone – a lost lover from his salad days in Transylvania.'

'He's from Transylvania?'

10

'That was a joke, Sammy.'

'Ah.'

'I don't know where he comes from. From hell, for all I know. Which is where I'd like to send him. In maybe about an hour.'

The clock on the dashboard showed 11:05 p.m.

'I thought you wanted *me* to kill him,' I said.

'It'll be a joint effort. I'll keep him busy while you sneak up on him.'

'With what?'

'I've got a hammer and stake you can use.'

'Jesus,' I muttered.

'You can hide in my bedroom closet.'

'Sounds like you've given this a little thought.'

'I've wanted him dead for a year. And like I said, I've tried a few times myself. I just can't pull it off. He has to be taken by surprise.'

'Don't vampires have psychic powers?' I asked.

'Do they?'

'So I've heard.'

'If Elliot's psychic, he's done a good job of keeping it a secret.'

'Then you don't think he'll have a vision of me hiding in the closet?'

'He might *sense* that something isn't right. But it'll be vague. And he's usually focused on just one thing when he shows up – me. It won't even cross his mind to look in the closet.'

'Hope not,' I said. 'You're expecting him around midnight?'

'Exactly midnight.'

'What if he's early?'

'Then we're screwed,' she said. 'But he's never early. He's an extremely punctual vampire. Probably comes from all that worry about the time of sunrise.'

'A joke?' I asked.

'Yep. I don't know how he feels about sunrises. He never sticks around that long. And he's never mentioned it. He doesn't talk about vampire stuff. He says that knowing his secrets would give me power over him.'

'What makes you think he *is* a vampire?' I asked.

Her head turned toward me for a moment. She said, 'He

11

bites.' Then she faced the windshield again. 'He sucks my blood.'

'*I* could do that.'

'Could you come and go whenever you please in a house that's locked up tight – without ever leaving a clue as to how you did it?'

'Not me, but a lot of people probably can. Locksmiths, certain talented burglars, magicians...'

'He *is* a vampire, Sam.'

'How do you know?'

'A lot of ways.'

'Have you ever seen him do something ... supernatural?'

'Like turn himself into a bat?'

'Yeah, like that.'

While I waited for an answer, I turned my face to the window and had a chance to see where we were. Westbound on Montana Avenue in Santa Monica.

'I *know* he's a vampire,' she said. 'But no, I can't think of anything supernatural I've seen him do.'

She turned right onto a quiet street. Cars were parked on both sides and in most of the driveways, but ours seemed to be the only car in motion. Cat drove slowly.

'Does this mean you don't want to help me?' she asked.

'It doesn't mean that at all. Of course I'll help me. I just want to know what I'm dealing with.'

'Elliot's a vampire, and he'll show up at midnight to suck my blood. You'll see for yourself before too much longer.'

I looked at the clock.

11:14 p.m.

'How far's your place from here?' I asked.

'Two blocks.'

'Guess we'll make it before midnight.'

'Barring calamity.'

This neighborhood looked like a good place for calamity. Between the streetlights were heavy patches of darkness. Thick, leafy branches loomed overhead, throwing shadows onto the pavement. The houses looked old. Most of them had second stories, and very few windows had lights in them. A few porch lights were on, but not many. Overall, this part of town seemed way too dark.

12

It reminded me of where I grew up, near Chicago, before my family moved across the country to California – long before I ever met Cat Lorimer.

It reminded me, especially, of Halloween nights when I was a kid, roaming up and down the dark and windy streets, scared half out of my wits most of the time.

In those days, I'd still believed in many things.

Including the things that go bump in the night.

Such as, among other things, vampires.

Cat said, 'Here we are,' and swung into a driveway.

3

Like so many old houses in Southern California, this one had a two-car garage in a far corner of the back yard. The headlights lit it up. We didn't go there, though. Cat stopped her car on the driveway while we were still in front of her house.

The dashboard clock read 11:18. It went dark when she shut off the engine.

'Made it with time to spare,' she said, and plucked the key out of the ignition. When she opened her door, I opened mine and climbed out.

I waited for her beside the car. She came around the rear, adjusting her robe with one hand. In her other hand were the keys. 'This way,' she told me.

'My bag,' I reminded her.

'Let's leave it in the trunk and get it later,' she said. 'We don't want to take a chance on Elliot seeing it.'

'Fine.'

I suddenly wondered why I needed the bag at all. If I was supposed to kill this guy at midnight, couldn't I just go home afterward?

Maybe Cat didn't want to be alone tonight.

Or maybe she planned to reward me.

I intended to comply with her wishes, whatever they might be. Anything to be with her.

We took a concrete walkway. It led from the side of the driveway, across the lawn to the front stoop. A yellow light

13

glowed above the door. Cat hurried up the steps ahead of me. As I followed, she swung open the screen door and stepped past it. It swung back at her. She stopped it with her rump. I pulled it away from her, and she unlocked the main door.

We both went in.

The main door appeared to be solid oak. After shutting it, Cat secured it with a deadbolt.

We turned our backs to the door. We were standing in a foyer with a hardwood floor under our feet and a chandelier overhead. In front of us, a stairway led to the upper floor. A narrow hallway, to the left of the staircase, stretched toward the rear of the house. On both sides of where we stood were entryways, but no lights were on in the rooms beyond them. The only light came from our chandelier. Which was obviously on a dimmer; its bulbs gave off little more light than if they'd been candles.

The house seemed very quiet.

'Any chance he might be here already?' I whispered.

'No chance.' She grinned a little. 'You don't need to whisper.'

'It's so dark in here.'

'Let's go upstairs.'

She led the way. I stayed a few stairs below her. My eyes were level with her rear end.

'You oughta be carrying a candle,' I said. 'We could have a scene from *The Old, Dark House* or something.'

'You sound nervous.'

'I am nervous.'

'Everything'll be fine,' she said.

'Only if Elliot's a figment of your imagination.'

'That'd let *you* off the hook, but it'd mean *I'm* bonkers. Which I'm not,' she added.

As we approached the top, I noticed that the stairwell was open along its left side. My head rose above floor level, and I looked out through the uprights of the wooden railing. Dim light came from somewhere. I was able to make out a stretch of carpeted floor alongside the stairwell, and a couple of dark doorways. Twisting my head around, I saw that the light came from a room near the front of the house. Its door stood wide open, letting brightness flood into the hallway.

Cat reached the top. She stepped around the bend in the banister, put a hand on the wooden railing, and looked over her shoulder at me.

'You don't believe in lights?' I asked.

'I was getting ready for bed.'

Getting ready for Elliot.

As she walked toward the room, the light from its doorway seeped through her robe and turned the silk translucent. I could see her legs – all the way up. And when she turned to enter the room, her right breast showed through the wispy material.

I followed her into the room.

A single lamp was on beside her king-sized bed.

The bed was turned down, ready for her.

The sheets were black and shiny.

Black, unlighted candles stood on the nightstands at both sides of the headboard.

'He likes black,' Cat explained.

'So I see. Halloween in July. I'm surprised he lets you wear the blue robe.'

'I don't wear it when he's here.' She said it in a way that made me feel lousy.

I didn't ask.

We both picked the same moment to look at the digital clock on her headboard.

11:23

Then our eyes met.

I saw the worry in hers.

She probably saw worse in mine.

In thirty-seven minutes, a stranger was supposed to show up. A stranger to *me*, anyhow. And I was supposed to kill him.

I could hardly believe it.

Everything about tonight, starting at the moment of Cat's arrival at my door, seemed oddly unreal, out of whack.

She needs me to kill a vampire for her?

In thirty-seven minutes, he would be here. *Someone* would be here. Unless Cat had lied to me. Or unless she was nuts. Or I was nuts.

11:24

'You sure he won't be early?' I asked.

15

'He's never early. But we'll go ahead and get you set up right now, okay?'

'Sure.'

She crossed the room ahead of me, walking toward a large, oak dresser. It was topped by a mirror that must've been six feet long and about four feet high.

In the mirror, I saw that the front of her robe had loosened slightly. I glimpsed a long, narrow V of skin down to her waist.

A mirror?

'He allows mirrors?' I asked.

'He loves mirrors.'

'Does he show up in them?'

'Sure.' Cat crouched in front of the dresser and pulled open one of its bottom drawers. 'The deal about mirrors,' she said, 'is that they used to have backing made of real silver.'

'Yeah?' I stepped up close behind her and looked down. The drawer seemed to be full of neatly folded sweaters.

'That's why vampires were supposed to shun them,' she said, and dug down into a gap between two stacks of sweaters. 'Just because of the silver. Something to do with Judas being paid in silver. A *Bible* thing.'

Her hand came out of the sweaters with a hammer.

Not exactly a hammer.

A *mallet*.

A short-handled mallet with a steel head about the size of a large coffee mug. It looked brand new. The pale wooden handle had a sticker on it. The barrel head of the thing was painted sky-blue except for the striking surfaces, which were gray and shiny like a polished nickel.

Cat reached it up to me, and I took it from her.

It must've weighed five pounds.

'Jesus,' I muttered.

She stuffed her hand deep into the sweaters again. 'Anyway' she said, 'they stopped using silver for the backings. Ever since then, vampires have been able to enjoy mirrors.'

'Did Elliot tell you all that?'

'Nope. It's like I said, he never tells me dip about vampires. But I've read a few things.'

16

Her hand came out of the sweaters, this time clutching a shaft of wood.

She raised it overhead. 'Here you go,' she said.

I took it from her.

It looked like fourteen or fifteen inches of dowel, about two inches in diameter. It was flat at one end. The other end tapered to a sharp point. 'You whittled this?' I asked.

'Yep.' She straightened the sweaters, then slid the drawer shut, stood up and turned to face me. 'Do you think it'll do the trick?'

'I should think so.'

She really meant me to *murder* this guy.

Though the night seemed more out of whack than ever, it also, for some reason, was starting to feel more real.

Maybe because I held the hammer and stake in my hands.

Making a crooked smile, Cat said, 'The Van Helsing method.'

'Tried and true.'

'Go for the heart.'

I took a deep breath and nodded. And hoped she couldn't see that I was trembling.

'You'll want to nail him while he's on top of me. That's when he'll be most vulnerable. Slam it right into his back.'

'What's to stop it from going through him and getting *you*?' I asked.

'Let me see it.'

I gave the stake to her.

She took it by the pointed end, and held it in front of her chest.

'It's fourteen inches long,' she told me.

The way her robe hung open, I had a hard time looking at the stake. The gap was now a couple of inches wide between her breasts. It narrowed on its way down. It went down a long way. I glimpsed her navel. Below the loose knot of her sash, the edges of the robe were still slightly parted.

'Elliot's about twelve inches thick through the middle of his chest,' she said.

I raised my eyes. She was still gazing down at the stake. 'How do you know that?' I asked.

'I measured some guy I met at the Home Depot when I went

17

there to buy the dowel and hammer. He seemed to be about Elliot's size. Came to twelve inches.'

'When was that?' I asked.

'Months ago. I've had this stuff hidden away for ... I don't know, a *long* time. I knew I'd need it someday.' She shrugged. 'Anyway, I don't think Elliot's chest size has changed much since then. Unless it's gotten thicker.'

'This stake is longer than twelve inches,' I· said.

'It's fourteen.'

'So only two inches will go in you?'

Cat raised her head and smiled up at me. 'Don't pound it in all the way, genius.' Lowering her head again, she spread the thumb and forefinger of her left hand a couple of inches apart and put them against the wide end of the stake.

About two inches behind the demonstration, her robe draped the curve of her left breast. Her nipple was stiff. The silk took on her shape like a veil of blue water.

'Leave about this much sticking out of his back, and I'll be fine.'

I shifted my gaze to the stake. 'Okay. I can do that.'

'And that should take care of him.'

She handed the stake to me.

Our eyes met.

'Are you all right?' she asked.

'I've never killed anyone before.'

'This isn't a person. This is a vampire.'

If you say so.

'I've never killed a vampire, either,' I explained.

'But you'll do it?'

I gave her a brave grin. 'Hey, kid, for you ...'

She lifted a hand and caressed my cheek. 'You'll be saving my life, Sammy. I can't go on having him ... come to me like this. It has to end.'

'Well, I'll do what I can.'

'That's all I can expect,' she said. Her hand slid behind my neck, curled and held me while she gazed steadily into my eyes. 'The thing is, don't even try if you aren't willing to go all the way. If you hesitate ... if you aren't quick enough or strong enough ... it'll turn out very bad. For both of us.'

I nodded.

18

'What I mean is, just stay hidden unless you're ready to kill him.'

'Okay.'

'Just wait till he leaves, and go on home. All right?'

'Fine. But don't worry. I'll take care of him.'

She gave my neck a gentle squeeze, then said, 'We'd better finish getting ready. Do you need to use the bathroom?'

'How much time have we got?'

'How long's it gonna take?'

I cracked a smile. 'About a minute.'

'There's time. Right in there.' Letting go of my neck, she nodded toward an open door just a few paces to the left of the dresser. 'I'll hold these for you.'

I gave her the hammer and stake, then turned around and checked the clock.

11:29

Before I could turn my eyes away, it changed to 11:30.

Though we still had half an hour, my stomach seemed to shrivel.

I hurried into the bathroom, flicked its light switch, and shut the door. I was surrounded by mirrors. Suddenly, there were several Sams walking past the sink and bathtub.

I still hadn't shaved or combed my hair. I still wore my old vulture T-shirt and blue jeans.

Who let this guy in?

I looked more like the fellow who might show up to repair the toilet than to use it.

But use it I did.

Someone had positioned a mirror behind the toilet, so I was forced to face myself. When I went, it looked like my twin was taking a leak on my knees.

I finished and got out of the bathroom as fast as I could.

Cat was sitting on the edge of her bed, hands resting on her thighs, the hammer in one hand and the stake in the other. She appeared to be gnawing on her lower lip.

I glanced at the clock.

11:32

'You all right?' I asked.

'Just a little scared. If anything goes wrong . . . I'm starting to wish I hadn't gotten you into this.'

19

I stepped up to Cat and placed my hands on her shoulders. 'Hey,' I said, 'you made my day.'

'This'll probably get both of us killed.'

'We'll be fine,' I told her. 'You've just got a case of the last-minute jitters.'

'That's 'cause I know what he'll do to us.'

'He won't do anything. He'll be dead.'

'God, I hope so.'

I gave Cat's shoulders a gentle squeeze, then bent over and took the hammer and stake from her hands. 'Where do you want me?' I asked.

'Over there.' She nodded to her right.

The far wall, about fifteen feet beyond the foot of the bed, looked like a series of sliding doors. There were several of them side by side, all painted white, all with golden handles, all shut. At the end of the row, way over to the right, the door to the hallway stood open.

'It's all one closet in there,' Cat said, getting to her feet. 'Come on, I'll show you.'

I followed her to the doors.

She slid one open.

Leaning in, I looked both ways. The closet was long and narrow. Light slipped in from cracks around the doors. There was plenty of room for me. Near the doors, the floor was clear of shoes and other obstructions. Clothes on hangers stretched along the entire length of the closet, but they were set back a couple of feet; I wouldn't bump into them if I stayed close to the doors.

Though the hangers were spread out to eliminate major gaps, the closet looked half-empty.

Emptiness thanks to her dead husband.

I realized that I didn't even know his name.

And didn't want to.

I pulled my head out of the closet and nodded at Cat. 'Looks fine,' I said.

'Elliot never checks in here,' she told me. 'I don't think I've *ever* seen him open any of these doors. So you should be perfectly safe as long as you don't make any noise.'

'I'll try to be quiet.'

'The room'll be fairly dark. Nothing but candle light. And

once he's on the bed, he'll have his back this way. He won't notice if one of these doors is open an inch or two.'

'Fine.'

'Any questions?'

'Nothing that can't wait, I guess.'

After I said that, we both looked at the clock.

11:35

A tremor rippled through me.

'Maybe I'd better go ahead and get inside,' I said. 'In case he shows up early.'

'He won't. But that's all right. I have a few things I need to do, so go on ahead and wait in there if you'd like. It'll give you a while to check things out.'

Nodding, I stepped into the closet. I turned around to face her and said, 'I do have one question.'

She lifted her eyebrows.

'Should we have a signal?'

'For what?'

'For when I should jump him?'

Her eyebrows lowered. She clamped her lower lip between her teeth, and shook her head. 'I don't think so. Just watch us. Wait till he's on top of me and busy sucking. Then be really quick. When I know you're coming, I'll try to hold him. Slam that stake into his back and *pound* the sucker in.'

'Okay,' I said. I was *really* shivering now.

'One more thing. It's bound to be a mess. If you don't want to get your clothes bloody, you'd better take them off.'

'Okay.'

'You'll want to do that *before* he shows up.'

'Okay.'

She smiled slightly. 'You're blushing.'

'Am I?'

'You're so sweet,' she said.

I didn't like the sound of that. But then she put her hands on my shoulders, leaned forward until her body met mine, and kissed me on the mouth.

A tender kiss.

Her lips felt great. She had that wonderful aroma of cotton candy and spearmint chewing gum. I felt the soft, firm pressure of her breasts against my chest.

21

But none of it lasted very long.

When it was over, she eased away and gazed into my eyes and said, 'You're probably the only guy in the world who would do a thing like this for me.'

'Oh, I don't know about that,' I said.

'I do,' she said. 'And I love you for it.'

11:37

I slid the door shut in front of me.

4

Standing there in the closet, I stared through the darkness at the door a couple of inches in front of my face and thought about what had just happened.

I felt two different ways about it: great and horrible.

I'd only held and kissed Cat a few times in my life, and not at all for the past ten years. During all those years, I'd missed her. I'd longed for her. And now, she'd taken me into her arms and kissed me.

Unreal.

But great, just great. Like a fantasy come true.

And she'd said, 'I love you.'

Except 'I love you' wasn't what she'd really said.

She'd said, 'I love you for it.'

Meaning she 'loved me' for coming to her aid . . . loved me in gratitude. Just as she'd embraced and kissed me in gratitude, not because of any amorous feelings toward me.

Some things never change.

As much as I'd loved Cat, back in our teenaged years, she had never seen me as much more than a good friend. The guy who was always 'there' for her. At least until she moved to Seattle. Hard to be there for someone a thousand miles away.

My commitment to Cat had obviously made an impression on her, though. After all, she'd kept tabs on me. And she'd come back to me when she needed a hit man.

At least she came back.

At least I'm here with her tonight.

And, with luck, maybe tonight wouldn't be the end of it. She would at least keep me around as long as she had uses for me.

That was something.

That was a lot.

I didn't *need* for Cat to love me. What I needed was to be with her, to be able to look at her and talk with her, and maybe sometimes touch her.

So this would do.

It would have to do.

The closet, already dark, suddenly became darker. The strips of light had vanished from the cracks.

I wondered what time it was.

How much longer before Elliot came?

Though I never wear a wristwatch, I have a fairly good sense of time. My brooding over Cat had probably lasted two or three minutes. Which would make it about 11:40.

Twenty minutes to go.

I couldn't see anything.

So I tucked the stake under my right arm. Slowly sidestepping to the left, I drifted my empty hand along the surface of the door in front of my face. Soon, my fingertips found the crack where it met the other sliding door.

I pried the edges apart.

A slit of murky light came in.

'How's it going in there?' Cat asked. Her voice didn't sound nearby.

'Fine so far,' I answered. 'Did I make a noise?'

'I didn't hear anything.'

'Okay. What time is it?'

'Quarter till.'

Fifteen minutes to go.

'You'd better get your clothes off if you haven't done it yet.'

'Okay.'

I figured I'd better go ahead and get it over with. It wasn't easy. First, I turned sideways and set the hammer and stake on the floor. Then I had to perform a balancing act to get my shoes and socks off. That seemed like the tricky part. But it went all right. When I tried to peel off my T-shirt, though, my elbow thunked against the door.

Cat, somewhere in her bedroom, let out a startled gasp.

23

'Sorry,' I said.

'Are you all right?'

'Fine. It's just a little tight in here for a striptease. And a little dark,' I added.

'Well, don't hurt yourself.'

'Thanks.'

Compared to the T-shirt, my jeans were easy. When I unfastened them, they fell. Dropped down around my ankles, and I stepped out of them.

Using my feet, I got my clothes out of the way by sweeping them toward the back of the closet.

I kept my shorts on, by the way. It made sense to take my clothes off so they'd stay clean, but I wasn't going to stand around *naked* in Cat's closet. Much less go scampering out bare-ass to do the job on Elliot the Vampire. Not me.

Besides, my shorts gave me a good place to keep the stake while I waited. I shoved it down under the waistband, over by my left hip. And that gave me an empty hand.

With my right hand, I held the hammer down low against the side of my leg.

I was ready.

I turned slowly toward the door.

How long till midnight?

Ten or twelve minutes, probably.

Leaning forward, I put my eye to the narrow gap between the doors. The room fluttered with soft, golden light. Part of the bed was visible, but I couldn't see Cat. So I crept the fingers of my left hand into the crack. Very slowly and carefully, I eased the door sideways. It slid a little and didn't make a sound. Once again, I peered out.

Though the gap was no more than an inch wide, it gave me a great view. I could see the entire bed. And the nightstands on both sides of it, where candles burned. A pair of tall candle holders now stood at the foot of the bed, near each corner. They hadn't been there, before. They were about waist-high. Each held two black, burning candles.

The black satin bedsheet shimmered like a midnight lake surrounded by fires.

Where's Cat?

I couldn't see her *or* hear her. Had she gone away?

24

She'd mentioned having things she needed to do. Chores of some sort, to get ready for him.

What if he shows up and Cat's not here?

She'll be here, I told myself.

Then I had a nasty thought. A thought that maybe I was being set up.

She wouldn't do that to me.

Or would she? I hadn't seen her in ten years. Maybe she'd gone bad.

Everything she'd told me tonight might've been a lie.

The holes in her neck are real, I reminded myself.

Maybe self-inflicted.

But if she wanted a fall-guy, why the insane story about needing to be saved from the clutches of a vampire? And why arm me with a couple of lethal weapons?

To throw me off?

I hated having such thoughts. I suppose they were inevitable, though. Partly because her story was so hard to believe in the first place, but mostly because she'd stuck me in the closet and gone away.

Had she left me behind for Elliot?

Ridiculous, I told myself. The guy's probably not even a vampire.

Probably?

Then I had an even more ridiculous thought: *maybe they're both vampires.*

No such thing as vampires, I told myself.

Besides, if I'm supposed to be tonight's meal, why did she give me the hammer and stake?

Just so I'd have a fighting chance?

'Almost time,' Cat said.

I jumped, and the hammer pounded the door.

She yelped, 'Shit!'

'Sorry,' I said. I still couldn't see her.

But I heard her panting. 'It's all right,' she said. 'You startled me, that's all.'

'I thought you were gone.'

'I just came out of the john.'

'Oh.'

Big set up. I'm tonight's main course. Right.

'What was that, the hammer?' she asked.

'Yeah. It slipped.'

'Hope that doesn't happen when *he's* here.'

'I'll be careful,' I told her.

'Anyway,' she said, 'it's five till twelve.'

'Okay, thanks.'

'Everything all right in there?'

'I'm just a little nervous, that's all.'

'Nothing to be nervous about.' Even though I couldn't see Cat, I knew she had to be smiling when she said that. It gave me a good feeling.

'What, me worry?' I asked.

And heard her make a quiet laugh.

'We'd better not talk anymore,' she said. 'It's almost time.'

'Okay.'

'Good luck.'

'You, too.'

A moment later, she stepped into view, coming from the direction of the bathroom. Her robe was gone. She seemed to be wearing nothing but oil.

Never looking in my direction, she crawled to the middle of the bed and lay down on her back. The bed had no pillow, and no covering other than the glossy, black bottom sheet.

Face toward the ceiling, Cat stretched her arms out to either side and spread her legs.

She lay there like some sort of primitive offering.

Her skin gleamed in the candlelight.

His slut, his midnight snack.

I gaped at Cat in shock, hardly able to believe she was sprawled in front of me this way. This girl I'd loved and longed for, dreamed about, desired.

Only in my most exotic, feverish dreams and fantasies had I ever seen her naked.

Even in those, she hadn't looked like *this*.

Never golden like this with candlelight, oiled and shiny, with her nipples standing stiff on top of her breasts, with her pubic mound hairless and glistening, with her legs wide open as if for no other reason than to show me the glistening cleft between them.

But I knew that none of this was meant for me.

It was for her vampire, not for me.

It sickened me with jealousy and lust.

I wanted her. I'd *always* wanted her, dreamed of her, ached for her. And she was doing *this* for some kind of sadistic intruder who liked to bite her neck and suck her blood.

I'm a nice guy – how come *he's* the one getting Cat?

What gives?

Is there some sort of rule that the assholes of the world get the best of everything?

I hated him.

I almost hated Cat for playing along with his games.

But I still loved her. And pitied her for debasing herself this way. And longed to save her. And ached to throw open the closet door and run to the bed and throw myself onto her and . . .

Something black slipped in from the side, blocking my view of Cat, blocking out the entire bed and the nightstands and most of the candlelight.

At first, I didn't realize what had happened. All I knew was that Cat had vanished.

Then I figured it out.

Elliot was standing in the way, his back only a few inches from the gap between my doors. I *hoped* it was his back.

I held my breath, and wondered if he could hear my heartbeat.

He was *awfully* close.

'Come here,' Cat said, her voice husky.

He didn't say a word, but started walking toward the bed. As he put some distance between himself and the door, I was able to see more than a mass of blackness. He seemed to shrink down and become visible.

But he didn't shrink much.

A few strides away from the closet, he halted.

My guess, he was six-foot-six. He had blond hair in a *buzz cut*, of all things. Jug ears, a long and skinny neck, and narrow shoulders draped by a black cape.

He wasn't exactly what I'd expected.

I'd imagined Elliot would be something along the lines of Tom Cruise: handsome, well groomed, nicely built.

Not this *goon.*

How could Cat...?

Scared of him, that's how. Fear works wonders.

My feelings of jealousy came to a quick stop.

I suddenly felt nothing except hard, cold anger toward this geeky son-of-a-bitch.

His cape fell to the floor.

He was naked.

He was way too skinny and way too white.

Suddenly, he no longer seemed like a goon.

And I no longer felt like a grown-up.

I was a kid again, scared half out of my wits. A kid who once again believed in the things that go bump in the night.

5

As Elliot walked toward the bed, Cat's feet and ankles came into view on either side of him. I could see to her knees when he stopped.

'Where to begin?' he said. He sounded amused. 'Such a gorgeous feast laid out before me.' Shaking his head, he muttered, 'Decisions, decisions.'

'Anywhere you wish, darling.'

I really expected him to crawl onto the bed. But he didn't. Instead, he took a step to the right, bent over and lifted Cat's leg. With him off to the side like that, I could see nearly all of her.

He raised the leg slowly and pulled it, sliding Cat toward him. Then he began rubbing the bottom of her foot against his skin. He started at his thighs and worked upward, taking his time, sliding her foot against his groin and belly and chest. After rubbing it all over his chest, he bent over, opened wide, and stuck it into his mouth as if it were a sandwich. He seemed to get about half of it in there.

Cat acted as if she liked what he was doing to her foot. Moaning and squirming, she slid her other foot up and down on the sheet. Her knee rose and fell and swung from side to side. Sometimes, when her knee was high, she shoved at the mattress and thrust her pelvis in his direction. Her breasts shook with the motions of her body. Her mouth hung open, and she rolled her head.

Keeping her foot trapped inside his mouth, Elliot began to massage her calf and shin with both his hands.

I stood watching from the closet, enthralled and disgusted, wanting to stop him.

It's too soon, I told myself. *Gotta wait till he's on the bed.*

Holding her leg by the calf, he pulled his mouth away. Cat's foot came out. She stopped writhing and moaning. As he lowered her leg slowly to the mattress, she let her other leg unbend and slide out straight on the sheet.

Still focused on her left leg, Elliot leaned over the mattress and did something to her ankle with his mouth. I couldn't see what. His rear was in the way. But then Cat's foot appeared between his legs. In the candlelight, her toes were shiny with spit.

The lower half of her foot gleamed with blood. The blood appeared to trickle from a pair of holes in her sole.

He'd done it – sunk his fangs into Cat right in front of me – and I hadn't even realized what was happening!

He'd slipped it past me.

What's he doing now?

Though I couldn't see his head, he appeared to be kissing or licking his way up Cat's left leg.

Biting?

Whatever, it seemed to be driving her crazy. The higher he went up her thigh, the wilder she acted. She flung her head from side to side and clawed at the sheets. She thrashed about, arching her back. Her right leg seemed to be in a frenzy, jerking up and down and sideways.

Then Elliot squirmed over the top of her leg.

Cat raised both her knees.

He was between them, belly down on the mattress, his butt at the end of the bed, his long, skinny legs hanging off, his toes against the carpet.

With his hands, he started to stroke the underside of Cat's upraised thighs.

His head went down.

She gasped, 'Yes!'

No!

Hooking my fingers through the crack, I started to ease the door open. I wanted to *hurl* it wide and run out and put an end to all this. But I forced myself to hold back.

I took my time. Opened the door slowly. Quietly.

Because this guy *did* scare me. I was afraid of what might happen if he heard me coming.

As the door slipped out of my way, I crept sideways to stay with the opening. And I watched. Cat was bucking and thrashing and whimpering, acting nuts. Maybe it wasn't acting, I don't know.

Slurpy wet sucking sounds came from Elliot's mouth. His hands were busy on Cat's thighs. His white buttocks were flexing. He looked as if he'd dug his toes into the carpet to anchor himself in place.

At last, the door's gap seemed wide enough. I stepped out of the closet and crept toward the bed.

They kept at it.

The hammer felt slippery in my hand.

Ever since Elliot's arrival, I'd been pretty much oblivious of my own body. Now I found that I was trembling violently and drenched with sweat. My wet shorts were clinging to me.

I pulled the stake out of my waistband.

Cat lifted her head off the mattress and saw me. She gasped, 'Yes! Oh! Don't stop!' Her arms reached down. She clutched the back of Elliot's head and pushed it as if mashing his face into her body.

I was almost to his feet. I stepped around them and moved alongside his legs.

As I crept toward the end of the bed, Cat blurted out, 'Oh, yes, yes! Suck! Ahhh! Suck me good! Yes! Don't stop! Suck me, suck me!' Her eyes were on me. They looked feverish, wild, and a little dazed. 'Yesssss!' she hissed. 'Suck me dry!'

My knees were only a couple of inches from the mattress when I stopped.

Elliot still sucked.

Cat still clutched his head.

I raised the hammer, turned a little toward Elliot, bent over at the waist and jabbed the stake down in the middle of his back. Not exactly in the middle – up near the base of his left shoulder blade. Over his heart, I hoped.

The instant the point touched his skin, I slammed the hammer down. His skin popped. His back opened and sucked in half the stake.

A rough spasm jolted his body.

One more blow . . .

As I swung the hammer down to drive the stake home, he freed his mouth from Cat and flung himself upward, breaking her hold on his head. The heavy steel mallet missed the stake and crashed against his back instead.

He surged up fast, turning, roaring at me.

His face came at me, mouth wide. I didn't try to study it; I tried to cave it in with my hammer. But somehow I happened to notice that it had no eyebrows or eyelashes. I found that odd. What I found horrible was the mouth. Spread wide open, it seemed way too large.

And full of blood and steel.

Cat's blood.

His top and bottom canine teeth – slender, curving fangs – looked like steel.

As I swung the hammer at his face, his roar flung specks of Cat's blood at me.

He knocked my arm out of the way. I tried to hold on to the hammer, but it flew off somewhere. Then he was on me. Still roaring and blowing blood in my face, he caught me by the shoulders and pounced, driving me backward, *riding* me backward and down to the floor.

The floor slammed my back and pounded my head. Then *he* came crushing down on top of me, his face against my shoulder. I'd been knocked nearly senseless.

He raised his head and glared at me.

Blood dripped from his mouth onto my lips and chin.

A couple of smart quips ran through my mind. *My, what big teeth you have.* And, *Does this mean you love me?* Give him a gutsy, macho wisecrack to remember me by. But I was too scared to talk. Also, I didn't want my last words to be some sort of phoney movie-star crap. Better to go out with some dignity and my mouth shut.

He opened wide and went for my neck.

I got my arm up. It caught his teeth. They chomped me midway between my wrist and elbow.

Then he turned his head aside. He didn't want my arm in his mouth. He wanted my neck. I tried to keep my arm jammed in there, but pretty soon he used his hands. Even with a stake in his back, he was too strong for me. In a couple of seconds, he pinned both my wrists to the floor.

Then he went for my neck.

Came down at it fast like a dog.

I jerked my head up and snapped at his face. Though I missed, he flinched away. Then he roared and made another lunge for my neck.

I was set to bite him. This time, I figured he'd probably eat my mouth.

I went for him anyway.

Our mouths were about to collide when I heard a heavy *thunk!*

Elliot flinched rigid, threw back his head, and shrieked. I felt something poke my chest.

Elliot's shriek turned into a gurgling choke. Blood gushed out of his mouth. I shut my eyes. The blood hit my face like a bucket of warm syrup – not just a mouthful, a stomach load.

Blind, I felt Elliot twitching and shuddering on top of me.

Then came a grunt that sounded as if it came from Cat, and Elliot tumbled off.

I wiped the blood out of my eyes.

Cat was crouching beside me, a worried look on her face. Her right hand, resting atop her knee, held the hammer. 'You did great,' she said.

'Not great enough.'

'You did most of the job,' she told me. 'It just took one more whack.'

'He ... almost had me.'

Reaching down with her left hand, she patted my chest. 'Couldn't let him kill my hero.'

For a while, I didn't feel like moving. I just stayed on my back, gasping for air and trying to calm down. We didn't talk. Cat put the hammer on the floor, sat cross-legged beside me, and held my hand.

I stared at her. She didn't seem to mind, even though she was naked and my eyes kept dodging down to her breasts. Every now and then, she squeezed my hand. A few times, she gave me that smile of hers.

It felt good, being her hero.

Except for my arm. That hurt like hell, but didn't seem to be bleeding very much.

I finally turned my head the other way and looked at Elliot. He lay on his back. Over near his left nipple, the pointed end of the stake was jutting out. It was bright red, and stuck up more than an inch.

If Cat had hammered it that far, I would've felt more than a little poke. The floor had probably shoved it in deeper when she rolled Elliot off me.

He was a real mess.

His mouth was full to the brim with blood.

I met Cat's eyes. 'How come he isn't turning to dust?' I asked.

One corner of her mouth tilted up. 'Should he?'

'Christopher Lee always did.'

'Maybe he's not old enough to crumble.'

I glanced at Elliot, then returned my gaze to Cat. 'I guess this means we'll have to get rid of the body.'

'Afraid so,' she said. 'Why don't you take a shower first? Then we'll worry about the rest of this.'

6

I tried not to drip on my way across the carpet to the bathroom.

Cat stayed behind.

I thought about asking her to join me. She might've done it. After all, I was her hero. But I didn't ask.

Inside the bathroom, I turned on the light and shut the door. Then I saw myself in the mirrors. I looked like the two-sided man: my back fairly clean, my front a bloody mess. The blood on my hair, face and neck – from Elliot's mouth and stomach – had probably belonged to Cat until shortly after midnight. The blood on my chest and belly came from Elliot's stake wounds. And the blood on my right arm was pretty much my own. Of course, some of everyone's blood had probably ended up everywhere, to one extent or another. *Most* of the blood on my face was Cat's. I was sure of that.

It gave me sort of a nice feeling. That is to say, I didn't mind having my eyes and nose and mouth drenched with *her* blood. I won't say I relished it, but if I had to be soaked with blood, better that it was hers.

There was something intimate about it.

But most of it had paid a brief visit to Elliot's stomach before spewing onto my face. Which made it somewhat less attractive.

AIDS crossed my mind, but didn't scare me. I had no reason to think that Cat or Elliot was infected. Also, I'd just come within an instant of getting my throat ripped out. When you're that close to death and you survive, you don't worry about the distant future.

I felt dazed by all that had happened. Dazed, astonished, excited, somewhat euphoric, horrified, disgusted, jittery ... other things, too. I felt very weird and confused. So I was only vaguely aware of climbing into the bathtub, turning the water on, sliding the glass door shut and starting the shower.

Then the hot water met the wounds on my arm and I let out a yell. Luckily, the real pain only lasted for a few moments. As for the tiny hole in my chest, it hardly hurt at all.

After a while, the water around my feet stopped swirling with pink.

I peeled down my shorts, stepped out of them and kicked them to the rear of the tub so they wouldn't clog the drain.

Then I inspected my arm. It was deeply dented by Elliot's teeth, but only his steel fangs had actually broken my skin. They'd left two punctures on top of my forearm, two more underneath. Those wounds were deep. They ached, and kept dribbling small amounts of blood while I showered.

For a while, I took my time. Getting done would mean returning to Cat's bedroom, cleaning up the mess and dealing with Elliot's body.

I wondered what we should do with him.

But mostly I thought about Cat. *Dwelled* on her as I stood

34

beneath the hot spray, soaping myself, then rinsing off the slippery suds.

It's a funny thing about me and Cat: when we're together, I'm pretty much able to treat her as a regular person. But when we're apart, I get weird. I become obsessed with her.

There's probably a simple explanation. Like maybe I'm nuts.

Anyway, I got awfully eager to be with her again. Also, I didn't like the idea of Cat being alone with the body. So I quickly shampooed my hair, rinsed it and put an end to my shower.

After drying myself, I reached into the tub and picked up my shorts. I wrung them out, then looked them over. A lot of the blood had been washed off, but not all of it. I put the shorts on, anyway. They clung to me and I could mostly see right through them, so I wrapped the towel around my waist.

The bathroom was hot and steamy. I wanted to get out of there, but my arm was bleeding slightly.

In the medicine cabinet, I found several tins of adhesive bandages. I pulled down one of them, took out four bandages, peeled off the wrappers, and covered my fang bites. Then I threw away the wrappers.

Keeping the tin, I opened the door and entered the nice, cool air of the bedroom.

Though the candles still burned, twin lamps on the night tables filled the room with light.

Beyond the end of the bed, Cat was squatting over Elliot's body. She still hadn't put on any clothes, but she was wearing a pair of pale leather moccasins on her feet. I walked toward her, gazing at her bare back and buttocks. Her skin glistened. It looked smooth and flawless except for the bite marks.

None looked fresh. Most were hardly visible – tiny dots a shade or two darker than her skin. A pair here, a pair there. Twin dots always the same distance apart. Usually a matching pair a couple of inches lower. I probably wouldn't have noticed many of them if the lamplight hadn't been so bright.

She looked over her shoulder at me, smiled, and said, 'You're out.'

'Are you going to take a shower?' I asked.

'Pretty soon. Some of this is so messy, though.' She returned to her job.

'Want some bandages?' I asked.

'He's way past bandages.'

'For you.'

'Ah. Thanks. Not right now.'

'Aren't you bleeding?'

'Yeah, but not that much. He didn't bite me the way he bit you. He was never trying to kill me . . . just suck my blood and . . . you know, get his jollies.'

I couldn't tell what Cat was doing until I stepped around Elliot's feet and got a look at her from the front.

She had a turkey baster in his mouth.

One of those big, hollow plastic tubes with a rubber bulb at one end. It's meant to be a cooking implement. You use it to suck up grease from the pan and dribble it over your turkey . . . I've also heard of gals using the things to inseminate themselves.

This one was sucking blood out of Elliot's mouth.

'What're you doing?' I asked.

'See?' She lifted the tube out of his mouth, swung it over to a large drinking glass in her left hand, and squeezed the yellow bulb. The blood squirted out. By the time the baster was empty, the glass was almost half full.

'Planning to drink it?' I asked.

'I just didn't want it spilling out all over the place when we go to move him. There's a big enough mess without this.' Keeping the bulb squeezed, she went back for a refill.

She plunged the tube down into Elliot's mouth and opened her grip on the bulb. With a slurping noise, more blood climbed the baster. Then came a rattly sound like you get with a straw at the bottom of a milk shake.

Cat squeezed the blood into the glass. Then she raised the glass from between her knees, swept it sideways and up toward me. 'Here,' she said. 'Would you dump this for me?'

Nodding, I took the glass from her hand. Her fingers had put bloody smears on it. 'Where?' I asked.

'I don't care. The sink, the toilet, the tub . . .' She shrugged.

'Okay,' I said.

'Can you take this, too?' She handed the baster to me. I still had the canister of bandages in one hand, so I stood the baster upright inside the glass of blood. 'Just give it a rinse,' she told me. 'I can put it in the dishwasher later.'

'Right back,' I said. In the bathroom, I set down the bandage tin, took out the turkey baster and dumped the blood into the sink. Then I ran the glass and baster under hot water until they looked clean. I left them in the sink and returned to the bedroom.

Cat was on her way out. Stopping in the doorway, she twisted halfway around. She held the black bedsheet bundled against her chest. 'Back in a jiff,' she told me. 'I'll just throw this in the wash.'

'Okay,' I said.

She left.

Alone in the room, I thought about getting dressed. It didn't seem like a good idea, though. I would've felt odd, being fully clothed while Cat had nothing on except her moccasins.

Besides, there appeared to be more bloody work ahead.

Staying in my towel and shorts, I stepped over to the bed. It had a white plastic mattress cover. Which I guess is a smart thing if you're being visited regularly by a guy like Elliot. The cover looked fairly clean. I saw only a few small places where blood from tonight had seeped through the sheet. A damp cloth should take care of them nicely...

I thought about wiping them off, myself. But Cat probably had a certain way of going about things. Most gals do. They get miffed if you try to help and use the wrong rag or something.

So I sat down on a corner of the bed to wait for her.

Elliot still hadn't turned to dust.

He probably wasn't going to.

I tried not to look at him. But I must've *wanted* to look, because my eyes kept sneaking over there.

He'd died with a snarl on his face, lips peeled away from his teeth. It reminded me of cats I've seen from time to time; you see a dead one on the road, it nearly always has a freaky snarl.

But you never see a cat with steel fangs.

37

I'd never heard of *vampires* with steel fangs, either. My guess, this Elliot was a geeky nut-case, a sadist with a taste for blood, a wanna-be vampire. And possibly a dentist. Those fangs were custom jobs. Perhaps he'd made them himself – *all the better to bite you with, my dear.*

My eyes snuck down to his penis.

All the better to fuck you with . . .

I suddenly wanted him covered, so I stood up, adjusted my towel, and headed for his cape. It still lay on the carpet between the end of the bed and the closet.

It appeared to be made of black satin like the bedsheet. It had no lining. When I picked it up, the air in the room made it ripple and billow. Still, it seemed to have more substance than Cat's robe. I could see the lights through it, but only dimly.

I headed toward Elliot with it.

'Try it on,' Cat said from behind me. I turned around. She stood in the doorway, smiling, her head tilted to one side.

'I'm not a cape person,' I told her.

She still wore only her moccasins. She'd picked up a pair of scissors, a spool of duct tape and a coil of rope, but they were in her hands by her sides. She made no attempt to cover herself.

She must've washed the blood off downstairs.

But she hadn't bandaged tonight's wounds. I glimpsed a pair of red holes down low on the curve of her pubic mound. The holes were about an inch apart. Elliot's upper fangs must've made them. She probably had two more holes underneath where I couldn't see them.

My towel started rising. The cape wouldn't save me; it was hanging by my side. So, trying to appear nonchalant, I turned my back to Cat and said, 'I thought I'd throw this over him.'

'Why bother?'

'He's naked.'

'Why ruin a good cape? It might come in handy next Halloween. Anyway, I thought we'd wrap him up in the mattress cover.'

'Ah. Okay.'

38

'We'll tape it up really good so he won't leak blood all over everything.'

'Sounds good,' I said.

I tossed Elliot's cape out of the way, then bent over the bed. Cat went to the other side. Together, we started to peel off the mattress cover.

I kept glancing at her. Not only because it excited me to see her naked, but because we were close to the lamps. For the first time, I could see the marks of the old bites on her shoulders, upper arms and breasts. Like those on her back, most were faint remnants on their way toward vanishing.

They appalled me.

There were so *many* of them.

Especially on her breasts.

I was damn glad we'd killed the guy. I only wished we'd done it a year ago.

My towel fell off while we were removing the mattress cover. I let it stay on the floor. It wasn't going to stay on, anyway. And I was wearing shorts, which is more than can be said for Cat.

We carried the cover away from the bed and spread it out on the carpet just above Elliot's head.

'I'll take his feet,' Cat said.

I nodded. While I stepped onto the plastic sheet and crouched over Elliot's head, Cat walked around to the other end. She squatted down. Reaching out with both arms, she grabbed him by the ankles. She swung his legs together and stood up, lifting them.

'All set?' I asked.

'All set,' she said.

I shoved my hands under his shoulders, hooked him by the armpits, and lifted.

For such a skinny guy, he seemed to weigh a lot.

We didn't try to pick him up completely. I waddled backward and Cat came forward. Elliot sagged between us, his ass dragging on the carpet. Which worked fine until his rear met the edge of the mattress cover. At that point, he started scooting the cover in front of him, rucking it up.

So then I had to hoist him all the way off the floor.

I staggered backward fast and Cat scurried forward. This shook up Elliot a lot. His penis, hanging limp across his thigh, wobbled and bounced. I turned my eyes to Cat. She seemed to be watching it.

She looked like someone pushing a wheelbarrow over rough ground. Grim. Sweaty. Her breasts jiggling as she rushed along.

I saw that she now had thin trickles of blood below the fang holes on her pubic mound.

We set down Elliot in the middle of the plastic sheet.

When Cat stood up straight, she noticed her problem. She frowned without much concern and swiped her fingers across the area, smearing the blood. Then she gave me a crooked smile and said, 'Leakage.'

I blushed. 'Want me to get the bandages?'

'I guess I'd better take care of it. And my foot – before the blood starts slopping out of my moccasin. The last thing we want's more mess on the carpet.'

She stepped off the plastic sheet. Instead of heading for the bathroom, she walked over to where she'd set down her duct tape, scissors and rope. She left the rope on the floor, but picked up the tape and scissors.

She tossed the roll of tape underhand, and I caught it.

'Please don't toss me the scissors,' I said.

'Chicken.' On her way over to me, she said, 'Would you mind taping his ankles together? And his wrists? I think it'll make him easier to handle. He won't flop around so much.'

I nodded and said, 'Fine. Good idea.'

She gave the scissors to me. 'It'll just take me a few minutes to slap some bandages on, and then we can wrap him up and . . .'

'If you'd like to go ahead and take your shower now,' I said, 'I'll finish up with Elliot.'

She looked pleased. 'Wrap him up?'

'Sure. No sweat.'

'That'd be great. Thanks.'

'You're welcome.'

'I'll try to be quick.'

'Take your time. I'll have him all taken care of by the time you're out.'

'Fabulous. Just make sure the stake stays where it is.'

I smiled. 'Why's that?'

40

'You know why.'

'He'll come back?' I suggested.

'He might.'

'I doubt it.'

She raised her eyebrows. 'If you're gonna pull the stake, let me know now so I can get dressed and evacuate the premises.'

'Oh, don't do that. I'll leave the stake right where it is. In fact, I'll *tape* it so it can't come out.'

7

Cat shut the bathroom door, but not all the way. She left it open a few inches. Maybe so the hot, steamy air would have a way out. Maybe for some other reason.

I stayed away from the door; I had a job to do.

While I worked on Elliot, I listened to the sounds of Cat's shower: the water coming on, the glass door sliding shut, the whispery hiss of the spray. I tried to concentrate on how she must look.

Cat standing in the hot spray.

Not Elliot stretched out dead on the mattress cover.

Cat sliding a bar of soap over her shiny skin.

Not me binding Elliot's ankles together with duct tape. Not me taping his hands together, crossed over his belly.

Cat slipping a sudsy hand between her legs.

Not me taping Elliot's penis down and covering his genital area with broad strips of tape.

Cat rubbing shampoo into her short, golden hair.

Not me pressing strips of tape across Elliot's snarling mouth and open eyes.

The shower was still going when I wrestled Elliot into a sitting position. I pushed him so that he slumped forward, head drooping over his knees. Then I wound the tape several times around his chest and arms and back. In front, the point of the stake popped through the tape and skewered it. In back, the blunt end made the tape bulge. Pretty soon, I had the stake secure. It wasn't going anyplace – not without a lot of help.

Soon after the shower went silent, I lowered Elliot onto the mattress cover, folded it over him, applied duct tape...

When I finished, he was sealed in a cocoon of white plastic and wide silver tape.

My hands and knees red from the bloody job, I sat on the corner of the bed to wait for Cat. Some quiet sounds came from inside the bathroom. I heard her snap the lid of a bandage tin shut. I heard her humming a tune from *The Sound of Music* – the one about 'a few of my favorite things.'

Finally she came out.

She didn't have a towel. She looked clean and new. Her short hair was combed and parted.

She carried her moccasins. Side by side on the instep of her bare left foot were two adhesive bandages. Though 'flesh' colored like those on my forearm, they weren't strips. These bandages were circular, about an inch in diameter, and looked as if they'd been designed to cover puncture wounds. She probably wore a couple more on the bottom of her foot, where I couldn't see them.

She wore two on the smooth slope between her legs. Others, I guess, were under her and out of sight.

The old pair of holes on her neck hadn't been covered. They seemed to be a darker shade of red than before. Her other old wounds also looked more conspicuous, the way blemishes often do after a shower. Probably because of the heat.

Her body was a *map* of the places where Elliot had sunk in his fangs.

He'd been almost everywhere.

Even her belly, though it was flat and must've been hard to bite.

Smiling at me, Cat said, 'Looks like *you* need another shower.'

'I'll just wash up a bit.'

She held on to her moccasins and took a few strides toward the end of the bed. Stopping, she gazed at Elliot. Her head tilted to one side. '*Very* nice,' she said.

'Thanks.'

'Thank *you*. God, though, it sure looks like a body.'

'It *is* a body.'

42

'We'd better not let anyone see it like this.'

'Do you have a plan?' I asked.

'Too bad he *didn't* turn to dust. I could've just run the vacuum cleaner...'

'Too bad,' I agreed.

'Now we've got a *stiff* on our hands. Like we're murderers, or something.'

'Yeah.'

She scowled at the stiff in such a fierce way that it made me grin. Then she looked at me and raised her eyebrows. 'Any ideas?' she asked.

'I don't suppose he'll turn to ashes if we put him out in the sunlight.'

'What sunlight?'

'We'd have to wait till morning,' I explained. 'Unwrap him. Lay him out on your lawn.'

'Oh, swift.'

'Works great in the movies. The direct sunlight hits a vampire, he goes up in a puff of smoke.'

'I've seen a few like that,' Cat said, nodding. 'You end up with a pile of ashes, and the wind comes along and scatters them.'

'But I have a feeling it won't work that way in real life.'

'I've got that feeling, too,' she said. 'So, I guess, what we've gotta do is *dispose* of the body. Like bury it somewhere.' She turned the fierce scowl on me. '*Not* in my back yard, thanks all the same. I don't want him anywhere near this place. It'd be too creepy.'

'And too dangerous,' I added. 'If he gets found, you don't want him on your property. We need to take him somewhere far away.'

'The farther, the better.'

'So, I guess he has to go in the trunk of your car.'

'Oh, what fun,' she said, but didn't look like she meant it.

After a little more discussion, I returned to the bathroom. Most of the blood was on my hands and knees, though some had also found its way onto my arms, chest and thighs. Not wanting to waste time with another shower, I stood in the tub, ran the water out of the faucet and used a washcloth to mop myself clean.

43

After that, I carried the damp washcloth into the bedroom. I found Cat standing on one leg in front of her dresser, putting on a white sock. 'With you in a jiff,' she said.

'No problem. I can take care of this.'

Staying away from the bloody area of the carpet, I squatted down beside Elliot and started to wipe the tape and the white plastic of the mattress cover. It wasn't a terrible mess – but bad enough. We needed it to be spotless before we could carry it down to the car.

While I worked at cleaning it, Cat put on another sock and a pair of black panties. There wasn't much to the panties. After seeing her without any for such a long time, though, they looked like a lot.

Next, she took a pair of white shorts out of a drawer. Before starting to put them on, she turned around and watched me wipe away some blood. 'Do you think he'll leak?' she asked.

'I don't think so. Not if the duct tape holds.'

'I mean, we don't want to leave a trail through the house. Bad enough he's wrecked the carpet up here.' She went ahead and stepped into the shorts. They were halfway up her legs when she stopped. Pulling them down, she said, 'White might not be the greatest idea, huh?'

'Probably not,' I agreed.

So she put them away and took out shorts that were fire-engine red. 'Better?'

'If you don't want blood to show, you'd better wear black.'

She smirked. 'Black? It'll probably be ninety degrees tomorrow. I'm not wearing black in that kind of heat.'

'Your panties are black,' I pointed out. And blushed.

'That's different. They're under*neath*. That's how come you call 'em *under*wear. I'd *cook* in black shorts.'

Grinning, I said, 'Well, it's up to you. Just don't wear red shorts thinking they'll hide bloodstains, that's all.'

'I know that. I'm a woman, for godsake. Not to mention Elliot's been visiting me for the past year. I'm the world's leading *expert* on blood stains.'

'Okay.'

'Ah! I know.' Turning her back to me, she squatted and

pulled open one of the bottom drawers. She rummaged about for a while, then stood up and faced me holding a pair of faded old cut-off blue jeans. They really had no legs at all. The leg holes were fringed with tatters of denim thread, and the bottoms of her pockets hung out below them. 'These'll be nice and cool,' she said. She bent over, stepped into the jeans, and pulled them up. 'Nobody'll even notice if they get a little blood on them.'

She was right about that for a couple of reasons.

Mainly because of how she looked in such ragged and skimpy shorts, especially with her top bare. Like some sort of fabulous, back-country primitive.

But also because the shorts were spattered and smeared with an array of colors: mostly beige, purple, bright yellow and a rusty reddish brown.

'My painting pants,' she said. 'See that?' She pointed at one of the rust colored patches. 'Redwood stain. I did the fence a couple of years ago.'

'Perfect,' I said.

My washcloth had become a little too saturated to do the job properly, so I hurried into the bathroom and squeezed it into the sink. Most of what came out was red. I rinsed the washcloth and wrung out the excess water. This time, the color was pink. I rinsed it again, squeezed it and rinsed – until finally the squeezed water looked clear. Then I returned to the bedroom.

Cat was now wearing a shirt. It appeared to be brand new: crisp and fresh, with brilliant checkers of red and yellow and blue. It had short sleeves. Untucked, it hung down low and hid the front of her cut-off jeans.

'Nice shirt,' I said.

'Thanks.' She undid her jeans and started to stuff her shirt tails inside. 'I figured, go multi-colored.'

'I don't think we'll be getting very messy.'

Crouching over Elliot, I resumed my task of cleaning off the blood stains.

Cat finished tucking in her shirt. When she was done, she looked very tapered and trim. But some of the shirt protruded from her leg holes like the ear tips of a gaudy, plaid bunny. Cat didn't notice, or didn't care.

Dressed as she was, none of her marks showed. Elliot had obviously been careful only to bite her in places that would usually be hidden under clothes.

Sly bastard.

While Cat walked over to her closet, I rolled Elliot over. This side of the plastic sheet had very little blood on it. I mopped it with my washcloth.

Cat took a pair of high-top walking shoes out of her closet, then turned around to put them on. They were brown leather.

'There goes the multi-colored motif,' I said.

'But these'll be easy to clean. A damp cloth...'

I tossed my damp cloth into the air, and caught it.

'Exactly. Let's bring it with us. You never know.'

'I seem to be about done,' I said. 'Let me just go and rinse this out again.'

'Go on.' She squatted down to tie her laces.

I went into the bathroom and once again cleaned the washcloth.

'We'll take this, too,' she said when I came out. Ducking quickly beside her bed, she snatched my towel off the floor. 'Probably a lot of stuff we should take,' she added. She swung the towel over her right shoulder. Letting it hang there, she headed for Elliot.

I followed.

She stopped near the body, put her hands on her hips, and scowled down at it. 'We'll probably need a shovel. And I brought that rope up from downstairs. It might come in handy. What else?'

She looked at me, her eyebrows rising.

'I guess it might depend on where we're taking him.'

'Any suggestions?' she asked.

'For starters, we oughta get him out of LA.'

She smiled. 'Too bad we can't ship him back to Transylvania where he belongs.'

'I don't think we'd better try to *ship* him anywhere.'

'Fly him away on TWA?'

'I wish. What I suppose we *should* do is drive him out to the mountains or desert...'

'Out of state,' she added.

'Sounds good to me. Maybe Arizona or Nevada. They're not *that* far away, and they both have plenty of nice, desolate places.'

'We'll have to drive all night,' Cat pointed out. 'Are you up to it?'

'Hope so.'

'Do you need a nap before we start?' She nodded toward her bed.

Would I be able to fall asleep in the same room as Elliot? Or in the same room as *Cat,* for that matter?

Not likely.

'I don't need a nap,' I told her. 'We should get him out of here – make as many miles as we can before daylight.'

I looked at the clock on her headboard.

1:33

'We don't have a lot of time before dawn,' I said.

'Is dawn our deadline?' she asked.

'We might want to plant him under cover of darkness.'

'There's always tomorrow night.'

'True.'

'I'll pack some things,' she said. 'A few days' worth.'

Trying not to look like a kid on Christmas eve, I said, 'My stuff's already in your car.'

8

Cat started packing a bag for our trip.

I went to her closet and retrieved my clothes. As I put them on, I asked, 'What about your carpet?'

'It'll keep.'

'Should we try to clean it before we go?'

We both turned our eyes to the swamp of blood near Elliot's wrapped body.

Cat shook her head. 'I guess it's beyond anything we can clean up.'

'We can't just leave it this way,' I said.

'Sure we can. I'm not expecting anyone. When we get back, I'll call up the carpet people and have it taken out.'

'They'll see the blood.'

'I'll tell them my dog exploded.'

A laugh took me by surprise and leaped out. 'Do you *have* a dog?' I asked.

'Not anymore. My dog, Poppy? It had a gas problem, went *boom.*'

'You think they'll believe that?'

'They're carpet guys, not cops. They won't even *ask* about the blood. But if they do, they won't know what the hell I'm telling them; they barely speak English. They'll just grin and nod. That's all they ever do. Grin and nod and say, "Veddy good, veddy good."'

'I hope you're right,' I said, and fastened my belt buckle.

'I'm right. I know these guys. But if the cops do get brought in and find out it's human blood, I'll just make up something. Maybe I came home and found the carpet this way, don't know *what* happened.'

'That might work.'

'Yeah. I'll just plead ignorance. What can they prove? Especially with the body nowhere to be found. They won't know who the blood came from. They won't even know for sure if anyone died. But I really don't think it's gonna come up. My guys'll get rid of the carpet, bring in a new one, and that'll be the end of it.'

'Done it before?' I asked, just kidding around as I pulled on one of my socks.

Cat met my eyes. She suddenly looked grim. 'Yeah. Last year when my husband was killed. There was a *lot* of blood, and they didn't ask any questions. Not the carpet guys, anyway.'

I suddenly found myself at a loss for questions, too. Her husband had been killed *here*?

'I thought it was a car accident,' I said.

She looked a little confused. 'I didn't tell you that.'

'I guess I just assumed . . .'

'He was murdered here in the bedroom.'

'My God,' I muttered.

Her eyes suddenly brimmed with tears. 'Can we talk about it later?' she asked.

'Sure.'

She wiped her eyes and sniffed. Trying to smile, she said, 'You'd think I'd be over it. I mean, it's been a year. Not to mention, Bill was such a jerk.' She shrugged one shoulder. 'I've gotta finish packing.'

With that, she turned away and headed for her dresser.

I put on my sneakers.

While I watched Cat, I thought about carrying Elliot down to the car.

Hauling him out the front door of the house and across the lawn to the driveway didn't seem like a great idea. L.A. never sleeps. Neither does Santa Monica. A neighbor might pick the wrong moment to look out a window. A dog-lover might stroll by with the pooch. A car might come along. And there are the derelicts: winos, druggies, crazies. You never know where one might be lurking.

If all that didn't make it risky enough, a police patrol car might roll by just as we lugged the body out. Unlikely, but possible. We'd be a lot more likely to encounter rent-a-cops from a private security company.

'You have a back door?' I asked.

She came out of the bathroom carrying a toilet kit. 'What do you mean?'

'Your house? It has a back door, doesn't it?'

'Sure.'

'Where is it?'

She gave me a tilted smile. 'At the rear of the house?' she suggested, as if trying to answer a riddle.

'On the driveway side?'

'Yeah. It goes out from the kitchen.' She tucked the kit into her overnight bag. 'I was thinking maybe we ought to take Elliot out that way,' she said.

'That's what I was thinking.'

'We could pull the car back there . . .'

'Want me to move it while you finish packing?'

She flashed a smile at me. 'Wait a minute and I'll go with you. I'm almost done.'

'Okay.'

So I waited. We were losing a few minutes, but I didn't mind. We still had several hours of darkness. There was no reason to hurry.

The mind is funny. A corner of my mind never forgot one thing, no matter what else was going on that night: as soon as we finished taking care of Elliot, Cat would probably send me home.

I wanted that moment to be far, far away.

Delays were my friends – so long as they didn't put us at extra risk.

When Cat finished packing, I took her overnight bag. She loaded herself with her keys, the washcloth and towel, the coil of rope, and a flashlight she took from one of her nightstands.

I noticed the hammer on the floor, so I hurried over and picked it up. 'Don't want to leave *this* behind,' I said.

'Right. The murder weapon. Give it here, I'll wrap it in the towel.'

'Just a second.' I took the hammer to the bathroom sink and washed off the blood. Then I brought it back to Cat. She swaddled it with the towel and tucked the bundle under one arm.

'What about the scissors and tape?' she asked. They were on the floor near Elliot. 'Should we take them with us?'

'Maybe leave them up here till we're ready to go. Just in case.'

Then we headed downstairs. Instead of going out the front door, we walked to the rear of the house. The kitchen was dark. We kept it that way. I waited inside while Cat went for her car.

Keeping the headlights off, she drove slowly up the driveway and stopped just beyond the back door. When the engine shut off, I stepped down onto the driveway with her bag.

This section of the driveway looked dark and private. We were a good distance from the road. The narrow driveway had Cat's house on one side, a six-foot high redwood fence on the other. Bushes loomed over the top of the fence. I couldn't see the neighbor's house beyond all that.

Cat still hadn't climbed out of the car.

It was dark inside.

Curious, I peered through the back window. She seemed to be twisted around in her seat, both arms high, her hands busy with the ceiling light.

A couple of minutes later, no light came on when she opened her door.

Cat, the master criminal.

She came to the rear of the car.

Instead of throwing her bag into the trunk, we took mine out. We put the washcloth and towel-wrapped hammer in the trunk. Both bags went into the back seat, along with the rope.

'What about a shovel?' I whispered.

'This way.'

I followed her past the front of her car and up the driveway toward the garage. She held the flashlight, but didn't turn it on. We had good moonlight, and there were few trees back here to throw shadows.

The garage door didn't seem to have an automatic opener. It wasn't locked, so I stepped in front of Cat and rolled the door open.

As we stepped in, she flicked her light on. She swung its beam to the left, where all sorts of tools hung from nails on the wall. The beam swept here and there for a moment, then settled on a spade.

I went and got it. I also grabbed a large, heavy pick-ax. 'This might come in handy,' I whispered.

'Anything else?' Cat asked.

'I don't know. Never done this sort of thing before.' Hanging nearby were a couple of saws and an ax.

Back in the old days – in real life, not in the movies – peasants used to deal with vampires by cutting off their heads. I'd read about it for a report in high school. From what I could recall, there was business about stuffing a vampire's mouth with garlic, cutting off his head, and burying him at a crossroads.

I wanted nothing to do with anything like that.

Shovel in one hand, pick in the other, I said, 'This should do it.'

Cat didn't suggest an ax or a saw.

Apparently, she and I had learned our vampire lore from different sources. She knew about mirrors, but not about decapitation.

She shut the garage door.

Following her down the driveway, I felt guilty about keeping my mouth shut. As if I'd lied to her. But if I'd mentioned decapitation, we probably would've had to take the ax. Sooner or later, I would've been forced to chop off Elliot's head. Better the guilt than that.

I stowed the shovel and pick-ax on the backseat floor of her car. She put her flashlight on the seat. We shut the back door of her car. Leaving the trunk open, we went back inside the house to get Elliot.

We found him as we'd left him; bundled in white plastic and silver tape upstairs on the bedroom floor.

Cat lifted his legs, and I raised his back off the floor. I stood there, bent over him, his head resting against my knees, and tried to get a firm grip on his upper arms through the mattress cover. Each time I attempted to pick him up, he slipped and dropped.

Cat lowered his legs. 'Let me try,' she said.

I let her.

She had no better luck than me. After dropping him a couple of times, she said, 'It's the mattress cover. You can't get a good hold on him.'

'I know. Plus, he weighs a ton.'

Cat took a step away from the body. Scowling down at it, she swung her hips over to the left. She shook her head. She put her hands on her hips. Shaking her head some more, she said, 'I guess we'll have to drag him.'

'I could try a "fireman's carry."'

'Throw him over your shoulder?'

'It's worth a try.'

Cat grimaced. 'He's awfully heavy. I don't want you to hurt yourself.'

'No harm in trying.'

'Not if you don't bust a gut or fall down the stairs, or something.'

'Let's see how it goes,' I said.

We both crouched down and lifted Elliot into a sitting position. Then I went around to the front, straddled him, sank to my knees and hunched down so that my left shoulder was snug against his belly.

'Okay,' I said. 'Let's load him up.'

As I hooked an arm around him, Cat shoved him forward. He flopped onto my back.

I yelled, 'OW!'

'What?'

'SHIT!'

'What?'

'THE STAKE!'

Cat tugged Elliot off me. As I scurried clear, his back and head thudded the floor.

I stayed on my hands and knees.

'You're bleeding,' Cat said.

'That doesn't surprise me.'

She came over and pulled up my shirt. 'I don't think it's very deep,' she said.

I raised my head. About two inches of the stake's bloody tip was jutting up through white plastic against Elliot's chest. 'Guess it didn't go in me *more* than two inches.'

'A lot less, I think.'

'Hope so.'

'Don't move, I'll get something.' She rushed off.

I remained on my hands and knees. The hole in my back burned. It didn't feel two inches deep, but it felt deep enough. Blood was welling out, spreading around my back, dribbling down the sides of my ribcage and falling, making a new red design on the carpet.

Cat returned and knelt beside me. She pulled my T-shirt the rest of the way up my back, over my shoulders and head, and down my arms. I lifted one hand off the floor at a time as if stepping out of pants.

Cat took the T-shirt. She wadded it and started mopping the blood off my back.

'It got you pretty good,' she said.

'Hoist with my own petard,' said I.

'Does it hurt?'

It hurt like hell.

'A little,' I said.

'I'm going to push against it.'

'Good idea.'

She pushed. I arched my back and gritted my teeth and hissed.

53

'I'll just hold it there for a few minutes,' she said. 'Maybe you'd better lie down.'

The carpet looked clean under me – except for dribbles of my own blood. So I eased myself down, stretched out, and folded my arms under my face. Cat kept pressure on my wound.

'Do you think it'll be all right?' I asked.

'I think so. I'll bandage it up in a while, and we'll be on our way.'

'What a stupid move,' I said. 'I didn't even *think* about the stake.'

'Maybe you weren't supposed to.'

'What do you mean?'

'Elliot's revenge.'

She was probably kidding, but it gave me the creeps.

I smiled anyway and said, 'If that's the worst he can do, I think we'll survive.'

Cat was silent for a long time. She just stayed on her knees beside me, pressing the T-shirt against my wound. Finally she said, 'I thought it would be over. Like magic. Put the stake through Elliot, and everything bad would suddenly end. But it's not going to be that way.'

'This was just a little accident,' I said.

'I'm not so sure.'

'I'm sure.'

'Maybe he's out to get us.'

'Elliot?'

'Yeah.'

'Elliot didn't have anything to do with it. I should've been more careful, that's all.'

'I hope that's all,' Cat said.

9

After a while, Cat stopped pushing against the hole in my back. She bandaged it. Then she brought a warm, damp washcloth from the bathroom and rubbed my back and sides. It felt good.

'Sit up,' she said, 'and I'll get your front.'

I started to push myself up. Fire rammed through my back. I cried out, but didn't let the pain stop me. When I was on my knees, I felt a little better.

Cat looked worried.

'Guess it messed me up a little,' I said.

On her knees in front of me, she started swabbing my chest with the moist cloth. There was almost no blood there, but I didn't object to the treatment. My skin was itchy from the carpet. The warm cloth felt great. And I liked having Cat care for me.

'Do you think you'll be all right?' she asked.

'Eventually.'

'Should we take you to an emergency room?'

'Nah. I'll be okay. As long as things don't get worse.'

'You'd better take it easy.'

'I'll take it easy *after* we get Elliot in the car.'

Her hand roamed lower, rubbing the warm cloth over my sides and belly. When she edged it down a little under the waistband of my jeans, I had to squirm. She grinned.

'Are you feeling any better?' she asked.

'Better all the time.'

She started working her way upward again with the washcloth. 'I'll have to find you a shirt to wear.'

'Mine's ruined, huh?'

'It's seen better days.'

'I liked that vulture.'

'You can probably keep the shirt around as a junker. I'll leave it soaking while we're gone.'

'That'd be nice. Thanks.'

'But you'll need something for the trip.' With that, she got to her feet. She took the washcloth and my T-shirt into the bathroom. Water ran for a couple of minutes. Then she came out and walked over to her wall of closets. She slid open a door near the far left end.

Her back to me, she said, 'I kept some of Bill's old things.'

'I'd rather wear something of yours.'

She grinned over her shoulder at me.

'If you've got a shirt that's really huge on you . . .'

'I don't have any *that* huge.' She returned her attention to the closet.

'I've got a spare one of my own down in your car,' I explained.

'How's this?' She pulled a shirt off its hanger and whirled around with it. The shirt looked similar to the one she was wearing: short sleeves, bright checkers.

I must've made a face.

'What's wrong with it?' she asked.

'Nothing.'

'It's a perfectly good shirt.'

Why fight it?

'Well, okay,' I said, and got to my feet.

Cat brought the shirt over. Behind me, she slipped it up my arms and onto my shoulders. Then she came around to the front and started to button it.

'It's perfectly fine,' she said.

'I suppose so.'

'He didn't *die* in it, you know.'

'Huh?'

'Bill. My husband. If that's what you're worried about. He wasn't wearing *anything* when he died.'

I hadn't needed to know that.

'I just don't like wearing someone else's stuff,' I said.

Especially not stuff that had belonged to Cat's husband, dead or otherwise.

She fastened the last button and said, 'I'm the one who bought it. Does that make a difference?'

It made a big difference.

'I guess so,' I said.

Hands on my shoulders, she leaned forward and kissed me. I felt her lips on my mouth, the soft push of her breasts against my chest, but only for a second. Then she eased away and said, 'Ready?'

'For what?'

'For him.'

We both turned and stared down at Elliot.

I stared especially at the bloody, wooden point sticking up out of him.

'Maybe we'd better just drag him,' I suggested.

Cat nodded. 'Exactly.'

I stepped over to the bundle, bent down and grabbed Elliot

56

by his ankles. Ignoring the pain from my wounded back, I lifted his legs off the floor and swung them toward the bedroom door.

'Not that way,' Cat said. 'Bring him over here.'

She was striding past a corner of her bed.

At first, I thought she meant me to drag Elliot into the bathroom. Which didn't make sense. But she walked past the bathroom door and continued toward a window.

Her king-sized bed and its twin nightstands were positioned between two windows.

She went to the window on the right, spread its curtains apart, slid it open, then turned around and smiled at me. 'Guess what's below,' she said.

'The ground?'

'The driveway.'

I lowered Elliot's legs and hurried to the window. It had no screen. I leaned out.

Straight down was the narrow, concrete driveway.

Turning my head, I saw Cat's car off to the right.

The neighbor's house on the other side of the driveway had a couple of upstairs windows facing our way. They were dark.

I stepped back from the window and nodded. 'If nobody sees us from the house next door...'

'They've gone to England for three weeks.'

'The place is definitely empty? No house-sitter?'

'I've got the keys. I went in just this morning to water Betty's plants. Nobody's there.'

'In that case, the window seems like a jolly good idea.'

'Wish I'd thought of it before you caught the stake in your back.'

Smiling, I said, 'Me, too.'

'Anyway, if we use the window, we won't have the stairway to contend with. And we won't have to drag Elliot all through the house. It'll make things a lot easier, especially now that you're hurt.'

'A lot easier.'

'We don't even have to worry about taking off the screen. Thanks to Elliot. I wrecked it a year ago trying to get away from him.'

I gazed at her.

She shrugged.

'You tried to jump?' I asked.

'A long way down, huh?'

'Sure is.'

'It was the night he killed Bill.'

'*Elliot killed Bill?*'

She stared into my eyes. Nodding, she nibbled her lower lip. After a few seconds, she said, 'Yeah, he did. I tried to dive out the window to get away from him. It was wide open, but I whammed against the screen. Demolished the thing. But it slowed me down so Elliot had a chance to grab me and pull me back in.'

'My God. It's a good thing he did. You might've been killed.'

Looking away from me, she said, 'That would've suited me fine.'

'Jesus,' I muttered.

She faced me again. 'I'm not exactly suicidal. I just wanted to get out fast, no matter what.' She made a twitchy attempt at a smile. 'Anyway, so that's how come the screen's off. Shall we have Elliot exit via the window?'

I didn't want to try talking. Not just then, with the tightness in my throat. So I nodded and returned to Elliot's body. I picked up his legs and started to walk backward, dragging him. My back hurt. So did my forearm, though the fang bites were not nearly as painful as the puncture from the stake. The injuries, at least, helped take my mind off Cat.

With my back to the window, I set down Elliot's legs. 'I'll run down and get the rope,' I said.

Cat squeezed my shoulder. 'Don't bother.'

'It'll just take a couple of...'

'We won't need the rope.'

I saw the look in her eyes.

'You're kidding,' I said.

'I don't think so.'

I said, 'Jesus,' again.

The look in Cat's eyes was very much like the old glint of impish mischief that I'd seen in them so often when we were teenagers. But the old look had been bright with innocent fun. The new one had a hard, sharp edge.

'Just drop *him*?' I asked.

'It'll be fast and easy.'

'Hard on *him*.'

The look of mischief spread to her mouth. 'He's dead, Sammy.'

'We can't just *drop* him.'

'Afraid he'll get a little banged up?'

'Well, yeah. It could bust him up pretty bad.'

Shaking her head, she laughed softly. 'We're gonna bury him, not sell him. He doesn't have to be in mint condition.'

'It's just ... no way to treat someone.'

'Seems like a *fine* way to treat Elliot.' The humor suddenly vanished from her face. 'I'll take care of it. You go on downstairs, or something.'

She stepped around Elliot, crouched down over his head, and started to wrestle him up. Not saying a word, I joined in. Cat didn't thank me, but she gave me a pleased glance. Together, we hauled Elliot into a standing position.

'Hold him up a second,' Cat said. 'I'll make sure the coast is clear.'

While I struggled to keep Elliot from toppling, she leaned out the window and gazed toward the street. The seat of her cut-off jeans was faded and didn't have much paint on it. She had a pair of old bite marks just below her right buttock.

Seeing the faded red dots, knowing that Elliot had put his mouth there and sunk his fangs in, I was suddenly reminded of other places where he'd put his teeth into Cat.

Dropping him out the window no longer seemed like a bad idea.

Cat turned around. 'Looks fine out there.'

'Maybe we should turn off the bedroom lights before we do it,' I said.

'Good idea.'

I continued to hold Elliot upright while Cat hurried around switching off the lamps and putting out the candles. She blew out all but two candles. They were in a tall holder by an end corner of her bed. 'I'll leave these going,' she told me. 'We oughta have *some* light.'

'That's fine,' I said. The room was fairly dark by then, and I liked how Cat looked in the shimmery glow.

She came over to me. 'If you can just get him a little closer to the window,' she said, 'I'll take over and shove him out.'

'Fine.'

I had my arms around his chest, just below the protruding point of the stake. I sidestepped toward the window, swinging him along, his feet dragging.

Cat suddenly pranced in front of us.

Put herself between Elliot and the window.

'Be careful,' I said.

She reached up, grabbed Elliot by the shoulders and pulled downward. He bent at the waist.

The three of us hurled toward the window.

'Cat!'

With a savage grunt, she wrenched him out of my arms and whirled, flinging him headlong. She stumbled out of the way. Elliot lunged for the window.

His legs whammed the sill at about thigh level, but momentum was on our side. The upper part of his body plunged through the window, and his legs followed. The white of his plastic wrapper vanished.

I stayed put.

Cat got to the window in time to see him land.

I *heard* him land.

It was the sound you might get if you slapped a garment bag against concrete – if the bag was packed with meat instead of suits . . . and maybe, instead of shoes, a coconut.

Cat faced me and grinned.

'Worked like a charm,' she said.

10

Down on the driveway, I stood by Elliot's body while Cat brought the car toward us in reverse. She did it quietly, headlights off. There was nothing she could do about the back-up lights, though.

I kept an eye on the street.

Expecting a patrol car to cruise by at any moment.

Or a neighbor to stroll along, out for a walk with Rover.

Anybody getting a good look at the large, untidy package at my feet would be sure to suspect foul play. For one thing, the bundle was shaped like a man. For another, the tip of the stake was poking out.

And the white plastic cover was bloody.

Up in Cat's bedroom, I'd put a lot of effort into wrapping Elliot and cleaning off the blood. But he'd popped open when he hit the concrete. Not a lot, but enough.

He'd leaked.

And he was very well lit for a few moments when Cat's car neared us. In addition to the back-up lights, the brake lights came on, flaring red.

I imagined myself being confronted by police.

No, officer, you see, I know it looks bad, but the deal is, we really didn't murder this guy. You see, he's a vampire.

The car went dark.

As Cat climbed out and approached, I continued to watch the street.

She opened the trunk.

'Let's get him in,' she whispered.

We didn't try to pick him up at each end. That method, tried upstairs, hadn't worked out well. Instead, we both crouched over his head and raised him to a sitting position.

'Why's he so slippery?' Cat whispered.

'He sprang some leaks.'

'You mean this is *blood*?'

'Probably.'

'Great,' she muttered. 'Let's put him down.'

We lowered him.

'Should I try to tape him shut again?' I asked.

Cat made a sound like a growl. 'It'd take too long,' she said. 'Anyhow, the tape obviously doesn't work all that well.'

Maybe if we hadn't thrown Elliot out of a second-story window . . .

'Wait here,' she said. 'I'll go get a tarp. Be careful you don't get blood on your clothes.' Being careful herself, she kept her hands high as she hurried past her car.

She continued on alongside the house, and I realized she was heading for her garage.

61

I stayed with Elliot's body.

For a while, nothing went wrong.

Then I heard a car engine. It sounded far away. But slowly it grew louder. And louder.

I muttered, 'Oh, shit.'

Down past the foot of the driveway, the street pavement brightened.

Standing, I was a lot more conspicuous than the bundle.

I glanced around fast, seeking a place to hide. The house wall was on one side, the redwood fence on the other. Cat's car looked like the only nearby cover.

No time to race around to its front.

No time to open a door and duck inside.

Hop into the trunk?

I glanced at the headbeams of the approaching car. They were tapering down like cones.

'Shit!' I gasped, and threw myself flat on the driveway.

Keeping my head down, I heard the car come cruising by. Along with its engine and tire sounds, I heard hissy crackles and voices from its radio.

Female voices.

Spouting a mostly incoherent jumble of numbers and words. But pieces here and there made sense.

'See the man...'

And 'Two-eleven in progress...'

And 'Euclid.'

I held my breath.

The sounds faded and finally disappeared.

Raising my head, I saw that the road was empty. So I pushed myself up – with mild pain from the fang wounds in my forearm and considerable pain from the stake hole in my back – then walked through the narrow space between Cat's car and the wall of her house.

I stayed in front of her car, sheltered from the street, until she returned with the tarp.

'What's wrong?' she asked.

'Cops came by.'

'*What?*'

'It's okay, they didn't stop. I hit the deck, and they kept on going.'

'They must not've seen you.'

'That's a safe bet.'

'We'd better get going.'

Cat in the lead, we made our way to the rear of her car. There, I helped her unfold the tarp and spread it open inside her trunk. It was way too big, overlapped the sides, and sort of drooped in the middle.

We wrestled Elliot to his feet and shoved him into the trunk. He dived in head first. His head, shoulders and chest whapped the tarp, knocked the air out from under it and mashed it down against the floor of the trunk.

He still hung out from the waist down, so we grabbed his legs and swung them up and shoved them in sideways. By the time we were done, Elliot was curled on his side with his knees bent.

We folded the loose sides of the tarp down on top of him. Then we shut the trunk.

Cat whispered, '*Dah-dahhhh!*'

'Mission accomplished,' I whispered.

'Never thought it'd be this tough,' she said. 'It's never this tough in the movies when they have to get rid of a stiff.'

'That's the movies for you. Can't trust them.'

'This is definitely the last time I kill someone in my own house,' she said.

I looked at her. She seemed to be smiling. 'Hope so,' I said.

'Now we'd better go back inside and clean up.'

'Again.'

'Again.'

She unlocked the door, let us in and turned on the kitchen light. Our hands and forearms were smeared with Elliot's blood. Cat had a smudge on her right cheek, where she'd probably rubbed an itch with her hand. I liked how she looked with it, but told her about it anyway. She didn't seem to have any blood on her shirt. If there was some on her cut-offs, it was well hidden among the various other stains. She had a broad smudge of blood on the front of her left thigh.

She cleaned herself off at the kitchen sink, using warm water and paper towels.

Then I washed up. Cat assured me that my face was clean. My shirt looked fine. I had a couple of smears on the legs of my blue jeans. They could've passed for paint stains, but I wetted them down and scrubbed them with a paper towel, just to take off the worst of the blood.

When we were done, we inspected each other.

'Clean as a whistle,' Cat told me.

'You, too.'

'So I guess we're ready to go.'

'Do you have overalls and gloves we can take with us?' I asked, mostly kidding.

'No overalls. How about gloves and aprons?'

'No apron for me,' I said.

'Gloves aren't a bad idea, though.' She opened the cupboard beneath the sink. After rummaging around for a minute or two, she found two pairs of yellow rubber gloves – the kind people sometimes wear when washing dishes or scrubbing floors. One pair was still inside its clear plastic package. 'This'll be good,' she said. 'We might not be able to wash up, wherever we end up unloading the bastard.'

She pulled a fresh, unwrapped roll of paper towels out of a cupboard. Clamping it under one arm, she said, 'I've also got a pack of wet wipes in the car.' She raised her eyebrows. 'What *about* aprons?'

I figured she would look good in one. But I said, 'We can get by without them. He'll probably be pretty dry, anyway, by the time we get where we're going.'

'Anything else we should take? Last call.'

'We might get thirsty along the way.'

'And hungry,' she added. She handed the gloves and paper towels to me, then went to the refrigerator. 'Pepsi okay?'

'Fine.'

'And I've got some bottled water.'

'That'd be a good idea.'

'Beer?' she asked.

'No thanks. It's gonna be tough enough to stay awake.'

'Should I make a pot of coffee?'

I shook my head. 'That'd take too long. We should get going.'

'Then I guess you don't want me to cook up a breakfast?'

'I'd love it. But how about a rain-check till we get back from this?'

'I'll just grab a few things.'

Within a few minutes, Cat had filled a shopping bag with six cans of cold Pepsi, six plastic bottles of spring water, a package of double-stuffed Oreo cookies, a sack of potato chips, a dry salami, an aerosol can of cheddar cheese, and a box of crackers. Then she turned around in a circle, scanning the kitchen and saying, 'Let's see, what else? What are we forgetting?'

'A tablecloth?' I suggested. 'Plates?'

'Smart ass.'

'Knives, forks and spoons?'

'A knife! Gotta have a knife for the salami!' She rushed to the counter, pulled open a drawer and came up with a steak knife. It had a wooden handle and a five-inch, serrated blade. She slipped it, point first, into the bag. 'Remember it's in here,' she warned. 'I don't want you hurting yourself again.'

'I'll be careful.'

'Is that it, then?'

'That should pretty much do it,' I said.

'Okay, then. I think I'll take a quick one before we hit the road.'

She hurried to a bathroom just down the hallway from the kitchen. When she returned, I took my turn. This one didn't have mirrors in funny places. And it had a fresh, flowery aroma that seemed to come from the bar of soap on the sink. After relieving myself, I washed with hot water and used the scented soap on my hands and face.

In the mirror above the sink, I still had messy hair and whiskers. I looked like a bum in a very nice shirt.

A lucky bum, I thought.

Real lucky. You've murdered a guy, you'll be damn lucky if you don't end up doing life in San Quentin.

But I saved Cat, I reminded myself. That bastard will never touch her again, never put his mouth on her, never sink his fangs into her neck or breasts or ... anywhere else.

I suddenly found myself picturing them together.

The way they'd looked on the bed when he was sucking her.

It made me feel hot and squirmy, so I got out of the bathroom fast and went back to Cat in the kitchen.

'I grabbed some matches,' she told me, and patted the left pocket of her shirt. The patting made her breast jiggle under the bright, checkered fabric.

'Matches?' I asked.

'You never know. We might want to light a campfire or burn down a school.'

'Endless possibilities,' I said.

'Be prepared. That's my motto. So, are we all set?'

'I guess so.'

'Let's hit the road,' she said.

I carried the grocery bag, the roll of paper towels, and the gloves. Cat shut off the lights and locked the house. When we reached the car, Cat opened a rear door and I set everything on the floor behind the front seat.

Then she headed around to the driver's side.

'Do you have a hose?' I asked.

'A hose?'

'A garden hose. One that'll reach the driveway.'

'Ah. Yeah, good idea. There's one just around the corner.'

'This'll only take a minute,' I said. 'You can go ahead and get in.'

It took more than a minute to find the hose, turn it on, drag it over to the driveway and hit the concrete with a good, hard stream of water. But it seemed like time well spent. When I was done, no visible traces of Elliot's blood could possibly remain on the driveway.

I put away the hose.

At last, I climbed into the car, sat down in the passenger seat, and swung the door shut. Cat reached over and squeezed my thigh. 'My guy,' she said.

'Glad to be of service, ma'am.'

'I didn't even *think* of the driveway.'

'Between the two of us,' I said, 'maybe we won't forget anything important.'

'We seem to be doing fine, so far.'

'If you don't count our wounds.'

'They'll heal.' She patted my leg and added, 'Mine always do.'

Then she took her hand away, twisted the ignition key and started the engine. Keeping the headlights off, she backed the car slowly down her driveway and swung it into the street.

No cars were coming.

She drove to the end of the block, then put the headlights on and said, 'We're off!'

11

At two-thirty in the morning, about the only people traveling on Los Angeles area freeways are drunks, killers, and cops.

I suppose we fit into category number two.

At least the traffic was light, and we made good time.

Cat tooled along at about five miles per hour above the speed limit. She did this without any advice from me. As if we'd both figured out the same rules for driving California freeways in the wee hours with a stiff in your trunk.

If you go too slowly, cops might think you're drunk and pull you over. Or you might get mowed down by a cannon-balling truck (the drivers of which are often *on* speed), slammed into by a speeding drunk, or shot by a speeding lunatic for getting in his way. If you go too *fast*, on the other hand, you might get pulled over for violating the speed limit. So you choose the middle ground, not too slow and not too fast.

In all matters risky, blending in is your safest course.

Blending in, and keeping your eyes open.

I had no trouble keeping my eyes open. I should've been asleep hours ago, and I'd gone through a lot of major stuff. It seemed, in ways, as if *weeks* had gone by since Cat's arrival at my door. But in other ways, it seemed as if only a few minutes had passed, that I'd only just begun to be with Cat again after years of missing her.

I felt exhausted, delighted, disoriented, excited and worried. But not sleepy.

I kept watch for hazards: reckless speeders, cars weaving and swerving from lane to lane, nearby vehicles carrying an unusual number of passengers (four guys in one car being a *very* bad sign), and Highway Patrol cars.

When any such hazards appeared, I warned Cat and she took evasive actions – usually changing lanes, slowing down, or speeding up to stay out of trouble.

It kept things from getting dull.

As we headed down from Sepulveda Pass on the northbound 405, Cat said, 'I've got maps in the glove compartment. Maybe we'd better figure out where we're going.'

'Where do we *want* to go?' I asked.

'Arizona? Nevada? Either one. Whichever is closer, I guess.'

'Arizona might be closer by an hour or so. But we should've gone through downtown and headed out the other way. We could still do it, though.' I stopped talking, opened the glove compartment and pulled out a stack of maps.

'Arizona's awful deserty,' Cat said. 'I'm not terribly keen on deserts.'

'But it has a lot of good, isolated places.' Why was I sticking up for Arizona? Nevada, farther away, would give me more time to be with her. 'Hot, though. This time of the year, it'll be miserable. Whereas Nevada could be pretty nice, especially if we go into the mountains.'

'Up near Lake Tahoe?' Cat asked. 'I love it there.'

'Tahoe might be a little crowded for disposing of a body,' I said. 'But we could head in that general direction. We'll probably go past plenty of good, desolate places.'

'So, how do we get there?'

'Where'd you put the flashlight?'

'Here.' She patted the console between our seats.

I found the flashlight, then spread the map of California open in front of me. The map, about a yard square, included the western portions of Nevada and Arizona, which was helpful.

Not so helpful was the fact that the southern half of California (including us) was on one side of the map, the northern half (including Tahoe) on the other. I had to keep flipping the map over, which was a good trick since it took up most of the space in front of me.

At last, I managed to find a route down from Lake Tahoe to our side of the map, and backtrack into familiar territory.

'Looks like we want 395,' I said. 'It'll take us all the way up, once we get onto it.'

'How do we accomplish that?' Cat asked.

'All we have to do is stay on the 405 till we run into the 14. Which oughta be up around Newhall...'

'Near Magic Mountain?'

'Before that. I think it's up the hill as you start to leave the valley. All we do is get on it, heading north, and keep going till it hits the 395 somewhere up past Edwards Air Force Base and Mojave.'

'Sounds simple enough.'

'Should be,' I said, then put away the flashlight and maps. Looking out the windows, it took me a while to figure out where we were. When we came to a sign for the Devonshire exit, I got a fix on our location and knew we were pretty far north in the valley – about to start climbing into the hills. Maybe about five minutes to our turnoff.

Headlights were rushing toward us from the rear, but they seemed to be in a different lane. A hundred yards ahead of us, an old pickup truck with one dead taillight was doing about forty in the slow lane. The bed of the truck appeared to be loaded with people.

'Better watch this one,' I said.

As we closed the gap, we got a better look at the group in the back of the pickup. They were kids – six or eight boys and girls of various ages. One of the girls appeared to be holding a baby.

'I don't think they're gang-bangers,' Cat said.

'Future gang-bangers,' I corrected her.

'If they live that long,' Cat said, shaking her head. 'They could end up scattered all over the freeway, riding like that.'

'Probably on their way home from a family outing,' I said.

'The parents must be nuts.'

'Or poor,' I added.

'Poor is no excuse for risking your kids that way. There *is* no excuse.'

When we passed the pickup, a few of them waved at us. I waved back. Cat didn't look at them.

But we both glanced over at the driver. He was a heavy guy with a black moustache and a white cowboy hat. Two other people seemed to be crowded into the seat with him. The guy smiled cheerfully at us. I smiled back at him, and then we left him and his brood behind.

'Ignorant s.o.b.,' Cat muttered.

'Yeah,' I said.

'I hate it.'

'Are you all right?'

'Doesn't he know what'll happen to those kids if he crashes?'

'He probably figures he won't crash.'

'Stupid bastard.'

I'd never seen Cat this way. I reached over and put a hand on her thigh. It was meant to comfort her, settle her down. But I wasn't ready for the feel of her bare skin. I gave her a couple of gentle pats, and quickly took my hand away.

She glanced at me. 'Somebody oughta sharpen up stakes and go after all the stupid, careless people in this world. I sometimes think they're worse than the Elliots. Maybe they aren't *evil*, but they do as much damage.'

'Maybe more,' I agreed. I wondered where she'd come up with such ideas – and why she was so vehement about them.

'Only thing is, there aren't enough forests.'

'To make enough stakes?'

'Right.'

I smiled a little nervously. Trying to lighten things up, I said, 'Sounds like you've been taking sensitivity training from Vlad the Impaler.'

She laughed softly. 'That's me. I'd leave the crooks to someone else. Just give me the ignorant, careless creeps who drive around with their kids loose in the back of a pickup truck. Give me the drunk drivers. Give me the ones that tailgate you, and cut you off, and run stop lights. And the parents who turn their backs and let their kids drown in pools or get hit by cars or shredded by dogs or snatched up by serial killers. I hate 'em all.'

'What ever happened to "love thy neighbor"?'

'I love my neighbor's victims.' She smiled over at me and said, 'Sorry. Certain things bother me.'

'I remember when your biggest concern was having a great suntan.'

She let out a soft laugh. 'Seattle and suntans don't mix. You've never seen so much rain. That's one reason I moved back to LA as soon as I was old enough.'

'You got it,' I told her.

70

'Got what?'

'The great tan.'

'All over,' she said.

The memory of Cat, naked, surged through me in vivid color. I blushed, but she couldn't see it. I also started to stiffen up; she couldn't see that, either.

'Elliot liked it that way,' she explained.

Who wouldn't? I thought.

'I do, too,' she said. 'Not so much having the tan as getting it. Just to be outside like that with nothing on. You feel so free and . . . real. You feel the sunlight on your skin. You feel the slightest breezes. And it's *fabulous* in the rain. You feel all the raindrops pattering against you.'

'Sounds great, all right,' I said.

'Anyway, things happened. Mostly after I met Bill. I started to worry about stuff. It probably came from watching the news on TV. Bill got me into that. When I was growing up, you know, we almost always ate supper in the kitchen. We only got to eat in front of the TV for special events. But Bill liked to eat in the living room every night and watch the news. He was sort of a news junkie, I guess.'

'What did he do for a living?'

'He was a doctor. An obstetrician.' She let out a small laugh. 'That was a good one – an obstetrician who hated kids.'

'He hated kids?'

'Hated kids, but loved to watch the TV news. I think maybe he just liked to ogle the info-babes.'

Why would he want to ogle them when he had you? I thought it, but kept it to myself. I usually know better than to actually say corny stuff like that.

'Anyway, I had to sit there and watch the news with him. It wasn't just at supper, either. But that was when I couldn't get away from it; I had to sit there and eat with him, so I ended up getting at least an hour, night after night, of one God-awful horror story after another. It's nothing but death and destruction . . .'

'And good stuff that'll kill you if you eat or drink it,' I added.

'Which includes everything,' Cat said.

'Pretty much.'

'The thing is, I didn't want to *know* all these things. But I got them shoved down my throat along with my meat and potatoes. And it just ... you start to see patterns. The terrible things that happen to people, some happen because of rotten luck – you're in the wrong place at the wrong time – but most of it's because people just don't think or don't care. You know?'

'Yeah.'

'They don't even seem to give a thought to what might happen.'

'On the other hand,' I said, 'you don't want to spend your life worrying about "worst-case scenerios."'

'You'll live longer if you do. So will your kids.'

'But you might not have much fun.'

She glanced at me. 'Do you know how many kids die because their mothers leave them alone to chat on the phone or visit a neighbor or have a couple of toots at the local bar?'

'No,' I admitted.

'Plenty,' she said. 'And these kids who get abducted all the time by pederasts? God only knows what sort of hell they must go through, getting tortured and raped and murdered by those animals. But most of those kids ... they got snatched in the first place because their damned *mothers* didn't care enough to watch over them.'

'Or their fathers,' I suggested.

'The buck stops with the mom. She's the one who gives birth, and she's the one with the ultimate responsibility for the safety of her kids. When something happens to them, it's almost always because she dropped the ball.'

'What about the bunch we just saw in the pickup truck?' I asked. 'That was probably the father behind the wheel. You called him a stupid bastard, didn't you?'

'Yeah. And he is. But the mother of his kids is the idiot who got herself knocked up by him. She never should've had kids with him. But since she *did*, she shouldn't let *anyone*, father or otherwise, drive around on freeways with her kids in the bed of a pickup truck.'

'With a dead taillight,' I added.

'If she didn't want to watch out for them, she shouldn't have *had* them. Stupid bitch.'

I looked at Cat. There wasn't enough light to see the expression on her face, but she was facing straight ahead, gazing out through the windshield, her fists clenched on the steering wheel. I could almost feel the tightness of her muscles, the heat of her rage.

'If I had kids,' she said, 'I'd take care of them. They wouldn't end up drowning in the tub or burning up or getting mauled by a dog . . . or grabbed off the street by some sick pervert. I'd be *with* them. I'd keep them safe.'

'Something can always happen,' I told her.

'Sure. I know that. But most of it happens because somebody got careless. Somebody was stupid and careless and *let* it happen.'

'You and Bill . . .' I paused, not quiet sure how to ask.

'He didn't want kids. He hated kids. And he didn't want me to get fat.'

'Nice guy,' I muttered.

'*I* wanted kids,' she said. 'And I finally got pregnant, in spite of him. But I made the mistake of telling him. I didn't realize . . . I figured he'd be happy about it. Stupid. But the thing is, this would've been his *own* kid. You know? When it's your own, it's not like some stranger. You don't hate it because it's loud or annoying or something, you love it because it's yours. At least that's what I thought. But Bill didn't see it that way.'

'He made you get rid of it?' I asked.

'*He* got rid of it. He gave me an abortion.'

'Your *husband* did?'

'In our own house. In our own bed. He . . . slipped a drug of some kind into my . . . It was a Friday night, so I made clam chowder for him. It was a favorite of his. But he put a drug in my bowl and knocked me out. Then he carried me up to bed and . . . while I was out cold, he did it. Went into me with . . . forceps or whatever. It was over by the time I woke up. The bed was all bloody. Seems like my bed is *always* all bloody.'

'Jesus,' I muttered.

'He told me he'd flushed the baby down the toilet.'

'The dirty bastard . . .'

'But I'm the stupid bitch who married him. I'm the stupid

bitch who let him knock me up. I'm the stupid bitch who let him murder my baby. That's how come I'm such an expert on stupid bitches.'

She barely got that out before she started crying.

12

'Maybe I should drive,' I suggested.

What I really wanted to do was hold Cat in my arms, hug her and make her hurts go away.

But I just sat there in the passenger seat and offered to drive.

Cat shook her head and choked out, 'I'm all right,' through her blubbering.

'Can you see where you're driving?'

'I'm fine.' She wiped one eye, then the other.

'Here comes the 14. Better get over one lane.'

She changed lanes and got us onto the 14 without any trouble, even though she was still bawling pretty good as she did it. After a while, she began to settle down. She sobbed and sniffed and wiped her nose and knuckled tears out of her eyes. And finally she made a deep, shaky sigh.

'Wow,' she said. 'Sorry.'

'Nothing to apologize for.'

'I don't know what happened.'

'You sort of let go.'

'I'll say.' She glanced at me and said, 'At least I kept hold of the steering wheel.'

'Lucky for us.'

'I didn't think it would . . . I've never told anyone about any of that . . . about the abortion.'

'You're kidding.'

She shook her head.

'Nobody?'

'Who would I tell?'

I thought about it for a few seconds. It wasn't the sort of thing you'd want to tell your parents. Probably not even your friends, unless they were especially close. Anyone sane hearing about it would despise Bill forever. 'The police?' I suggested.

'Thanks, but no thanks.'

As she drove along the highway through the moonlit night, I felt the solemn glory of being the one-and-only person to whom she'd revealed her terrible secret.

After a while, I said, 'What he did to you ... he must've broken a ton of laws. An abortion like that, against your will? Drugging you? Unauthorized surgery? Not to mention a possible murder charge for ... destroying the child. They probably could've thrown him in prison for years.'

'I didn't want him in prison,' Cat said. 'I wanted him dead.'

That got my attention like a sledge hammer coming through the windshield.

I muttered, 'My God.'

She said, 'He murdered my baby.'

'Did he ... what else?'

'What do you mean?'

'When he was doing that to you, did he ...?' I couldn't think of a good way to ask it. Finally, I said, 'Are you still able to have babies?'

'Oh.' She nodded. 'Yeah. I am.'

'Thank God,' I said, feeling great relief. Because it was obvious how badly she wanted to have children someday. And because I harbored certain hopes – farfetched or otherwise – of being their father.

'I went for a checkup a week later to make sure I was okay. I didn't want Bill to find out about it, so I drove all the way out to San Bernardino and used a fake name, paid cash ... But then he noticed the mileage on the car and he made me talk.'

'*Made* you?'

'He always had ways to make me talk. I admitted everything. And he laughed.'

'He *laughed*?'

'He said I must be nuts to think he'd do a thing like that. He said he could hardly wait for me to get pregnant again so he could rip *another* baby out of me. Apparently, he'd gotten a charge out of it.'

I just gaped at her. I could hardly believe what I was hearing.

Not for the first time.

Ever since showing up at my apartment, Cat had been hitting me with strange, wild stories that were pretty hard to swallow.

But turned out to be true.

'He really said he wanted to do it *again*?'

'Do you think I'd make that up?'

'No, but it's ... How could someone say a thing like that?'

'How could someone *do* a thing like that?'

I just shook my head.

'Anyway,' Cat said, 'that's when I decided to kill him. I'd thought about it before. Right after I woke up and he told me what he'd done. So that's the main reason I didn't tell anyone. Everybody thought we were happily married. I figured to keep it that way, so I wouldn't have an obvious motive if he should happen to turn up dead. But it was ... you know, just sort of a thought at that point. A fantasy. I hadn't actually decided to *do* it. But then, when he laughed and told me how he *wanted* me to get pregnant again ... It was a little more than that, actually.'

She took a deep breath, glanced at me, and faced forward again.

'He raped me,' she said. 'Right then and there. On the driveway. He'd dragged me out to show me the car's odometer and ... you know, interrogate me about the mileage I'd put on with the trip to the doctor's office.'

'He raped you outside?'

Her head nodded with quick little jerks.

'Was it dark out?'

'No. More like dusk. It was a summer night, only about eight o'clock. I think the sun had just gone down. But there was plenty of light. If there hadn't been enough light, he probably would've dragged me inside the house to do it. He always wanted to be able to see me when we were ... you know, having sex.'

'What about the neighbors?'

'I don't think anyone saw us. The car was back near the kitchen door, and we were down on the concrete in front of it. What with the fence and everything ... But I had to stay quiet. Even when he was making me talk, we kept it down to

76

whispers. And I didn't dare cry out. No matter how much he hurt me, I kept quiet. I didn't want anyone to know.'

'Bastard,' I muttered.

'He was trying to make me pregnant again right there on the driveway. That was the whole point. Before that night, he'd always used condoms. Always. He used to say things like, 'Leave it to you, we'll be up to our ankles in rug-rats.' So I never used any sort of birth-control device. Didn't have to. Didn't *want* to, anyway. I wanted to have a baby, but Bill always wore a rubber.'

'How did you end up pregnant? Did you tamper with his stash?'

'Nah. I wouldn't do something like that. One of the damn things must've leaked. They do that. They leak all the time. Sometimes they come off inside you. But anyway, he didn't use one the night he raped me on the driveway. It was a first. And he kept saying stuff while he was . . . doing it. Telling me how he could hardly wait for me to get pregnant so he could . . . rip the baby out of me. And how this time he wouldn't drug me, he'd tie me to the bed so I wouldn't miss anything. He'd . . . show me its pieces. He said that stuff while he was . . . raping me.'

She went silent for a while.

Outside, the moonlight glowed on rocky bluffs where countless western movies had been filmed in the early days of Hollywood. So I'd heard. And I believed it. Some of the slopes and crevices almost looked familiar. Maybe I'd seen them on old TV reruns of *The Lone Ranger* or *The Gene Autry Show*.

Back when I was a little kid watching such things, I couldn't even have imagined the sort of evil that Cat had just described to me.

It had probably been going on, though.

I just hadn't known about it.

It's too bad that anyone ever has to find out about that sort of thing.

After a while, Cat broke the silence by saying, 'Anyway, it didn't take. I didn't get pregnant that night, in spite of everything.'

'That's lucky,' I said.

'I guess so. Not that Bill would've had a chance to . . . take it out of me. He was dead a month later.'

'Killed by Elliot,' I said.

'That's right. Killed by Elliot.' She turned her head and looked at me for a moment, then faced the front again.

'You had something to do with it?' I asked.

She nodded. 'I had everything to do with it. Elliot was my hitman.'

I gaped at her.

'You're kidding,' I said.

'You think so?'

'We just put a stake through the heart of the guy you *hired* to murder your husband?'

'Well, I had no idea he was a vampire. Not at first.'

'Didn't you wonder about his steel teeth?' I asked.

'He didn't have them on. Not the night I met him.'

'How *did* you meet him?'

'Just lucky, I guess. I went looking for a killer to hire, and . . . The thing is, I wanted Bill dead, but I didn't want to end up in prison. The prisons are *full* of women who killed their husbands. I did a little research. It doesn't matter how abusive he might've been, what he's done to you . . . the only circumstance where they *allow* you to kill your husband is if you do it while he's in the middle of trying to kill *you*. Otherwise, they call it murder. They don't just let you off because you've got a good sob-story and he deserved to die.'

'A jury might,' I told her.

'Sure. No telling *what* an LA jury might do. They've been known to ignore every shred of evidence and acquit you because they like your smile or skin color or think you're cute. But what if they *didn't* like me? Anyway, just to go through the trial, I'd probably have to spend a year in jail. They don't always let you out on bail when you're accused of murder.'

'That's true,' I admitted.

'Which sort of puts the lie to that crap about being 'innocent until proven guilty.' If you're so innocent, why do they keep you in jail?'

'Sort of a contradiction, I guess.'

'Or sort of a lie.'

'Yeah.'

'Anyway, I didn't feel like throwing myself on the mercy of the system. Not for killing the man who murdered my baby. So, what's the best way to avoid being arrested for murder?'

'Don't do it?' I offered.

'Exactly! Get somebody *else* to do it. When you're the spouse, you're automatically a prime suspect. They'll be *looking* for ways to incriminate me. But if I didn't actually do the killing, they'd never have more than a fairly weak case based on circumstantial evidence. They couldn't *possibly* get physical evidence that I'm the killer, because I'm *not* the killer. You know?'

'Makes perfect sense.'

'That's the way I saw it. So I went out looking for a killer.'

'And you found Elliot.'

'I found a *lot* of guys. A few women, too. Or they found me. Just go out anywhere in the middle of the night and make a little eye contact, you'd be amazed who'll start talking to you.'

'Killers, drunks, and cops,' I said.

'Yeah. For sure. But that's just for starters. The only sort of person you *won't* meet is somebody who's normal, well adjusted, law-abiding . . .'

'Like me.'

She looked at me, and I saw the hint of a smile in the darkness. 'I'm not so sure about that.'

'Maybe not after tonight,' I said.

'Maybe you were law-abiding before tonight. I don't think you've ever been normal and well-adjusted.'

'Really?'

'You were *always* obsessive about *me*.'

I actually laughed, even though I was suddenly blushing. 'I tried to hide it.'

'It always showed.'

'Sorry.'

'Nothing to be sorry about. It's flattering.'

I didn't much like the sound of that.

'Anyway,' Cat said, 'I spent a few weeks prowling the night . . .'

'Where was Bill while all this was going on?'

'Sometimes out of town on business trips. Sometimes just gone ... hitting the sheets with assorted sluts, probably. Sometimes, he was asleep in our own bed.'

'You snuck out of bed?'

'Sure.'

'Did he ever catch you?'

'Sometimes.'

'What'd he do?'

'Make me talk.'

I grimaced. 'He hurt you?'

'Sure. He loved to hurt me.'

'What did you tell him?'

'The truth.'

I was astonished. 'You *told* him you were looking for someone to kill him?'

'I had to. It was the only way to make him stop.'

'What'd he think about that?'

'He'd laugh. He'd say, "You mean you don't love me anymore?" Or he'd say, "If you'd like a divorce, just ask." That was because he didn't really believe me. What he thought, really, was that I was out getting laid behind his back. Because that's what *he* was doing every chance he got. People always think you're the same sort of shit that they are. Whereas, in fact, we're all shitty in different ways.'

'So he never believed you were really looking for someone to kill him?'

'I don't think it ever entered his mind.'

'Weird.'

'You've gotta remember, he was a doctor.'

'What does that have to do with it?'

'All doctors think they're God. God is immortal. Bill is a doctor. Therefore, Bill is immortal. It's inconceivable that someone would try to kill that which can't *be* killed.'

As I shook my head, I found myself smiling.

'Maybe it was a good thing that he caught me a few times,' Cat said. 'Otherwise, I might've quit looking. Because it was scary out there. And frustrating. There were so many freaks. I was always afraid of being attacked. Hell, I *was* attacked. More than once. But you know? What those guys did to me was no worse than what I was used to getting from Bill. So it didn't matter that much. I could take it. You'd be surprised what you can take.'

It made me feel sick, hearing her talk that way – being forced to imagine what people had done to her. *I could take it*. Cat should never have had to *take it* at all. She deserved a wonderful life, not any of that. It made we want to cry.

I wished like hell that I could've been with her and saved her from all those agonies. Watched over her and kept her safe from every harm.

If only I'd known.

'I wish you would've come to me,' I said.

'I thought about it,' she said. 'But I didn't want you mixed up in something like that. It was actual murder. I couldn't ask you to murder someone for me. Not you.'

'Why not? Bill deserved to die. I would've killed him for you. Gladly.'

'It would've been wrong. It would've ... made you dirty.'

'What am I, Mr Clean?'

'That's right. And I wanted to keep you that way.'

'Then why did you bring me in to kill Elliot? Not that I'm complaining, but ...'

'That was different. That wasn't murder.'

'Of course it was.'

'No. It's only murder if you kill a human being. Elliot is a vampire. Therefore, you didn't murder anyone.'

Under different circumstances, I might've laughed. But I knew that Cat was serious. And I felt honored that she thought of me as some sort of unsullied champion who could only be used for honorable tasks.

'Aside from that,' she said, 'vampires are supposedly *already* dead, right? "The undead?" '

Elliot sure seemed alive to me.'

'To me, too,' she admitted. 'But the fact remains, alive or undead, he wasn't a *human* being, so killing him wasn't a homicide. Killing Bill, *that* was a homicide. So I didn't ask you to do it.'

'We could've gotten together a year ago,' I told her.

'We're together now,' she said. Reaching over, she gave my leg a gentle squeeze.

Then the tire blew out and the car swerved.

She gasped and jerked her hand away from me and wrestled with the steering wheel.

13

The car, thumping and bucking, acted like a beast that wanted to slam us into the nearest obstacle and kill us.

Lucky for us, there was no traffic.

We were alone on the desolate, moonlit highway.

Fighting the wheel, Cat kept us on the pavement and slowed down. Then she steered all the way over to the right.

'Better keep going,' I called out.

'What?'

The car limped along, making loud *THUNK* noises with every revolution of the right front tire. *THUNK-THUNK-THUNK-THUNK-THUNK-THUNK-THUNK.*

The pounding was quick and hard and steady and seemed endless.

'We've gotta get off the road!' I yelled. 'We can't change the tire here!'

Cat nodded.

We both looked for a place to go.

On both sides of the highway, the terrain was rough. There were rock piles, bluffs, nasty drop-offs. But no connecting roads – not even dirt tracks that we might take to get away from the highway.

Cat slowed down. The more she slowed down, the less the car jolted us and the less rapidly the thunks attacked our ears. 'Nothing's coming,' she said. Though she spoke loudly, she no longer had to shout. 'Maybe I oughta just pull over now. If we change the tire really fast . . .'

'You do have a spare, don't you?'

'Yes.'

'But it's in the trunk?'

'Afraid so.'

'And the jack?'

'They're together in the trunk.' She glanced at me. 'Underneath Elliot.'

'That's what I figured.'

'What'll we do?'

'We've *gotta* get away from the road. That's all there is to it.'

'Hang on,' Cat said, and steered farther to the right.

It suddenly became a very bumpy ride. Though Cat was driving slowly, the rough ground tossed us about as if we were riding the rapids. We bounced in our seats. We were thrown from side to side. If not for our seatbelts, we probably would've banged our heads on the ceiling.

Banging my head might've been a pleasant change from the punishment my wound was taking. No matter how I tried to lean forward or brace myself, I kept being thrown backward. I felt as if an old, too-friendly pal was gleefully slapping me on the back – smacking my stake puncture again and again.

Soon, we were descending a rocky slope.

'Easy,' I said.

Cat turned her head. I looked, and saw a pale slice of grin on her dark face.

'Don't go anywhere we won't be able to get out of!' I shouted.

'Aye-aye, sir!'

I saw a boulder dead ahead.

'Look out!'

She swerved. The car missed the boulder, but then skidded downhill sideways. I expected it to flip over and roll to the bottom. Before it could flip, however, Cat jerked the wheel and our front swung around so that we seemed to be diving headfirst down the slope. We picked up speed, our flat tire banging *THUNK-THUNK-THUNK-THUNK-THUNK* quicker and quicker.

The headlights revealed a leaping landscape of gray and tan: rocks, bushes, gravel, ruts, stunted trees, boulders, cactus.

Cat, hunched over the steering wheel, missed the big stuff.

The little stuff hurled us about, bounced us and battered us. I flinched each time my pal, the seatback, slapped the hole in my back.

After several skids and close calls and one complete 360 degree spin, Cat finally brought the car to a stop.

The noises ceased. Abruptly, no more roar of engine or *THUNK* of flat or crunching wheezing scraping scuffing of tires fighting for traction on the rocky gravel slope, no more rattle and clunk and squeak from the car itself.

Silence.

Cat shut off the headlights. Then, as if worn out, she let go of the steering wheel and slumped back in her seat. She let out a big breath. Then she said, 'At least we're off the highway.'

'We're that.' I leaned forward. The bandage on my back felt warm and slippery, but I didn't feel any trickles. So far, at least, the new leakage was apparently being absorbed by the gauze pad.

'And we aren't dead,' Cat added.

I laughed.

Then we just sat there, staring out the windshield. We seemed to be at the bottom of a small valley. I couldn't see any signs of civilization in front of us. Just moonlit desert cluttered with rocks and scrubby bushes and some nearby stark hills and bluffs.

After a while, Cat muttered, 'Boy.'

'What?' I asked.

'Guess maybe the flat tire's ... it's like the *least* of our troubles, now.'

'I'd better get out and inspect the damage.'

We both climbed out. Cat had taken care of the ceiling light, back in Santa Monica, so the car remained dark. We left our doors wide open. I checked the tires on my side. The front one, as expected, was a shredded ruin. But the rear tire looked okay.

Cat came around the front. 'The tires are fine on the other side,' she said.

'Thank God,' I said.

'Unless one of them has a *slow* leak.'

'We won't worry about slow leaks.'

'Good idea.'

She crouched beside me. We both stared at the flat tire.

'What do you think happened to it?' she asked.

'I don't know.'

'They aren't supposed to blow like that, are they?'

'I guess anything can happen. Is it an old tire?'

'It's less than a year old. They all are. Brand new, top-of-the-line steel belted radials. They probably don't have a thousand miles on them.'

'Should've been okay.'

'Do you think somebody might've *shot* it out?'

'Possible,' I said. 'Sure *felt* like it could've been something like that.'

'*Blam!*' Cat said.

'There weren't any other cars around. But somebody might've fired from a distance, I suppose. Sniped us. Or maybe you ran *over* something.'

'Nothing I saw.'

'We'll probably never know.'

Swaying, she bumped gently against me with her upper arm. 'Maybe I ran over a *stake*,' she whispered.

'A beef steak?'

'A *vampire* stake.'

'Wouldn't surprise me at all,' I said.

'Hey!' She elbowed me.

'Ow! I was just playing along.'

'You're not *supposed* to play along, you're supposed to *reassure* me.'

'Oh. Sorry. Okay. It wasn't a vampire stake.'

'Thanks.'

'You're welcome.'

'I mean, I was just kidding. I *know* I didn't drive over a stake.'

'You probably drove over something.'

'Unless somebody shot at us.'

'Certainly a possibility,' I admitted.

We didn't say anything for a few moments, just crouched there, side by side, staring at the flat. I knew what I needed to do next. Which was why I stayed by the tire.

'Still think there's nothing going on?' Cat asked, putting an end to the silence.

'Huh?'

'First, you get stabbed in the back with the stake. Then we suddenly have a mysterious blow-out on the freeway.'

'Elliot's Revenge?'

'Things have been going wrong ever since we killed him.'

'A few mishaps are to be expected,' I pointed out. 'If you look on the other side of things, we've been fairly lucky. Neither of us has been seriously hurt or killed.'

'So far,' she added.

'And the car's only problem seems to be the flat tire. Which is *very* lucky. Soon as I get that changed, we'll be on our way.'

'On our way where?'

I looked over my shoulder. And up toward the freeway.

I couldn't *see* the freeway, but I knew it had to be up there. As I searched for it, I heard the distant noise of a truck engine. Soon, a pale glow drifted out over the slope.

Way up there.

'I guess we'll have to find an alternate route,' I said. Then, reluctantly, I stood up.

Cat walked beside me as I headed for the trunk.

The bandage felt sodden and slidy against my back. But the hole didn't hurt much. My main problem, at the moment, was the nasty chunk of dread that seemed to be growing in my belly with every step I took toward the rear of the car.

Trying to distract myself, I said, 'At least we shouldn't have to worry about getting caught in the act.'

'Thanks for mentioning it.'

'Welcome.'

At the trunk, Cat studied her collection of keys. She held them up to the moonlight, picked one, then bent over and inserted it into the lock. When she turned it, the lock gave a little *kunk* sound and the lid began to rise.

I had an urge to take a few steps backward, but resisted.

As the lid swung up, crackly sounds came from the plastic tarp.

Gazing into the trunk, I expected to see Elliot curled on his side, wrapped in his mummy suit of white mattress cover and tape.

But the raised lid cast a moonshadow that hid the trunk's interior in thick blackness.

'Dark,' Cat said. 'Want me to go around and grab the flashlight?'

'I'd rather try to get by without it.'

'Okay.'

'I can't see him.'

Cat was silent for a moment. Then, sounding a little nervous, she said, 'That's 'cause it's dark, bozo.'

'I know.'

'He didn't *go* anywhere.'

'I know.'

Leaning forward, she reached with both hands into the trunk. It was like sinking her arms into black water. They vanished up to her elbows.

Then she yelped and jerked her hands back.

'What?' I gasped.

'I touched him.'

'You were *trying* to touch him.'

'I touched *him*. Not plastic, *him*. Elliot. *I touched his bare skin!*'

She took a step backward. I did, too, just to stay with her.

Then I put a hand on her back. She flinched, so I jerked my hand away and said, 'Sorry.'

'No, it's all right.'

'He must've come unwrapped with all that bouncing around.'

'Yeah. That's gotta be it.'

'Not surprising, really.'

'Really,' she agreed. 'I damn near came unwrapped, myself.'

I let out a nervous laugh.

'And now I've come unglued,' she added.

I saw her smiling, so I put my hand on her back again. I rubbed her a little through her shirt. 'You're fine,' I said.

'I'm jumpy as hell.'

'You and me both.'

'But hell,' she said, 'we have a right to be jumpy, right?'

'Every right. We'd have to be nuts not to be jumpy.'

For a while, neither of us had any more to say. We stood there, staring at the blackness of the trunk, my hand on Cat's back.

Then she whispered, 'What'll we do about the tire?'

'Change it,' I said.

'What about Elliot? We can't change it with *him* in the trunk.'

'I'll take care of him. But maybe we're going to need that flashlight, after all.'

She went off to get it. I didn't like being left alone so close to the trunk – and Elliot. Besides, it was my duty to keep an eye on Cat. So I took a couple of sidesteps. She had already opened the right rear door, and was leaning in. I could only see her bare legs and the seat of her cut-offs. After a few seconds, she backed her way out, straightened up and turned around. She held the flashlight in her left hand, something pale and floppy in her right.

'Figured we might want these,' she said, waving them at me.

'What are they?'

'The gloves.'

'Good idea.'

She tossed a pair to me. They were still in their plastic wrapper. I tore them open as Cat approached. Then I stuffed the cellophane wrapper into a pocket of my jeans and followed her over to the trunk. I was about to put the gloves on when she turned on the flashlight.

I guess I'd expected her to give me fair warning.

Ask if I was ready, maybe.

Maybe count to three.

But none of that.

She flicked the switch and a strong, pale beam flooded the trunk.

14

It could've been worse, I suppose.

But it was bad enough.

Elliot still had the big, blue tarp underneath him. The edges of it that we'd folded down over him, however, had all been flattened against the sides and floor of the trunk so that they didn't cover him at all.

And he was no longer wrapped in the white plastic mattress cover from Cat's bed. It lay mashed beneath him. It was smeared with blood.

So was Elliot.

'What *happened?*' Cat whispered. She sounded appalled.

'He had a bumpy ride,' I said. 'Without benefit of seat belts.'

'But *Jesus!*'

'He must've popped out of the mattress cover and spent a while tumbling around in here.'

Elliot had come to rest on his back, in something like a fetal position, his knees up and tucked down against his chest. While being tossed every which way, he'd probably gotten jammed into that position, his knees against the lid. It looked awfully strange.

'You just hold the light,' I told Cat. 'I'll take care of him.' Then I clamped the gloves between my teeth and took off the shirt that Cat had given me. I didn't want it to end up bloody. I took it to the open passenger door and tossed it onto my seat. As I returned to the trunk, I pulled the gloves on.

Then I hauled Elliot's body out.

It probably took about two minutes.

It felt like two hours.

He was slippery and heavy, and I had to be careful not to get stabbed again by the stake jutting out of his chest.

By the way, that's the good news: in spite of his rough ride in the trunk, the stake hadn't become dislodged. I guess the duct tape can be thanked for that. Though it had failed to hold the mattress cover together, it hadn't come loose where I'd wrapped it around Elliot's torso to secure the stake.

Also, his hands were still bound. So were his ankles.

The strip of tape across his eyes remained in place.

Not the strip on his mouth, though. It looked as if it had been torn loose, then reapplied – crooked, so the left side of his mouth was bare. I glimpsed a steel fang imbedded in his lower lip. He must've bit himself while being tumbled about.

The tape at his groin had also pulled loose. One side of the big, silver patch clung to his right hip and thigh, but it was flapped back so it no longer covered his genitals.

I noticed all that after reaching into the trunk and pulling his legs down away from his chest. I also noticed how Cat's light touched Elliot's penis, then swung away so fast that it seemed to slice a gash through the darkness.

Anyway, I reached in and wrestled him out of the trunk and threw him down onto the ground. I didn't get stuck by the stake, but I got pretty messy.

With Cat lighting the inside of the trunk, I wadded the mattress cover, then folded down the tarp. I lifted them out and dropped them onto Elliot. Then she told me how to take out the floor pad. Underneath it, I found the spare tire and the jack nestled together in a well. They were fastened down with a bolt that was easy to remove.

Having just dealt with Elliot, changing the flat seemed like a simple, almost pleasant diversion.

I had no trouble jacking up the car, removing the lug bolts, pulling off the ruined remains of the old tire, and putting on the one from the trunk. Mostly, I did it by moonlight. Cat stood beside me, helping in small ways, helping mainly by staying nearby.

The moment of truth came when I jacked the car down.

The new tire held firm.

'We're in business,' I said.

'Thank God.'

'And Mr Goodyear.' Squatting by the flat, I said, 'Let's take a better look at this.' Cat switched the flashlight on. I set the flat tire upright and turned it this way and that, inspecting it. The thing was a wreck. Trying to find the source of the blow-out was like looking for a knife wound in a victim of hand grenades. 'Do *you* see anything?' I asked.

She squatted down on the other side of the tire, shined her light on it with one hand and explored its tattered rubber with the other. I turned the tire around so she could study its other side.

'It's so torn apart,' she finally said.

'Could've been anything,' I said.

'Oh, well.' She stood up. 'What now?'

I stood up, lifting the tire. 'Take this with us. I'd rather not have it in the trunk, though. How about the back seat?'

'Fine.'

I put the tire and jack on the floor behind the driver's seat – on top of the pick and shovel from Cat's garage. Then I returned to the rear of the car. Elliot was out of sight underneath the jumble of the mattress cover and tarp.

Cat stood at the other side of the pile, her flashlight off. 'You know,' she said, 'we *could* bury him right here. Get it over with.'

'We could,' I admitted.

But I didn't like the idea. If we buried him here, our mission would be ended. There'd be no long journey into the mountains of Nevada. We would simply return to Cat's house. My reason for being with Cat would all be over.

'I thought we wanted to take him out of state,' I reminded her.

'But this looks like a pretty good place. And we're here, you know? If we bury him here, we'll save ourselves a long trip – and maybe avoid a lot of bad stuff. I mean, things haven't exactly gone smoothly, so far. And we're hardly even an hour away from home.'

'I guess there's no *rule* that we've gotta take him out of state.'

'We're making up our own rules,' Cat said.

'Do you want him to be this *close* to where you live, though?'

'Not really. Hell, I'd like him to be on another planet, but...'

'Also, we're awfully close to the freeway.'

Cat gazed up the hillside. 'It's out of sight.'

'Just barely. I think this is just too ... public. We need to take him out into the real *boondocks*, where the chances of anyone finding his body are slim to none.'

'I guess so.'

'Besides, we might have trouble getting out of here. We don't want to bury Elliot, then find out we need a tow truck, or something.'

'Do you think we *will*?'

'Need a tow truck?'

'Yeah.'

'I don't know. You haven't got four-wheel drive on this baby, do you?'

She shook her head.

'Even if you had it, I doubt if we'd be able to go back the way we came. Probably slide right down again. But since you don't have four-wheel drive...'

'What'll we do?'

'I'll put Elliot back in the trunk, for starters. Then, I don't know. We can either start driving, or wait for morning and see how things look in the sunlight.'

'Sounds like a plan,' Cat said.

'Not much of one.'

She put on her gloves, then helped me spread the tarp inside the trunk.

'Any point in trying to wrap him up again?' I asked.

'I don't think so. Why bother? He'll just come apart.'

Together, we put the mattress pad down in the middle of the tarp.

'Okay,' I said, 'stand back.'

Cat stepped out of my way. 'Do you want the flashlight on?' she asked.

'No thanks.'

With Cat watching by moonlight, I arranged Elliot on the ground so that he was lying straight on his back, his feet toward the car. Then I crouched behind his head, lifted him to a sitting position, hugged him around the chest (being careful of the stake's jutting point), and hauled him up. When I had him vertical, I lunged forward and flung him head first into the trunk. He only made it half way. Then I had to grab him low and hoist his legs over the edge of the trunk. Doing that, I ended up pressing a cheek against his dead, bare ass. It grossed me out. But it didn't last long.

The moment his legs vanished into the dark trunk, Cat slammed the lid. '*Dah-dahhhh!*'

'Mission accomplished,' I said, pulling off my gloves.

'Now we need to clean you up.'

I followed her to the passenger side of the car. Ducking inside the open front door, she bent down and searched for something. Pretty soon, she came up with a plastic container of wet wipes.

With one hand, she shined the flashlight on me. With the other, she used several of the cool, wet paper towels to clean my face and chest and arms. She even gave the front of my jeans a few quick rubs. I squirmed a little.

'Don't get excited,' she whispered.

'Maybe you'd better stop doing that.'

'Ooooo.'

'Or don't.'

'Just trying to get the blood off.' She continued a while longer, then inspected me from face to foot with the flashlight. 'Clean as a whistle. How's your back?'

'Any blood on my back is my own,' I said, and turned around.

'Dandy,' she said.

'Bad?'

'Not too bad. We'd better change the bandage, though.'

Ducking into the car again, she found the roll of paper towels and a first-aid kit. Then she had me squat down. Standing behind me, she peeled the sodden bandage off my back.

'Nasty hole, camper,' she said.

'Do I wax whimsical about *your* wounds?'

'You may.'

'I might.'

'Any time,' she said. 'Feel free to enjoy yourself at my expense.'

I laughed.

Cat stopped talking and held a dry paper towel against my wound for a couple of minutes. Then she applied a fresh bandage.

While I put my shirt on, she threw the old bandage and all the used papers into a sack. She tossed our gloves in, too.

'We might need those again,' I said.

'I'm not throwing any of this away. Not just yet. But I figure we don't want to leave stuff behind.'

'You're right,' I said. 'We're killers, not litterbugs.'

She laughed softly. 'We're not *killers*, we're ... vampire exterminators.'

'I hope the DA sees it that way.'

'We're not going to get caught.'

'From your mouth to God's ears.'

She laughed, turned away, and set everything down on the floor behind the front seat.

'Now,' I said, 'I guess it's time to see if we can get out of here.'

'Maybe you'd better drive,' Cat suggested.

'So it'll be my fault if we get stuck?'

'It's about time for *something* to be your fault.'

'Good point.'

She gave my arm a swat.

'Real nice,' I said. 'Hit a guy, why don't you?'

93

Stepping in front of me, she grabbed the chest of my shirt with both hands. She jerked me toward her. 'How about if I hit you with my lips?' she said.

I grinned like a fool. I was tempted to ask if she'd been reading Mickey Spillane. But this didn't seem like the best of all times to start a literary discussion. So I shut up and let her hit me.

The punch of her lips knocked my breath out and almost put me on the canvas.

I don't know how long it lasted. I don't know why it got me the way it did.

Maybe being in love had something to do with it.

The way she held me, all I could feel were her fists against my chest and her mouth against my mouth. Sometimes, the tip of her nose touched my face. I could feel the hot breath from her nostrils.

I felt her tongue a few times. Mostly, though, only her lips, soft and firm and wet, and the moist hole between them.

Then her knuckles pushed me back and her mouth went away.

'You drive,' she whispered.

15

Cat gave me the keys and I went around to the driver's side. She climbed into the passenger seat. We shut our doors. As soon as we had our seatbelts on, I started the engine.

'Maybe you'd better keep the headlights off,' Cat said.

I nodded, shifted, and eased my foot down on the gas pedal. We started rolling forward, the car rocking and bouncing. Ahead, the way looked rough but possible. The moon cast a gray, dusty glow over the ground, rocks and bushes.

There were also patches and streaks of blackness where shadows fell. I didn't know what might be waiting for us in such places, but there were too many of them to avoid.

'What's the plan?' Cat asked.

'A slow and careful drive.'

'To where?'

'Out of here, I hope. I don't even want to *try* going up to the freeway, though. That could be a disaster. But there's a chance we might run into some sort of road down here. If we don't get stuck before we can find it.'

A few seconds after saying that, I drove into a narrow strip of shadow. The front tires dropped, then pounded and bounced up hard, hurling both of us off our seats. The belts grabbed us and pulled us down. The back of my seat slapped my stake wound. I hit the brakes.

'Elliot probably just did a double back-flip,' Cat said.

I was going very slow when the rear tires met the gap. They descended and climbed out smoothly.

Then I stopped the car.

'I'm not so sure about trying to do this by moonlight,' I said. 'It'll be tough enough if we can *see* where we're going.'

'Should we put the headlights on?'

'We'd stick out like a UFO. God-only-knows who might show up to investigate.'

'One of us could jump out and walk ahead,' Cat suggested.

'That's not a bad idea.'

'Check things out with the flashlight, make sure it looks safe for the car.'

'Great.'

'It's a plan?' she asked.

'An excellent plan. Which would you rather do, scout or drive?'

'I'll scout.'

'You sure?' I asked.

'Do *you* want to scout?'

'Not necessarily. But if you'd *rather* drive . . . I mean, you'll be alone out there.'

She looked at me and smiled. 'I think I can handle it.'

'I'm sure you can. Just be careful, okay?'

'Yeah. The way things have been going, I might just fall in a pit or get chomped by a rattlesnake.'

'Try not to.'

'I'll try real hard.' With that, Cat climbed out. She retrieved the flashlight from behind the seat, then shut the doors and started walking. With her back to the car, she switched on the flashlight. She swept its beam this way and that a few times to get a general idea of what lay ahead, then turned it toward the ground just in front of her. Apparently satisfied that there were no immediate hazards, she shut off the light and beckoned for me to follow her.

I started driving slowly, keeping my eyes on Cat.

The car windows were up. They'd been up the whole time to keep out road noises. We had vents open for air. Now, I wanted to be able to hear Cat if she should call out, so I cranked my window down. She didn't have automatic windows. I would've had to lean way across her seat to get at the passenger window, so I let it stay shut.

Anyway, my window seemed to do the trick. The warm, dry air came in. So did the sounds of the tires crunching their way over the rocky ground.

At such a low rate of speed, the bouncing wasn't too bad. The car still got jostled around, but not in a drastic way.

Nothing that would make Elliot do a double back-flip in the trunk.

I didn't much like being left alone with him. Even though he was locked away and out of sight, his presence made me nervous.

It's amazing, the difference another person makes. With Cat in the car, I hadn't been bothered much at all by the idea of Elliot being in the trunk. He'd worried me only to the extent that I didn't want us to get *caught* with him.

Thinking about him back there hadn't given me the *creeps*. But now it did. Because we were alone together, now that Cat was scouting ahead.

Trying not to think about Elliot, I concentrated on driving. And on Cat.

She rarely used the flashlight. She put it on only for seconds at a time, then switched it off and walked by the glow of the moon.

Sometimes, I found myself gaining on her and had to ease off. Other times, she got too far ahead and I stepped on the gas to catch up. When she came upon obstacles or stretches of terrain that might cause trouble, she waved me off and led me in a new direction. Though our route took many twists and turns, we were able to keep going.

Which was the object, really.

Keep going long enough, and we were bound to find our way to a road.

Probably.

As I drove along, I kept having a fantasy that Cat, roaming on ahead, would suddenly whirl around and race back to the car and blurt out, 'I found it! A road! Dead ahead!' And I'd shout, 'Yes!'

So when she *did* suddenly whirl around and come running for the car, I figured she must've spotted a road.

I kept driving toward her.

I wished she would slow down. The way she was dashing full-tilt, leaping and dodging, she looked as if she might take a header at any moment and bust herself up.

'Take it easy,' I muttered.

And suddenly realized she didn't run like someone eager to report a wonderful discovery; she ran like someone fleeing.

At the last moment, I stopped the car. She jerked open the passenger door, leaped in, and slammed it. She was panting for breath.

'What happened?'

'Saw someone,' she gasped.

'*What?*'

'There's a *guy!*'

'A *man's* out there?'

'Yeah.'

'Where?'

'Up ahead. I ... God! Scared the hell outa me.'

I gazed out through the windshield and saw the same desolate, moon-gray desert. Though I tried to spot the stranger, I saw only brush, cactus, stunted trees, and clusters of rocks.

'What was he doing?' I asked.

'Nothing. Just standing there.'

'Alone?'

'Yeah.'

'Did he have a car?'

She shook her head. 'He didn't have anything. He was just ... *standing* out there. I didn't think it was a person. I thought it must be a ... maybe Joshua tree or a cactus or something. 'Cause he wasn't moving. He didn't move a muscle, just *stood*

97

there. But then I got closer and shined the flashlight on him. And he ... had a face. And his eyes were open. He was ... *staring* at me.'

'Did he say anything?'

'No. Huh-uh. Nothing. Didn't make a sound, didn't move. Just ... *stared* at me. And kind of ... kept giving me this queer smile.'

'Did you say anything to him?' I asked.

'Are you kidding? It was all I could do not to scream. I ran like hell. You should've seen him. He looked like ... I don't know what.'

'How was the terrain?'

'What are you going to do?'

'Keep going, I guess. Check him out.'

'We might not want to do that.'

'Maybe he can help us find a way out. If he's familiar with the area ...'

'This isn't a guy we wanta mess with. Believe me. He's some kind of a creep.'

'He's just up ahead?' I asked.

'Yeah. See that big clump of rocks?'

I saw it, and nodded. The boulders, about fifty feet away, formed a mound the size of a small house.

'He's just around on the other side of it,' Cat said.

'Doesn't look like he's coming.'

'Maybe he's just being sneaky about it.'

'You never saw him move at all?' I asked.

She shook her head.

'Are you sure he wasn't something like a scarecrow, a mannequin?'

She didn't answer right away. Then she said, 'If that guy's a dummy, he's good enough to be in Madame Tussaud's. I mean, he had a glint in his eyes.'

'You're pretty sure he's real.' I didn't make it a question.

'Pretty *damn* sure.'

'So why didn't he move? Why didn't he say anything?'

'Because he's a creep.'

'Are you sure he was alive?'

Again, Cat was silent for a while. Then she said, 'I don't know. I mean, he *looked* alive. He was standing on his own two feet. He was *staring* at me like a damned lunatic and giving me this godawful *smile*. He didn't look dead to me. I haven't seen that many dead guys, just Bill and – I don't know if you can call Elliot dead, but – Bill *really* looked dead. I mean, my God. If that's what dead looks like, this guy's fit as a fiddle.'

'Maybe I should go have a look at him,' I said.

'I've got a better idea. Why don't you turn left? We can parallel the highway for a while and see what happens.'

'What if this guy needs help?' I asked.

'If he wanted help, he could've asked me for it. He didn't have to just stand there and stare.'

'Maybe there's something wrong with him.'

'Probably a *lot* wrong with him. I've finally got Bill and Elliot out of my life and you want to get us involved with *this* freak? My God. I need a break, Sam.' Then she blurted, '*I need a fucking break!*'

Her outburst shocked me.

Not saying another word, I turned the car to the left and started driving slowly away. It was a risky business, trying to cross such rough land by moonlight and without Cat out front to guide me. But I had to put some distance between us and the stranger she'd encountered.

I felt a little guilty about it. Maybe the guy was in some sort of trouble and needed our help. But my first duty was to Cat.

I needed to get her away from him.

After a while, she said, 'Sorry about that.'

'It's all right.'

'I don't usually ... scare so easily. You'd think nothing would bother me, after the stuff I've been through with Elliot ... and Bill. I oughta be immune to fear. But I guess it doesn't work that way. That guy freaked me out, and he didn't even *do* anything.'

'I'm just glad it was you and not me.'

She made a quiet laugh. 'Oh, thanks a heap.'

Then she twisted in her seat, cranked her window down, put her head out and looked back.

'Any sign of him?' I asked.

'So far, so good.' After a few more seconds, she brought her head in and raised the window. 'I guess we're all right,' she said.

99

'What do you think he was doing out there?' I asked.

'God knows.' She faced me. 'Maybe he was waiting for us.'

'You trying to give *me* the creeps?'

'Sure.'

I'd been aware, even while making the turn to the left, that our way would soon be blocked by a hump of rock that rose out of the ground like the back of a great white whale. I'd counted on finding a way around it. Now was the time. Another left would've taken us into steep, impossible terrain below the highway. So I turned to the right.

'*What're you doing?*'

'We don't have much choice.'

'But *he's* this way.'

'All the way over there.' I nodded to the right.

'It's not that far,' Cat said, and lowered her window. We both looked out.

The house-size mound of rock, which stood near the area where she'd seen the stranger, was a lot closer to us than I'd hoped. It's hard to tell distances when hills and mountains are involved, but this was probably no more than a quarter of a mile away.

A guy could walk that sort of distance in less than five minutes.

Run it in less than two.

A good sprinter could probably cover it in about *one* minute, except that the land was no track and he'd probably wind up on his face.

'Just keep your eyes open,' I said, and turned my attention to the area ahead. 'If he wanted to come after us, he probably would've done it by...'

'Oh, my God! Here he comes!'

16

I leaned forward to see past Cat's head.

The guy was charging straight at us from the side, no more than fifty yards away. He looked big. He ran with short, powerful strides.

'Where the hell did *he* come from?' I yelled.

And stepped on the gas.

The car surged forward and struck a rock with such force that we were both thrown off our seats. Even as our seatbelts grabbed us, we pounded against another rock. I yelled, 'Shit!' and slammed on the brakes.

'Go!'

'We can't outrun him. We'll wreck the car.'

'Sam!'

The guy kept coming. He had long, pale hair that flowed behind him.

'Okay, look,' I said. 'I'll get out. You stay in the car. There's no reason to think this guy means us any harm.'

'What if he does?'

'We took care of Elliot, right? We can take care of this guy, if we have to.'

Waiting no longer, I leaped out of the car and slammed my door. The stranger was rushing at us from the other side. I jerked open the back door, ducked in, reached under the flat tire and grabbed the pick-ax. When I tugged at it, the tire came tumbling out. The damn thing hit my leg and nearly knocked me down, but I managed to stay on my feet.

I threw the door shut. With the mattock in both hands, I hurried around the car. I put my back to Cat's door and faced the guy.

He'd already slowed to an easy jog.

But he was only about twenty feet away.

'You'd better hold it right there,' I called out.

He covered about half the distance between us before settling to a halt. He seemed to be a little winded, but not much. Hands on his hips, he hung his head and took some deep breaths. His hair looked white in the moonlight. But I'd seen him running, and figured he was no old man.

He was a couple of inches taller than me, and looked strong. He wore a buckskin jacket with long strands of fringe all over the place. It was open down the front. At his waist, it was cinched in with a belt. A hunting knife hung on the belt by his right hip. The buckskin jacket reached halfway down his thighs. It had fringe at the bottom that dangled almost to his knees. He appeared to be wearing blue jeans and boots.

'What's up?' he asked. He sounded oddly cheerful. 'Gonna dig a hole with that? Or are you fixing to brain me?'

'I won't brain you unless I have to.'

'No call for that,' he said. 'I'm harmless. Name's Snow White. That's what they call me on account of my hair.' Slipping a hand behind his neck, he gave his tresses a fling. A banner of pale hair drifted up into the moonlight.

'What do you want with us?' Cat asked from behind me. I glanced around. Her window was halfway down.

Snow White answered, 'Nothing you don't want to give.'

'You came running over here,' I said. 'What for?'

'Give me a ride? My Harley got shot out from under me.'

'Got shot?'

'Yep. I was bushwhacked.'

'Where'd that happen?' I asked.

'Up on 14 about an hour ago. Some low-life shithead put a slug through my gas tank.'

'Are you sure?' Cat asked him.

'I heard the caps a-poppin' at me. Reckon he was using a .223. Either an AR-15 or a Ruger Mini-14, more than likely. Put a hole the size of a pencil in my tank. I ended up down here. Over yonder, that's where my gas ran out.'

'Something knocked out one of our tires up on the highway,' I told him. 'We thought it might've been a gunshot.'

'Likely was,' Snow White said. 'Sounds like the same damn shithead got both of us.'

As he said that, Cat opened her door and climbed out. She stood up beside me. 'Sorry I ran away from you back there,' she said. 'You gave me sort of a fright.'

'Well, you give me a good scare, too. The both of you did. I was just standing there, lamenting the loss of my hog, when all of a sudden I seen this car a-coming at me. And you, honey, walking out front with a flashlight. I figured you was hunting me.'

'Is that why you didn't say anything?' she asked.

'I was trying to make up my mind. I was either gonna run like hell or rush in and kill you with my knife. Figured I'd maybe take my chances on a rush, but then you run off like your ass got scalded.'

'Good thing I did,' Cat said.

'Yep. Would've been a shame to cut you down, you being such a beautiful young lady and all. And here you two ain't the shooters, after all.'

'What makes you so sure?' I asked, feeling a little angry with all this talk of knifing Cat.

'I knew you two was okay when she run off. If you had yourself an AR-15 or such, she would've just called out and you would've blasted me, right? 'Stead of that, off you go. When I seen you heading back this way, I figure maybe you'll give me a lift. So how about it?'

'We're pretty much stuck out here, ourselves,' I said.

'Well, I'll risk it.'

'What about your bike?' Cat asked.

'Gotta leave her here for now. I'll have to round up some buddies. We'll come back and take care of her. So if you'll give me a ride into a town, I'd sure be obliged.'

'We haven't got much room in the car,' I said.

I didn't *want* him riding with us. Also, I had no idea how Cat felt about it.

'I could probably make some room for myself in the back seat,' she said. To me, she added, 'We really can't just leave him stranded out here.'

Sure we can, I thought.

This wasn't exactly the middle of nowhere. Even though it *looked* like a desolate wilderness, we were only about half a mile from a major, well-traveled highway. Where Snow White would have no trouble finding help.

But maybe, like us, he needed to avoid the Highway Patrol.

'Be glad to chip in with some gas money,' he offered.

'That's not necessary,' Cat told him.

'If you can help us get to a road,' I said, 'we'll drive you to the nearest town.'

'Well, we're in business.' Reaching out his hand, he stepped toward me.

I let the mattock swing down by my left side and put out my right hand to shake with him. Not that I *wanted* to shake the man's hand. He was a tough guy and I didn't trust him. But I didn't want to look snooty or chicken, so I did it. His hand felt big, dry and grimy. He didn't try anything, though.

After he let go, I said, 'My name's Sam.'

'And I'm Catherine,' Cat said.

Catherine? I'd hardly ever heard her use that name. Had she started going by 'Catherine' as a regular thing during the past ten years? I doubted it. More likely, she'd given the formal name to Snow White because she didn't want a guy like him to be calling her Cat.

'For the time being,' I said to him, 'why don't you take the flashlight and lead the way? We'll follow in the car.'

'You mean I'm s'pose to walk?'

'It's what I was doing before we ran into you,' Cat explained. 'We need someone to go on ahead and make sure we're taking a safe route. We don't have four-wheel drive, for one thing.'

'And we've already had one flat tire,' I added. 'So we don't have any more spares.'

Snow White nodded. 'You want me to take point and get us outa here.'

'That's about it,' I said. 'And keep an eye out for any terrain that might give us trouble. We're trying to avoid big rocks, ditches . . .'

'I get it. I'll do it.'

'We need a road that'll take us out of here,' Cat explained.

'No sweat. I'm your man. I'll find us a road in about two shakes of a snake's ass.'

Cat handed the flashlight to him.

Staying by her side, I asked Snow White, 'Do you need to go back to your bike before we head out?'

'You ain't gonna get rid of me that easy.'

'I'm not trying to get rid of you.'

'Just kidding, Sam.' The way he said my name, with sort of a snide turn to it, I could see that Cat had been smart to keep her true name a secret from him.

She climbed back into the car and shut her door.

'Go on ahead,' I told Snow White. 'We'll catch up.'

'Yes, sir.' He started to swagger off.

As soon as he was a safe distance from Cat's door, I hurried around to my side of the car. Stepping over the flat tire, I opened the back door. I stowed the mattock. I planned to leave the ruined tire on the ground, but then changed my mind.

Just because things are going wrong, you don't go against what you know is right.

So I hefted the tire and tossed it into the car.

Snow White, out in front, had the flashlight on and was shining it into his own face. For Cat's benefit, I assume.

He was movie-star handsome. Rugged and craggy, darkly tanned, with blue eyes, straight white teeth, a heavy jaw, and a stubble of white whiskers.

In spite of the white hair and whiskers, he looked no older than thirty.

As I climbed in and fastened my seat belt, he extended his arm so the light spread out, illuminating his upper body: his broad shoulders, his thick neck and the tapering expanse of bare, bronze skin down the middle of his chest and belly to where the buckskin jacket was belted shut at his waist.

'Lovely,' I muttered.

'Let's get going,' Cat said.

I started the engine, then lowered my window and called out, 'Let's go!'

Snow White winked at Cat, smirked at me, then whirled around with a flourish of swinging fringe and white hair. As he strode away, he raised the flashlight, twirled its beam at the sky, and swept it down ahead of him.

Cat said, 'Oh, boy.'

'Well,' I said, 'he's colorful.'

'He's a fruitcake. A *spooky* fruitcake.'

'I thought you wanted to help him.'

'I wanted to *humor* him. As far as I'm concerned, he's our good old pal till we get out of here. The biggest mistake we could make is to get him pissed off at us.'

'You're probably right.'

'If we'd told him to go away,' she said, 'things might've taken a turn for the ugly.'

'Well, I'm glad to hear you aren't suddenly *smitten* by the guy.'

'Hardly.'

He stopped, turned around, and waved us forward with the flashlight. I started driving slowly toward him.

'I think he likes *you*,' I said, partly teasing her, partly worried by the idea and wanting to warn her.

'Don't count on it.'

'What do you mean?'

'Maybe he likes *you*.'

I cringed. 'That's a pleasant thought.'

'You never know,' Cat said. 'It wouldn't surprise me. You look at how he's dressed . . . and the way he strikes poses. Don't you think so?'

'Now that you mention it. I guess we'd both better watch out.'

'I don't want him touching me,' Cat said.

'Same here.'

'So don't let him. If he tries anything with me, you've gotta stop him. And I'll do the same for you.'

'It's a deal,' I said. 'Let's just hope it never comes up.'

'*Something's* gonna come up. You can bet on that.'

'What do you mean?' I asked.

'Maybe he isn't interested in raping either of us, but he'll be attacking us one way or another. You can tell by looking. The guy is a criminal.'

Exactly, I thought.

'Maybe he wants to rob us,' she said. 'Steal the car. Maybe he's even planning to kill us.'

'Maybe he's just a biker who needs a ride into town,' I suggested, though I hardly believed it.

'I didn't see any motorcycle.'

'*What?*'

'When I saw him the first time – when I wasn't quite sure whether he was a person – I had a pretty good look at the area around him. You know? Because I was trying to figure things out. There wasn't any motorcycle. Not that I saw.'

17

'Maybe it was behind a rock, or something,' I suggested.

'Possible. I'm just saying I didn't see it.'

'He sure *looks* like a biker.'

'Looks like Davy Crockett, king of the wild frontier.'

'Or Hawkeye.'

'Those guys weren't bikers,' Cat pointed out.

'Where do you think he got that hair?' I asked.

'Out of a bottle?'

'I don't think so. His whiskers...'

'I was kidding.'

'Maybe he scared himself in a mirror.'

'Real nice, Sam.'

'He scares *me*.'

'Good thing he can't hear us,' Cat said. 'He'd probably kill us right now for bad-mouthing him.'

'We'd better get in all our wisecracks while we've still got the chance.'

'Right,' Cat said.

'How about that name. Snow White?'

'And you think he *isn't* gay?'

'He might just be cheerful.'

Cat laughed. So did I. It felt good to be laughing with her, but I had some very bad feelings. I felt as if I had a chunk of cold steel down inside my stomach.

Snow White might be a guy who wanted nothing more from us than a ride into town. But we both knew the odds were against it.

'I'd feel a lot better about things,' Cat said, 'if his name was Cinderella.'

Out in front of the car, forty or fifty feet away, he looked over his shoulder at us.

A shiver scurried through me.

'Just kidding, big guy,' Cat muttered.

He faced forward and continued leading the way.

Cat sighed.

'What'll we do about him?' she asked.

'I don't know. Nothing, I guess. Unless he gives us trouble.'

'Maybe he won't,' Cat said.

'He might not. Maybe we're just being paranoid.'

'Wouldn't that be nice?'

'If he wanted to attack us,' I said, 'he could've done it right away.'

'You had the pick.'

'I'm not sure it would've done much good.'

'But who'd want to risk getting hit by a monster weapon like

107

that? Maybe he was being cautious. He probably wants to wait until he can take us off guard.'

'So we'd better not turn our backs on him,' I said.

'When we give him the ride, you drive and I'll take the back seat. If he tries anything, I'll get him from behind.'

'With what?' I asked.

'Where'd we put the hammer?' she asked.

For a moment, I didn't know what hammer she was talking about. Then I remembered the steel-headed mallet that we'd used for pounding the stake into Elliot. Afterwards, she'd wrapped it in a towel . . .

'Did we put it in the trunk?' she asked.

'Yeah. Guess so.'

'That'd be a good thing to have. We've got the salami knife, but the hammer'd be a lot better. If Snow White gives us any trouble, I can bash him on the head with it.'

'But it's in the trunk.'

'We oughta have it. We could knock his brains out with a thing like that.'

'You're right.'

'I'll get it,' Cat said.

'If we stop the car . . .'

'Just keep going the same speed.'

On the steering column just behind the wheel, a black leather case with half a dozen keys dangled below the ignition. Leaning toward me, Cat reached out. It took both hands and a small struggle, but she managed to unclip the ignition key. She sat up straight with the rest of the keys. Head down, she searched through them. 'Here we go,' she muttered.

'The trunk key?' I asked.

'Yeah.'

'You can't just pop the trunk from in here?'

'Nope. Bill didn't like car gadgets. Automatic windows, locks, headlights, trunk openers . . . He hated that stuff. Said it took away your control.'

'Sure would be nice if we could control the trunk lock from inside.'

'Can't,' Cat said. 'Did you happen to see the hammer while you were back there?'

'No. But I wasn't looking for it.'

108

'It has to be there,' she said.

'I never took it out.'

'Neither did I.'

'It was wrapped in a towel,' I reminded her.

'It probably isn't in the towel any more.'

'I doubt it.'

'Must be under the tarp.'

We both stared at Snow White as we talked. He was still a fair distance in front of us. Once in a while, he glanced back. Mostly, though, he studied the area ahead. He rarely used the flashlight.

'We don't want him to know we're up to something,' Cat said. 'So just keep driving. I'll hop out and...'

'While we're moving?'

'It'll be all right.'

'You'll fall on your butt.'

'Maybe. But you're not exactly breaking any speed records: I'll survive. Just keep driving. I'll get around behind us, open the trunk and grab the hammer. If we're lucky, I'll be in my seat again before he even looks back.'

'I don't know,' I said.

'I do. It'll be fine. Just don't stop or speed up suddenly or anything weird like that.'

'Okay. But be quick about it, okay?'

'I'm the wind.'

She leaned over and kissed me on the cheek. Then she sat up straight. We both stared at Snow White. He had his back to us.

'Very good,' Cat whispered. 'Don't slow down.'

'Be careful.'

'*Adios.*' She swung open her door, then swiveled in her seat. Holding the door wide with her left hand, she lowered her feet toward the ground. And hesitated.

'I'll stop for a second,' I said.

'No, don't.'

I did it anyway, and kept my eyes on Snow White. He still had his back to us.

Cat hopped out. The moment I heard her feet hit the ground, I started the car moving again. When I glanced over, she was jogging alongside, easing the door shut.

Snow White was still scouting the area ahead.

Cat dropped back. She vanished for a few seconds, then appeared in the rearview mirror. She was running slowly behind the car, bent over at the waist, her left hand on top of the trunk to steady herself, her right hand low and out of sight. Though I couldn't see it, I knew she must be trying to fit the key into the lock of the trunk.

And trying.

Having trouble.

No wonder.

Even at such a slow speed, the car was being jolted and bounced by the rough, rocky ground.

Must've been like trying to thread a needle on the back of a galloping horse.

I thought about stopping. A brief stop would give her time to slip the key into the lock. On the other hand, she wasn't expecting a stop. Taken by surprise, she'd probably crash into the back of the car.

I grimaced as I watched her in the mirror.

How long could she trot along back there? Sooner or later, she was almost sure to stumble.

Lowering my eyes from the mirror, I looked out the windshield at Snow White. He was fifty or sixty feet ahead of us, descending a shallow slope, his head down.

Down at first, then rising and turning. His shoulders turned. Still walking forward, he twisted halfway around and looked back at us.

He'd done this before, apparently just to check on our progress.

Before, however, Cat had always been in the passenger seat.

We had no lights on. She'd shut her door enough to make it latch. But could Snow White see that she was no longer beside me?

Could he see her jogging behind the car?

If he noticed anything unusual, he didn't let it show.

What if Cat gets the trunk open while he's watching?

I checked the mirror. She was still running behind the car. Head down, she probably didn't even realize that Snow White was looking at us.

'Don't open it now,' I whispered.

And wondered if I should take the risk of shouting to her.

My window was open; Snow White might hear a shout.

I knew a sure way to prevent Cat from opening the trunk: speed up. But she would probably fall on her face.

Suddenly, she straightened her body and pulled back her left hand. The trunk lid leaped up.

I winced. 'That did it,' I muttered.

But when I looked at Snow White, he had his back to us. He was walking slowly away, sweeping the area ahead with our flashlight.

'Okay,' I whispered. 'Just keep walking, Snowman. Don't look back. Whatever you do, don't look back. Nothing to see back here.'

Nothing except the lid of our trunk pointing at the sky.

It completely blocked my view of Cat.

I pictured her running behind the car, one hand on the edge of the trunk to brace herself as she reached in with the other. Reached in and felt around in the blackness, seeking the hammer.

It would probably be hard to find.

She would likely end up touching Elliot.

The hammer might be *under* him. Or on the far side of his body, out of reach.

Unless she climbs in.

The lid remained up.

I glanced again at Snow White.

'Keep going,' I urged him. 'Don't look back.'

I stared at the trunk lid in the mirror.

'Put it down, Cat,' I said in a voice meant only for myself. 'Come on, shut the damn thing. Grab that hammer and get it shut. Or forget the damn hammer. Come on. He's gonna look!'

He looked.

'Shit!' I blurted.

He not only looked, but swung around and came running.

I slammed on the brakes. As the car lurched to a halt, I heard a yelp from Cat and knew it had been a mistake to stop so fast. A moment later, the car shook slightly.

The way it might shake if you throw a heavy piece of luggage into the trunk.

'Oh, no,' I muttered.

Though Snow White didn't seem to be running all-out, he was rapidly closing the distance between us. I shut off the engine. Trying to stay calm and look casual, I climbed out and swung the door shut.

I was trying to decide whether to go for the mattock, but Snow White huffed out, 'Found us a road! Ain't much of one, but it oughta...' He slowed to a walk. 'What's going on? Where's Cathy?' He frowned in the direction of the open trunk.

No expert at impromptu lies, I said, 'She had to get something out of the trunk.'

He swaggered over to investigate. I hurried after him.

At the rear of the car, he shined the flashlight on Cat.

From feet to knees, she was sticking out over the edge of the trunk. The rest of her was sprawled inside – across Elliot's body. Squirming and shoving, she tried to scurry out. Before she could make much progress, though, Snow White planted a hand on the seat of her cut-off jeans and stopped her.

'Hey!' she yelled.

'Take your hand off her,' I said.

He shined the light in my face and said, 'Shut the fuck up.' Then, still pressing down against Cat's rear end, he aimed his flashlight into the trunk.

Aimed it at Elliot, who was currently stretched out on his back: face in the far left corner, legs straight, feet in the near right corner. His face was turned away. You could tell that he had tape across his eyes and mouth, but you couldn't see the side of his mouth where the fang was exposed.

You could see the silver tape that I'd wrapped around his chest – and the bloody wooden point of the stake jutting out of it.

You couldn't see Elliot's tape-bound hands because of Cat. They were down at his belly. Cat could probably feel them under her left breast.

She could probably feel his *penis* between her breasts.

There was no sign of the hammer. Apparently, she hadn't been able to find it before my sudden stop had hurled her into the trunk. It must've been somewhere underneath the crooked, rumpled blue tarp that covered most of the trunk's floor.

'Would you get your hand off my ass?' Cat said.

'No,' Snow White said.

'Let me out of here!' she yelled.

He swatted her.

'OW!'

I went for him.

But never got there.

I was still on my way, snarling 'Bastard!' and ready to tear him apart, when he pivoted and kicked me in the stomach. I folded. My knees pounded the ground, but I caught it with my hands and saved my face from crashing.

18

Down on all fours, I fought to suck in air. My lungs felt flat and empty.

Even though there hadn't been any loud noises, my ears rang.

Barely audible through the ringing and the sounds of my own lousy attempts to snag a breath, I heard Cat cry out, 'Sam! Sam, are you all right?'

'Shut the fuck up,' Snow White said.

'Up yours,' she said.

I heard a sharp smack.

'Eat shit and die,' she said. Though her words were tough, her voice was too high-pitched. She was crying.

'Sam's okay,' Snow White told her. 'I just kicked him a little, okay? Had to defend myself. But I didn't hurt him much as I coulda, so calm down.'

'Let me out of here!'

'I don't wanta hurt nobody. But you gotta tell me what's going on. I mean, you got a fucking *stiff* in there.'

I raised my head enough to see Cat's feet sticking out of the trunk, Snow White still beside her with his hand reaching in to hold her down.

'You two a couple of bad-ass killers?' he asked.

'Let me up!'

'Talk to me, honey.'

113

'He had an accident.'

'Don't look like no accident to me. Looks like he's got a sharp stick through him.'

'It's a stake,' Cat said.

'A stake? He had himself a *stake* accident?'

'He got killed setting up a circus tent.'

'That's real funny,' he said, and smacked her again. When the blow landed on her rump, her legs jerked.

'Don't!' I gasped out.

'Shut the fuck up and stay down, or you're *both* gonna have an accident. I want me some answers.'

'We did it,' I said. 'Let her up.'

'Wasn't no accident?'

'No!'

'So I got me a couple of murderers. When'd you do it?'

'Tonight,' I said.

'So you flung him in the trunk and took off, huh? Figured to dump him off someplace. Only you got yourself a flat, and here you are.'

'That's right,' I told him. Pushing at the ground, I rose to my knees.

'Don't try nothing.'

'I won't.'

'Took the sap outa you, did I?'

I didn't bother to answer.

'Now, somebody's gotta tell me what sorta stunt you was trying to pull with the trunk.'

'She needed to get something,' I said.

'Like what?' He slapped her rump, but not as hard as before. 'Cathy? What was you sneaking around in there trying to get?'

'Nothing.'

He gave her the hardest one yet. She yelped and her feet flew up.

I started to get up, but Snow White struck me in the jaw with the flashlight. The blow knocked my head sideways and I flopped on my back.

'What was you after?' he demanded.

'I just wanted to cover him up,' Cat blurted, her voice high and trembling. 'Okay? He got uncovered when ... when we changed the tire. That's all. We ... we were afraid you might

... look in the trunk and see him. Figured if I could ... just get the tarp over him ...'

'Sounds like a loada mule shit.'

'It's the truth!'

'Wanta change your tune?'

'She told you the truth,' I said, raising my head off the ground.

Not saying another word, Snow White stuffed the big flashlight into a pocket of his buckskin jacket. Then he suddenly grabbed Cat by both ankles, picked up her legs, twisted them sideways, and thrust them into the trunk.

He slammed the lid shut.

Then he pulled his knife out of the sheath at his hip and ambled toward me. I scuttled backward.

'Settle down,' he said. 'I don't aim to hurt you.'

I stopped trying to get away. A stride from my feet, he halted.

I could hear Cat yelling inside the trunk, but her voice was muffled.

'What do you want?' I asked.

'Nothing but the truth.'

'Okay.'

'What's in the trunk? Not counting Cathy and the stiff.'

'A hammer.'

'She went in for a hammer, that it?'

'Yes.'

'What for? As if I didn't know.'

'In case you tried something.'

'What, you *scared* of me? A couple of bad-ass killers like yourselves?'

'We killed that guy in self-defense. He was attacking us. We were afraid *you* might attack us. We thought you might ... be a criminal.'

He grinned. His teeth were pale in the moonlight. 'Do I *look* like a criminal?'

'You're a biker.'

'You prejudiced against bikers?'

'We just wanted to play it safe. I mean, we planned to give you a ride in our car. For all we knew, you might want to rob or murder us.'

115

'So you aimed to beat me to the punch?'

'No! We weren't going to do anything unless you attacked us. We just wanted to be able to *defend* ourselves. Now, will you let her out of the trunk? Please? My God, she's in there with *him*!'

'That brings us to another subject.' Squatting down near my feet, Snow White rested his elbows on his knees and tapped the knife blade against his chin in a way that seemed contemplative. 'Who is he?'

'His name?'

'For starters.'

'It's Elliot.'

'This one of those deals where you snuff the hubby?'

'He wasn't her husband.'

'You and Cathy started getting it on, figured to knock off the mister?'

'He *wasn't* the mister.'

'Maybe collect some life insurance . . .'

'No.'

'I seen that movie. Fred MacMurray and that gal, the one that was in *The Big Valley*.'

'Barbara Stanwyck.'

'Yeah, she's the one.'

'*Double Indemnity*.'

'Yeah, that's the movie. He threw that crippled guy off the back of a train, and . . .'

'This isn't like that.'

'Looks like it to me.'

'Looks like a different movie to me,' I told him.

'Yeah? What movie's that?'

'*Dracula*.'

I shouldn't have said it, but I couldn't resist. For one thing, he'd started in with movies. For another, I didn't like the idea of Snow White or anyone else getting the wrong idea about why we'd killed the guy. Also, it seemed like a good idea to throw him a curve. Give him something to think about.

A moment after I popped out the '*Dracula*' remark, Snow White said, 'Fuck.'

'Elliot's a vampire,' I explained. 'He'd been attacking

116

Catherine almost every night for a year. Coming to her bedroom and biting her. Sucking her blood.'

'Bull-fucking-shit.'

'It's the truth. She asked for my help. So tonight I hid in her closet and waited for him. When he showed up and started sucking her blood, I nailed him with the stake. That's how you kill vampires. You pound a wooden stake...'

'Yeah, I know all about it. I seen the movies, too. Seen a million of 'em. I love them vampires. Only one problem – it's all bullshit. No such thing as vampires. They're *just* in the movies.'

'That's what I thought. But I watched him suck her blood. She has bite marks. Open the trunk and let her out. You can see the marks on her neck. They're from *his* teeth.'

He shook the knife at me. 'You just want me to open the trunk.'

'*Yes*, I want you to open the trunk! How would *you* like to be trapped in there with a dead guy?'

'Serves her right for giving me shit.'

'Would you let her out? Please?'

I suddenly realized that it might not be easy to let her out. If she'd been thrown into the trunk with the keys in her hand or pocket...

'How do I know she ain't got a gun in there?'

'She doesn't.'

'Easy for you to say; you ain't the guy she'll try 'n cap.'

'She was looking for the *hammer*. And she couldn't even find that. If we had a gun – believe me, it wouldn't be locked in the trunk.'

'You would've already dropped me, huh?'

'I didn't say that.'

'I can read your mind. Get up.'

While I pushed myself off the ground, Snow White stepped around behind me. With his left hand, he clutched the hair on top of my head. His right hand held the knife to my throat. Then he walked me toward the car, his chest pushing at my back.

He halted me at the rear bumper.

No sounds came from inside the trunk. For some reason, Cat had quit yelling.

'We're going to let you out,' I said, speaking loudly.

Snow White jerked my hair so that I winced and went up on my tiptoes. 'Shut up,' he whispered.

'Okay, okay.'

'Now open it.'

Keeping hold of my hair and still pressing the knife against my throat, he straightened out his arms so I could bend over the trunk.

The lock hole was hidden by shadow.

When I put my hand down there, however, I felt the dangling key case. The trunk key was still inside the lock. I pinched it and gave it a twist. With a quiet click and thump, the lock disengaged and the lid swung up.

All I could see was a trunk full of blackness.

'You all right?' I asked.

Cat didn't answer.

A couple of awful possibilities ran through my mind, but then she said, 'Are *you* all right, Sammy?'

'Sure.'

'Where's *he*?'

'Right here,' Snow White said. As he spoke, he pulled me by the hair until I was standing up straight. Then he walked me backward a few steps. 'All set to open up Sammy's gullet,' he added, 'if you give me any shit.'

'I'll be good.'

'What've you got in there?' he asked.

'Nothing.'

'What was you *looking* for?'

I said, 'I already...'

He jerked my hair.

'OW!'

'Don't hurt him!' Cat blurted.

'I'll slit his throat!'

'No! I was trying to find a hammer!'

'Did you get it?'

'No!'

'Got *anything*?'

'No!'

'A gun?'

'I don't have *anything!*'

118

'Better not. Down on your knees, Sammy boy.'

He shoved at the top of my head. As I sank to my knees, he took the knife away from my throat. But he stayed behind me, clutching my hair. A few seconds later, he switched on the flashlight and pointed it at the trunk.

'Come on out, honey. Your hands better be empty.'

Cat pushed herself up. On hands and knees inside the trunk, she turned her head and squinted into the flashlight's beam. Her eyes were shiny. Her cheeks were lined with tear streaks. She had a small smear of blood on the left side of her face – probably Elliot's.

She reached up, took hold of the trunk's edge, then swung one leg over and climbed out. On her feet behind the car, she turned toward us. She raised her open hands. 'Empty,' she said.

I saw that she had a few smudges of blood on her hands and arms. I didn't notice any on her shirt, but the checkered pattern might've concealed them. Her legs looked fine: smooth and slender and clean.

'Get your shirt up,' Snow White said.

It had come untucked, and hung down so far that it hid the front of her cut-off jeans.

She unfastened the top button.

'Don't gotta take it off.' He chuckled. 'Not unless you wanta. Just pick it up some.'

Cat lowered her hands. She took hold of the shirt, down near her hips, and lifted it. Her hands were almost up to her armpits before we could see bare skin above the waist of her cut-offs.

'Turn around slow,' Snow White told her.

He kept the flashlight aimed at her midriff while she followed his instructions.

When she was facing us again, he said, 'Anything in your pockets?'

'No.'

'Come over here. Keep your shirt up.'

Holding it high, she walked toward us.

'Here.' He pointed to my left.

Cat stopped beside me.

'Stay put,' Snow White told me. 'I don't want no trouble.'

Then he let go of my hair and took a step to the side. Standing directly in front of Cat, he used his left hand to pat the two front pockets of her cut-offs.

I watched closely.

He didn't try any funny stuff.

'Turn around,' he said. She did, and he patted her seat pockets. 'Okay. You can put your hands down.'

She lowered her shirt, turned to face him, and took a couple of steps backward.

Snow White knocked on my shoulder with the flashlight. 'Get up.'

I stood and went to Cat. She squeezed my hand. We both faced Snow White.

'Sorry you made me rough you up,' he said. 'Ain't every night I run into a pair of killers.'

'We're not killers,' Cat said.

'Oh. Right. Pardon me. This dude in your trunk, he's a *vampire.*'

She glanced at me.

'I told him,' I admitted.

She nodded.

'Show me your bites,' Snow White said.

The top button of Cat's shirt was still unfastened. Reaching up with one hand, she slipped the checkered fabric toward her shoulder.

Snow White stepped up close to her. He shined the flashlight on the side of her neck, leaned forward and peered at the same pair of wounds that Cat had shown me early that night in my apartment.

'You got a couple holes there. Sure do. Course, that don't mean...'

'Look at his teeth,' Cat said.

Snow White stepped past us. Bending over the trunk, he reached in and turned Elliot's head. The strip of silver tape across his mouth, which had been rearranged during our earlier rough ride, was still crooked enough to expose the right corner of his mouth. And the shiny steel fang that curved down like a nasty dental tool. Its tip was still buried in Elliot's lower lip.

Snow White ripped off the entire length of tape.

And gasped, 'Yah!' and leaped back as Elliot's mouth sprang wide open.

19

Cat and I, standing behind him and over to the side, also jumped and let out gasps when Elliot's mouth leaped open. She grabbed my arm.

The beam of Snow White's flashlight jittered wildly.

All four of Elliot's fangs gleamed like silver.

None of us spoke. I guess we were all waiting for his next move. But he just lay there, mouth agape.

After a while, our biker ventured, 'What the fuck?'

'See those fangs?' Cat asked.

'Fuck the fangs! You see what he done? He was gonna *bite* me!'

'It was probably the stickum,' I said.

'Huh?'

'The stickum on the back of the tape. When you tore the tape off his mouth, the stickum held and jerked his jaw down.'

'Yeah!' He let out a brash laugh. 'That was it. Sure. You got it right on the money, Sammy boy. Had me going, though. Ha! Shit! Just goes to show you, don't it? You start talking this vampire shit, all of a sudden you got some dead as a dirt asshole trying bite you. The mind's a funny thing, huh?'

'Sure is,' I said.

He said, 'Shit,' again, and shook his head. Then he muttered, 'Fuck.' Then he said, 'Enough of *him*,' and backed away from the trunk and slammed the lid shut. Bending over, he plucked the key out of the lock. He swung around and tossed the keys to me. I stuffed them into a pocket of my jeans.

'So you believe us?' Cat asked.

'You got them holes in your neck from that freak? Yeah. Shit. Weird. Let's see.' He stepped up to Cat for another, closer look. As he studied the pair of holes in her neck, he shook his head. 'Just sunk 'em right in you, huh? Them iron fangs?'

'Yeah.'

121

'And he, like, drank your blood?'

Cat nodded.

'Pukin' Judas. Did it hurt?'

'Sure.'

'Musta. Ouch. Can I touch?'

'Okay.'

He shifted the flashlight to his left hand. His right hand, forefinger extended, moved slowly toward one of the wounds as if going for a doorbell that might give him a shock. He touched it and his hand jumped away. Then he tried again. He fingered one hole, then the other. 'These ain't real fresh,' he judged, and stepped back.

'They're a few nights old,' Cat explained.

'Did he get you tonight?'

'Yeah.'

'Where at?'

I remembered, and heat suddenly rushed through my body.

'My foot,' Cat said.

Ah. I'd forgotten about that.

'He sucked your *foot*?' Snow White sounded astonished and appalled.

'Blood's blood,' Cat said. 'He wasn't particular where he sucked it from.'

'But your *foot*?' Snow White cast a glance at the trunk. 'What kinda weird fuckin' geek *is* that guy?'

'Too weird to live,' I threw in.

He looked at me and nodded. 'Right on, man. I'd of killed him my own self.'

Cat put her hand out. 'Glad to hear it, friend,' she said.

Smiling, the biker reached out his hand and shook with her.

'From now on,' she said, 'you can call me Cat.'

'Yes, ma'am. You can call me whatever you damn want. Sorry about the spanking.'

'That's all right.'

'Okay if I do it again sometime? Sure felt good.'

She laughed and shook her head. 'Please don't.'

Letting go of Cat's hand, he turned to me. 'Hope I didn't hurt you much,' he said and extended his hand.

I didn't feel enormously friendly toward the guy. For one thing, I detested him for spanking Cat. For another, my stomach and jaw still ached from the blows he'd dealt me. But I was glad he hadn't pulled any cute stuff with Cat when he was searching her for weapons. Also, I felt a certain relief that he now – apparently – considered himself to be on *our* side.

Not that I wanted him on our side.

I didn't trust him.

I preferred him gone.

But at least he was no longer battering us – quite an improvement.

When we shook hands, I remembered Cat's comment about humoring him, so I said, 'Glad to have you aboard.'

He gave my hand a good, solid shake, then let go and said, 'Found us a road. I was just coming to tell you...'

'Really?' Cat asked.

'You were in the trunk,' I reminded her.

'For which I've been intending to thank you.'

'I messed up.'

'Guess I'll forgive you this time.'

'Did you get hurt at all?' I asked.

She shook her head and said, 'Not much.' To our new friend, she said, 'But I sure didn't like getting locked in. You should try it sometime.'

'Well, it looked like a good idea...'

'It wasn't.'

What had happened to humoring him?

'I messed up,' he said, stealing my line. I didn't appreciate it.

But I said to Cat, 'It was understandable. He thought we were a couple of murderers.'

'You *are* a couple of murderers,' he said, a grin lifting half his mouth. 'Only thing is, now it looks like you killed a guy that needed it. Which is okay by me. The less fucking freaks we got walking the world, the better. You ask me, kill 'em all.'

'That was my theory,' Cat said, 'when I tried to get the hammer out of the trunk.'

Snow White had a good laugh about that, and slapped her on the arm a couple of times.

Then he said, 'Let's get a move on. You're driving, Sam.

The road's dead ahead. Ain't much, but I reckon it'll likely get us outa here.'

Leading the way, he opened the front right door of the car. Instead of climbing into the passenger seat, however, he gestured for Cat to take it. When she was in, he shut the door. He opened the door behind it, and swung his big body into the back seat.

I slid in behind the steering wheel.

Just what we didn't want – Snow White riding behind us.

But we went along with it. After all, he was bigger and stronger than us, and he had the better knife.

We *had* a knife, of course. Our salami knife. I'd watched Cat put it into the food bag, back in her kitchen. I hadn't seen it since then, though. She'd mentioned it just before making her try for the hammer.

I suspected that she might know where it was.

She didn't seem to have it on her.

Not that it really mattered. With both of us sitting in front and Snow White at our backs, the knife would've done us no good at all.

Besides, he was now our friend.

Sure.

Cat and I put on our seatbelts. I started driving slowly in the same direction that we'd been taking before the trunk incident.

We bumped over ruts and rocks.

'Take it easy,' Snow White said.

'I'm trying. It's hard to see what's coming.'

'Turn on the headlights.'

'I'd rather not. They'll make us ...'

'Do it.'

I did it.

Snow White said, 'They ain't gonna hurt nothing.'

With the help of the headlights, I could see what was ahead and steered around a good many obstacles that I might've hit, otherwise. The ride still wasn't smooth, but at least we avoided the worst stuff. And I picked up speed.

'You're coming up on it,' Snow White said. 'Better slow down.'

'Which way should we go when we get there?' Cat asked him.

'Left, I reckon.'

'Sounds good,' Cat said.

Soon, an unpaved road appeared in the headlights. It wasn't just a pair of ruts, the way a lot of them are. This road was a narrow strip, not much wider than a large car, with low banks of dirt on both sides. It almost looked as if it had been scraped across the desert floor by a snow plow.

I steered in at an angle. We climbed the embankment, front rising, the whole car tilting sideways. I stepped on the gas. We bounded over the top and swooped down the other side.

After crossing so much rough terrain since leaving the highway behind, this road felt almost smooth in spite of the way it rattled the car and shook us with its washboard surface.

The washboard wasn't terrible. I've been on worse.

I made it better by picking up speed. I probably could've made it go away entirely if I'd had the guts to hit fifty. But that would've been too dangerous in the dark – even with headlights on. So I held to about thirty-five. At that speed, we cut the shaking down a good deal, plus we covered ground at a pretty fair clip.

'I hope this gets us somewhere,' Cat said after a while.

'They don't got roads to nowhere,' Snow White said from behind us.

'No, they don't,' I agreed. 'But some lead off into places you can't go. Especially if you don't have four-wheel drive.'

'Which we don't,' Cat added for his benefit.

'If this don't take us where we're going,' Snow White said, 'we'll just turn the buggy around and go back the other way. Don't matter to me. I ain't in no hurry. You in a hurry?'

'Not really,' I said. 'It'd be nice to get onto a real road, that's all.'

'What're you aiming to do with Dracula?'

'His name's Elliot,' Cat said.

'Yeah. So what're gonna do with him? Bury him?'

'I guess so,' I said.

'You got your pick and shovel right back here.'

With a glance over her shoulder at him, Cat said, 'Maybe you'd like to help us dig.'

125

'What's in it for me?'

'The satisfaction of a job well done.'

He laughed. Then he said, 'Reckon I'll take a pass on that. I got nothing against working up a sweat, but not for nothing.'

'You want cash?' Cat asked.

'Might.'

Time for my two-cents worth. I threw in, 'I think we can get along without hiring anyone to help us dig.'

'It'll be a lot easier if we get Mr White to help us.'

'Mr White,' he said. 'I like that.'

'I think we should get Mr White to the nearest town,' I said, 'so he can make arrangements to retrieve his motorcycle.'

'I got no big rush,' he said.

He'd sounded somewhat amused through all this.

'It's all right,' I said. 'No trouble at all.'

'Still wanta get rid of me.'

'It's for your own good,' I explained. 'We've got a murdered man in our trunk. Do you really want to be riding with us if we should happen to get pulled over by the Highway Patrol?'

'Take my chances.'

'The sooner you get away from us, the better off you'll be.'

'Nah. I'll stick with you, help you dispose of the remains. Fact is, I've had me some experience along them lines.'

'Great,' I muttered.

Cat looked back at him again. 'You've gotten rid of bodies?'

'Now and again. Sure have.'

'People you've killed?' Cat asked.

I was wondering that, myself, even before the words had popped out of her mouth. But I never would've asked.

'Some,' he answered.

'Ah,' said I. 'So you *are* a serial killer.'

Luckily, he laughed.

'Nah,' he said. 'I don't get no thrill out of it. I just kill folks that need it. You know, like if they try and fight me. Or if they cross me up, cheat me, rip me off or piss me off one way or another. I never killed nobody that didn't have it coming.'

'Guess we'd better be nice to you,' I said.

'Yep,' he said.

'So,' said Cat, 'do you have any recommendations on the subject of body disposal?'

'Sure. Main thing is, don't plant nobody in the dirt. It's a big waste of sweat and time.'

'We don't want anyone to find the body,' Cat pointed out.

'So what you do, just heave it down a chasm. Or a mine shaft, that's better yet. I know all kinds of mine shafts, chasms, dried up wells, sink holes. Anything'll do, long as its deep and dark and out in the boonies so you don't get a lot of visitors. All you gotta do is drop him down, he's gone forever.'

She looked at me. 'That sounds like a pretty good idea.'

'If it'll save me from digging a grave,' I said, 'I'm all for it. The thing is, I don't really think we should drag Mr White all over the place. He needs to get back to his bike before someone *else* finds it out there. Don't you think so, Mr White? That's a valuable machine. A Harley? If the wrong person should happen to see it out there in the middle of nowhere, that'll be the end of it.'

'Don't let it worry you.'

If *he* wasn't worried about his bike being stolen, he probably didn't have one back there. Right from the start, Cat had suspected as much.

'Nobody touches my bike,' he said.

'I wouldn't count on that.'

'Last guy tried to steal it, he's *still* down at the bottom of a hole. Least I reckon he is. It ain't real far from here, matter of fact. Might make a good place to drop off Dracula.'

'Elliot,' Cat said.

'Old Brock, he could use some company. Must be mighty lonesome down there.'

'Well,' I said, 'we appreciate the advice. Maybe we will look for a good, deep hole somewhere. But I think we should let you off as soon as possible this morning. There's no point in dragging you into this business.'

'Already in,' he said. He sounded cheerful.

'I think we'll all be better off,' I pointed out, 'if you don't know where we leave the body.'

'Nah,' he said.

'Nah?'

'I'm coming with you.'

'Why?'

''Cause I feel like it. Who's gonna stop me, you?'

Cat looked at me. I couldn't see what sort of expression she wore, but my guess is that she was giving me one of those looks meant to warn me off and shut me up.

Before I could say anything, she glanced over her shoulder and said, 'You can stay with us on one condition.'

'A condition?'

'When we get there, *you've* got to throw Elliot in.'

'Why's that?'

'Sam has a bad back.'

'Aw, poor Sam.' He chuckled. Then he said, 'What's in it for me?'

'Agree to throw him in, and we'll let you enjoy the pleasure of riding with us till we get there.'

'You drive a hard bargain, Cat.'

'I'm a hard woman.'

He got a real kick out of that one, and sat in the back seat giggling as if he might never stop.

A couple of hundred yards ahead, a pickup truck went by pulling a horse-trailer.

We'd found a real road.

20

I turned left onto a paved, two-lane road. No more shaking, rattling, bouncing, jolting. Just a nice, smooth ride.

'Ah, this is great,' Cat said. 'Think it'll take us back to 14?'

'It might.' After saying that, I turned my head and asked, 'Do we still want 14, Mr White?'

'Good enough,' he said.

'Well, where's the hole?'

'Hole? What sorta hole?'

'The one you threw Brock into. Isn't that where we're going?'

'Sounds good to me.'

'Do you know how to get there?'

'I wouldn't be taking you to it if I didn't know where it was.'

'Where *is* it?' I asked.

'Not gonna tell.'

Cat looked over her shoulder at him. 'If you don't tell us where it is, how are we supposed to get there?'

'Simple. I'll tell Sammy boy when to turn. Sam? Just keep going till I say to do something different.'

'All right,' I said.

'Is it far?' Cat asked him.

'Ain't saying.'

'Okay,' she said. 'Well, I'm going to take a nap.'

'Suit yourself.'

To me, she said, 'You must be getting awfully tired, too.'

'I'm fine,' I told her. 'Go on and get some sleep.'

'If you get drowsy, wake me up and I'll drive.'

'I will,' I said, though I intended to stick it out for as long as she might remain asleep.

Nodding, she faced forward and unfastened her seatbelt.

'What're you doing?'

'I can't sleep with this on,' she told me. 'Try not to crash.'

I was tempted to argue. But she had a right to go without the seatbelt. Also, I'd never crashed a car in my life.

We were tempting fate, of course.

With Cat unstrapped and a stiff in our truck, we seemed ripe for a traffic accident.

When the belts were out of her way, she scooted down in her seat a little, rested her hands on her lap, lowered her head and shut her eyes.

'Go ahead and get on 14 when it comes up,' Snow White said.

'North?'

'North.'

When I looked over at Cat a couple of minutes later, she seemed to be asleep.

Snow White stopped talking. Soon, rough snores started to come from the back seat.

They were great to hear. It was as if he'd gone away and left me alone, again, with Cat.

I started looking over at her.

The night wasn't quite as dark as before; dawn was on its way. I couldn't see Cat clearly yet, but I saw her well enough to make me hurt.

Her face had a calm about it, a softness, an innocence as if sleep had changed her to the way she'd been when I'd known her before. She seemed to be fourteen, maybe fifteen years old.

Though she had grown into a shockingly beautiful woman – a woman with intelligence and wit and strength and tenderness – it made me ache to see such a reminder of how she used to be. Maybe because she'd grown up away from me; I'd missed so much. But more likely because she'd changed. She hadn't *stayed the same*, and that seemed like a terrible thing.

It made me ache.

As I sat there, glancing over at her and feeling an awful sorrow in my chest, I told myself that it was right for her to grow older. Even if I had the power to make her stay fourteen forever – or fifteen or sixteen – I would be extremely tempted, but I would not do it.

Though I'd loved everything about her at those earlier ages, I couldn't cheat her out of growing into a woman.

Still, I felt miserable for the loss of the way she'd been.

It's a little like how you might miss a puppy or a kitten after it becomes a full-grown dog or cat. So much has been lost: the cute, quick, fun, bumbling liveliness. It almost breaks your heart.

But there are compensations.

The playful, endearing kitty has turned into the sleek and gorgeous Cat.

You hate to see the one go, but you'd sure hate to miss the other.

And you can't do a damn thing about it, anyway. Just sometimes think back on what was lost, and mourn its passing. And hold on to the present for dear life.

Cat's face had been gray with the promise of daylight when I'd first looked over and noticed she was asleep. After that, I was pretty much lost in a maze of regrets and hopes and odd thoughts.

I didn't crash, though. Didn't get lost, either. Without paying any real attention to my driving, I'd returned us to Highway 14.

Though we were northbound, the sun rising over to the right soon spread gold out in front of us. It glared so that I could hardly see out the windshield. But I could see Cat just fine in the seat beside me.

She still slept.

Snow White continued to snore.

I squinted out at the road often enough to avoid mishaps. Much of the time, however, my eyes lingered on Cat. I'd missed her so much, for so many years. And here she was, sleeping in the seat beside me. I could hardly believe it. This was almost like a miracle – but more like a very strange and wonderful dream.

The girl of my dreams, riding with me at dawn, near enough to touch . . .

This was the first time in a decade that I'd seen her in sunlight.

I studied her: the mussed tangle of her boyish, golden hair; the curve of her left eyebrow (the right side of her face was mostly out of view); the faint lines near the corner of her eye where she might someday have wrinkles; the sprinkle of light brown freckles on her brow and eyelid, cheek and nose; the downy hair on her cheek and above her upper lip; the way her lips pursed out a little.

Her head was down, so her chin was hidden by the collar of her shirt.

Because of how she slouched in the seat, the front of her shirt was rumpled. It appeared to have a few small waves up the middle. Being a woman's shirt – or blouse, I suppose – it buttoned so that the overlap faced my way.

I could see in.

An opening between two buttons, a bulging rumple and my eyes were all lined up to let me see inside the shirt and view the left side of her right breast.

She wasn't wearing a bra.

The previous night, Cat must've been naked in front of me for an hour. I'd seen every inch of her body. So it's strange that I found myself enthralled by this view of her breast.

I could hardly force my eyes away.

Most of her breast was out of sight. I was only able to see a small portion of it, down where it began its rise from her chest. Part of its side and underside. For some reason, my view of the underside – the smooth, curving *bottom* of her breast – seemed like an astounding, surprising treat.

I kept looking at it.

I felt guilty, felt like a Peeping Tom. But the view made me breathless and hard.

It also put a stop to my regrets about Cat growing up.

Only the present moment mattered.

The perfect moment, the special view.

Sneaking glimpses while she slept, while Snow White slept behind us, while I drove without sunglasses on the glaring highway.

In no danger at all of falling asleep.

Hidden by her shirt from the morning sunlight, the visible section of Cat's breast was dusky with a soft, mellow glow – a glow like the light that finds its way through curtains into a bedroom on a sunny day.

It turned her breast the color of honey.

The small portion that I could see looked warm and smooth and, for no good reason, more *naked* than any skin I had ever seen before.

Finally, I needed to stop staring at it and get myself back under control. I fixed my eyes on the windshield, squinted into the sunlight, took deep breaths and tried to think about something else.

There were plenty of matters worth thinking about: Snow White in the back seat and Elliot in the trunk, the dangers they could mean for us, how we might get rid of them...

But my mind kept sliding back to the view I was missing.

It's like *spying* on her, I told myself. Invading her privacy.

She was running around stark naked in front of me last night; she wouldn't mind me peeking into her blouse.

Don't count on it.

She'll never find out.

What's the harm in looking, anyway? I asked myself. You don't turn away from a rainbow, a brook in the woods, a field of bright flowers. You don't glance at it, then decide you're wrong to look, and shut your eyes. Hell, no. You stare at it. You savor it. You're supposed to. Otherwise, you're missing out. You're cheating yourself.

Using that rationale, of course, it would be okay to spy on strangers through their bedroom windows. A line needed to be drawn...

Staring into Cat's blouse was clearly on the wrong side of it.

But I couldn't *not* look.

Soon, my head turned and my eyes again probed the gap between her buttons, went into the murky light and lingered on the skin that was there.

Lingered as much as I dared before needing to check the road.

A few seconds, maybe.

After making sure I was still in my lane, then looking all around for about half a minute, I returned my attention to Cat.

Something had changed.

I could hardly believe my luck.

The gap in her shirt had grown; a button must've come loose while I was looking away. Now, through the pursed opening, I could see probably *half* her breast – halfway up the smooth slope of its side, halfway up its curved bottom.

The view jerked my breath out. My mouth suddenly felt parched. And I grew awfully hard.

I squirmed, but it didn't help much; I still felt as if my jeans were crushing me. They weren't made to fit comfortably in such circumstances. Nothing short of opening them would've helped, and I wasn't about to try that.

Nor was I about to solve the problem by focusing my attention on the road. I *had* to check the road every few seconds to keep us safe, but I was always quick to return my eyes to Cat's breast.

I could see so *much* of it, now.

But I started to worry that Snow White might be sharing the view. His snoring was no guarantee. A glance at the rearview mirror didn't satisfy me, either. I twisted around and peered over my shoulder.

He was slumped down crooked in the seat behind Cat, chin

133

at his chest, white hair hanging down past both sides of his face. His buckskin jacket gaped open, showing a great deal of his broad, tanned chest.

I had no interest in his chest.

He was in no position to see Cat's; that's what mattered.

Facing forward, I made sure we were in no peril of running off the road or smashing into a nearby car or truck.

No other vehicles were near enough to worry about.

So I looked over at Cat.

Impossible!

The gap had expanded again!

Cat must've squirmed in her sleep, twisting her shirt sideways. The entire left side of her breast was now bare. Her shirt no longer covered it, but draped the far side and top of her breast like a hood.

A hood held aloft as if tossed over a peg.

Held aloft by her nipple.

Her nipple was dark gold under the shirt's edge. Below it, sunlight washed the left side of her breast.

Though the car was warm, she had goosebumps.

There'd been no goosebumps before.

I liked them.

And I liked the curls of shiny golden down that I could now see, just barely, on the sunlit side of her breast.

I liked the freckles, too. Maybe half a dozen of them. Dark brown specks on the tan slope.

In a way, I even liked the scars.

So many of them. Twenty? Fifty? All up and down the side of her breast, but faint. You needed very good light to see them at all.

A few, fresher than others, were slightly pink. Most looked white. There were thin marks of different lengths – white threads where she'd apparently been nicked or slit by a blade. There were also curved scars where she'd been carved. But most of her scars, by far, were dots where holes had healed.

Holes made in her breast by Elliot's steel fangs.

Where he'd sunk them in and sucked her blood.

I thought about how it must've felt. Having her breast in his mouth. Squeezing it between his teeth. Puncturing it, sucking on it.

134

For a while there, I envied him.

Hated him.

Hated him for hurting her, but mostly for *having* her.

I was glad we'd killed him.

But still, I liked the scars he'd put on Cat's breast. Because they belonged to her, I suppose. They were part of her, like her freckles or the color of her eyes.

They weren't ugly.

They were like secrets written in magic ink that could only be seen when the light was just right.

I wanted to kiss them. Kiss each and every one of them. And kiss her nipple, too, while I was at it. Take it between my lips, lick it, test it with my teeth, suck on it...

Squirming and more breathless than before, I turned my head away and studied the road and tried to calm down. The traffic was still light. In the rearview mirror, though, I saw a truck rushing toward us. I changed lanes to get out of its way. The eighteen-wheeler sped by, roaring and buffeting us with wind. When it was ahead of us, I turned my eyes to Cat.

My mouth fell open, but I didn't make a sound.

No moan, no mutter of 'My God!' or 'Holy Cow!'

I didn't even breathe.

My heartbeat, however, sounded like a wild drum.

What the hell's going on around here?

Cat's shirt, draping her breast like a hood when I'd last seen it, had now fallen aside.

Her entire right breast was bare in the bright sunlight.

Snow White still snored. I glanced back at him. He hadn't changed position – and I don't believe that his buckskin jacket had opened any wider than last time I'd looked.

Glad he was still out of the picture, I latched my gaze on Cat's breast.

It suddenly hopped.

A small, upward lurch.

Up and down, a quick hop followed by a slight jiggle.

We'd struck no bumps or potholes. Nor had Cat's left breast made any abrupt movement.

Some sort of muscle twitch?

It happened again.

This time, I spotted a quick flex of muscles above the breast.

135

I looked at Cat's face. Her head was still down, her eyes shut.

Her breast hopped again.

She suddenly squeezed her lips together. Her chin trembled. Tremors shook her shoulders and chest and bare breast. At first, I thought she must be starting to cry.

Then her left eye opened, her head turned slightly, and she slyly peeked at me.

Then winked.

If we'd been alone, she probably would've exploded with laughter. Because of Snow White, she held it in like a sneeze. The effort made her shake all the more. Her eyes even watered.

After wiping them and regaining control, she sighed deeply and looked over her shoulder.

I looked, too.

Snow White still snoozed and snored.

We turned to the front again. Cat took another deep breath, then lowered her head and suddenly seemed to notice her exposed breast. She went, 'Huh?' Then she frowned at me, puzzled. 'How'd that get out?' she whispered.

'Don't ask me,' I said.

Shaking her head, extremely perplexed, she drew the shirt over her breast and started to fasten the buttons. 'Terribly embarrassing,' she muttered. 'You didn't do it, did you?'

'Not I.'

'Must've been ghosts.'

'More than likely.'

'So, anyhow, I had a nice little sleep. How did the driving go?'

'Just fine.'

'You haven't had any trouble staying awake?'

'Not a bit.'

She grinned and nodded. 'Glad to hear it. I was a little afraid you might get bored and doze off.'

'Never came close.'

'Would you like me to take over the driving for a while? I'm good and rested.'

'You're good, all right.'

'Oh?' Grinning, she hoisted her eyebrows.

'I'll keep on driving for a while. Maybe you'd like to take another nap.'

'I'm not tired anymore.' She pulled the seat belt down across her chest and lap, and latched its buckle.

21

A while later, Snow White let out a loud snort and woke up. Then he made all sorts of noises: coughing, sniffing, clearing his throat, sighing and groaning. There were some leathery sounds as he changed positions.

Cat and I stayed quiet.

'Mornin', pilgrims,' he finally said.

'Morning,' I said.

Cat twisted sideways, looked back at him, and asked, 'Sleep well?'

'Not bad, not bad. Me and all your junk. Look at all this you got back here. You going out to dig a grave, or have yourselves a picnic? Maybe you're aiming to throw in a honeymoon.' He tittered. 'By gravy, you even got a salami.'

'Help yourself,' Cat said. 'We've got crackers and cheese, too.'

'That ain't no breakfast for a man. What the hell time is it?' Before either of us had a chance to answer, he said, 'Quarter till eight.'

'You're wearing two wristwatches,' Cat told him.

'Sure.'

'What for?'

'Got two eyes, don't I?'

'So you need a watch for each eye?'

'You got it, honey. Right on the nose. Now, where the hell are we?' he asked.

'Still on 14,' I told him. 'We passed Mojave about half an hour ago.'

'Half an hour ago, you say? Got it. Know precisely where we are.' He must've chosen that moment to look out the window. 'Why, this here is Red Rock Canyon!'

'It's beautiful,' Cat said. 'Almost like the Grand Canyon.'

137

She was right. I hadn't been paying much attention to the landscape, but suddenly noticed that we were passing through an area of steep canyon walls – bluffs of rich, red rock so vivid and colorful in the morning sunlight – and so unexpected – that they hardly seemed real.

'Are we still on the right track?' I asked.

'Huh?'

'We're on our way to Brock's hole, aren't we?'

'Yup,' he said.

'We didn't miss a turn, or anything?'

'Nope. We're looking for the junction with 178. Oughta be half an hour up the road. We'll take it on over.'

'Over to where?' Cat asked.

'Brock's hole,' Snow White told her.

'And where is that?'

'Tell you when we get there. First thing we gotta do is get on 178. We can find us some breakfast over at Inyokern or Ridgecrest.'

'In the meantime,' Cat said, 'I'm dying of thirst. There should be some bottled water back there. Probably on the floor. Everything got tumbled around. Could you find one of the bottles and pass it up here?'

'You asking me to pass water?'

'That's about the size of it,' Cat said.

'Haw!'

'Ho ho ho,' said Cat, with just a touch of sarcasm.

'Glad to oblige, honey.'

Pretty soon, he handed a clear plastic bottle to Cat. She thanked him and said, 'Have a bottle yourself, if you'd like.'

'Nope. That's rich-kid shit, bottled water.'

Neither of us responded to that.

Cat faced forward. 'Want some?' she asked me as she twisted off the cap.

'You go first.'

She put her lips around the mouth of the bottle, tipped her head back, and gulped the water. I watched her throat work. As she drank, a single trickle dribbled off her lower lip. It slid down her chin, down the sloping underside, and down the front of her neck. It left a silver trail.

'Watch where you're driving,' Snow White said.

'Sorry,' I muttered, and looked forward.

Cat was done drinking by then, anyway. She handed the bottle to me. I put my lips around it, just as she'd done. Then I tilted up the bottle and drank.

The label said it came from a mountain spring. It tasted like it. Cool and delicious, with a mild woodsy flavor. Maybe it was actually LA tap water that had been aged in oak barrels, I don't know. But it sure was great. I drank quite a lot of it, then gave the bottle back to Cat, who drank some more.

When she was done, she capped the bottle. She turned her head a little and said to Snow White, 'How far is it to Brock's hole? Or is that also a state secret?'

'It ain't real far from here.'

'I think that's what you said last time I asked, which was probably a hundred miles back.'

'That ain't far.'

'Give us a clue,' Cat said. 'Will we get there *today*?'

'I reckon. If we don't have no mishaps. Only thing is, we're likely to get there a long spell before dark.'

'Well, good,' Cat said.

'Not so sure it's a *good* thing. Thinking maybe we oughta lay up somewhere and wait till sunset. Find us a motel . . .'

'Why on earth would we do that?' Cat asked.

'Well, we don't wanta open the trunk on your old pal till it's dark out.'

'Why not?'

'Might ruin him.'

'What?'

'He's a vampire, ain't he?'

'I don't know, *is* he?'

'You both been telling me how he's a real-life vampire. Hell, I seen where he bit you, honey.'

'He *did* bite me.'

'And he sucked your blood, right?'

'Yeah.'

'So, don't that make him a vampire?'

She shrugged. 'I guess so.'

'Sammy!'

'Yes?'

'You told me he's the same as Dracula. Right?'

'I guess I said something like that.'

'I know you did.'

'I guess so.'

'You weren't lying to me, were you?'

'I suppose he might be a vampire,' I said. 'He, uh, behaved like one. He *looks* like one. I mean, he has those fangs. He even sort of looks like that Nosferatu from the old silent movie.'

'I seen it,' Snow White said. 'That guy was a tad uglier than Elliot.'

'Anyway,' I went on, 'we *figure* Elliot's a real vampire. Look at the way we killed him. If we hadn't assumed he might be the real thing, we could've just shot him or strangled him or . . .'

'So you *do* have a gun?'

Cat shook her head. 'We don't have any gun.'

'But Sam just said . . .'

'I didn't mean we *have* one,' I tried to explain. 'We *don't* have a gun. I was just trying to make a point; we killed him with a *stake* because we assumed he was a vampire.'

'If we'd thought he was a normal person,' Cat said, 'we would've done it differently.'

'Or not at all,' I added.

'That's true. Of course, if he *was* normal, he wouldn't have kept biting me. We only had to kill him *because* he was a vampire.'

'So you weren't lying to me?' Snow White asked.

'No,' I said.

'Far as the both of you know, he's the real McCoy?'

'Right.'

Raising his voice in triumph, Snow White said, 'So if he is, he'll catch fire and burn up and turn to ashes if the sunlight gets him. Ain't that so?'

'Supposedly,' I said.

'It's certainly what happens in the movies,' Cat added. 'Whether or not *Elliot* would burn up . . .' She shrugged.

'It'll be easy to find out,' I said.

'We ain't gonna find out,' Snow White said. 'Gonna keep him nice and safe in the trunk till after dark.'

Cat and I glanced at each other. I thought, *What kind of a nut is this guy?* Cat looked as if her thoughts might be running along the same lines.

'You're in charge, Mr White,' I said. 'The only thing is, it won't be dark until ... probably about nine o'clock tonight. That's an awfully long time to be driving around with a corpse in the trunk. Besides, I don't really think the sunlight will hurt him.'

'Hurts *all* them vampires,' Snow White protested. 'I don't know what goes on in books – ain't much for reading – but I seen a million vampire movies.'

'Have there been that many?' Cat asked.

'Been plenty,' he said. 'And I seen them all. You just *touch* one of them fuckers with sunlight, he's a gonner. Goes up like a match.'

Cat and I looked at each other, nodded, and didn't laugh.

'I've seen a few of those movies, myself,' I said. 'You're right about the sunlight. But what about a stake through the heart? Don't the vampires always crumple and turn into dust if they get staked?'

'Some do, some don't.'

'Elliot didn't,' Cat pointed out.

'I reckon that's 'cause he ain't a real *old* vampire.'

'How old was Elliot?' I asked Cat.

'He never told me. But he didn't look a day over forty.'

'See how it is,' Snow White said, 'only the really *ancient* vampires fall apart and turn to dust when you stake them. Like if they're a couple hundred years old.'

'Sounds reasonable to me,' I said.

'So if he ain't real old, he can stay in one piece when you stake him.'

'Like Elliot,' Cat said.

'That's right.'

'Now it all makes sense,' she said – and didn't crack a smile.

'See,' Snow White said, 'here's the thing. They live damn near forever, these vampires. I reckon maybe they *do* live forever if nobody comes along and kills them or they don't get caught in the sun or something.'

'More than likely,' I agreed.

Cat gave me a look.

'And they don't get old, see. Take Elliot, maybe he's been creeping around and sucking folks for fifty years or something. But he don't look his age. All he looks is, like, forty or whatever.

141

'Cause that's how old he was when he started *in* on being a vampire.'

'Shouldn't he look ninety now that he's dead?' Cat asked.

Snow White didn't answer right away. Apparently, he was pondering the situation. At last, he said, 'You got me stumped on that one. All I know is what I seen in the movies.'

'He doesn't look ninety,' Cat pointed out.

'We haven't seen him recently,' I said.

'Or in daylight,' she added.

'You ain't *gonna* see him in no daylight, so get that outta your heads. You'd ruin him.'

'He's already ruined,' I said. 'We killed him.'

'Maybe, maybe not.'

'I don't see much room for maybes,' Cat said.

'Maybe the stake only just ... holds him down. You know what I mean?'

'No,' I said.

Though I knew otherwise. I'd done research and knew a few things that weren't in the movies.

In olden times, stakes were apparently pounded through vampires for the very purpose of holding them down – physically pinning them to the ground at the bottom of their graves in order to keep them from climbing out and wreaking havoc on the countryside.

'What I'm getting at,' Snow White said, 'is I seen movies where the stake comes out and guess what? Old Bruce Lee wakes up just as good as new.'

'Christopher Lee,' I said.

'Huh?'

'Not Bruce Lee. Christopher Lee.'

'Bruce Lee kicked ass,' Cat said. 'Christopher Lee sucked blood.'

'Oh, yeah. Right. I knew that. Anyhow, that ain't the point. Point is, stakes don't *kill* vampires, just ... sorta keep them down. Like going to sleep.'

'Like the poison apple,' Cat said.

'Huh?'

'You know, the poison apple. The wicked witch? Who's the fairest of them all? *Snow White?*'

His hand flew out over Cat's seat and swatted her head. I

happened to be looking when it happened. His open hand caught the right side of her head, up near the top. The blow wasn't hard enough to hurt her much, but it took her by surprise. It jolted her head. Her hair bounced as if struck by a sudden gust. And her entire face seemed to twitch with shock.

She yelped 'AH!' and ducked.

Twisting around in my seat, I yelled, 'Leave her alone!'

His open hand slammed me in the face.

Then he dropped backward and slumped in his seat and muttered, 'Fucking wiseass cocksuckers.'

22

Everybody stayed silent and glum for a while after that.

I wanted to beat the crap out of Snow White. Maybe I should've stopped the car and given it a try. But he had a knife. Also, he was bigger than me, tougher than me. Unless I could take him by surprise, he would win.

Then he might tear into Cat.

I didn't want her to get hurt again.

That's what *really* frosted me – that he'd given her a smack. She'd taunted him, but she didn't deserve to get hit for it.

As I drove, I kept picturing it in my mind. I also kept remembering the way he'd spanked her bottom, not just once but over and over again when she'd been stuck head-first in the trunk.

I started having fantasies about killing him.

Cat, meanwhile, sat low in her seat with her head down. Mostly, she stared straight forward and seemed to be deep in thought.

Now and then, she looked over at me. I'm not psychic, but I'd swear I knew what she was thinking. *Did you see what he did to me? What're we going to do about him? The bastard'll probably end up killing us if we don't do something about him.*

If she could read my eyes, she got, *He never should've touched you. We'll figure out something. We'll take care of him. He'll wish he'd never laid a hand on you.*

'Anyone hungry around here?' he asked. It must've been

twenty minutes after he'd knocked us around. We'd left 14 behind and were on 178, making our way down the main drag of Inyokern.

We didn't answer Snow White's question.

'Hey, buckeroos. Quit your pouting. Pull in up here, Sammy boy. Breakfast time.'

Just ahead of us, on the right, was a place called Lucy's Kitchen. I swung into its parking lot and found us a space between a couple of pickup trucks.

When I shut off the engine, Snow White said, 'Hand me back the key.' I gave it to him. 'Rest of them, too.' So I had to dig the key case out of my pocket and turn it over to him.

'Afraid we might drive off without you?' Cat asked.

'Nope. Not anymore.'

'If you didn't go around hitting people, you wouldn't need to worry about stuff like that.'

He laughed and said, 'Let's go eat.'

I opened my door, but Cat looked over her shoulder and said, 'Could you pass me my purse? It's probably on the floor back there...'

He lifted a brown leather purse into view by its strap.

This was the first time I'd ever seen it.

From what I could recall, Cat had been without a purse of any kind from the moment she'd stepped into my apartment last night. It should've struck me as odd: women usually take their purses everywhere they go. But it's a lot more odd to have a gal show up at your door dressed in nothing but a silk robe. *Where's her purse?* isn't exactly the first question that comes to mind.

From what I could remember, she hadn't carried a purse from her car to her house, either. Nor had I noticed one in her bedroom or kitchen ... or anywhere else.

The whole time, it must've been in the back seat of her car. Or on the floor back there.

Now, Snow White was holding it up by the strap. 'This it?' he asked.

'Thanks.' She took it from him.

We all climbed out of the car. Cat slipped the purse strap over her shoulder and hurried across the parking lot ahead of us.

'Slow down,' Snow White called out.

She glanced back. 'Just trying to stay out of striking range.'

'Real funny,' he muttered.

Cat waited for us at the door to Lucy's Kitchen. Stepping past her, I tried to pull it open. Snow White shoved a big hand against it.

Holding the door shut, he said, 'Don't go and start nothing inside. You're the ones that murdered Elliot, okay? Wasn't me. I'm just a guy with a broke-down Harley and you was nice enough to give me a ride.'

Which, I realized, was the absolute truth.

'We know,' I told him.

'Can we go in now?' Cat asked. 'I need to use the restroom.'

'Sure.' Taking his hand away, he said, 'Sammy boy, you stay with me till she gets back.'

I opened the door, and we entered the restaurant. A waitress called out that we could sit anywhere. Snow White and I went looking for a table while Cat headed off to the restroom. Even though the place was crowded, we didn't have any trouble finding a table. We sat down across from each other.

When the waitress came along with menus and a pot of coffee, I let her know there were three of us. She placed three menus on the table and filled three cups with coffee before sauntering off.

'She better not pull nothing,' Snow White muttered.

'Who?'

'Who you think?'

'The waitress?'

He didn't look amused. 'Cat,' he said.

'What could she possibly pull? Are you afraid she might phone the cops? Or run away?'

'I don't know. Don't much trust her, though.'

'Maybe if you didn't go around *hitting* her.'

'Fuck off.'

'It's no way to make friends.'

'I got all the friends I need, and they ain't smart-mouth wiseass know-it-all *rich* kids.'

'Rich kids? That'd be nice. Me, I'm too poor to be rich and too old to be a kid.'

'How old?'

'Twenty-six.'

'That's a kid. I'm damn near twice your age.'

'No kidding?' I didn't have to fake my surprise. 'How old are you?'

'Pushing fifty.'

'Amazing. You really look young for your age. Except for your hair, of course.'

'You got a problem with my hair?'

'No. It's fine hair. You wouldn't be Snow White without it.'

Just after I said that, Cat showed up. She sat in the chair beside me, took a sip of coffee and asked, 'Have you ordered yet?'

'We were waiting for you,' I told her.

We spent the next few minutes with our faces in the menus. Then the waitress arrived to take our orders. Cat asked Snow White to go first. He ordered the Bombardier Special: orange juice, three eggs, sausage links, hash browns, flapjacks and toast. (The meal must've been dubbed the Bombardier Special in honor of the naval weapons center at nearby China Lake.) I went next, asking for Breakfast #1. It lacked an exotic monicker, but it promised two eggs, bacon, hash browns and toast. Then Cat ordered a bagel with cream cheese and a side of sausage patties.

'That all you're gonna eat?' Snow White asked her.

'It's plenty.'

'I'm paying, so you just go on and order up whatever you want.'

'I ordered what I want,' she said. 'Thank you.'

After the waitress was gone, Cat frowned at Snow White and said, 'You're planning to pay for all of us?'

'Sure.' He gave her a narrow look. 'Think I can't afford it?'

'Why should I think that? For all I know, you might be Howard Hughes.'

'Hughes is dead,' I pointed out.

She gave me half a smile. 'Maybe he is, maybe he isn't.' She faced Snow White. 'If you *are* Howard Hughes, maybe you'll put us in your will. I mean, we gave you a ride out of the desert.'

'We sure did.'

'Maybe saved your life.'

'Yeah,' I said. 'You could've died out there.'

'*Are* you Howard Hughes?' Cat asked him.

'Nope. But I know who *you* are.'

'Who am I?' she asked, and took another sip of coffee.

Leaning forward, Snow White whispered, 'You're a smart-mouth wise-ass rich-kid cocksucking bitch.' Then he grinned.

Cat slowly set her cup down on the table. Then she met his eyes and said, 'I'm not exactly a kid anymore, but thanks for the compliment.'

'Snow White's pushing fifty,' I quickly threw in.

She grinned at him. 'Knocking at heaven's door.'

His grin went crooked. Wobbling his head from side to side, he said, 'You're cruisin' for a bruisin', baby.'

'Let's knock it off,' I said. 'Nobody's going to bruise anyone, okay? We're in a public place, here.'

'I gotta take a leak,' Snow White said. He shoved his chair back. 'You're coming with me, Sam.'

I started to get up, but Cat put a hand on my leg and said to Snow White, 'He'll be fine right here with me.'

'The fuck he will.'

'What's the matter?' she asked loudly. 'Do you need someone to hold it for you?'

Snow White, on his feet by then, glanced around as if worried that someone might've heard Cat say that. Which I found funny, considering the language that had been spewing out of *his* mouth.

Funny, but not very. I sure wasn't laughing.

What had happened to *humoring* the guy?

Had Cat lost her mind?

Snow White might be afraid to assault her in a crowded restaurant, but our breakfast wouldn't last forever.

In a subdued voice, she said, 'Go ahead, Mr White. Do you know where the men's room is?'

'Reckon I can find it,' he muttered, glaring at her.

'Just past the cash register...'

'Yeah, yeah.'

'We won't start eating without you.'

He nodded. His mouth twisted itself into a sickly smile and he said, 'Yeah. Okay. See you later.' Then he swaggered away, his long white tresses and jacket fringe sweeping through the air.

The moment he was out of sight, Cat gave my leg a squeeze.

I turned my head and stared into her eyes.

'Saved you,' she said.

'Thanks. Only two problems. One, he's gonna kill you. Two, I've got to go.'

'One, he'll have to catch me first. Two, if I were you, I wouldn't go in front of that guy. I'm *not* you, and I wouldn't.'

Smiling, I said, 'Glad to hear it.'

'So,' she said, and patted my leg. 'Shall we be off?'

'*What?*'

'Make like a tree and *leave*? Make like the wind and blow?'

'What are you talking about?'

'Let's *haul ass*.'

'You're kidding. We can't. He's got the car keys.'

She slipped a couple of fingers into the left breast pocket of her shirt and pulled out a white plastic card. It was about the size of a credit card, but thicker. In the middle was a cut-out shaped like a key. 'Look what I found when I was in the john.'

'What is it?'

'An emergency door key for those who are careless enough to lock themselves out of their cars. Courtesy of the auto club.'

'It's *yours*?'

'It came out of *my* billfold.'

'Does it work?'

'It'll get us into the car. After that, we'll have to rely on the spare ignition key I keep in the glove compartment.' She scooted her chair back. 'So. Ready to go? Or would you rather stick around and enjoy a nice breakfast with Tinkerbell?'

'Snow White.'

'Whatever.'

'Let's scram,' I said.

23

I snatched out my wallet. Snow White wasn't likely to stick around for breakfast – or pay for it – so I tossed ten dollars onto the table before hurrying after Cat. She was striding across the

148

restaurant, well ahead of me, a hand on her purse to keep it from swinging.

Nobody seemed to be paying attention to us.

I didn't see our waitress.

The cashier was busy making change for a customer.

Cat walked past the customer's back and veered toward the door.

Off to the right of the cash register, the hallway to the restrooms looked empty.

I quickened my pace.

A man about to enter the restaurant opened the door for Cat. Smiling and saying, 'Thank you,' she stepped outside.

He came in.

Down the restroom hallway, a door started to swing open. It opened outwards. The sign read, 'Gents.'

Not waiting to see who might come out, I hurled myself at the restaurant door. It flew open and I lurched into the sunlight.

Cat was already halfway to her car, sprinting like a champ. I poured on the speed. In seconds, Cat reached the car. She stopped at the driver's door and bent over slightly. I didn't have a lot of faith in her plastic key. But she suddenly flung the door open and scurried into her seat. By the time I reached the passenger door, she was leaning over to unlock it. I jerked the door open.

'Wait wait wait!' she gasped.

Bracing herself up with her right hand on the seat, she opened the glove compartment with her left.

I looked back.

Snow White wasn't charging toward us. There was no sign of him.

I heard the glove compartment slam.

'Got it!' Cat blurted.

I leaped in and shut the door.

She shoved the key into the ignition and gave it a twist. The engine roared. 'Is he coming?' she asked.

'Not yet.'

She shoved the gear shift into reverse and stepped on the gas. We ripped backward out of the parking space, skidded when she brought the front around, skidded again when she hit

149

the brakes, then threw up a spray of gravel and dust as we lurched forward.

We sped past the door of Lucy's Kitchen.

It swung open. A tall, skinny cowboy stepped out and adjusted the angle of his ten-gallon hat.

Seconds later, we were on the highway.

Cat gave me a wild, fierce grin and cried out, *'We did it!'*

'Sure did.'

'My God, I can't believe it! It worked! We really did it! Ha!' She reached over and grabbed my thigh and shook my leg back and forth. 'Can you believe it! I never thought we'd make it to the door, much less . . .' She shook her head and gave my leg a few more shakes. 'He didn't even come running after us!'

'Hard to believe,' I said.

'Pretty slick getaway.'

'He must've taken his time in the john. I kept expecting him to come out . . .'

'Me, too! God, I was so scared!'

'Can't imagine what was taking him so long.'

'Can't?' She laughed.

'Perhaps he needed to relieve more than his bladder.'

'Perhaps. And it never occurred to him that I might have spare keys.'

'Most people don't carry them.'

'I'm trickier than most.'

'That you are.'

She squeezed my leg, then returned her hand to the steering wheel. She sighed deeply. 'Free at last,' she said. She glanced at the rearview mirror, then eased off the gas a little. 'Sorry *you* didn't get a chance to go.'

'That's okay.'

'But I think he was planning to pound you.'

'He might've,' I agreed.

'He was pretty mad.'

'Not at me.'

'He would've pounded you to pay me back. Or done something vile to you. I sure didn't want you ending up alone in the john with him.'

'Who knows, I might've cleaned his clock.'

'Sure! And twice on Sunday!'

150

'If I had a hammer.'

'Anyway, it would've ruined the big plan. As soon as I made sure I still had my plastic key, it was just a matter of getting him away from us. I figured he'd almost *have* to make a pit stop. I mean, you don't have breakfast at a place like that and *not* use the toilet. I just had to make sure you didn't go with him.'

'You did an excellent job of it,' I told her.

'Thanks. The only problem now is that he's got us on the wrong highway. What road did we want?'

'We were heading for 395. It was supposed take us north to the area around Lake Tahoe.'

'So where does this one go?'

'I'm not sure.' Opening the glove compartment, I said, 'We're on 178?'

'Yep.'

I pulled out the map of California, unfolded it, and started to search for 178 and Inyokern.

'We could probably just turn around,' Cat said, 'and go back the way we came. That'd take us past the restaurant, though. Not sure we should do that. Have you found us yet?'

'Not . . . Yeah, here we are. We're coming up on Ridgecrest pretty soon, so . . . After that, there's not much. A place called Trona, then . . . Death Valley.'

'*Death Valley?* My God. Do you think Snow White was taking us to *Death Valley?*'

'Looks that way.'

'Cute.'

'That must be where he disposed of Brock.'

'He probably planned to dispose of us there, too.'

'Wouldn't put it past him,' I said.

Suddenly, we were entering Ridgecrest.

On its way through town, the road turned into China Lake Boulevard and took some odd turns. We stopped discussing other things, and gave all our attention to staying on 178. About halfway through town, it made a left turn and we soon found ourselves in the desert again.

Nothing to either side of us except a rolling, rugged wilderness of dry land and cactus, with mountain ridges off in the distance. On the low slopes of the mountains, I saw a few ruins of old shacks and mines.

'You know,' Cat said for no apparent reason, 'I didn't *mind* Snow White coming with us. He was a little weird and creepy, but he didn't seem ... I don't know, *awful*. But God, he was such a bully. I can't stand it when a guy just hauls off and clobbers you like that.'

'I felt like I wanted to kill him.'

'A guy like that, we're lucky he didn't kill *us*. But he was okay, sometimes.'

'Almost human.'

'And I sort of wish he'd shown us where to throw Elliot. That would've been handy, you know?'

'I'm sure we won't have any trouble finding a place,' I said. 'There are all kinds of old mines and stuff out there.'

'But he knew a really good one.'

'Shall we go back to Lucy's Kitchen and see if we can find him?'

'I don't think so.'

'What about going back to 14, though? I mean, we don't want to go driving into Death Valley, do we?'

I looked at the map. 'This 178 ... It sort of forms a big U with 395 on the western side. Which is where we'd *like* to be.'

'Are there places to cut over?'

'Yeah. Looks like fifty or sixty miles from here, up near the entrance to Death Valley. But those roads heading west – they don't look very direct. I don't know what we'd be getting into. It might be better if we *do* turn around and go back to 14.'

'Maybe I should take a look.' She checked the mirrors and started to slow down.

Peering over my shoulder, I saw some approaching traffic. Nothing was on top of us yet, and the road had a good, broad shoulder.

'Looks okay,' I said.

Cat swerved onto the shoulder and stopped.

I started to pass her the map.

'No, wait.' She gazed at her side mirror. 'After these go by.'

I watched over my shoulder.

For a few seconds, nothing happened. The cars and trucks grew larger, that's all. Then a semi roared by, shaking us. It was followed by three or four more of the monstrous trucks, all in the lane nearest us, all missing us – but not by very much. With each passing, the car shuddered. I could feel the vibrations in my chest as if I were standing too close to a drum corps.

While the huge semis went by, so did a small crowd of other vehicles. Mostly pickup trucks and four-wheel-drives, a couple of campers . . .

No motorcycles.

A Highway Patrol car.

'Uh-oh,' Cat said.

'Maybe you'd *better* look at this,' I said, and shoved the map in front of her at about the same time the patrol car was bearing down on us.

The map blocked her view out the windshield.

The patrol car sped by.

'Is he stopping?' she asked.

'Not so far. No. No, he's still going.'

'Thank God.'

I lowered the map so she could watch the Highway Patrol car vanish in the distance.

Looking out the rear window, I saw that the road was empty behind us. 'Why don't you check out the map?' I said. 'I'll be right back.'

She grinned at me. 'Watch out for snakes and lizards.'

'Thanks.' I climbed out.

Except for the highway, we were pretty much in the middle of nowhere. Just desert and distant mountains. So I hurried off and made my way down a nearby embankment. The slope was dirt and gravel, mostly gray, with a few scrawny bushes here and there. The bottom looked like a dry creek bed.

From down there, the road was out of sight. I couldn't see our car, either, but I turned my back to it before unzipping my jeans.

I pulled out my penis and aimed high.

It felt great to be standing down there in the sunlight, releasing all that pressure, feeling the breeze . . .

Then I heard a car coming.

It's all right, I told myself. Nobody can see me down here.

The windy sound of its engine and tires came from my right. From the east. From the direction of Ridgecrest, Inyokern . . . Lucy's Kitchen.

Just our luck, it'll be Snow White.

153

The chances were remote. But not *that* remote.

I tried to stop going, but I'd only just begun.

The car slowed down. The hiss of its tires changed to crunching sounds.

It's pulling over!

I suddenly realized that it was probably the Highway Patrol. The officer must've changed his mind about us, decided that maybe we needed assistance, after all – then turned around and come back.

Better him than Snow White.

Heat suddenly flooded my face.

A cop's gonna bust me!

Not if he doesn't see me, I thought.

The way things were going, however, he could probably hear me.

A car door thudded shut.

Keeping my back to the embankment, I twisted my head from side to side. I couldn't see either car. I couldn't see anyone.

But finally I finished.

Moments later, I was safely zipped. No longer in danger of arrest for outdoor pissing or indecent exposure, I started to climb the side of the ditch. Just a few steps, and I could see over the top.

My guess about the Highway Patrol had been dead wrong.

Stopped a few yards behind Cat's car was an old, faded gray van with a blunt hood, a running board under the passenger door, and a row of windows along each side. I could see the two front seats through the windshield. They were empty. The area behind the seats was shut off by a hanging curtain. The side windows appeared to be curtained, too. I couldn't see into the rear of the van, at all.

Nor could I see its driver.

The driver *had* to be Snow White. He must've stolen the van from the parking lot of Lucy's Kitchen.

But where was he?

Only a couple of minutes earlier, I'd heard a door shut.

The door on my side of Cat's car still stood open, just as I'd left it. I couldn't see whether hers was open or shut. The two front doors of the van were shut.

154

Who had shut what door?

Where was Snow White?

I could hardly imagine Cat just *sitting* in the car if White had climbed out of the van and started walking toward her. She probably would've either sped off or tried to run him over.

From where I stood, partway up the slope and a little to the rear of my open door, I couldn't see what might be happening on the other side of her car. For that matter, I could only see the upper two-thirds of the side that faced me.

I climbed slightly higher.

Still no sign of anyone at the van.

I peered into the space between Cat's undercarriage and the ground.

And spotted a pair of feet on the other side.

I knew Snow White wore black motorcycle boots and Cat wore high-topped, brown leather hiking shoes.

These feet were bare except for flip-flop sandals.

They were the only feet in sight.

I took a couple of careful sidesteps to the right. My open door gave me a partial view into the car. Cat still sat behind the wheel. Her head was turned toward her window, where a young woman was speaking to her.

With the engine running and some traffic rushing closer, I couldn't hear what was being said.

She noticed me watching, and must've told Cat.

Cat looked over. In a loud voice, she said, 'Come on up. We've got a problem.'

24

Feeling a little sick, I climbed higher. I looked all around. No sign of Snow White.

Maybe the 'problem' had nothing to do with him.

As I reached the top, a Peterbilt came thundering along. The woman beside Cat's door, apparently worried about getting hit, stood up straight and stepped up against the car. We looked at each other over the roof.

She must've been about eighteen years old.

She was crying. She had very pale blue eyes. They were red and wet. Her face seemed pretty, but too thin: cheekbones too prominent, cheeks too hollow, chin too sharp. She tried to smile, but her face crinkled and trembled out of control.

The wind from the passing truck seemed to grab her long hair and fling it in about ten different directions. A lot of the hair fell across her face and stuck to her tears.

The tops of her shoulders were bare except for a couple of dress straps.

'Get in, Sam,' Cat said.

I hurried forward and climbed into the passenger seat. As I shut my door, Cat said, 'This is Peggy Thompson.'

I looked past Cat. The young woman was bending down, her face in the open window. She wore a sundress that was almost the same pale-blue color as her eyes. Except for the shoulder straps, the dress didn't start until just above her breasts. I assumed breasts were there, though you couldn't really tell by looking. 'Hi, Sam,' she said.

'Hi, Peggy.'

She sniffed and wiped her eyes. She had long fingers and a bony wrist.

I'd rarely seen such a bony girl. I wondered if she had an eating disorder. Then I wondered if she might be a fashion model.

'Why don't you tell Sam what you told me?' Cat said.

'Well . . . he's got my little brother. They're over in my van. Him and Donny. He's got this knife? He says how you've both gotta do whatever he says, or else he'll kill Donny.'

Cat glanced at me and said, 'Snow White. He jumped them in the parking lot, back at the restaurant.'

'Snow White?' Peggy asked.

'That's what he calls himself,' Cat explained. 'It has to do with his hair.'

'How did he get you?' I asked Peggy.

'We were about to go in and have breakfast. Me and Donny? He's only a little fellow.' Her chin started trembling. Fresh tears spilled down her cheeks. 'He's only *twelve*. He's all I've got. You've gotta help us.'

Cat nodded, but didn't say anything.

'You're supposed to follow us,' Peggy went on. 'That's what

156

he told me to tell you. Snow White? I'll be driving the van, and he'll have his knife on Donny. He says if you don't stay behind us or if you try any funny stuff, he'll ... he says he'll cut off Donny's head. He'll ... toss it out the window. And then he'll kill me.' For a while, she cried too hard to go on. Then, sobbing and sniffling, she wiped her eyes and said, 'Will you do it? Please? You don't even know us, but ...'

'It's our fault you're in this mess,' Cat told her. 'We'll do whatever we have to.'

'Why's he doing this?'

'I'm not sure. We gave him a ride, then we tried to get rid of him. Now this.'

'How's our gas?' I asked.

'Just under half a tank.' To Peggy, she said, 'You'd better tell White we're below half a tank. We can't go more than about a hundred more miles without a fill-up. How's your gas?'

'We're full. I got it in Inyokern right before breakfast – so I'd have a chance to wash my hands?' Even as she sobbed, she lifted a hand to her face and sniffed its fingers. Then she blurted, 'Why's this *happening*?'

'Bad luck,' I said.

'Bad choices,' Cat added.

'We never ...'

'Mine,' she said.

Behind us, a horn honked.

'I've gotta get going,' Peggy said.

'Tell him about our gas,' I reminded her.

'And tell him we'll do whatever we wants,' Cat said.

'Okay. Thanks. Thanks a billion. Bye.'

'Be careful,' Cat said. Then suddenly blurted, 'No, wait!'

'He'll get mad if ...'

'Look, tell him we're sorry we tried to ditch him back at the restaurant. He doesn't need to do this with you two. Tell him we won't give him any more trouble. Okay? We'll wait here, and he can come up and get right back in the car with us. We'll take him wherever he wants to go. All right? Tell him that.'

'I don't think he'll go along with it.'

The horn blared again. Peggy flinched as if she'd been pinched.

157

'Ask him,' I said.

'Okay, but...'

'Go,' Cat said.

'Okay.' Peggy nodded, checked the road for oncoming traffic, then swung away from our window and walked toward her van with long, quick strides. I watched her over my shoulder. Her sandals kicked up dust. Her thin, bare legs seemed to rise forever before encountering her dress. The skirt swayed as she walked. The upper part of her back was bare except for the straps rising to her shoulders – and the straight, light brown hair that hung down almost to her waist.

I looked for Snow White, but the sun was glaring on the windshield.

By the side of the van, Peggy stopped and pulled open the driver's door. Instead of climbing in, she started talking. I watched her mouth move. Then she appeared to be listening, shaking her head. Finally, she turned toward us and shook her head from side to side.

'He isn't going for it,' Cat said.

'I didn't think he would.'

'I wonder if he'd go for a hostage exchange.'

'I doubt it.'

Peggy climbed into the van. As she shut its door, Cat unlatched her seatbelt.

'Hey!' I grabbed her right arm.

She threw her door open. 'Let go, Sam.'

'No! Are you kidding?'

'I got them into this.'

'It won't do any good.'

'Let go!' She jerked her arm free.

I caught her by the nape of her neck. Squeezing it with my left hand, I twisted sideways and clutched her thigh with my right.

'Ow!' she cried out. 'Damn it! Stop it, Sam! Let go of me!'

As she yelled and struggled, the van rolled by.

'Shit!' she yelled. The fight suddenly went out of her. 'Okay, okay. You can let go of me, now. They're gone. Let me shut my door.'

Though I was prepared for a trick, I released my holds on Cat. She leaned out, grabbed her door, and pulled it shut.

Then, not bothering to refasten her seatbelt, she shifted and stepped on the gas. As we picked up speed along the shoulder, she checked the side mirror. Then she swung onto the highway. She quickly closed the gap between us and the rear of Peggy's van.

When we were about fifty feet behind it, she eased off the gas.

She gave me a quick, angry glance.

'Sorry,' I muttered.

'If he had me, he might've let them go.'

'Not a chance. Think about it. He's already abducted them and stolen their van. They're victims. They can identify him, testify against him. He can't exactly drop them off by the side of the road. Not alive, anyway.'

'I would've told him that I'd be his hostage and they could ride with you.' She nailed me again with her eyes. 'You think *that* might've worked?'

'Maybe,' I admitted. 'I'm sure he'd love to get his hands on you.'

'Better me than those kids.'

'Not the way I see it.'

When she looked at me this time, the hardness was gone from her eyes. 'My guy,' she said.

'You'd better believe it.'

'Too late to try it now, anyway.'

'Thank God,' I said. 'He might've kept all three of you. Or kept you, and killed them. He wouldn't need them if he had you.'

She nodded. 'So what do you think we should do?'

'I don't know.'

'Turn around and take off?' she asked.

'No.'

'I'm sure we could lose him. That old van wouldn't stand a chance.'

'Neither would Peggy and her brother.'

'So you *do* care.'

'Of course.'

She gave me a smile. 'Just wanted you to admit it. You'd like to save them, but you don't want to get me hurt in the process. Is that about right?'

'That says it all.'

'So how do we accomplish such a feat?'

'God only knows.'

'And he's not talking.'

'I guess we need a plan,' I said.

'I'll try to come up with one. Maybe you'd better try to get some sleep.'

Sleep. It sounded like a great idea. I'd been awake much too long already.

'You won't do anything strange, will you?' I asked.

'If I get an urge along those lines, I'll be sure to wake you up.'

'Okay.' I loosened my seatbelt, but kept it latched. Then I settled back, rested my hands on my lap, lowered my head and shut my eyes. Though I felt tired and dazed, my mind in a foggy chaos, I doubted that sleep would come. I was way too tense for that.

And way too sick at heart.

Things had started fairly simple: weird but simple. I was supposed to ambush Cat's vampire and kill it.

With Cat's help, I'd succeeded.

That should've been pretty much the end of our problems. Instead ... a flat tire, a wild downhill ride, Snow White inviting himself aboard. Suddenly, we'd not only had Elliot dead in the trunk but Snow White alive in the back seat. Alive and running the show.

Now he was *still* running the show, but in the van ahead of us with Peggy and Donny as hostages.

We'd expanded to six.

We'd grown into something big, complex, and out of control.

Sitting there with my eyes shut, I searched my mind for a way to save us from disaster. Not just Cat and I; the two of us could simply turn around and speed off. But we couldn't do that without risking the lives of Peggy and Donny. What we needed was a way to save them *and* ourselves.

A plan.

A great plan.

The real problem, I told myself, was Donny.

I pictured Snow White inside the van, his knife at Donny's throat. But I didn't know what the twelve-year-old boy looked

160

like, so my imagination turned him into his sister. She cried and squirmed in Snow White's grip.

Instead of pressing the knife to her throat, he used it to cut the straps of her dress. As the top of her dress started to fall away from her breasts, she turned into Cat.

While Snow White clutched Cat from behind, Elliot, resurrected from the dead and kneeling in front of her, pulled the dress down to her feet. Naked, she squirmed between her two attackers.

It surprised me to find Elliot there. He had a horrible, bloody wound in his chest.

Leave her alone! I shouted. And ran at them.

I had the stake in my left hand, the hammer in my right. They ignored me.

I ran as fast as I could. But they were too far away.

Noooo!

Elliot clamped his teeth into her crotch.

Snow White slit her throat.

I let out a yell and woke up, gasping and sweaty but hugely relieved to find myself in the passenger seat of Cat's car.

'Nightmare?' Cat asked.

'A doozy.'

But I suddenly felt as if I'd traded one nightmare for another.

The highway pavement was red and leading us, a few car lengths behind Peggy's van, through the middle of a desolate industrial town – a town that looked half dead and stank like hell.

To the right were power poles, then a barren, white wasteland that seemed to spread out for miles across the valley. Up ahead, smokestacks shoved white clouds of stench into the sky.

The air smelled like bad eggs.

We seemed to be surrounded by heaps of a dirty white substance that looked like mountainous piles of old snow.

Strings of railroad cars were scattered about as if waiting to take away survivors.

But I saw nobody.

'Welcome to Trona,' Cat said. She was cupping a hand over her nose and mouth.

161

'What the hell is the matter with this place?' I asked.

'A chemical plant.'

'People *live* here?' I asked.

'Half the place looks abandoned,' Cat pointed out. Then she took her hand away from her mouth, let out a laugh and pointed over to the right of the road.

The saloon looked old and a little dismal.

And deserted.

The sign across its roof read, 'Searles Dry Lake Yacht Club.' Perched on the roof were three colorful, life-size turkey vultures.

'I guess somebody has a sense of humor around here,' I said.

'You'd almost have to.'

25

'Do you want to try again?' Cat asked.

'Try what?'

'Sleep.'

'Not right now. How can I sleep while we're driving through downtown Hell?'

'Maybe we can keep some of the stench out. Let's roll up our windows and I'll put the air on. Besides, it's starting to get hot.'

As I cranked my window up, I said, 'I'm glad your husband believed in air-conditioning.'

'He had his moments.' Cat slid a couple of levers to the right, and air started to blow in through several vents. It felt warm at first, but soon grew cool.

'Nice,' I said, though I could still smell the nasty, rotten aroma of the town's chemical industry.

'I wonder if *they* have air.'

'Peggy and them? I'd be surprised if it works. That van looks like an old heap.'

'It must be miserable in there,' Cat said.

'Aren't you glad I made you stay?'

She cast her eyes my way and said, 'That's a subject best left behind.'

162

She was right.

'Some people get nothing but bad breaks,' she said.

'You mean them?'

'Yeah. Where the hell are their parents? What's Peggy – seventeen, eighteen years old? And she's driving a broken-down piece of junk through the middle of nowhere with her twelve-year-old brother? My God. What the hell's going on?'

'Did she say anything about her parents?' I asked.

'Just that stuff about Donny being all she's got.'

'Yeah. Their folks must be out of the picture, one way or another.'

'Hope they have a damn good excuse. You don't just abandon your kids. I mean, I feel like absolute shit because it's all my fault they got snatched by Snow White. But they shouldn't have been out here in the first place. They should've been *home*.'

'I've got a feeling maybe they *are* home,' I said.

'Live in the van?'

'Wouldn't surprise me.'

'Their parents ought to be shot.'

'Maybe they have been.'

'That'd be about their *only* good excuse.' She gazed out the windshield, her eyes narrow and fierce. 'Those kids never should've gotten into this situation. It isn't fair.'

'Maybe we can save them,' I said.

She turned her eyes to me and said, 'We've *got* to.'

'I've been thinking about it,' I told her. 'I haven't figured out a solution, but I think I've isolated the problem. It's Donny.'

'Donny? You sure the problem isn't Snow White?'

'We ditched him, remember? We're really only in this, right now, because of Donny.'

'What about Peggy?'

'She could've jumped into the car with us; we'd all be safe. It's Donny.'

Cat nodded. 'I see what you mean. White's only in control of the situation because he's got Donny in the van.'

'He could kill the kid in a split second,' I said, 'and there's no way we'd be able to stop him. Or if there is a way, I haven't figured it out yet.'

Frowning out of the windshield, Cat said, 'We need to separate White and Donny.'

'For starters.'

'How?'

'I don't know,' I said. 'The thing to do, I guess, is play along. Keep on doing whatever White wants, and hope we get a break.'

'What *does* he want?' Cat asked. She glanced at me. From the look on her face, I got the feeling that she already had a pretty good idea for an answer.

So did I.

'He wants us to follow him and not try any funny stuff,' I said.

'Why? Where are we going?'

'To Brock's hole, I suppose.'

'Why?'

'To dispose of Elliot.'

'That's what *he* says. Like he just wants to help us out.' Making her voice gruff to mimic Snow White, she said, '"Hey, don't wear yourselves out digging no grave for this guy, just throw him down a hole. I know where to find us a dandy one."' In her normal voice, she said, 'Bull. Why should he care what we do with Elliot's body?'

'I figured he was just looking for an excuse to stay with us for as long as possible.'

'I think you're right,' Cat said. 'It probably started that way. Maybe he was interested in a little romance with one or the other of us. But somewhere along the line, his real interest turned to Elliot. All of a sudden, we're not supposed to open the trunk till *after dark*. Because . . . ?' She looked at me and raised her eyebrows.

I followed her lead, fairly sure of the destination. 'Because sunlight destroys vampires,' I said. 'In the movies.'

'Right on.'

'And Mr White seems to think that the stake doesn't kill them – just holds them down.'

'Right,' Cat said. 'A temporary measure.'

'So his big plan is to wait until dark, then haul Elliot out of the trunk and remove the stake.'

'Why?' Cat asked.

'So he'll finally have the opportunity to meet a real, live vampire.'

'Right. He figures Elliot will wake up.'

'Sure looks that way,' I said.

'Now, why would he want to revive a vampire?'

'Elementary, my dear Catherine.'

'Yeah. Elementary if you're a moron.'

'I'm not sure he's a moron,' I said. 'He's simply pushing fifty and wants to live forever.'

'It takes a moron to think that a vampire'll do the trick for you.'

'Hey,' I protested, 'it works in the movies.'

'What doesn't?'

'You'll be singing a diffent tune, young lady, if he pulls out the stake and Elliot *does* wake up.'

'A different tune? I'll be peeing my pants.'

'That was crude and unnecessary,' I pointed out.

'I don't think it'll happen.'

'Because you're a champ at holding your water in times of crisis?'

'Not exactly,' she said. 'Right now, we're Elliot's transportation. But as soon as we get where we're going, Mr White probably won't see any more reason to keep us alive. Also, he won't want us to be interfering in his nefarious plans. So he'll kill us before he opens the trunk. If not sooner. So we won't get a chance to watch him pull out the stake.'

Not quite able to hold up my end of the banter now that the subject had turned to our deaths, I said seriously, 'Well, we don't have to let him.'

'Think we can stop him?'

'We did a pretty good job on Elliot.'

'That we did,' Cat agreed. 'Of course, we had surprise on our side.'

'You're tricky,' I pointed out. 'You ought to be able to come up with something.'

'You're right about Donny. He *is* the key. We need a way to get him out of Snow White's reach.'

The turn signal on the right rear corner of the van began to blink. My stomach fluttered. 'They're pulling over?' I asked.

'I'm not ... ah! A gas station. About time.'

165

Moments later, I saw it, too: a big old station, apparently an independent, at the very end of Trona. A wooden sign on poles out front read 'LUCKY'S FOOD & GAS'.

'Lucky for us they decided to stop,' Cat said.

'Running out of gas might've worked for us,' I told her.

'I don't know. I'd hate to get stranded somewhere. It's always nice to have a way out.'

As we neared Lucky's, we saw that it looked old and run-down and very busy. There were eight gas pumps out front, all in use, with several cars and pickups and vans waiting their turn. Off to the side was a parking lot. It looked pretty full. Plenty of people had apparently stopped in for breakfast.

'Busy place,' I said.

As the van slowed down, we approached its rear. It made a right turn into Lucky's, and we followed.

'Do you suppose he'll let us have breakfast?' Cat asked.

'Oh, I'd bet on it.'

We grinned at each other.

Then Cat focused on driving. The place was a tangle of vehicles trying to move in on suitable pumps or trying to squirm their way out. We had a couple of close calls, but Cat managed to keep us on the van's tail until we were safely stopped behind it.

The van was third in line at a row of pumps.

Cat shut off our engine and started to roll her window down. 'This may be a while,' she said.

I rolled my window down. A warm breeze came in. Though we were still in Trona, the horrible, sulphur stench had been left behind.

The air was a little whiffy with gasoline fumes. Sometimes, that odor sickens me. This morning, though, I found myself liking it. For one thing, it smelled almost sweet after the rotten-egg stink of the town's chemical fumes. But also, it reminded me of when I was a kid off on a long vacation drive with my parents. It smelled of unknown places, of adventure.

'We could almost be on a trip together,' I said.

'We are on a trip together.'

'I mean, like a vacation.'

'Too bad we aren't,' Cat said. 'If we could just make our two friends disappear . . .'

166

'Snow White and Elliot?'

'Yep.'

'Let's not be too hasty about Elliot,' I said.

'What do you mean?'

'He's the only reason *I'm* here.'

Cat turned her head. A corner of her mouth lifted slightly. Reaching out, she put her hand on my thigh. She squeezed it and said, 'I'd get rid of him and keep you.'

'Thanks.'

I wondered if she would keep me *after* we'd gotten rid of Elliot.

If we're not dead by then.

'Here comes Peggy,' Cat said.

I couldn't see the girl until she stepped past the end of her van. She walked stiffly as if struggling to control her movements. Her jaw looked tight, and her lips were squeezed together. This time, she was wearing sunglasses.

She stopped beside Cat's window, bent down, and put her hands on the sill. She seemed to be breathing through her nostrils, though I couldn't hear the hiss because of so much nearby noise.

'Are you all right?' Cat asked.

'He's been ... messing around with us.'

'My God.'

'Who's driving?' I asked.

'Me. But he ... does stuff to me anyway. I have to sit there and take it. He just ... does whatever he wants. He's got Donny tied up in the back.' She took quick, deep breaths. 'It's awful. He's got Donny's clothes off, and ...' She shook her head. 'We can't stop him. We can't do anything. He says he'll kill us if we give him any ... trouble. I don't want him to kill us.'

'You'll be all right,' Cat told her. 'You've just gotta hang in there.'

Peggy's chin started to shake.

'Is he hurting either of you?'

'Yes.'

'Badly?'

She nodded, then shook her head. 'Not so it shows. But the ... the awful things ... He's sick.'

'Sick?'

167

'In the head.'

'We'll get you out of this,' Cat said. 'Okay? You and Donny both. You're going to be fine.'

'We aren't fine anymore.'

'Just hang in there. This won't last forever.'

'It'll probably be over tonight,' I told her.

'Did he send you back here for a reason?' Cat asked.

Peggy sniffed and wiped her nose. 'He ... he says *you're* supposed to pump the gas for both of us. You, not Sam. Sam's supposed to stay in the car. He says you should pay for it all, too. The gas.'

'Okay,' Cat said. 'I'll take care of it.'

'And he wants your food and drinks. I'm supposed to get it for him. He says you cheated him out of breakfast.'

'That we did. Help yourself. It's all in the back.'

'I'm sorry,' Peggy said.

'No problem.'

She stepped to the door behind Cat, then shook her head. Probably at the sight of the luggage, shovel, pick and ruined tire blocking her way.

'You'd better come around to this side,' I told her.

So she walked around the rear of the car, came up on my side, and opened the back door. Leaning in, she started gathering food off the back seat and the floor. Most of it had spilled out of the grocery sack.

'Take whatever you want,' Cat told her, and twisted around to watch. 'Make sure you get the Pepsis.'

'I don't wanta take *all* your stuff.'

'Go ahead. Fill up the bag. Take everything. We'll be fine. When was the last time you and Donny ate?'

'Last night. We had us a couple of Big Macs.'

'Is that all?'

'We don't got a lot of money.'

'Where are your parents?'

'Left us.'

'They *left* you?' Cat sounded shocked and appalled.

'Well, Dad's doing twenty-five to life. Mom hanged herself three weeks back.'

Cat muttered, 'Jesus.'

'So Donny and me, we're on the road.'

A horn beeped. Cat turned to the front, leaned a little to the left, and said, 'You'd better go. The line's starting to move.'

Looking back, I watched Peggy duck backward with the full grocery sack clutched to her chest. It had a rip halfway down one side, but she held it together so that nothing fell out.

'Come back if he'll let you,' Cat said.

'Sure. Thanks.' Peggy shut the door with her knee, then hurried forward. She crossed in front of our car and disappeared alongside the van. Soon, I heard a door thump shut. The van started rolling.

We followed, and stopped close behind it.

'Those poor kids,' Cat said. 'My God. And I thought *I* had it tough.'

'You *did* have it tough.'

She shrugged one shoulder as if to pass off her husband-and-vampire troubles as nothing. 'Now they've got Snow White screwing around with them.'

Twisting sideways, I looked down behind our seats. 'At least they won't starve,' I said.

'Did she take everything?'

'She left behind the squeeze-cheese and crackers. And two bottles of water.'

'I told her she could take everything.'

'Well, I guess she took pity on us.'

'Can you reach the stuff?'

'It's on the floor. I'll have to get out.'

'I don't think he'll cut off Donny's head over something like that.'

'Hope not.' I threw open my door, climbed out, opened the back door, crouched and picked up the cheese, the crackers, and one of the water bottles. In my seat again, I started to rip open the cracker box.

'What about the knife?' Cat asked.

'We don't need it. Peggy made off with the salami.'

'I know that. Where is the knife?'

'I didn't see it back there.'

Nor did I see it after kneeling on my seat and peering down at the rear floor and seats for a couple of minutes.

'It doesn't seem to be here,' I reported. 'It might be underneath something...'

'She probably took it,' Cat said.

26

We pulled forward one more time, and Cat got out. She crossed in front of our car, stepped around the right rear corner of the van, and opened its tank.

After she started pumping the fuel, I stopped watching her and climbed over the console to the driver's seat. I couldn't see her from there, but I had a view up the left side of the van. I could see Peggy's closed door, but not Peggy.

Soon, the van pulled away from the pumps and Cat motioned me to drive forward. When she signalled for me to stop, I shut off the engine. Turning my head, I watched her open the gas tank and put the nozzle in. As soon as she had the gas flowing, she came over to the passenger window.

'I'll have to pay inside,' she said. 'Any hot ideas about what else I might do while I'm in there?'

'Like tell someone to call the Highway Patrol?'

'Along those lines, yeah.'

'I wouldn't do that,' I said.

'Me neither.'

'Donny might end up dead.'

'Yeah. I don't see how the cops can help us much. Anything else? I think there's some kind of convenience store.'

'If it's convenient, pick up a couple of guns.'

'If only.'

I shook my head. 'Even if they did sell guns, we'd be screwed by the waiting period.'

'I'll see what I can come up with in the way of weaponry.'

'Probably not much.'

'At any rate, I'll pick us up some goodies.'

With my attention on Cat, I'd lost track of the van. I looked around and found it parked at the far side of the lot.

Cat had already spotted it. 'It's *way* over there,' she said.

'I'll say. He probably can't even see us very well.'

'Of course, he really doesn't have to. If we pull anything, he can kill Donny. Or Peggy. Or both of them.'

The pump clicked off.

'Want to hand me my purse?'

'I've got some cash,' I said.

'Save it. I'll use a credit card.'

I reached under the passenger seat, found Cat's purse, and passed it out the window to her. She swung its strap over her shoulder and hurried off.

After hanging the nozzle on the pump, she capped her gas tank. Then she made her way to the front entrance of Lucky's and vanished inside.

I waited.

A few minutes went by, and I started growing nervous. I kept an eye on the van. Snow White had to be getting nervous, too. Or angry. Though I couldn't see him, I figured he was probably watching us in the side mirror. Watching us, and wondering what was taking so long.

I half expected him to leap out of the van and come running over in a rage.

But then I realized he couldn't.

Not unless he brought Donny along.

With all these people around, he sure couldn't drag a twelve-year-old-kid hostage over here. Even if he wanted to, he would have to untie the boy first. And get him dressed.

Basically, Snow White was trapped inside the van.

We were safe.

But they weren't.

I doubted that he would carry out his threat to kill Donny, though. Not here. Not now. Not in anger because Cat was spending a little too long in Lucky's.

He might be nuts. He might be moronic about some things. But he was cagey, too.

Cagey enough to know that he needed his hostages. They were his only hold on us. Killing Donny would ruin everything for him. For starters, Peggy would go berserk. He would lose his messenger *and* his driver.

If he had to kill Peggy, he would lose us.

At least as soon as we found out about it.

All that aside, he might figure that molesting them wouldn't be as much fun if they were dead. So he'd be reluctant to kill them. He'd save it as a last resort.

I hoped so, anyway.

Finally, Cat emerged from Lucky's. She was carrying a twelve-pack of beer by her side and clutching a large paper bag to her chest.

I leaned across the seat and opened the door for her.

She lowered the twelve-pack toward the floor and used it to sweep the can of squeeze cheese, cracker box and water bottles underneath the seat.

Holding the bag to her chest, she climbed in. I started the engine. The cool air began to blow. The moment her door shut, I stepped on the gas.

'Took a while,' she said. The bag resting on her lap, she cranked up her window.

I rolled up my window, too. 'You had me worried,' I told her.

'Scared Whitey might come over and kick your ass?'

'The bastard can't leave the van. Took me a while to figure it out, though.'

'It didn't occur to me,' she admitted, ''till I'd been in the store for a couple of minutes. After that, I sort of slowed down and took my time.'

'You didn't have to do that.'

'What was he going to do about it?'

'Nothing, I guess.'

'Precisely.'

Ahead of us, the van pulled out of its parking space. When it turned toward the exit, I glimpsed Peggy through her open window. The passenger seat beside her looked empty.

Snow White was probably in the rear with Donny.

'I also figured out,' I said, 'that he won't kill Peggy or Donny unless he really has to.'

Cat nodded in agreement, then said, 'But he can't not kill them, either. Sooner or later, they've gotta go. Same as us.'

'Except we won't let him.'

'Right.'

I followed the van onto the road. As we picked up speed and left the town of Trona behind, I asked, 'What'd you buy? I presume you weren't able to get your hands on a sniper rifle.'

'Afraid you're right. However! I picked up a ton of beer.'

'So I see.'

'We might have a long wait for nightfall, so I figured we should have the ingredients for a party. Or who knows, maybe Whitey'll confiscate it, get drunk out of his skull and useless so we can jump him.'

'Sounds good either way,' I said.

'They didn't have any hard stuff, unfortunately.'

'Too bad.'

'Want a beef stick?'

'Sure.'

She reached into the bag and pulled a long, brown tube of meat. It was encased in a clear plastic wrapper. She tore one end of the wrapper with her teeth, then slid the beef stick partway out and handed it to me.

The casing was greasy. When I bit in, juice spurted into my mouth. I ripped off about an inch, and started chewing. The beef was teriyaki-flavored and tasted great. 'Good,' I said.

'I bought a few of those. I mean, who knows how long it'll be before we get to have a real meal?' She peered into the sack. 'Didn't get any chocolate. Figured it'd melt on us.'

'Good idea.'

'Got pretzels, though. And a can of mixed nuts.'

'They'll go good with the beer.'

'Potato chips, some of those cheese and cracker packets, sugar cookies, a few more bottles of water, a can of WD-40 . . .'

'For the squeak in the door?'

'It's by way of a weapon. Spray it in Whitey's eyes. Also, I've heard you can light the spray on fire, make yourself a flamethrower. So I got us a couple of lighters, too.'

'Lighters. Good idea.'

She reached deep into the bag. After a brief search, her hand reappeared clutching two cigarette lighters. 'One for you, one for me. Here you go.'

I clamped the beef stick between my teeth to free my right hand, and took one of them. I dropped it into my shirt pocket. Cat stuffed her lighter into the right front pocket of her cut-offs.

'Also bought a can of lighter fuel. The clerk gave me all kinds of crap about it, too. He didn't want to sell it to me. Kept trying to explain that these lighters are disposable and you can't refuel them. I told him I knew that, but I wanted the stuff anyway. He kept saying I didn't need it, couldn't use it, I'd be better off spending my money to buy a few more lighters 'cause I sure couldn't refill any of them. As if any of this was his business, anyway.'

'But he finally let you have it?'

'I threatened him with you.'

'Yeah?'

She nodded and suddenly smiled. 'I said, "Just sell me the stuff, okay? It's for my boyfriend. If he has to get out of the car and come over here, he'll be very unhappy with you." So he looked out the window at you, then just said, "Suit yourself, lady."'

'So I saved the day, huh?'

'Yep. I almost made you my husband, but I'm not wearing a ring.' She held up her left hand to show me. 'Only reason he gave me all that trouble, he was trying to hit on me. Thought he was God's gift to dumb broads who don't know the ins and outs of cigarette lighters. I should've told him the truth.'

'Which truth? That he's not a gift, that you're not a dumb broad . . . ?'

'Why I *really* want the lighter fluid.'

'Anything to do with Snow White?' I asked.

'Good guess.'

'Looks like we're well prepared to burn him down if we get half a chance.'

'Yep. I also bought this.' She searched the bag and came up with a corkscrew.'

'Did you buy wine?'

'Nope. Bought *this*, though.' She reached in again and came up with a church key.

'The beer cans have pop tops,' I pointed out.

'I know.'

'Did the clerk explain this to you?'

'By then, he was strangely silent.'

'We're supposed to use these on Snow White?' I asked.

'They didn't have any knives. Not for sale, anyway. Maybe I could've gotten my hands on one in the kitchen . . .'

'Maybe a *big* one.'

'I didn't want to create a situation. Besides, these'll be easy to conceal. Which would you rather have?'

174

'Your choice,' I said.

'I'll take the corkscrew.'

She handed the church key to me. It was a simple, cheap tool: about five inches of flat steel, almost an inch wide, with a bottle cap-opener at one end and a can-piercer at the other. This wasn't exactly a Bowie knife.

No worse than a corkscrew, though.

While I steered with one hand and held the church key with the other, Cat put the corkscrew into the glove compartment.

'You're not going to carry it?' I asked.

'I'll know where it is if I need it.'

'Want to toss the church key in there?'

'Church key?'

'This.'

'That's a church key?'

'That's what they call it.'

'Why?'

'I don't know. Maybe it's for people who figure beer is divine. I don't even know why they still make the things. Bottle caps twist off. Cans pop open.'

'Not all of them,' Cat said. 'Anyway, maybe they're intended for emergencies. Like ours.'

'Maybe *that's* why they're called church keys.'

'Why don't you put it in your sock?' Cat suggested.

'What?'

'The church key.'

'I'm trying to drive.'

'I'll do it for you.'

'Okay.' I gave the can-opener to Cat and said, 'Be careful of the point.'

She leaned forward and stuffed the bag in front of the twelve-pack. With her lap clear, she ducked toward me. Hunched over the console, left hand clutching my thigh to brace herself, she reached down to my ankle with her right hand.

I tried to keep my foot steady on the gas pedal.

She fumbled around down there, lifting the cuff of my jeans, slipping fingers inside my sock. 'I'll put it on the outside,' she said. 'Easier for you to reach.'

'Point outward, okay?'

'Point out and down.'

She slid the tool in against the side of my leg, just above the ankle. Its steel felt smooth and warm. Nothing poked me. Cat held it with a couple of fingers while the rest of her hand dealt with my sock. When she let go, the sock held the church key snugly in place. She pushed herself up and gave my thigh a squeeze.

'There you go,' she said.

'We're loaded for bear,' I said.

'Is that a crack?'

'Nah.'

'At least we've got something,' she pointed out. 'Plus, we have the pick and shovel. *And* the hammer in the trunk.'

'And the tire tool in the back seat,' I added.

'The *what*?'

Our heads jerked toward each other. Our eyes locked.

'The tire tool,' I muttered.

'Oh, my God,' she said.

It was a heavy iron rod a couple of feet long.

The jack handle.

The lug wrench.

I'd used it last night to change the flat tire. Then I'd tossed it behind the driver's seat along with the ruined tire and the rest of the jack.

And forgotten all about it.

'You put it there after fixing the flat,' Cat said.

'Yeah. I sure did.'

'My God,' she said again. 'I never gave it another thought.'

'Neither did I. Until just now. I don't know what made it pop into my mind all of a sudden like that. I mean . . . *the tire tool in the back seat* . . . as if I'd known about it all along.'

'I guess we both knew about it all along,' Cat said.

'Yeah. Apparently.'

'I wouldn't have gone for the hammer last night.'

'Probably not.'

'No. Not a chance. Not when we've got a tire iron in the back seat. I would've stayed in the car . . . never opened the trunk.' Looking stunned, she shook her head slowly from side to side. Then she said, 'White never would've found out about Elliot. None of this would be happening.'

176

'It sure would've changed things,' I admitted.

'How could we forget about the *tire iron*?'

'Well,' I said, 'it was out of sight by the time we started worrying about weapons.'

'So was the hammer.'

'But we'd *used* the hammer as a weapon. We'd only used the tire tool for changing the flat.'

'We should've thought of it,' she said.

'Yeah. I know. We should've. I can't believe we didn't.'

'It's the damn curse.'

'*The Curse of the Vampire.*'

'I'm not some sort of superstitious nut, but this much stuff shouldn't be going wrong. It's crazy. We're cursed.'

27

Cat reached back through the gap between our seats, but couldn't find the tire tool.

'I hope it's still there,' she said.

'It's probably down on the floor under everything. I didn't even see it when I was back there. I just hope Peggy didn't take it.'

'With what she was wearing, she had nowhere to hide it.'

'For that matter,' I said, 'where'd she hide the knife?'

'Down her front?' Cat suggested.

'Wouldn't it fall out the bottom?'

'Did you see how she was clutching the bag against her chest?'

'Maybe she put it inside the bag.'

'The tire iron?'

'The knife,' I said.

'Not if she's smart. She'd probably have to hand the bag over to White right away. *I* sure wouldn't try to hide a knife in it. If I was in an outfit like that, I'd put it down my front. Or slip it under the side of my panties ... but she couldn't do that.'

'Why not?'

'Got none on.'

'How do you know that?'

'I'm observant.'

'So am I, but I never noticed *that*.'

'Well, I had certain advantages. For one thing, I could see her climbing in and out of the van. That dress is so short...' She wiggled her eyebrows at me. 'No bra, either. Don't tell me you didn't notice that.'

'Well, I saw that there didn't seem to be any bra straps on her shoulders.'

'That's because she's not wearing one. She's not wearing *anything* under that dress, as a matter of fact. When she was leaning in through the door to get the food, I could see all the way down its front, all the way down to her legs – another reason I happen to know she doesn't have panties on. Too bad you missed it.' Cat threw me an impish grin. 'Not that there was much to see.'

I laughed. '*You're* nice.'

'I know. Terrible. You didn't miss much, that's all. I wanted to set your mind at ease.'

I shook my head and asked, 'What makes you think I care?'

'You're a guy. Guy's always care about such things.'

'But she's not my type.'

'Yeah, right. Are you saying you wouldn't have looked?'

'Who, me?'

'You. The truth. Never lie to the Cat.'

'I might've taken a little peek,' I admitted.

'A little peek, huh? Like the little peek you took at *me* this morning?'

'You *are* my type.'

She suddenly went quiet and serious. She stared at me. I mostly kept my eyes on the road, but glanced at her every few seconds. Pretty soon, she leaned over and curled a hand around the back of my neck. She pulled me closer to her and kissed the side of my face. Then she whispered, 'My guy' with her breath tickling my cheek. Then she kissed me again. Her other hand roamed slowly over my chest and belly.

I turned, wanting to kiss her on the mouth.

She pulled her head back. 'No no no,' she said. She looked as if she were trying not to smile. 'Not while you're driving. We'd crash for sure. Especially with Elliot's curse hanging over us.'

'I'll risk it,' I said. But I wondered if this would be a good time for taking such a risk. After leaving Trona, we'd been driving through a fairly flat area of desert. Now, however, the road was climbing into a ridge of mountains. We had rocky bluffs on both sides. A swerve off the road could mean a nasty crash.

Cat sat there, staring at me and not moving.

I didn't hold onto a single hope that she would change her mind about kissing me on the mouth. But she suddenly said, 'Okay. Just for a second, though.'

She pulled me toward her. I turned my head and met her open mouth. Her lips were moist and soft. They writhed against my lips. I felt her breath going into me. Then she sucked my tongue into her mouth.

As my tongue went in, her hand gently pressed against the front of my jeans. I was already hard.

A moan slipped out of me.

She took her mouth and hand away. With her face still close to mine, she said, 'That reminds me, I'd better get the tire iron.'

I blushed fiercely and turned my eyes to the road. We were still okay. From the openings among the rocks ahead, however, I sensed that we were almost to the top of the pass.

Cat gave me a quick, light kiss, then turned and knelt on her seat. After surveying her destination for a few seconds, she started to climb the seatback. Not exactly a kid, she was too big for such a maneuver. She had to fight her way up, squirming and crawling, then squeezing her way between the top of the seat and the car ceiling.

I had a fine view of her bare, thrashing legs.

Her heels pounded the windshield a couple of times, but not hard enough to break it. Once, she almost kneed me in the face.

Finally, she dropped off the top of the seat and vanished.

'Ah,' she said. 'That was fun.'

It took her a while. Keeping my eyes on the road, I didn't watch what was going on back there. But I heard things being shoved about. The back of my seat was bumped a few times. Cat grunted now and then, and muttered several curses. Then she said, 'Gotcha, you bugger! Ha!'

'Well done,' I said.

'A case where "better late than never" doesn't necessarily apply.'

'At least we've got it now.'

'Makes me want to scream. If we'd only remembered it last night ... People may *die* because I went hot-footing it to the trunk for that damn hammer that we didn't even need.'

'Nobody's died yet,' I pointed out.

Not counting Elliot, I thought. *Or her husband, Bill. But – they were before she went to the trunk.*

'Not yet,' Cat muttered. 'I don't know how the hell we're going to get out of this mess, though, without *somebody* getting killed.'

'You never know,' I said.

'I'll probably buy the ranch just trying to climb back over...'

'Oh, my God,' I muttered, my stomach dropping.

We'd suddenly left the pass behind. It was like coming out of a tunnel. In front of us stretched a vast expanse of sky. Below us – far, far below us – was the floor of a desolate valley. The van was already on its way down, swerving this way and that on the curves of the narrow, two-lane road.

Behind me, Cat said, 'Whoa!'

'You'd better stay there,' I warned her.

The road looked steep and dangerous. It curved its way down the side of the mountain, with steep rock walls rising on the left and a drop-off into the valley on the right – our side of the road.

A small mistake in that direction could drop us about a thousand feet to the desert.

I didn't want to go down that road. I had a strong urge to stop the car, turn around and drive the other way.

But we were already starting down.

There *was* no place to turn around. Not without risking a plunge over the edge.

We couldn't retreat, anyway, without betraying Peggy and Donny.

'Be careful,' Cat said.

'I'll try.'

'Jeez.'

'I guess that must be Death Valley, down there.'

'Aptly named,' Cat said.

Though we had the air-conditioning on, the steering wheel was slick in my sweaty hands. I felt dribbles of sweat trickle down my sides, untouched by my shirt.

'I'm not good with heights,' I muttered.

'Heights are okay with me,' Cat said. 'It's the possibility of abrupt descents that I don't like.'

As she said that, we took a curve too fast and our tires sighed.

'Eeeee,' Cat said.

I used the brake to slow us down. And had to keep pumping the brake pedal to keep our speed from growing. After about thirty seconds of that, I down-shifted to let the transmission do some of the work. But I still had to continue applying the brakes every so often.

'Peggy's doing all right,' I said as the van ahead of us took a sharp curve without going off the road. 'I *guess* she's driving.'

'If she makes it, we can.'

'People must make it all the time,' I said.

'Of course, they probably aren't driving under the curse of the vampire.'

'If we go, he goes.'

'And if we go,' Cat said, 'the trunk'll pop open on impact and *he'll* get cooked by the Death Valley sun.' Raising her voice, she said, 'Do you hear that, Elliot? If *we* crash, *you* burn.'

We glanced at each other and grinned.

Suddenly, the road leveled out ahead of us.

We'd reached the bottom.

I took a deep breath and blew it out.

'That wasn't so bad,' Cat said.

'At least it didn't last long. It looked a lot worse than it was.'

On both sides of us, now, the desert stretched out rugged but fairly flat. Though it had rises and ravines and clumps of rock, we were no longer in danger of a plunge to our deaths. The nearest mountains were a few miles to our left. There were mountains to our right, but they looked a lot farther away.

'You can come up now,' I told Cat.

'Guess so. Do you need anything from back here?'

181

'I don't think so.'

'Is there anything worthwhile in your overnight bag?'

I tried to remember what I'd packed. It wasn't easy. On about half an hour of sleep, my mind wasn't working the way it should. 'You can look if you want,' I said.

'Any weaponry?'

'Not that I ... nah. Just some clothes, my toilet kit ...'

'What do you shave with?'

'It's a Trac-II, or something. Not enough blade to matter. We'll do better with our corkscrew and church key.'

'Okay. Guess I'll come up. Or try to.' Reaching through the gap between the bucket seats, she set the tire tool on top of the console.

'Now *that's* a weapon,' I said.

The black, iron bar was about two feet long, and curved at one end. The curve led to a lug wrench. At the other was a pry wedge.

I let go of the steering wheel with my right hand and hefted the tool. It must've weighed four or five pounds.

'This baby's lethal,' I said.

'It's all yours. Maybe stick it under your seat, or something.'

'Maybe over here.' I switched it to my left hand, then reached down into the space between the edge of my seat and the door. I let go of the bar. It fell a few inches and thudded against the floor.

'Okay,' Cat said, 'here I come.' She put her hands on the top of her seatback. 'I used to do this when I was a kid,' she said. 'It was so easy. Guess that's what age will do for you.'

'It's not your age,' I said, 'it's your size. You're a lot bigger than you used to be.'

'Gee, thanks.'

'You're a *great* size ...'

'This gets better and better.'

'You're the *perfect* size, but not for climbing over seats.'

'You want me to stay back here?'

'I've got a better plan. I'll pull over. You can hop out and hop back in.'

'What about Whitey?'

'We'll only be stopped for about five seconds. He won't kill Donny over a little thing like that.'

Somewhere in my mind, a voice whispered, *The kid's doomed, anyway.*

I told that voice, *No, he's not. We'll figure something out.*

Which was more of a hope than a belief.

Checking the mirrors, I saw that the highway looked fairly clear behind us. 'Ready?' I asked.

'All set.'

I hit the brakes. As our speed dropped, I swung us onto the gravel shoulder. Then I mashed the brake pedal down. We were still skidding when Cat threw open the back door and leaped out. She stayed on her feet. Just as we came to a halt, she slammed her door. She rushed forward, jerked open the front door and jumped in. I stepped on the gas, and off we went.

'Slick,' Cat said.

Back on the road, we bore down fast on the van.

'White-ass probably doesn't even know we stopped,' Cat said.

'Even if he does, why should he care? We're back where we belong.'

Cat bent down, reached between her legs, and pulled a beer can out of its plastic holder. 'I'm having one,' she said. 'How about you?'

'I'm driving.'

'One beer isn't gonna impair you enough to matter.'

'But it's against the law.'

'So is murder.'

'I thought you said it's not murder, killing a vampire.'

She turned her head enough for me to get a look at her impish grin, then said, 'So who believes in vampires?'

'Snow White, for one.'

'Not the cops, though. As far as they'd be concerned, we did a homicide.' She tugged out a second can, then sat up. 'Don't let me drink alone,' she said. 'It ain't ladylike.'

'I'm no lady.'

'I know. You're my guy.' She popped open both cans, and offered one to me.

I took it. 'You're corrupting me.'

'Nobody's holding a gun to your head.'

'If only we had one.'

'Can't have everything. Here's to us.'

'To us,' I said.

We gently bumped our beer cans.

Before taking my first drink, I checked all around – looking for the Highway Patrol. I'm that kind of guy. A worrier. I'd deliberately broken very few rules in my life. And even fewer laws.

After killing a guy, everything else should come easy.

But it didn't work that way. I felt like a criminal, drinking the beer.

The can was wet in my hand. The beer was cool. It had obviously been refrigerated back at Lucky's. Though it must've lost some of its chill while sitting on the car floor, the air-conditioning had kept it from warming up too much. It tasted strong and very good.

I looked over at Cat. She stopped drinking and smiled at me. 'Good, huh?' she asked.

'Great.'

'Hits the spot.' She took a couple of swallows, then said, 'You wouldn't believe how hot it is out there. They must be dying in that van.'

'From the heat?'

'Yeah. But then, maybe they do have air.'

'No. They've got windows open. The driver's window, anyway. I get a glimpse of it sometimes on curves.'

'That's too bad. I wish they had air. It's hot as a mother dog out there, and it's still morning. A couple more hours . . .' She shook her head. Then she said, 'Well, there's nothing we can do about that. We might as well try to enjoy ourselves. What would you like to eat?'

'How about some cheese and crackers?'

'The aerosol cheese?'

'Sure.'

She set her beer on the console, then reached down under her seat. Soon, she came up with the can of cheese and the box of crackers. She pried the plastic cap off the cheese. 'It's bacon-cheddar flavored,' she said.

'My favorite.'

'Mine, too.'

We grinned at each other.

Up ahead, the van's right rear signal began to blink.

28

'Now what?' I muttered.

Cat leaned to the right. Her head against the side window, she said, 'I don't see anything up there.

Its turn signal still blinking, the van started to slow down. I eased off the gas to stay off its tail. The van dropped to about twenty miles per hour, and so did we. In the rearview mirror, I saw that nothing was coming at us from behind.

'Maybe they're having trouble,' Cat said.

'Or looking for something,' I suggested, and took a drink of beer.

Cat squirted some cheese onto a cracker. 'Why don't you have this?'

I clamped the beer can between my thighs and took the cracker.

The van kept creeping along.

I ate the cheese-loaded cracker. The cracker crunched in my teeth. The cheddar was smooth and tangy, and had a smokey bacon flavor. Cat had already made another.

'Here,' she said.

'You eat that one.'

'No, go ahead. I'll have the next.'

'Thanks.' I took it and ate it. Then I picked up the beer. As I drank and Cat squirted cheese on another cracker, the van swung to the right, veering off the road and kicking up dust and heading off into the desert on a strip of dirt road.

'There she goes,' Cat said.

'Here *we* go.' I swerved and followed the van. We dropped off the smooth pavement. Our tires crunching over the desert ground, I closed in until we entered the van's dust cloud. There, I couldn't see anything. It was like driving through a fog bank, but brighter. Almost white, like fog when the sunlight has almost burnt it off, but with a yellow tinge.

The dry smell of dust began to invade our car through the air-conditioning.

I backed off until we found clear air. Then I kept us at a safe distance behind the van and its huge, rising tail of dust.

In the rearview mirror, I saw that we were being chased by our own pale cloud.

Cat sank her teeth into a cheese-covered cracker. She bit off half the cracker and started to chew. Her eyes appeared to be locked on the rear of the van – or its dust. She had a small gob of yellow cheese on her upper lip, and licked it off before taking another bite.

I held on tightly to the steering wheel with my left hand, and drank the beer with my right.

We bounced and rattled about on the rough dirt surface, but not too badly. We weren't going very fast – between ten and fifteen miles per hour. There was no washboard. The road had a lot of unexpected dips and holes and twists, though. Going faster might've ruined us.

Cat took a drink of beer and said, 'I wonder if White knows where we're going. Or did he just happen to see this lousy excuse for a road and decide to take it?'

'It looked to me like they were trying to find it.'

'Maybe it goes to Brock's hole.'

'Wherever it goes,' I said, 'it isn't used very often.'

'What makes you think so?'

'No washboard. You notice how we aren't getting rattled apart?'

'It's pretty damn bumpy.'

'But not from washboard. There's none of that ribbing in the dirt. Which means this road doesn't get much traffic. He's taking us somewhere that doesn't have a lot of visitors.'

'I guess he would,' Cat said.

Holding the beer can between her legs, she took a cracker out of the box and up-ended the cheese can. As she pressed the plastic nozzle, cheese spiraled out onto the cracker until a lurch of the car made her hands jump. A snake of cheese looped down off the edge of the cracker and fell onto her left thigh. She said, 'Pooh.'

Then she stuck the whole cracker in her mouth. As she chewed, she reached down with her left hand. Her forefinger scraped the gob of cheese off the tawny skin of her thigh, lifted it, carried it over to my face and put it between my lips.

Surprised and pleased, I nibbled the cheese off her fingertip.

'Clean it off,' she said in a voice muffled by her mouthful of cheese and cracker.

So I licked her fingertip until it felt bare and slippery on my tongue.

'Thank you,' she said.

'Thank *you*.'

We both drank more beer. 'This is almost fun,' Cat said.

'It's not bad at all,' I said.

'If we could just forget about White,' she added.

'I forgot all about him when you stuck your finger in my mouth. And when we were kissing a while ago. And a few other times.'

'Me, too. It's nice to have distractions. The problem is, they don't last long enough and then it's back to worrying.'

'I guess there's always something,' I said.

'What a philosopher.'

'That's me. Just call me Plato.'

'Isn't he the guy who drank the hemlock?' Cat asked.

'It was either him or Socrates.'

'Screw hemlock, have another beer.'

'Don't mind if I do.'

I finished what was in my can while Cat took care of plucking another couple of beers from the twelve-pack on the floor. She popped both cans open. Then she took the empty away from me and tossed it over her shoulder into the back seat. She placed a cold can into my hand.

'Thanks,' I said.

'More cheese and crackers?'

'Sure, why not?'

'We might as well enjoy ourselves,' Cat said. 'God only knows what's coming next.'

'Brock's hole, probably.'

'And coming up soon.'

'Probably,' I said again.

'Though why *should* he take us there? He's planning to resurrect Elliot, not give him the old heave-ho.'

'The old heave-ho,' I said, 'is for us.'

'Likely so. Eat, drink and be merry, for tonight we may get the old heave-ho.'

We both laughed, oddly enough.

It probably had something to do with the beer. But not just the beer. Strange as it may seem, I think we were both having a good time. Hell, we were having a picnic in the car. We were driving in air-conditioned comfort through an area – or at least *near* an area – where thousands of people came each year for fun and recreation. We were 'off-roading,' a popular pastime for vacationers. We were venturing into the heart of the desert.

As for me, my passenger was the only girl I'd ever loved, she was more beautiful than ever, more *wonderful* than ever, and we were even messing around a little.

In some very big ways, this had been the best day of my life.

This was probably one of Cat's better days, too. I might not be the greatest prize, but she'd been showing a lot of affection for me. Also (and more important to Cat, probably), she was finally rid of Elliot, who'd gotten rid of Bill. For the first time in years, she was free from the cruelties of her husband *and* her vampire.

For now, at least, she was also free from White. He couldn't possibly harm her – not while he was up ahead of us in the van.

In fact, if we really wanted to escape, we could simply turn around and drive off.

We weren't the prisoners.

In a sense, we were volunteers here, on a mission to rescue White's hostages.

Like a two-person SWAT team.

We certainly had Special Weapons, and I figured we would come up with the Tactics sooner or later. We'd find a way to save ourselves, Donny and Peggy, when it came time for action. I hoped so, anyway.

In the meantime, we drove through the desert behind the van's cloud of dust, enjoying our beer and crackers and cheese, making jokes about our troubles, having ourselves a fairly good time.

I didn't want it to end.

When my second can of beer was empty, I smiled at Cat and handed it to her. She tossed it over her shoulder into the back seat.

'Another?' she asked.

'Better not.'

'Me neither. I don't want to get stewed. Just gotta stay loose as a goose. Gotta be ready for action at the drop of a hat.'

'Right,' I said, and laughed.

She laughed and slapped my leg. 'We'll give *him* the old heave-ho.'

'Absolutely.'

'Crackers?' she asked. 'Cheese?'

'I'm fine.'

'You're better than fine.'

'Thanks. You, too.'

She tossed her own beer can into the back seat, then picked up the box of crackers and the can of cheese. Bending forward with them, she reached down to put them into the bag on the floor.

While she was bent over like that, I leaned a little to the right and put my hand on her back. Her shirt was damp. I could feel the heat of her body through its fabric.

By then, she must've been done putting away the cheese and crackers. Instead of sitting up, however, she hung her head. I rubbed her back, and she moaned.

Continuing to rub her back, I snuck glances at her as I steered us along the dirt road. She was hunched over, her checkered shirt taut against her back, her arms hanging between her knees, her head low. She swayed and shook with the motions of the car. Her head wobbled slightly. Her short hair, shining like gold in the sunlight, shimmered and bounced.

I moved my hand up her back and under the collar of her shirt to the bare nape of her neck. Her skin there felt moist and hot. The muscles underneath were hard.

As I caressed her neck, rubbed it and squeezed it, I felt the soft brush of her hair against the upper edge of my hand.

She swayed gently. She seemed to be limp and drifting toward sleep.

Then her collar loosened. She must've brought up a hand from below and unfastened a button on the front of her blouse. Or the button had popped open on its own. Either way, her collar was no longer tight against the back of my hand. I roamed lower down her neck, rubbing and squeezing.

She suddenly flinched, quick and hard, gasping 'Ah!'

I jerked my hand away.

She sat upright, grimacing. Lips peeled back, she panted for air and dragged the collar of her shirt sideways – away from her neck and down off her left shoulder.

She was bleeding.

Bleeding from the pair of fang holes down low on the curve of her neck.

The holes she'd shown me in my apartment·last night . . . and shown White to back up our vampire story.

I must've rubbed them open.

'Oh God,' I said, 'I'm sorry.'

She turned her head toward me. Her eyes were shiny with tears, but the worst of the pain must've faded. 'It's all right,' she said.

'I forgot about them. Your wounds.'

She sniffed and wiped her eyes. 'Me, too.' A corner of her mouth tilted up. 'Till you gouged those with your thumb.'

'I'm so sorry.'

'Don't be. It felt great ·for a while there. You've just gotta never forget I'm damaged goods.'

Damaged goods.

It made me feel sick to hear her say that about herself, even if she was trying to be flippant.

'You're not damaged goods,' I said.

'Yeah, I am.' Keeping the shirt off her shoulder with her left hand, she turned and reached for the console with her right.

The way she had her shirt pulled, her left breast was bare almost down to the nipple.

She swung up the lid of the console.

'Can I get something for you?' I asked.

'I've got it.'

She had some paper napkins stored there. She plucked out one of them, and I shut the console for her. She used the napkin to mop the two dribbles of blood off her neck and upper chest. Then she let go of her blouse collar. It came sliding up over the top of her shoulder while she used both hands to fold the napkin. She made the napkin into a square pad, then pressed it against the pair of holes. She held it there with the fingertips of her right hand. She let her left hand rest on her thigh.

'The first-aid kit's in back,' I said. 'Why don't I stop the car for a second and...?'

'No, don't bother. I have some bandages in my purse if I really want any. But I'm fine. This sort of thing happens. I've gotten pretty used to bleeding at odd moments.' She gave me a crooked smile. 'At odd moments, from odd places. Like I told you, damaged goods.'

'No, you're not.'

'Sure am. Battered and scarred – body and soul.'

'But not broken,' I added.

She smiled a little sadly and said, 'Nope, not broken yet. I guess White'll get that opportunity tonight.'

'We won't let him.'

'We won't go gentle into that good night,' she said.

I gazed at her, astonished. 'No, we won't. Where on earth did you pick up *that* line?'

'A guy I know.'

'You *remember*?'

'Are you kidding? You Dylan-Thomased me half to death that last summer. Remember when you had us do the "Fern Hill" duet in the parking lot?'

'My God,' I said. I hadn't thought about it in a long time. It used to always hurt, remembering the fine moments with Cat, so I'd trained myself to stay away from them as much as possible, tried to keep my mind in the present and stay away from things that made me ache with the loss of them.

'Those were great times,' Cat said. 'How about this one? "And you, in the dark, suck sweetly my heart's core down the secret corridors of my veins"?'

'Sounds familiar.'

'It ought to.'

'Did I write that?'

'What do you think?'

'And you remembered it? All these years?'

'I have a copy. I have lots of your poems.'

'You *kept* them?'

'Of course. And that one ... I always loved it. I knew it by heart long before Elliot came into my life. And after that ... I mean, you write me this incredibly erotic vampire poem when I'm like sixteen years old – starring me as the vampire – and

191

then one fine night I end up on the sucking end. I mean, that's uncanny if you ask me. Weird.

'After things got started with Elliot, your poem ran through my mind all the time. He'd be ... doing horrible things to me ... and I'd be thinking, "Your dark bite stuns my blood, plunders me, quakes me with such rough aches, I rage for the coming dusk."'

Though I could feel myself blushing fiercely, I smiled and said, 'Pretty good.'

'Do you know the title?'

I shrugged and said, '"Do Not Suck Gentle"?'

She gave me a look that made me feel bad about joking.

'Sorry,' I muttered.

'"My Vampire Bride."'

'Ah.'

'That poem ... it was like my companion during all those times with Elliot. It kept me company and ... made things not quite so bad.'

'That's nice,' I said.

I didn't know what else to say. I felt very strange about it. Naked in bed with Elliot, she'd had my poem in her mind. While he humiliated her, while he tortured her, while he bit her and sucked her blood, while she writhed beneath him in agony and maybe sometimes in delight, my poem had been in her mind.

'It's probably the reason I went to you last night,' Cat said. 'Your poem ... it had become so much a part of me, a part of the whole ordeal. So, in a way, it was as if *you'd* been going through it with me.'

'I wish,' I said.

'Wish?'

'That I *had* been going through it with you.'

She looked a little perplexed.

'I don't know,' I said. 'It's just ... if I could've been there and helped ... somehow saved you.'

'Saved me from Elliot?'

'Yes.'

'You did.'

'But not until last night.'

'I got no worse than I deserved,' she said. 'When you do

192

something like that, you know . . . arrange for someone's death . . . even if he's the scum of the earth . . . you end up paying. You've gotta suffer for it. It's in the rules.'

29

'Would you do it over again?' I asked.

'You've got to be kidding.'

'Is that a no?'

'It's a no, all right.'

'What would you have done differently?'

'Knowing what I know now? Everything. For starters, I wouldn't have married Bill. That's number one. If I hadn't married him, none of this would've happened. I'm having another beer. You want another beer?'

'Sure, why not?'

She bent over to get two more cans. 'So what if we get a little sloshed? We'll have plenty of time to sober up before Snow White tries anything with us.'

'As long as he waits till after dark,' I said.

'Well, that's how we've got it figured.' She sat up, clamped one can between her thighs, and opened the other. 'I think we've got it figured right, don't you?'

She handed the open can to me. I thanked her and took a sip. The beer was still somewhat cool.

'Who knows?' I said. 'It's completely crazy. Nobody really believes all that crap about vampires being immortal.'

'Nobody but Snow White.'

'What can you expect from a guy who's named after a fairy tale?'

Cat laughed. 'Don't let *him* hear you say that. The boy's sensitive about his name. He *whacked* me for making that crack about it.'

'Yeah. The poison apple business.'

'He's whacked me any number of times,' she pointed out as if it were a curiosity that deserved to be noted. Then she frowned out the windshield toward the van and the pale cloud of dust rising behind it. 'Those poor kids.' She shook her head, then raised the beer can to her mouth and drank. Then she said, 'We should've just stayed with him, back at breakfast. Whatever he's doing to them, its our fault. *My* fault. They're paying for my mistakes.'

Wanting to take her mind off Peggy and Donny, I asked, 'What was mistake number two?'

'Number one was marrying Bill,' she said, and drank some more beer. 'Number two ... had to be getting involved with Elliot. Well ... maybe ... *morally* speaking, number two must've been *deciding* to kill Bill. I could've divorced him, right? Maybe that would've been the *moral* thing. But he'd murdered my baby.' Her voice started to get strange. 'Pulled it out of me, piece by piece. Flushed it down the toilet.' She faced me and I saw that her eyes were brimming and shining with tears. 'When somebody kills your baby, you've gotta do something about it.'

'Yeah,' I said. 'You do.'

'So I don't ...' She sniffed, then took a deep breath. After wiping her eyes, she had another drink of beer. 'I don't see that as a mistake – deciding to kill him. Not really. I had to. Something's not a mistake if you don't really have a choice. I don't think so, anyway. A mistake's when you have options and you pick the wrong one. So I guess mistake number two was getting Elliot to do it.' She shrugged and shook her head as if disgusted. 'Who'd have thought the bastard was a *vampire*? I don't even *believe* in vampires. Or at least I didn't.'

'Not many people do,' I pointed out.

'White does.'

'Just our luck.'

She let out a quick, grim laugh and said, 'Think it's luck? I think it's the damn curse.'

'*The curse of the vampire.*'

'Exactly. Elliot's doing all this to us 'cause we killed him.' Turning slightly, she scowled over her shoulder and called out, 'Hey, Elliot! Give us a break, huh? You bastard!'

Our eyes met, and she gave out that peculiar little laugh again.

'I'm losing it,' she said.

'Nah.'

'Where was I? Oh, right. Mistake number two. That's right.

See, it never occurred to me there'd be any sort of . . . *aftermath*. I figured I'd hire a guy, he'd do the job, and that'd be the end of it. Only it wasn't the end of it. Boy, was there *aftermath*. We've got *aftermath* up the wazoo.' She shook her head. 'I never would've hired Elliot if I'd thought he was a vampire.'

'Why *did* you hire him?' I asked.

'For one thing, he wasn't wearing those steel fangs when I met him. Actually, I thought he was a pretty nice guy. He *looks* creepy . . . looks like a spook out of the silent movies, or something. Well, hell, you've seen him.'

'Looks like Nosferatu.'

'So I guess you *can* tell a book by its cover, huh?'

'In this case,' I said.

'Anyway, he was very nice to me.'

'Where did you find him?'

'He found me. I was down on the Santa Monica beach about two o'clock in the morning.'

It took a moment for that to sink in. Then I could hardly believe I'd heard her right. 'The *beach*? At two in the *morning*? That's crazy! You're lucky you didn't get killed.'

'Funny you should say that.' She gave me an odd look, raising both her eyebrows and one corner of her mouth. 'As a matter of fact, I probably came pretty close to getting killed that night. I ran into these three guys . . .'

'What the hell were you *doing* on the beach at that hour?'

'What do you think? Looking for someone to murder Bill for me. You're looking for someone like that, you don't go to the country club. You go to where the bad guys are.'

'But, my God . . .'

'Do you want to hear about it or don't you?'

'Yeah. I'm sorry. Go ahead.'

'So I had this run-in with these three guys on the beach. I knew right off, when I saw them coming, that they'd be trouble. So I ran for it. I almost got away, too. I'm pretty fast on my feet when I want to be. But one of them was *really* quick. Probably some sort of high-school sprinting champ, or something. He took me down with this flying tackle. Then all three of them . . . They pounded the crap out of me and raped me.'

She drank some more beer, then sighed, then stared out the

windshield for a while as if remembering it all. After a minute or two of silence, she said, 'They were gone when I came to. So were my clothes and purse. Everything. I was freezing my tail off and bleeding from all over the place. I hurt so much that I could hardly move. And I was wondering how in hell I would ever get home.'

'How far away was your car?' I asked.

'At home. I'd walked. It's only two or three miles from my place to the beach. I figured I'd have a better chance of meeting a potential killer if I went by foot. But walking home was going to be a big problem. I mean, I could hardly move, much less take a three-mile hike. And I was naked. I didn't want anybody to see me. Especially not cops; they'd pick me up for sure. I didn't know what to do. I cried, of course.'

'Sure,' I said.

'I cry a lot.'

'You've got a lot of reasons.'

'Nah, I'm just a weenie.' She tried to smile. 'Anyway, I was bawling my head off and crawling through the sand when Elliot showed up.'

'What was *he* doing on the beach at that hour?'

'God knows, probably out looking for dinner. But I wasn't it. Maybe he'd already dined by the time he found me. Who knows? He scared me at first. I could tell just by looking that he was a dangerous character. I half expected him to take up where the *three pigs* had left off – and then maybe finish me off. But he was fine. The first thing he did was whip off his cape and put it around me.'

'He was wearing his cape?'

'He *always* wore his cape.'

'Did he have anything on under it?'

'Sure. Black sweats.' She smiled. 'It was cold out there.'

'I thought maybe he *always* went naked under it.'

'No. Only indoors. And maybe on hot nights? I never asked him a lot of questions. At the time, I just figured he was some sort of flamboyant eccentric – a guy who maybe roamed around at night because he was too ugly for daylight. Anyway, I sure appreciated the cape. There's nothing colder than a beach at night, especially when you're dressed in nothing but your birthday suit. Makes you appreciate the heat.'

'Should we turn off the air-conditioner?' I asked. It was pumping a chilly wind into the car. I realized I was shivering and had goosebumps, but I don't think it was all because of the air-conditioning.

'Oh, I don't think so,' Cat said. 'I think we're just fine. Turn it off, and we'll cook.' She drank some more beer. 'So that's how I met Elliot. He came to my rescue. Not that he saved me from those dirty pigs that attacked me, but at least he came through for me in the aftermath. He wrapped me up in his cape and carried me to his car.'

'He had a car?'

'A hearse, actually.'

'Wow.'

'Figures, huh?'

'I'm surprised he didn't fly you home.'

'On bat wings? No. That would've aroused my suspicions for sure.'

'And the hearse didn't?'

'He told me he was a funeral director. But I wasn't in much of a suspicious mood at that point. I just wanted to get home, and I was thanking my lucky stars for Elliot. He acted like a real gentleman. Never tried any funny stuff. He drove me straight home and carried me to my front door.'

'Where was Bill during all this?'

'San Francisco. Some kind of medical convention. This was a Saturday night, and he wasn't due to get home until Monday afternoon, so he was well out of the picture.'

'How did you get into your house? It was locked, wasn't it?'

'Sure. But we kept a spare key back in the garage. I sent Elliot to get it, and I waited on the porch.'

'Just curious. I wonder about stuff like that.'

'The writer in you.'

'I guess. So, what happened after you got inside?'

'I took a bath for about an hour.' Giving me an odd look, she said, 'I always like to take a nice, long bath after I've been beaten up and raped. You're not supposed to, you know. You're supposed to call the cops, and they take you someplace for crime samples. Somebody swabs you out for semen specimens. They comb your pubic hair, if you've got any. I went through all that one time, but never again. A whole different story. The thing is, I know you're not *supposed* to take a bath, but I do it anyway. And I did it that night . . . morning. It was about three o'clock in the morning by then.'

'Had Elliot gone home?'

'No, he waited.' Shrugging one shoulder and giving me sort of a half-embarrassed smirk, she said, 'He stayed with me in the bathroom.'

'While you took your bath?'

'Sure. I didn't care. I mean, I was naked when he found me. He'd been nice. He hadn't tried to jump me or anything. I was still scared by everything that'd happened, and in a lot of pain. I figured if he wanted to keep me company, fine. Whatever. Besides, he was so ugly I sort of felt sorry for him. He probably didn't have much of an opportunity for this sort of thing. And I was glad to have someone there.'

'How nice for him.'

'Take it easy, Sam.'

'Well, jeez.'

'Maybe you'd rather not hear about this.'

'No, I do. I'm sorry. It's just . . .' I shook my head. 'You've got no reason to be jealous of Elliot.'

'I know,' I said.

I knew no such thing.

I envied him for finding Cat on the beach that night, for being able to wrap her in his cape and carry her to his car, for getting to be with her for an hour while she bathed.

I envied him for plenty more than that, too.

'We didn't *do* anything,' she said. 'I took my bath and he sat on the toilet seat and we talked. He seemed . . . very concerned about me. Worried. We talked for a very long time. After I was done with my bath, we went downstairs to the living room and I made us drinks and we kept on talking.'

'What . . . ?'

'I was wearing his cape. He put it on me after my bath, and . . .'

'I was going to ask what he had to drink.' That wasn't the truth. I had been about to ask what she'd been wearing.

'Ah.' She smiled. 'Vodka martinis.'

Her answer took me by surprise. 'He actually drank booze?'

'He had three martinis.'

'Do vampires *do* that?'

'He did. Anyway, I had no inkling he might be a vampire.'

'Thought he was maybe James Bond?'

'That's right. A very ugly James Bond. But he was suave and considerate and he seemed *very* concerned about my welfare. We kept talking and talking ... almost always about me. He was very vague and mysterious about himself.'·

'With good reason,' I said.

'Yeah. As it turns out. But I finally ended up telling him what was going on. It started with him wanting to know why I was on the beach at that hour of night. I beat around the bush for a long time ... I'd never actually *told* anyone that I wanted a killer. I'd always just ... felt people out and tried to decide whether I could trust them ... and decided I couldn't. But Elliot and I kept on talking and after I'd had a couple of drinks myself, I told him the truth: that I was out there looking for somebody to murder my husband. He stared into my eyes and held my hands and said, "Why would you want someone to do that?" So I told him.'

'About the abortion?'

'No. No, I couldn't tell him about that. I wanted to ... thought I *ought* to, but...' She shook her head. 'It hurt too much to talk about. What I told Elliot was that Bill was sleeping around and I was afraid he might give me AIDS, and that he beat me up all the time. Which was all true, by the way. Maybe he didn't beat me up *all* the time, but he'd done it enough. Elliot certainly seemed to believe me. He listened to every word and he got this *look* in his eyes. This wild, eager look. He actually seemed *enthralled* by it all. I could tell that I had him hooked, so I really poured it on. I told him some pretty nasty details about things Bill had done to me. Sexual things. Bloody things. Elliot got all breathless and kind of scary. I still had no idea he might be a vampire, but I figured he must be some kind of weird pervert or something to get that excited by what I was telling him. A sadist, maybe. Which seemed like a fine quality in a guy if you want him to do murder for you.'

'Is that why you came to me?'

'*Or* find a sweet guy who's nuts about you.'

'That's better.'

Her can was empty. She tossed it over her shoulder. I kept working on mine.

'I didn't even have to ask Elliot. We were on the couch in my living room. He was on his third martini. I just got done telling him about the time Bill carved his initial in my buttocks and licked the blood off, when . . .'

'He *did* that?'

'Bill? Sure. He did a lot of stuff. Including that. He did *that* with a scalpel on our honeymoon.'

'On your *honeymoon*?'

'It wasn't exactly a marriage made in heaven.'

'My God.'

'Anyway, Elliot was just *salivating* when I told him that one. Should've been a clue, huh? Then he blurted out, "*I'll kill him for you! I'll cut off the fucker's head!*"'

'And he did, too. Cut it off. Literally.'

30

'We didn't want the killing to look planned,' Cat said. 'We figured, if I knew it was coming, I might do something unusual. I might let something slip, or try to be away so I'd have some kind of alibi. I might, you know, make some kind of stupid mistake that'd seem suspicious to the cops. We wanted it to be as much a surprise to me as it was to Bill.'

'I bet that was your idea,' I said.

'Right.' Her smile seemed a little sad. 'I'm the tricky one.'

I finished my beer, and tossed it over my shoulder. It must've hit the handle of the shovel or pick-ax back there. I flinched a little.

'It was supposed to look authentic,' Cat said. 'That was the thing. The spouse is always a suspect, you know? We really had to make it look good. I'd be a victim, too. That was the idea. The only difference between me and Bill is that *I'd* survive the attack, and he wouldn't.'

'Wouldn't the cops see through a trick like that?' I asked.

'They'd try. I mean, people pull this stuff sometimes. They

200

shoot themselves in the foot, cut their own arm, that kind of thing, and say it was done by the attacker. The cops probably *look* for that. But I figured they wouldn't get suspicious if Elliot did a good enough job attacking me. So I made it clear to him. "You can't just rough me up a little," I said. "You've gotta do some real damage." He said, "Don't worry, I'll take care of it." Turns out, he meant it.

'The other part of the plan was to wait till I'd healed. I was pretty bashed up from the attack on the beach, and we didn't want the cops to think Bill had been a wife-beater. That would've given me a motive to have him killed, you know? So I suggested that I might give Elliot a call to let him know when I was healed enough. He said we shouldn't have any sort of contact till after the deed. And he said it wouldn't be necessary, anyway – he'd keep an eye on me. He'd know when I was ready. That seemed a little creepy to me, but I went along with it. Made it better, too. That way, I wouldn't know when to expect the attack and I'd be taken by surprise the same as Bill.

'And, man, *was* I. About three weeks went by. On the night it happened, it was the *last* thing I expected ... My God. We'd gone out to dinner. It was my birthday, of all things, and Bill took me to the Ruth's Chris Steak House in Beverly Hills. We had a couple of drinks, a fabulous dinner. Elliot was the farthest thing from my mind.

'When we got home, we drank champagne in the living room – knocked down the whole bottle. We both got a little looped. Then Bill gave me a birthday present. It was a nightgown from Victoria's Secret. See-through, of course. And beautiful. So we went up to the bedroom and I slipped into it. He had me model it for him. Then he put on some music and told me to climb up on the bed and dance. He wasn't interested in dancing *with* me. He just wanted me to do a solo, like a stripper. I didn't want to. But he insisted, and I knew how these things went. If I didn't do it, he'd get ugly with me. So I climbed up on the bed and started to dance for him. I felt like an idiot, at first. And embarrassed. It was awfully humiliating to stand up there and just ... show off like that. But then ... I don't know, I started getting into the spirit of things. I mean, I was a little smashed, anyway. And this *was* my birthday, and I was wearing this slinky, sexy nightgown and

Bill was gaping up at me like I was Salome doing the Dance of the Seven Veils. Before long, I was really going to town. Man, did I give Bill an eye-full! Elliot, too, as it turns out – he was hiding in the closet and watching everything.'

Like me last night.

A lot like me.

Only last night, I'd been the guy in the closet, Elliot the one messing with Cat.

'I didn't know he was there,' Cat said. 'I had no idea. After I got going, I hardly even knew that *Bill* was still in the room. I was just so caught up in the dancing. I was going totally wild. It felt great.

'Then suddenly Bill came up on the bed. Without any clothes on. I never saw him take them off. He was just suddenly leaping around naked on the mattress with me. I didn't like it. He'd interrupted, you know? He'd broken the spell. He'd ruined it for me. Just like he'd ruined everything else. So I stopped dancing and shoved him. It was a good shove, too. I sent him flying off the end of the bed and he landed on the floor. The whole bedroom shook. He wasn't hurt, though. He pushed himself up with his elbows and smiled at me. It was his bad smile . . . the one he uses when I'm about to really get it.

'Then he said, "Come down here."

'He had more than just that awful smile; he had an erection. His fall hadn't bothered that. It was sticking straight up, and I knew he had plans for it and me. I started crying. You should try crying some time when you're already out of breath. It *hurts*. And I could hardly talk. I kept trying to tell him I was sorry and I'd never do anything like that again and how he ought to spare me because it's my birthday, but I was gasping and sobbing the whole time. A real mess. You should've seen me, Sammy.'

I *wished* I'd been there to see her.

But I pictured her easily in my mind – especially the way she was breathless and sweaty from so much dancing. She looked as if she'd just finished running a mile. Her nightgown was clinging to her skin, transparent as a wet veil.

'If you'd been there,' she said, 'you would've helped me.'

I nodded.

'You wouldn't have just stayed in the closet and watched.'

'No way.'

'That's what Elliot did. Can you believe it? He didn't lift a finger to help. Bill kept telling me to come down off the bed, but I wouldn't do it. I stayed up there and cried and pleaded with him until he got up off the floor and came after me. He leaped up onto the mattress. I backed away from him, but he kept coming. Then I was stepping on pillows and my back hit the wall. He got me by the throat. And he gave me that smile again. The one that says, "You're really in for it now." Then he bounced the back of my head off the wall. Not enough to knock me out, just enough to hurt like hell. Then he used his other hand to rip the nightgown off me. He just shredded it. Then he started in on me. Held me against the wall with his left hand clutching me by the throat, and worked on me with his right.

'I couldn't fight back. I couldn't even breathe. I couldn't plead with him or scream. All I could do was stand there and take it.

'He used pinches and twists and slaps, things like that. Keeping it all below the neck. He always wanted to keep my face looking good, no matter what. So he concentrated on my breasts. And my ... you know, genital area. Sometimes he used to go for my rear end, but not that night. That night, I had my back to the wall so he was working on my front. And smiling while he did it.

'Elliot watched it all happen. Never lifted a finger. He was there to *kill* the filthy bastard, but he just stayed in the closet and enjoyed the show while Bill twisted my nipples and ... worked on me till I was shuddering against the wall like a sweaty piece of ...' She shook her head and didn't finish the simile. 'I couldn't even come *close* to standing up. When Bill finally let go of my throat, I just crumpled. He didn't let me fall, though. He caught me under the armpits and hoisted me up and slammed my back against the wall again and this time he shoved his cock into me.'

I took my eyes off the dirt road and looked at her.

She was gazing straight forward as if watching her story on a movie screen – and entranced and sickened by it.

'He had me up there pinned to the wall so my feet didn't even touch the bed. And he kept, you know, *ramming* into me. Holding me up there and ... grunting and ... I thought he'd never finish. It felt like he had me up there forever. Later, the backs of my heels were all black and blue from thrashing around and pounding them against the wall during the whole thing. But he finally ... He was grunting and ramming and whimpering and I could feel him starting to ... you know, come. And then all of a sudden he didn't have a head anymore.

'Elliot had waited till then. Having a good time watching, I guess. Enjoying the show. Letting Bill hurt me and ... Anyway, I had no idea he was there, not even when he sneaked out of the closet. Bill was doing that to me, and all of a sudden his head flew off his neck. It sort of leaped straight up at first, then went tumbling over and falling sideways. It was so odd. I had no idea what was going on. It was like seeing some sort of bizarre magic trick. Except for the blood. A spray of blood just *exploded* against me. Slapped me across the face like a wet rag. And my shoulders and chest. Afterwards, you could see where I'd been standing. I'd left like an empty portrait of myself on the wall – invisible girl, surrounded by blood.

'Anyway, when it happened, Bill kept standing there. He was still on his feet, pinning me to the wall with his hands under my armpits and his cock in me. It was like nothing had happened, except he didn't have a head anymore.

'Where his head used to be, there was blood spurting up. And I saw Elliot through it, standing back there, standing on the mattress near the foot of the bed with a sword in his hands. It was a huge thing. Like knights of the round table use in the movies.'

'A broad sword?'

'Yeah. One of those. God.' Cat squeezed her eyes shut and shook her head. 'His mouth was wide open. He had the fangs in. That was the first time I ever saw them. He looked like he didn't have any clothes on, but the cape was hanging behind him. That's all he wore. And *he* was aroused. He had this horrible, mammoth erection. I noticed all this in just about a second. Bill hadn't even let go of me yet, or ...' She hesitated a moment, then said, 'Elliot suddenly swung the sword again. This time, it chopped Bill in half. Right across the waist. That's when he let go of me. His torso went dropping off sideways, but ... the rest of him still stood there. And he was still ...' She shook her head roughly from side to side. 'I didn't have Bill holding me up against the wall anymore, so *I* fell. His legs and ... he went over backward ... his ... his bottom half ... and I fell on top of him.' Shaking her head, she muttered, 'I really can't ...'

She took quick, deep breaths and gazed out the windshield. I kept driving, staying a fair distance behind the van to keep out of its dust.

Pretty soon, I started to wonder when we were going to reach our destination.

We'd been on this back road for a long time.

Now that Cat had stopped telling her story, I realized how the beer had gotten to me. She was probably feeling the same way, but she hadn't mentioned it yet.

I could hold it a while longer, I supposed.

But Cat hadn't finished. She said, 'What happened after that ... after he chopped Bill in half ... I don't think I can talk about it. It's too ... horrible.'

'Worse than ...?'

'It was. If I ... just thinking about it ...' She shook her head some more, then took a deep breath and said, 'That's when I found out ... the truth about Elliot. The things he did ... He started in on Bill's body. I just watched. I must've been in shock from everything else. So I just watched what he did. But then it suddenly registered and I freaked out and ran for the window. I tried to dive out, but hit the screen. I told you about that, didn't I?'

'Yeah.'

'The screen stopped me, and Elliot grabbed me. He threw me on the floor. I landed on Bill's head.' She turned toward the side window and said, 'Then Elliot did his stuff to me.'

She went silent again, and kept staring out her window.

After a while, she said, 'I ended up in the hospital for two weeks because of what he did.' Facing me, she made a wry smile. 'The good news is, the cops never even came close to accusing me of the murder. *Nobody'd* go through what I did. Not on purpose. Not just to make it look good. So my plan was a smashing success. They thought we'd been attacked by some kind of maniac.'

'And they were right,' I added.

'Yeah. That's for sure. Anyway, they did a full investigation, but never came up with any good suspects. Never even found out anything at all about Elliot. But then one night about a week after I got home from the hospital, he showed up.'

'For his money?' I asked.

'No. I'd paid him up front the night we made our plans.'

'The night he brought you home from the beach?'

'Right. I had ten thousand dollars in cash hidden away, and gave it to him before he left so there'd be no reason to get in touch again.'

'You paid him the whole amount in *advance*?'

'It seemed safer that way.'

'He might've ripped you off.'

'I wish he *had*.'

'Yeah,' I said. 'Yeah.'

'Bill was no prize, but Elliot was worse. A lot worse. If I'd had any idea . . . But it's like they say, "You make your bed, you sleep in it." Except I didn't do much sleeping anymore.

'Do you know what Elliot did, that first night he dropped in? He brought me a present. A see-through nightgown from Victoria's Secret. Identical to the birthday present from Bill. Then he made me put it on and climb onto the bed and dance for him.'

'You're kidding,' I said.

'I didn't want to do it, that's for sure. But I was afraid to refuse. I mean, I'd seen Elliot in action. I wanted to stay on his good side.'

'I can understand that.'

'He wanted a *reenactment*,' Cat said. 'With me in the role of me, and him in the role of Bill. So I went along with it. We played it out . . . almost exactly the way it had happened that other night, the way he'd seen it happen from the closet. But at the crucial moment, when he had me pinned up against the wall with his hands jammed under my armpits and he was starting to come, just like Bill'd done, he sank his fangs into the side of my neck.'

Fucked her and sucked her.

Simultaneously.

'After that . . . he stayed for a few hours and had himself a lot more fun with me. Then he finally left, but he came back again the next night. And the night after that. I guess I've already filled you in on some of that. How he gave me nights off, once in a while, so I'd have time to recover.'

'Yeah,' I said.

'God forbid I should drop dead on him. Anyway ... it went on for about a year and felt like about a hundred. The stuff he did ... not just cruel stuff; some of it was *evil*. I can't even talk about it – things he did to me, and made me do. Sometimes with other people. Strangers he'd bring over. Prisoners. Most of them ended up dead. Sometimes, he made *me* kill them.'

'You *killed* people?'

She nodded, then said quickly, 'I've gotta take a leak or I'm gonna explode.'

'Me, too.'

'All that beer,' she said.

'I guess I'll just stop.'

'Maybe you'd better honk first. We don't want White to think we're trying to pull something.'

'Right,' I said, and beeped the horn.

Then I slowed down, beeped a couple more times, and stopped the car. Up ahead of us, the van came to a halt. Its cloud of dust blew sideways, spread out and sailed away on the breeze.

31

Because we were in such a hurry to get it done – afraid White might suspect a mutiny and hurt Donny or Peggy – we didn't go off into the desert to find privacy. Instead, we leaped out, left our doors open to obstruct the view of us from the van, and peed beside the car.

The heat out there was astonishing. It felt *heavy*. It pressed down on my shoulders and on my hair. I felt as if someone were ironing my shirt while I wore it.

Within about two minutes, I was zipped up and back in the car with my door shut.

Cat took longer. It seemed like a *lot* longer, because the air-conditioner couldn't compete with hot desert air coming in through her open door. At last, she flung herself into her seat with one hand holding her cut-offs up, swung the door shut, then sighed and zipped up her shorts. 'It's an oven out there,' she said.

'I noticed.'

'My God.'

I started driving forward, but the van didn't move.

It stayed put.

'Now what?' Cat said.

'I don't know,' I said.

I drove slowly up to the van and stopped a few feet from its rear.

Cat and I glanced at each other. She looked a little worried.

I had that sick feeling inside, the way you get when you're expecting bad news.

The driver's door of the van swung open.

Peggy hopped down, her dress rising so I saw for myself that she had no panties on.

The way the road curved, the van was at enough of an angle for Cat to see her, too.

'Told you so,' she said.

'Yeah.'

The wind flapped Peggy's dress against her skinny legs, tossed it this way and that, and flung her hair all around as she walked toward us.

I set the parking brake, then cranked my window down.

Bending over to look in, Peggy put her hands on the sill. But she suddenly gasped and jerked her hands off it as if they'd touched a hot skillet. She stood up straight. Then she took a couple of steps backward and bent her knees until her face was level with the window.

She had the sunglasses on, so I couldn't see her eyes. The rest of her face was shiny with sweat. Loops of hair clung to her forehead and cheeks. Above the top of her dress, her chest gleamed. The thin, pale blue straps of her top were dark with wetness. So was the fabric down both her sides and between her breasts. She looked awfully hot and miserable.

'What's going on?' Cat called to her from the passenger seat.

'He wants to trade,' Peggy said.

'What kind of trade?' I asked.

'Me for Cat.'

The bottom seemed to drop out of my stomach.

'I'm s'pose to ride with you,' she told me, 'and Cat goes in the van with him and Donny.'

'What for?' I asked.

''Cause he says so.'

'What does he want with her?'

'He didn't say.'

'I'll go,' Cat said.

I turned on her. 'No, you won't. Sit still.'

'She's gotta,' Peggy said. 'He'll kill Donny if she don't.'

'I have to do it,' Cat said. 'This is all my fault.'

'No. He wants to mess around with you.'

'I've been messed around with before.'

'Not on my watch.'

'I'll be all right.' She reached for her door handle.

I grabbed her left hand by the wrist and said, 'No.'

'Sam.'

'No. No way. We've been through this before. You don't go to the van.'

'He's gonna cut off Donny's head!' Peggy blurted.

'Let him. He's not getting Cat.'

'Sam. Let me go.'

'No.'

Cat studied my eyes. Her own eyes looked strange. They seemed urgent and angry . . . but grateful. 'I've got to do what Snow White wants.'

'No you don't.' I faced Peggy. 'Go back to the van and tell him that Cat stays here. If he wants a change of drivers, he can have me. He can trade you for me, but not for Cat.'

Peggy shook her head so hard she looked crazy. 'You're gonna get my brother killed!'

'He won't kill Donny,' I said. 'Just think about it. Donny's his only hold on us. So go back and tell White that he can have me if he wants me, but no way does he get his hands on Cat.'

Tears dribbled down from behind Peggy's sunglasses and ran down her cheeks. 'You dirty rotten bastard,' she said.

'Take it easy, Peggy,' Cat called to her.

'Well, he is!'

'Did you take our knife?' Cat asked. The question, such an abrupt change of subject, took me by surprise.

'Huh?' Peggy asked.

'The knife we had in the back seat. Did you take it when you were here for the food?'

She pulled off the sunglasses. Squinting, she wiped the tears from her eyes. She put the glasses back on, sniffed and said, 'So what if I did?'

'That's a yes,' I muttered.

'Did you take it for the salami, or what?' Cat asked.

'That's my business.'

'Planning to use it on White?'

'Maybe.'

'What are you waiting for?' I said.

'I can't just . . . He's so big. If I can't get him by surprise . . .' She shook her head. 'I've been looking for a good chance, but all I gotta do is go at him and blow it, and he'll kill the both of us.'

'Where *is* the knife?' Cat asked.

'Under my seat.'

'Underneath the driver's seat?'

'Yeah. I snuck it down under there when he wasn't looking.'

I said, 'If he wasn't looking, you should've snuck it into his throat.'

'Take it easy, Sam.'

'She wants to save her brother, but she's afraid to go for the kill.'

'I can't blame her for that. White's a monster. He'll be hard to kill. He probably would've taken the knife from her and shoved it up her ass.'

The van's horn tooted.

'We're taking too much time,' Peggy said. 'Come on, Cat. You've gotta . . .'

'She doesn't gotta,' I said. I still had a good, solid grip on Cat's wrist to enforce my point. 'You go back and tell White to forget about it. He can keep you for his driver, or he can have me. But he can't have Cat. And remind him that we've been very cooperative so far. We could turn around and drive away. The only thing stopping us is that we don't want you and

Donny to get hurt. Tell him that. And tell him we'll leave if he causes any more trouble. We can outrun that old van of yours. Tell him that.'

Peggy shook her head. 'Cat, you gotta help us.'

'I'd like to.'

Though she said it, she didn't try to break my grip on her wrist.

I said, 'Tell White I won't let her...'

The horn started honking again, this time beeping four or five times. Apparently, White was losing his patience.

'Better get going,' I said.

'I hate you, you dirty bastard.'

'Get going.'

She whirled away and walked toward the van.

'She'd probably make an interesting passenger for you,' Cat said.

'I'm not interested.'

'Do you want to let go of me, now?'

'Do you promise not to try anything?'

'Yeah. Hey, don't think for a minute that I want to ride with that guy.'

'I know,' I said.

Even as I let go of her wrist, though, it crossed my mind that maybe Cat *would* like to ride with him. Not consciously – aside from anything else, she'd been the one who got us away from White back at the restaurant – but perhaps she had something inside her that drew her to vicious men. She'd gone through hell at the hands of her husband and Elliot and at least a few strangers like those who'd attacked her on the beach.

She'd walked right into those nasty situations almost as if she *wanted* trouble: as if she had a secret urge for the pain and humiliation and brutal sex.

You can't blame her for...

I stopped thinking about all that when Peggy reached the open door of the van. She faced the door, but didn't climb in. Instead, she started to talk. Her lips and chin moved, but I couldn't hear anything she said. Not with the noises of the engine and air-conditioner and the wind outside.

'He's not going to go for it,' Cat said.

Peggy started shaking her head and making frantic gestures

with her hands. Whatever White was telling her, she didn't like it. She even pointed at me and jabbed the air with her finger. Then she faced the open door, shook her head from side to side and put out her open hands, palms up, as if she were pleading with a teammate to pass her the basketball.

'She's begging him,' Cat said.

Suddenly, Peggy threw her arms wide and cried out, 'NO!' I heard that, all right. The sound of it ripped my breath out.

The next instant, she leaped into the van. She seemed to be clambering over the driver's seat, probably on her knees. We could only see her feet sticking out. Then she suddenly dropped backward with a quick lurch as if she'd been punched. For a moment, she looked as if she were crawling upside-down. Then her back hit the ground. She struck it hard. Her arms slapped down on both sides of her. Dust flew up around the edges of her body.

The wind blew the dust away.

She lay there on her back with her knees in the air.

'I'd better go,' Cat said. 'This isn't looking good.' She opened her door.

I reached for her, but she'd already swung her left arm across her chest to keep it away from me. As she lunged out the door, I caught the side of her shirt. All I got was a fragile hold with my fingertips. She jerked away from me and ran.

Pulling myself up, I saw her rush around the front of our car.

Peggy, still on her back, lifted her head and tried to push herself up on her elbows.

I shoved open my door. As I climbed out, Cat shouted, 'I'll do it, White! I'm here! Leave the kid alone!' Holding her arms high as if surrendering, she jogged toward the driver's door of the van.

'Cat, no!' I shouted. 'Don't! Get back here! Please!'

She hurried straight for the van's door.

I dropped back down behind the wheel, released the parking brake, jammed the shift lever to drive and stomped the gas pedal to the floor. The engine roared. The tires shrieked. The car took off like a shot. Cat, standing on the running board, already had one foot in the van. She was reaching for the steering wheel.

Her head snapped sideways. Her eyes widened. Her mouth dropped.

She made a last-ditch effort to climb in. She didn't make it, though. She was one-foot-in, one-foot-out, and hadn't yet grabbed the wheel when I crashed into the rear of the van.

My arms folded and my forehead bounced off our steering wheel.

But I saw Cat twisting and prancing away·from the van, waving her arms and trying not to fall.

Keeping my foot on the gas, I plowed the van forward.

I didn't step on the brake until I was next to the women. The car stopped, but the van kept rolling. My guess – White was having trouble making his way to the brake.

I set our emergency brake, opened the door and jumped out.

Peggy was already on her feet, panting for air and gaping in shock at the van. A strap had slipped off her shoulder. Her top had fallen away, on that side, leaving her breast bare. It was a pale, low knoll, so small that it would probably go flat if she raised her arm overhead. But the nipple was big and dark and erect.

Though I thought she was watching the van, she had those sunglasses on. Somehow, she caught the direction of my gaze, said, 'Bastard,' and quickly covered up. With her breast out of sight and the strap on her shoulder, she turned her head toward the van.

So did I.

Just in time to see one of its brake lights come on – the one I hadn't smashed to oblivion with the car.

I looked at Cat. She was standing on a narrow ridge of dirt beside the road a little up the road from Peggy. She swatted dust off the seat of her shorts and watched the van stop.

I latched my eyes on the van.

I think we all expected it to back up.

But it just sat there.

We gazed at it.

A minute or two went by, the three of us just standing there and staring at the van. Then it started moving again.

But not toward us.

213

'He's leaving!' Peggy shouted. Then she yelled, 'NO! COME BACK!'

The van kept going, picking up speed, throwing dust into the air behind it.

'COME BACK!' Peggy shouted again. She broke into a run.

Not saying a word, Cat leaped off the ridge of dirt a moment after Peggy ran by and tackled her.

32

I'd been ready to chase down and stop Cat if she should make a run for the van, but I stood there shocked when she hurled herself at Peggy, wrapped her arms around the girl's waist and tore her off her feet.

Peggy went down hard on her side, skidding and rolling through the dirt, her sunglasses and both her flip-flop sandals flying off, Cat clinging to her. Dust flew up around both of them.

The van kept going.

Peggy fought to free herself from Cat. She thrashed and squirmed and kicked, grunted and whimpered. But it didn't last long. Very quickly, Cat scurried on top of her, straddled her hips, leaned forward and caught hold of her wrists and pinned them to the ground.

Peggy quit struggling. Sprawled on her back under Cat, she panted for air. The tackle had torn both of her dress straps loose. She was naked down almost to her waist. The pale blue dress was bunched around her middle – where Cat was sitting on it. Her legs were wide apart.

She had a few scratches and scrapes on her legs. There was a little blood, but not much. Her legs and groin were powdered with dust. In places where she was wet, the dust looked like pale clots of mud.

I didn't want to keep standing where I could see her like that, so I started walking forward.

And noticed that the van had come to a halt. It was stopped just beyond a curve in the road at least two hundred yards away.

'Get off me,' Peggy gasped.

Cat ignored her.

Still leaning forward and pressing Peggy's hands against the dirt, she raised her head to peer up the road. 'What's he doing?' she asked.

'He's stopped,' I said.

'Doesn't want to lose us.'

'I'm sure he doesn't.'

'Get off! Let me up! Damn it, you dirty bitch!'

'Shut up,' Cat said, her voice calm.

'*He's got my brother!*'

'Well, he doesn't have you anymore. Lie still, and I'll let go of you.' Not waiting for a reply, Cat released the girl's wrists and sat up straight.

The moment her arms were free, Peggy crossed them over her breasts. She scowled up at me and muttered, 'Bastard.'

'Sorry,' I said.

'Fuck you,' she said.

'Knock it off,' Cat said. She turned her head and looked up at me. 'I think we should keep her.'

'No!' Peggy blurted. 'Let me go!'

'Why let White have *two* hostages?' Cat said to me. 'He's still got Donny. We can still go along with things and try to save the kid, but this way at least Peggy's safe.'

'He also loses his messenger,' I pointed out.

'Yeah. This'll screw him up a little. The more we can screw him up, the better.'

'He'll kill Donny!'

'Not a chance,' I said. 'He might've killed him when he still had you, but now Donny's all he's got.'

Cat frowned at me and said, 'We should've done this sooner.'

Then we both stared up the road.

The van still sat there. White was probably watching us in the side mirror.

Cat looked down at Peggy. 'I'm sorry if I hurt you. But it just suddenly seemed like a good idea to keep you away from White. I think he would've done something to you. I mean, he'd already knocked you out of the van on your ass because we wouldn't make the exchange.'

Peggy's eyes suddenly brimmed with tears and she blurted, 'He said he was gonna cut off Donny's ear!'

'Things are getting better,' I said. 'He *was* going to chop off the tyke's head.'

They both ignored me.

'He won't cut off Donny's ear,' Cat told Peggy, sounding very sure of herself and shaking her head from side to side.

'He was gonna make me bring it to you – so you'd change your minds about the trade. That's when I tried to get back in the van. I had to make him stop. But he kicked me out. Now he's gonna do it!'

'He was just trying to scare you,' Cat said.

'No, he wasn't!'

'I've known guys like him. Donny's a cute kid, I'll bet.'

'Yeah.'

'Well, White'll want to keep him that way. He won't cut off any ears. He won't do *anything* to deface the boy. You can count on that. I've been there.'

Maybe they'd left Cat's face alone, but they'd been tough on the rest of her body. She didn't tell that to Peggy, though, and neither did I.

'We want you riding with us from now on,' Cat said. 'Okay? It's for your own good. You'll be safe with us.'

Peggy sniffed and blinked. Her tears were making trails through the dust on her face. Her nose was running. She needed to wipe her face, but her arms stayed locked across her chest.

'Let's get in the car,' Cat told her, 'and catch up to the van.'

'How can I get up if you're sitting on me?'

'Good point,' Cat said.

But she didn't make a move to climb off.

Looking up at me, she said, 'You know that rope in the back seat? Why don't you get it?'

I nodded and went for the rope. After a little searching, I found it on the floor behind the driver's seat, down there under the shovel, pick, flat tire and jack. I got hold of one end and climbed backward out the door with it. While I tugged out the rest of the rope and worked it into a coil, I purposely kept my back to the women. I did glance up the road, though. The van still waited around the bend.

Still looking away from the women, I called, 'What do you want me to do with the rope, Cat?'

'Bring it over here.'

I turned around. Cat and Peggy had gotten up off the ground. Cat was watching her, but not holding on.

Peggy wore her sunglasses. She had pulled up and straightened her dress, and her hands were busy holding up the front to keep her breasts covered. The broken straps dangled behind her back. I saw that her flip-flops were on her feet again.

'Tie the rope around her waist,' Cat said.

'No!' Peggy protested. 'Hey! Nobody's gonna tie a rope around me!'

'Just stand still and go with the program,' Cat said, her voice calm.

'No!'

As I stepped behind Peggy, Cat said, 'I don't wanta have to tackle you anymore, that's all.'

I swung an end of the rope around Peggy's front and caught it with my other hand. Even though the rope hardly touched her, she flinched. But she made no struggle, maybe because she needed both hands for holding her top up.

'I'm not gonna *do* anything,' she said.

'We'll make sure of it,' Cat said, then crouched down and untied one of her shoes.

While I put a couple of half-hitches in the rope and cinched it in snugly around Peggy's waist, Cat removed the laces from both her high-topped hiking shoes.

When she was done, she kept her shoes on and came over to us. With the laces out, the shoes looked big and floppy and their tongues bulged.

I let out some rope and stepped out of the way. For the next few minutes, Peggy stood motionless while Cat used her laces to reconnect the straps to the front of Peggy's dress. It was a real makeshift job, but it worked.

I kept an eye on the van. It never moved.

'I'll take the rope,' Cat said.

I handed it to her.

'You go ahead and drive, Sam. We'll put Peggy in the passenger seat, and I'll sit in the back.'

That's what we did. Peggy sat with the rope around her

217

waist, the knot to her left. Cat, seated behind her, held the coil. The connecting length of rope was draped through the gap between the seatbacks.

After the doors were shut, Peggy said, 'You got *air*.'

'Traveling in air-conditioned comfort,' Cat said from behind her.

I started to drive. The car had been idling ever since I'd crashed it into the van, and seemed to be all right. Now we were moving, and I couldn't detect any troubles. Apparently, the car had weathered the impact with no significant damage.

'Our air's busted,' Peggy said.

'Must've been awfully hot in there,' I said.

She gave me a sour look and said, 'It wasn't so bad. Rather be there than here.'

'I thought White was messing around with you,' I said.

'So what if he was?'

'You were *crying* about it, last time we saw you. Back at the gas station. Now it's just "so what?"'

'Fuck you.'

The rope suddenly jerked, giving her a tug.

'Ow!' She snapped her head around. 'What're you *doing*?'

'Try to be nice,' Cat told her in that same calm voice she'd been using lately. 'We rescued you. You don't have to kiss our asses, but at least be polite.'

'I want to be with Donny!'

'You can be with Donny all you want,' Cat said, 'after we've taken care of White.'

I eased off the gas as we approached the rear of the van. Though I couldn't see White, I figured he must be in the driver's seat and watching us.

The van didn't start moving.

I stopped the car a few yards behind it.

'What the hell is he up to now?' Cat asked.

'Whatever it might be,' I said, 'he can't get out and tell us about it.'

'I hope he isn't just going to sit there.'

'Look what you did to my van,' Peggy said.

The rear bumper was crunched and I'd smashed the lights on the left side. Also, the metal ladder going up its back was caved in a little near its bottom rung.

'Sorry,' I said.

'Sorry,' she said. 'Real nice.'

'I'll see that it gets repaired for you.'

'If we save your brother,' Cat said from the back seat, 'you should call it even.'

The van's horn beeped.

I beeped back.

Cat chuckled.

Peggy blurted, 'You *assholes*!'

'Let's just see what he does,' Cat said.

'What *can* he do?' I said.

'Steam.'

'You think you're funny?' Peggy said.

'Psychological warfare,' Cat explained. 'If we screw with him enough, he might mess up.'

I tooted our horn a couple more times.

Up ahead, an arm came out of the driver's window. A thick, dark, muscular arm. It came out almost to the shoulder. It was bare; White had obviously taken off his buckskin jacket.

We were at an angle that prevented the women from seeing the left side of the van.

'White just stuck his arm out the window,' I reported. 'Now he's giving us the finger.'

'Cute,' Cat said.

I smiled, but kept my own arm inside and didn't return the gesture.

'We've got him rattled,' Cat added.

'If he does anything to Donny . . .'

'Knock it off,' Cat told her.

White pulled his arm inside, and the van started moving forward.

'All *right!*' Cat cried out – as if we'd won some sort of victory. I let out a shout of joy, myself, I felt such relief.

'I don't know what you two are so happy about,' Peggy said.

'I'm happy because he didn't jump out and come after us,' I explained.

'One thing *I'm* happy about,' Cat said, 'is that he didn't throw a severed portion of your brother out the window.'

'Very funny.'

Finding Cat's face in the rearview mirror, I said, 'Didn't you say he wouldn't do anything like that?'

'Turns out, I was right.'

'But you weren't too sure, huh?'

'I've been known to be wrong.'

'You two think you're funny.'

'We laugh at danger,' Cat said.

'We spit in the eye of trouble,' I added.

'You're assholes.'

'Do you know what?' Cat asked. 'We've accomplished fifty percent of our mission. We're only going through all this to save you and Donny. We've already rescued you and it isn't even dark yet. So I think we've got some pretty good reasons to be pleased with how things have gone so far. Why don't you have a beer?'

'She's under age,' I pointed out.

'So, who's counting?'

'I don't know,' I said. 'We'd be contributing to the delinquency of a minor.'

'We'd better drink them up while they're still cold.'

I looked over at Peggy. She was facing the windshield, her lips pressed together. I suddenly felt bad about kidding around. She'd been surly with us and she'd caused us trouble but she had a right to be upset; her brother was still White's prisoner and victim, and might end up dead.

'Why don't you go ahead and have a beer,' I said.

'Grab three of them,' Cat told her.

Saying nothing, Peggy bent over to reach down for them.

'Now that you're here,' I said, 'White has to be his own driver. He's behind the wheel right now.'

'Yeah? So what?'

'So it means he can't be messing around with Donny. He can't do that and drive at the same time.'

'At the very least,' Cat said, 'it would be awkward.'

Peggy sat up, put her legs together and rested three cans of beer on her lap. 'I guess maybe you might be right,' she muttered. Then she raised one of the cans over her shoulder and Cat took it from her.

'Thanks.'

Peggy didn't say anything.

'My guess,' I said, 'is that he's got Donny strapped into the passenger seat. Maybe tied up – secured somehow so the kid won't be able to attack him or try for a getaway.'

Peggy popped open a can, muttered, 'Here,' and passed it to me.

I thanked her.

She said in a quiet, tired voice, 'He had Donny in the back of the van with a belt around his feet. It was to stop him from kicking. The belt. We've got all our stuff back there. If he wanted to tie Donny up, there's a hundred things ... But he won't have to tie him up at all if he's dead.'

'If who's dead?' Cat asked.

'Donny.'

'Donny isn't dead.'

'How do you know?'

'We know,' I answered for Cat.

'At least we think we know,' Cat answered for herself.

'If he kills Donny,' I said, 'he'll be missing the chance of a lifetime.'

'Several lifetimes,' Cat added.

'You're both getting stupid again. What are you talking about?'

'Whitey wants to be a vampire,' Cat said. 'And he can't do it without us. We've got the magic ingredient in the trunk of our car.'

33

Peggy popped open her can of beer, lifted it to her mouth and took a drink. She winced and made a face. Then she turned toward me, bringing a knee up and resting an elbow on her seatback. From this position, she could look forward at me or over her shoulder at Cat. She took another swallow of beer, made another face, and said, 'This stuff's awful.'

'Don't drink it,' I told her. 'More for the rest of us.'

'Is it s'posed to taste like this?'

'Pretty much.'

She tried again, then looked at Cat and said, 'You're trying to be funny again, huh?'

'In what way?' Cat asked.

'This vampire shit.'

'It's no shit,' Cat said. 'Snow White wants to be a vampire. Honest injun.'

'You can't say "injun" anymore,' I told her.

'Honest native American.'

'That's better.'

'He does,' Cat said. 'Want to be a vampire.'

'Who're you trying to kid?' Peggy asked.

'Are you trying to say you don't believe in vampires?' I asked her.

'You're talking about Dracula, right? Or like *Salem's Lot*? I seen that movie, *Salem's Lot*. And that *Interview with the Vampire*? Seen that one, too. That Brad Pitt?' She almost cracked a smile.

'So you know what vampires are,' Cat said.

'Sure. Who doesn't? Do I look like a feeb? Only I sure don't *believe* in them.'

'That's their strength,' Cat pointed out.

'Who said that?' I asked. 'Van Helsing?'

'I did. Just now.'

'You didn't invent it.'

'Nobody believes in vampires,' Peggy broke in.

'We do,' I said.

'Sort of,' Cat added.

'White *definitely* believes in them.'

'He plans to *become* one,' Cat explained. 'That's what this is all about. The whole problem is, he found out we've got one in the trunk.'

Peggy said, 'One what?'

'A vampire,' I said.

'Sure you do.'

'A *dead* vampire.'

'I think that's redundant,' Cat pointed out.

'Right, in theory they're already dead. They're *un*dead. But ours is dead in addition to that.'

'In addition to being undead,' Cat said, 'our vampire has a stake through his heart. Which we put there last night.'

'You two are out of your minds.'

'It's been a tough day,' I told her.

'A tough day following a tough night,' Cat said.

'We haven't had a lot of sleep.'

'But we *have* had some beer.'

'Maybe too much beer,' I said, and took another drink.

'Which might go far,' said Cat, 'in explaining our semi-ebullient mood.'

I laughed and shook my head. 'Our mood,' I said, 'has less to do with beer and more to do with desperation.'

'Exactly,' Cat said. 'Vampires are tough on the nerves. We laugh to stave off madness.'

'You're both already mad.'

'Or at least very nervous,' I said.

Shaking her head and frowning, Peggy asked, 'What's in your trunk? A dead guy?'

'Okay,' Cat said. In the rearview mirror, I saw her take a swig of beer. Then she lowered the can and wiped her lips with the back of her hand. Then she took a deep breath and said, 'Here goes. About a year ago, I got myself involved with this guy named Elliot who turned out to be a vampire.'

'Sure.'

Ignoring the remark, Cat went on. 'I never saw him turn into a bat or any of that and I've got no idea how old he is . . . was. He might've just been a really . . . creepy, vicious guy who got a charge out of biting me and sucking my blood. He *did* bite me and suck my blood. Look at this.'

I watched in the rearview mirror as Cat slipped the shirt off her left shoulder and twisted sideways to show the neck wounds to Peggy. Thanks to me, they looked fresh. The pair of raw holes had stopped bleeding, but they were bright and wet.

Peggy pulled off her sunglasses and narrowed her eyes. She stared at Cat's neck. Then she said, 'Bullshit.'

'It's not bullshit,' I said.

'Nobody's got teeth that'll do that.'

'He has special teeth,' Cat explained. 'They're steel.'

'Sure.'

'Just his fangs. His canine teeth. He can slip them on and off when he wants to.'

'His vampire fangs,' I said.

'Yeah, right.'

'We could show them to her,' I told Cat.

'Not without opening the trunk. And we can't do that.'

'Why not?' Peggy asked.

'The sun,' Cat said.

'Oh. Right. Sure.'

'We'll be opening it after dark,' I said. 'She can see the fangs then.'

'Is that makeup?' Peggy asked.

Cat said, 'Touch,' and scooted forward and leaned toward us.

Peggy had to shift the beer can to her left hand, twist further sideways and reach across herself with her right arm. The awkward position pursed out the top of her dress and shoved her breasts together so they looked larger. I don't think she did it for my sake, though. She was just trying to reach through the gap between the seatbacks and touch Cat's neck. I tried to keep my eyes on the dirt road as much as possible.

Peggy said, 'Ooooo.'

'See?' Cat asked.

'Does it hurt?'

'Not that much. Not if you're careful.'

She lowered her arm, but stayed twisted. 'The guy in the trunk did it?'

'Yeah. Elliot. They're not as new as they look, though. We had a little accident a while ago.'

Peggy nodded slowly, then said, 'So if this guy in the trunk's a vampire and he did that to you, how come you aren't dead?'

'He didn't want me dead.'

'But he sucked your blood, didn't he?'

'Not enough to kill me.'

'This is all such bullshit.'

'White doesn't think so,' I pointed out.

'That's the problem,' Cat said. 'If White thought it was bullshit, we wouldn't be in this mess. He's a movie buff, or something. He's seen a million vampire movies, so now he thinks this is his big chance for immortality.'

224

'Or at least longevity,' I added.

'His big plan is to pull out the stake so Elliot can come back to life and turn him into a vampire.'

'That's crazy.'

'Tell us about it,' I said.

'He's nuts.'

'Looks like it,' Cat said.

'Some people believe what they see in the movies,' I explained.

'Nobody'd believe *that*.'

'He would,' Cat said. 'He does.'

'But he can't do anything till after dark,' I told Peggy. 'If we open the trunk before the sun goes down, Elliot gets toasted.'

'If you believe what you see in the movies,' Cat added.

'And White does. He seems to believe *all* the vampire crap. Which is a pretty good trick, since so much of it's contradictory. Like about crosses. The concensus is that your cross will usually save you.'

'Do you have a cross?' Cat asked Peggy.

'Not on me.'

'But the cross won't *always* save you,' I continued. 'Depends on the movie. Or the book.'

'We don't think White reads.'

'Depends on the *vampire*,' I continued. 'You get a Jewish vampire and you're shit out of luck in the cross department.'

Cat laughed.

'Or an athiest,' I added. 'Or *any* non-Christian variety of vampire.'

'I'd still bank on a cross,' Cat said.

Surprised, I asked, 'Did you ever try one?'

'Oh, yeah.'

'With Elliot?'

'Sure did. I picked up a gold cross on a necklace the day after he paid me his first visit. After the hospital.'

'What were you doing in a hospital?' Peggy asked.

Cat met my eyes in the rearview mirror and said, 'I had a little car accident. It didn't have anything to do with all this. Anyway, Elliot attacked me for the first time about a week after I got out of the hospital. The next day, I went to a mall and bought the cross. I could hardly get out of bed, I was so messed up. But I did. You get sucked by a vampire, you get yourself a cross. It's one of the basic rules.'

'What about garlic?' I asked.

'Got that, too. Did I ever. Bunches of it. Do you know what the check-out girl at Von's said to me? She grins and says "Vampire trouble?" She thought she was making a joke. I played dumb and said, "Italian boyfriend."'

'What about holy water?' I asked.

'I considered it, but figured it'd be tricky to lay my hands on. I guess you'd have to steal it from a Catholic church, and I wasn't in any mood for something like that. Besides, I had my cross and garlic. I wouldn't need holy water if they worked.'

'You *really* did that?' Peggy asked. 'Got a cross and garlic?'

'Sure.'

'Outa your mind.'

'So what happened?' I asked.

'I hung the garlic around my bedroom door and windows, and I wore the cross to bed that night. When Elliot showed up ... I heard my door open, so I sat up. My room was dark. We hadn't started with the candles yet, but a light was on in the hallway behind him. He had his cape on. And one arm was cradling a bunch of my garlic against his chest. He suddenly started to *throw* the garlic bulbs at me like baseballs.'

'Good God,' I muttered.

'They hurt, too. He had a good aim and he threw *hard*. I covered my face, but it probably wasn't his target anyway. I don't even know how he could see me – light from the hallway, maybe. He really nailed me with a few of the things. I had bruises later on.

'Then when he was done bouncing the garlic off me, he switched on the lamps and came in. He was grinning, but he was mad. He came at me so fast his cape was flying out behind him. He called me a stupid, fucking bitch. Then got to the end of the bed and grabbed me by the feet and started dragging me toward him. That's when he saw the necklace. He said, "Oh, you think you're so smart!" Then he pulled me by my ankles till I fell off the bed. My back and head hit the floor. Then he picked me up – shoved my feet almost to the ceiling so I was hanging completely upside-down in front of him. And he shook me and shook me. I didn't even realize what he was trying to do. I just knew he'd gone ballistic again and I half expected him to kill me. I would've taken it off. The necklace. The cross. He didn't have to do all that. But he loved it. He loved that sort of stuff.

'Anyway, the necklace wouldn't fall off. It had gotten hung up on the bottoms of my ears, with the cross dangling between my eyes. So then he started swinging me. He turned around in circles and swung me by my ankles ... around and around. It was like you see sometimes if you watch figure skating – the pairs. The guy swinging his partner around by her ankles.

'Elliot swooped me up and down as he swung me. My head almost hit the floor sometimes. Other times, he'd swing me toward the ceiling. He turned my body, too, so that I was looking up for a while, then I'd be looking down. The worst was when he had me going sideways – not up or down, but looking at the walls of the room. I was afraid he'd slam me face-first into the dresser or something.

'Finally, the necklace flew off. It hit the mirror over the dresser and cracked it.' She paused for a moment, then said, 'Maybe *that's* where the bad luck's coming from, huh, Sam?'

'*He* broke the mirror,' I said. 'It should be *his* bad luck, not yours.'

'It was my cross.'

'Maybe the bad luck gets split between the two of you,' I suggested.

'Three and a half years each?'

'Or you get it for the whole seven years, but only half as badly.'

'For godsake,' Peggy muttered. 'Who gives a shit? What happened *after* the cross broke the mirror? That's what *I* wanta know. Did Elliot let go and send you flying?'

'No,' Cat said.

'What *did* he do?'

'Bit me. *While* he was swinging me.'

'How did he bite you if he was ... ?'

'It's not a how question, it's a where question.'

'Where?'

Through the blowing cloud of dust in front of us, I saw the van's brake light come on.

'Heads up,' I said.

The dirt road kept going, curving gradually to the left, but the van slowed to a stop. I eased off the gas pedal. My foot hovered over the brake.

Peggy turned to the front.

Cat leaned forward until her face appeared between the seatbacks. 'Now what's going on?' she asked.

'I don't know,' I said.

The van turned right and started rumbling over the rough desert ground. I saw no road there. But I saw no major obstacles, either. Scattered rocks, cactus, sagebrush. Nothing to stop us unless we had bad luck.

I turned off the road, and followed the van.

The land threw us around.

'Take it easy,' Cat said.

I took my foot off the gas. As our speed decreased, so did the bouncing and bumping.

'I've got a feeling we're almost there,' Cat said.

I had a feeling she was right: it felt like something cold and heavy in my stomach.

34

'Aye-yi-yi,' I said a while later, trying to keep things light. We had finished our beers and I used both hands for the steering wheel. Though the car was chilly inside from the air-conditioning, the wheel felt slippery and the sides of my shirt were soaked from the armpits down to my waist.

'It's okay,' Cat said. She was leaning forward to see out the windshield, and clutching the seatbacks with both hands. Her image in the rearview mirror shook so much that she looked like a blur.

Peggy had put her seatbelt on.

We were driving up a slope near the base of a mountain range. My big fear was that we might start to slide backward and not be able stop.

'We'll be fine,' Cat said.

'I doubt it,' I told her.

'We can go wherever he can.'

White's van was above us, still climbing.

I glanced at Peggy. 'Are you sure you don't have four-wheel drive on that thing?'

'I'm sure.'

We slipped sideways a bit. I gasped and called out, 'This sucks!'

'Where are we *going*?' Peggy wanted to know.

'Wherever he leads us,' I said.

'Maybe to Brock's hole,' Cat said.

'What's that?'

'It's where he gave some guy the old heave-ho,' Cat explained.

'Who?'

'A guy named Brock who tried to steal his Harley.'

'Huh?'

'Yes!' I cried out. Ahead of us, above us, the van found level ground and scooted forward. 'I think we'll be all right.'

A few seconds later, the front of our car lowered and pointed itself at a narrow opening between two steep, towering walls. The van was just starting into it.

'How in hell did he find a place like this?' Cat asked.

'Maybe he was a pal of Butch and Sundance,' I said.

'Yeah, right,' Peggy said.

'That was a joke,' I explained.

'*Supposed* to be a joke,' Cat corrected me.

We followed the van into the gap. The rock walls shrouded us with shadows that seemed darker than shadows ought to be. I felt as if I were driving along the bottom of a deep gorge, but there was no river down here – just a bed of dirt and rock not much wider than our car.

It seemed to go on for a great distance. I could see no traces of sunlight ahead.

But the gorge couldn't go on forever. Soon, I knew, we would leave it behind, leave the deep shadows and emerge as if from a tunnel into glaring sunlight.

And stop.

We would have to be stopping soon; we were climbing into mountains and the terrain would only let us go so far before halting us.

229

Maybe just on the other side of this passage . . .

It scared me to think about stopping.

We were okay as long as we kept moving; nothing bad would happen until we stopped.

Even there, wherever that might be, we should be okay until after dark. But the place we stopped would be where it all would happen.

What was going to happen would happen there, and I dreaded our arrival.

'This'd be a good place to pull something,' Cat said. 'It'd be hard for him to see much.'

I took my foot off the gas and we slowed down. 'What do you think we should pull?' I asked.

'I'm not sure. Any ideas?'

'You're the tricky one,' I said.

'Somebody could get out of the car, I guess. Me, for instance.'

'And do what?'

'Maybe sneak up on him after we stop. He'd think we're all still in the car. I'd have the element of surprise.'

'You wanta get Donny killed?' Peggy asked.

'I want to save him. That's the whole point.'

'But we don't know what's coming,' I said. 'Or what White'll do when we get there. You might not be able to sneak up on him. And what if he finds out you're not in the car?'

'I don't know,' Cat said.

Peggy said, 'He'll kill Donny, that's what.'

'No, he won't,' I told her.

'We have to try *something*,' Cat said.

'But not here,' I told her.

And not you, I thought. *We're not going to risk you for these people, even if you* do *think it's your fault.*

I told her, 'We have to wait till we get where we're going.'

'It probably isn't very far from here.'

'Probably not,' I agreed, 'but we can't be sure. And what if you can't find us?'

'The thing is,' Cat said, 'this'd be a great place to trick him. We could pull *anything* with the shadows like this.'

'Let's pull backward and scram,' I suggested.

'Just try it and I'll kill you.'

'Hey!' Cat snapped, her voice sudden and loud and close to Peggy's ear. The girl flinched as if she'd been slapped. 'Any more talk like that, and we *will* leave.'

Peggy's chin started to tremble.

'Just keep going,' Cat told me. 'I can't think of anything. Not with Peggy this way.'

'Too bad,' I said.

Cat was right about this place. If we did nothing, we might be missing a good chance for tricking White and giving us an advantage. Maybe we could stash some weapons here. Or I could hop out and try a sneak attack on White. But what if the destination turned out *not* to be just ahead? What if, at the other end of the gap, he drove on and on? Maybe he would lead us through another pass, or maybe back down into the valley.

'Wait,' Cat said.

'What?' I already had my foot off the gas, but I eased down on the brake pedal.

Up ahead, the van went around a curve and I couldn't see it anymore.

'Suppose we drop off Elliot?' Cat said.

'Here?'

'Yeah! Why not?' Her voice sounded hushed and excited. 'It'll really screw White up. He won't even know we did it till he opens the trunk tonight. Presto, no more Elliot. He'll shit!'

'Then he'll kill Donny,' Peggy told us.

'No, he won't,' Cat said. 'He's gotta have his hostage to the very end. And it doesn't end till he gets his hands on Elliot.'

'But you're gonna *wreck* Elliot,' Peggy complained. 'You can't open the trunk till tonight or he'll turn into toast. Isn't that so?'

'So what?' I said. 'By the time White finds out, it won't matter.'

'It's pretty dark in here, anyway,' Cat said. 'Maybe he'll be okay.'

To the extent that a dead guy can be okay, I thought. But I didn't say it. This didn't seem like a good time for banter.

We eased slowly through the curve where I'd last seen the

231

van. It came into sight again, maybe a hundred feet ahead of us, a vague shape in the gloom. An instant later, it vanished around another curve.

I stopped the car.

'Let's do it,' I said.

Cat suddenly groaned.

'What?'

'White has the trunk key. We'll have to use the fake one.'

'You still have it, don't you?'

'Yeah. Just hope it works.'

'It worked on the door.'

'I just don't have a lot of faith in plastic keys.'

'If it doesn't work, it doesn't.'

'You stay put, Peggy.' She gave the rope a quick tug.

'Ow!'

I unfastened my seatbelt.

'Here.' Cat reached forward. She had the white plastic key in her hand. 'You take it and open the trunk. I'll be right out.'

I took it.

'And turn off the engine. Take the ignition key. We don't want Peggy driving off with our car.'

'I wouldn't . . .'

'Glad to hear it,' Cat told her.

With both keys in my hand, I scurried out.

The enormous heat crashed down on me. I'd forgotten about the heat. The car had been chilly inside, and the shadows of the gorge looked cool, but the hotness was there waiting and dropped onto me.

'My *God!*' I gasped.

But I stayed on my feet and made it to the trunk. I switched the ignition key to my other hand, stuffed it into the left front pocket of my jeans, and inserted the white plastic key into the lock of the trunk.

It went in sluggishly, but it went in. It was hard to turn. But it turned.

I heard a door bump shut.

The trunk popped open. As its lid swung up, Cat came running from the other side of the car.

She stopped beside me.

She said, 'Judas H. Priest.'

'Yeah,' I said, though I didn't know whether she meant the weather or the look of the corpse or the idea of *touching* it.

Elliot hadn't changed much since the last time I'd seen him.

He looked hideous.

Skinny as a cadaver, with skin that looked blue in the gloom.

He was curled on his side, facing us. His wrists were still bound with tape, the same as his ankles. His knees were bent. Underneath him was the white plastic mattress pad from Cat's bed. Under that was the blue tarp. He still had the silver tape across his eyes, but White had torn the tape off his mouth last night. His mouth gaped open so that he looked ready to snap at us.

His naked body was smeared as if he'd been rolling in blood. The blood looked dark purple in the shadows – almost black.

'You don't have to touch him,' I said. 'I'll take care of it. Just hold this.' I pulled off my shirt as fast as I could and gave it to her, saying, 'I don't want it getting mucked up.'

Then I plunged into the trunk and grabbed Elliot.

I did it fast and rough, trying not to think about what I was touching, trying to ignore the feel of his skin, trying most of all to get it finished quickly.

Grunting, I hefted him out and pivoted and flung him to the ground. He landed with a heavy, dry sound. He rolled over a couple of times and ended up on his back. He looked like a blindfolded, naked maniac howling at the sky.

I glimpsed the point of the stake jutting out of the tape around his chest.

I glimpsed his penis hanging against his thigh.

Feeling a little sick, I turned around quickly and reached up for the lid of the trunk.

'Don't shut it,' Cat said. Stepping in beside me, she raised a hand to stop the lid. 'Go and start up the car. I want to find the hammer.'

'We've got the tire iron.'

'The hammer'd be good to have. If I can't find it fast, I'll give up.'

'Okay. Hurry.'

I started away.

'I'll keep your shirt,' she called after me. 'You'll get it icky.'

'Okay.'

She was right about getting the shirt icky. I couldn't do much about my arms and chest and belly, but on my way to the door I wiped my hands on the legs of my jeans. Then I climbed in behind the wheel. I fished the key out of my jeans pocket and slid it into the ignition. The car started fine. Cold air began to blow against me. It made the sweat feel chilly on my skin.

There was no sign of the van up ahead.

The car shook slightly. I figured it came from Cat leaning into the trunk. I couldn't see anything but the trunk lid in the rearview mirror. Nothing much showed in the side mirrors, either: not even Elliot's body.

I was glad I couldn't see it.

'What's she doing?' Peggy asked.

'Looking for something.' I didn't feel like going into a big explanation with her.

'Where's your shirt?'

'She has it.'

I watched the trunk lid in the rearview mirror. Then I looked through the windshield to where the van had gone out of sight around the curve. By now, White was probably wondering what had happened to us. He might already be backing up.

'Is that blood you've got all over you?' Peggy asked.

'Yeah.'

'*His* blood?'

'I guess so.'

'You're a mess.'

'I know.'

I stared at the trunk lid and *willed* it to shut.

What's taking her so long?

'Can you do something about this rope?' Peggy asked.

'Huh?'

'It's killing me.'

I'd hardly spared Peggy a glance after returning to the car.

234

I'd noticed she was still there, that's all. Now, I looked over at her to see what the problem was.

She raised her arms high so they were out of the way.

Cat had tied her into her seat.

After I'd gone to open the trunk, Cat must've jerked the rope across the back of Peggy's seat, then looped it around her front so that it crossed her waist and came back between the seatbacks. To make the arrangement secure, Cat had apparently taken the rest of the rope outside with her and shut the door on it.

I could see two loops of rope across Peggy's waist. Her dress was cinched in and bunched, and the tightness of the loops had drawn her skirt up so that it barely covered her lap. She had her thighs pressed together as if to keep me from seeing anything I shouldn't.

That didn't make any sense to me. Her hands were free; she could've adjusted her dress and hidden the area nicely if she'd wanted to.

It puzzled me, but I didn't linger on it. I didn't care much about Peggy's motives. They were probably bizarre, anyway.

'It's squeezing me,' she said. 'Do something.'

'There's nothing to do,' I said. 'I'd have to go around and open Cat's door. Just wait a minute, and...'

'You both hate me!'

'We don't hate you.'

The trunk thumped shut.

Peggy gasped, startled.

Looking over my shoulder, I saw Cat rush alongside the car. I put my hand through the space between the seatbacks and grabbed the rope where it slanted away behind Peggy's seat. It was taut and hard. When Cat opened the door, the rope went soft. I pulled it, but there was no need for that because Cat brought the rest of the rope inside with her.

As she flung herself into the back seat, I saw the hammer in her left hand. 'Found it,' she said, and slammed her door.

I didn't wait for anything; we'd been stopped too long. The moment Cat's door shut, I stepped on the gas. We jerked forward and picked up speed.

In the rearview mirror, I glimpsed Elliot's body stretched out in the shadows.

35

A glimpse of that was more than I really wanted. I jerked my eyes away from the mirror and looked at Peggy. She was using both hands to loosen the coils across her waist.

'Did that go slick, or what?' Cat asked.

'Pretty darn slick,' I said.

'I can't believe I found the hammer.'

'Took a while.'

'It was hidden in a corner. But persistence will out.'

'You hurt me with the rope,' Peggy said.

'We couldn't afford trouble,' Cat told her. 'You can take it off now. Just don't try and pull anything on us.'

I swerved around the next curve. The gloom of the narrow gap continued ahead of us.

There was no sign of the van.

I was glad about that, but puzzled. 'Where the hell is he?' I said.

'Don't worry,' Cat said. 'I'm sure he'll turn up. We might as well take it easy. We pulled it off. If he asks what happened to us, we'll tell him Peggy had to take a leak.'

'Very funny,' Peggy said, and pulled the two coils of rope up her body like someone peeling off a T-shirt.

I suddenly wondered what had become of *my* shirt. Cat had climbed back into the car with the hammer in one hand, the rope in the other. 'Where's my shirt?' I asked her.

'Right here.'

I glanced back at her. She was trying to open the plastic container of wet wipes. I didn't see my shirt. Concerned about crashing, I quickly looked forward again.

'Where is it?' I asked.

'You looked right at it.'

'Huh?'

'I'm wearing it.'

I glanced back again. Sure enough, she wore one shirt over the other. With their bright, checkered patterns, they were so similar that they blended into each other.

Peggy, arms high, reached back over her head and dropped a tangle of rope behind her seat. 'Thanks for nothing,' she said.

'You're welcome,' Cat told her. She got the wet wipes open, and a strong lemony aroma filled the car.

'Must've been hot out there with two shirts on,' I said.

In the rearview mirror, I saw Cat smile. 'I can take it,' she said.

'You're a tough cookie.'

'That's me. Anyway, I needed my hands free. You can have it back now. I sure don't need it.'

'Maybe I'd better clean up first.'

'My hands got icked up,' she muttered. 'The trunk's a real mess.'

'I'll wait till we're out of here,' I told her.

Soon after saying that, I steered around another curve. The van was still out of sight, but the shadows didn't seem so dark anymore. Around the next curve, I found out why. About fifty yards ahead was the end of the pass. It looked like a glaring pillar of sunlight holding up the sky. I had to squint and turn my head away.

'Ohhh, boy,' Cat said.

She sounded the way I felt.

'Nervous?' I asked.

'I feel like the time I got sent to the principal's office.'

'What was that about?'

'I pushed a guy off the monkey bars.'

'You *what*?'

'He had it coming.'

'Glad to hear it.'

'He stepped on somebody's fingers. A friend of mine. Her name was Ardeth. She was lower on the bars, climbing around, and he stepped on her fingers on purpose. Mashed them against the bar she was holding. He thought it was hilarious, but Ardeth almost fell. Anyway, that's why I shoved him. We were way up near the top. He got banged up pretty good, but I always figured he deserved it.'

I grinned at her in the rearview mirror. I felt a lot better. But the good feeling started to slip now that her story had ended and I had nothing to distract me from what was ahead.

'How old were you?' I asked.

'Nine or ten.'

'Tough cookie even then.'

'Better believe it. Vengeance is mine. But then I had to face the principal. That was the downside. Scared the hell out of me. I had to wait outside his office for about half an hour. I was a wreck by the time he told me to come in. Then he yelled at me and I wet my pants.'

'Jeez,' I said.

'Just one of those things.'

'Don't do that here,' I said.

We both laughed, but Peggy didn't. She was sitting up straight and stiff, her legs tight together, her hands clutching her thighs, her face forward. She had her sunglasses on, and seemed to be staring straight at the opening.

'Here goes,' Cat said.

We broke out of the shadows and into the blinding daylight. Hardly able to see anything, I stopped the car.

'Where *is* he?' Peggy blurted.

'He has to be around here someplace,' Cat said.

'Maybe I'll take those wet wipes now.'

Cat handed the package forward. I plucked out a few of the moist napkins and started to mop Elliot's blood off my chest and belly. Then I did my arms. By the time I finished, my eyes had adjusted to the sunlight.

We were still surrounded by steep walls of rock, but they no longer loomed over us and hid the sky. The area in front of us was a wide open field of baked dirt and rock. It generally looked flat enough to drive on. Scattered about, however, were any number of boulders and rock piles. They came in all sizes: some waist-high, others as big as refrigerators, as cars, as trucks – and more than a few were as large as a house.

I didn't see the van anywhere, but figured that it probably hadn't gone far.

Cat held up our trash bag and I tossed in the used wipes. Then I handed the plastic container to her.

'Ready for your shirt?' she asked.

'How's my back?' I asked, and leaned forward until my chest met the steering wheel.

'What happened to you?' Peggy asked.

'I got poked a little.'

Cat said, 'Looks fine to me.'

'The bandage feels all wet.'

A moment later, I felt a gentle pressure against it. I couldn't see whose hand was touching me, but figured it had to be Cat's.

'It's soaked,' Cat said, and the hand went away. 'Must just be sweat, though. There's no blood showing.'

'That's good. Thanks.' I leaned back. Hands on the steering wheel, I scanned the area ahead of us.

'What poked you?' Peggy asked.

'A sharp stick. I wonder where they are.'

'They have to be out there somewhere,' Cat said. 'Maybe you should just start driving.'

'Which way?'

'Straight ahead, I guess. Do you want your shirt?'

'Okay.'

Keeping my foot on the brake, I looked over my shoulder to watch Cat take off the extra shirt. It wasn't buttoned at all, just worn like a jacket. As she tried to pull it off, she arched her back, thrusting her breasts out against her own shirt and squirming a little. The over-shirt clinged to hers. It drew her shirt taut across the front and strained at the buttons. Two of them popped open in the struggle before she freed herself from the extra shirt.

'That was a lot of trouble,' I said.

'It didn't want to let go.'

Leaving her buttons unfastened, she leaned forward and passed my shirt through the space between the seats. Her shirt was open halfway down. In the space between its edges, her skin looked dark and gleaming. I glimpsed the side of a breast.

'You don't have to put it on,' she said. 'I wouldn't, if I were you. Unless you're cold.'

'I'm not exactly cold.'

'Can we get on with it?' Peggy complained. 'He's got my *brother*, for godsake.'

'Be nice,' Cat warned.

'You two keep *dicking around!*'

'White's not going anyplace,' I said.

'He's *already* gone! We've gotta *find* him!'

Cat said, 'He'll find us. Do you think he wants to ditch us? We're his *prize*. Or Elliot is, anyway. He isn't going to lose us.'

I finished folding my shirt in half, and put it on top of the console between the front seats. 'Nothing's going to happen before dark, anyway.'

As I said that, I lifted my foot off the brake. I stepped lightly on the gas pedal, and we started creeping forward.

'Thanks,' Peggy muttered.

'We aim to please,' I said.

She turned her head and gave me a look, but her sunglasses saved me from it.

'Anybody want another beer?' Cat asked.

'There're only three left,' I pointed out.

'Maybe we'd better save them, huh? I should've bought more when I had the chance.'

'Or we shouldn't have drunk them all up.'

'That's what they're for,' Cat said. 'And they were sure good to have when we had them. It's just too bad we don't have a bunch more. How did you like yours, Peggy?'

'It was okay.'

'Let's go ahead and drink the rest of them. That okay with you, Sam?'

'You don't want to save them?' I asked.

'They'll just get warmer. And who knows, White might take them away from us before we have a chance at them. Life's strange. You never know when it might throw you a curve and you miss out on your last beer.'

She grinned at me in the rearview mirror.

I grinned back. 'Let's have them,' I said.

I kept on driving slowly forward across the desolate basin while Peggy took off her seatbelt, bent over and reached down between her knees. I kept looking for the van. It was nowhere to be seen. I couldn't even find a trace of a dust cloud.

Worrying that White might circle around and come in behind us, I kept an eye on my rearview and side mirrors.

We weren't leaving much of a dust cloud, ourselves. A lot of the ground seemed to be bare rock.

Peggy soon sat up with three cans of beer in her hands. She placed them on her lap. One at a time, she popped them open and handed them out.

'Thanks,' I said, taking mine.

When Cat had her beer in hand, she said, 'Anyone for snacks? There's all kinds of stuff in that bag up there, Peg.

Potato chips, pretzels, nuts, cookies, beef sticks. Take a look. Help yourself. What do you feel like, Sam?'

'Makes no difference to me. I'm not very hungry right now.'

'Gotta keep up your strength.'

'You two can decide. As long as it's something that goes with beer. I wouldn't want any cookies right now.'

'What do you want, Peg? I know – your brother. You don't have to say it. Pick something from the bag.'

'I don't care.'

'Nobody cares. Okay. I guess it's up to me. How about grabbing the can of mixed nuts?'

Peggy reached down, searched inside the bag for a few seconds, then sat up with the can of nuts in her hand. She turned sideways and handed it to Cat.

'Thank you, my dear.'

I heard Cat pop the ring of the can's lid. Then came a ripping sound as she peeled the lid off. A warm, roasty aroma of nuts drifted through the car. She extended the open can through the space between the seatbacks and said, 'Help yourselves, gang.'

I needed one hand for steering, and the other held my beer can. So I put the can between my thighs. Then I reached for the nuts. I started digging for a handful.

And the van came at us.

I stomped on the brakes and jerked my hand out of the can. Nuts flew. As we started to skid, I grabbed the wheel and wrenched it to the right, trying to veer out of the van's way.

White had been waiting for us.

Waiting in ambush.

He must've counted on us coming this way. Either that, or he'd been keeping an eye on us and maneuvering among the rocks to put himself in a good position for his attack.

While I helped myself to the mixed nuts, we were passing through an area bordered on the left by scattered boulders, on the right by a cluster of rocks the size of a two-story house.

It was a very good place for his attack.

We had nowhere to go.

If I'd had time to throw us into reverse...

But there wasn't even time to stop.

Suddenly the van sped backward, coming in from the right, swerving around the corner from behind the house-sized mound of rocks, then rushing straight at us, rear first.

Somebody yelled, 'Shit!' I think it was Cat.

36

In the couple of seconds as the van rushed toward us, a lot of thoughts shot through my mind. Among them, that this was payback. I'd crashed into White. Now, he would crash into us.

If it was payback, it was payback in spades.

I hadn't done much more than bump his van and shove it forward: he slammed into us with everything he had.

None of us had a seatbelt on.

An instant before the van struck, my swerve crashed us into a boulder that stopped us dead. It was like the foreshock of a major quake. And probably saved us from worse harm; we'd already been thrown forward by the time the van smashed against us with ten times the impact.

It helped, too, that I'd managed to turn the car somewhat. The van blasted into our left front corner instead of nailing us straight-on.

I don't know much about physics, but I think we might've all been killed if I hadn't swerved and crashed into the boulder before the van hit us.

Not that the crash was any picnic.

Half a second after I struck the steering wheel, there came a din of bursting glass and metal caving in. I felt as if we'd been hit by a train. The blow came at an angle, whacking the car backward and crooked, shoving me off the wheel, smashing me against the door and bouncing my head off the window. I thought he'd killed us all.

Then there was stillness. The crash was over.

I heard gasping sounds that seemed to come from behind me. From Cat? Was she alive?

Was *I* alive? It hardly seemed possible.

I certainly thought myself to be conscious. I didn't think I could move, though. I felt as if my body had been hacked apart by a team of lumberjacks.

The car made pinging noises, clinks and clicks, hisses, splashy liquid sounds, metallic bonks and clanks as if it were trying to uncrunch itself. Pieces of glass and metal still seemed to be falling off and hitting the rocky ground under the car.

The engine was no longer running.

Maybe *that* had been the idea – to kill our car.

I wondered if there might be a danger of fire.

Those splashy sounds. Some of them were probably coolant, but some might be gasoline spilling out of the tank or broken lines. I couldn't smell gas, but I couldn't smell anything else, either. My nose didn't seem to be working.

We'd better get out of here.

I thought it, but could do nothing about it.

Then an engine wheezed and chugged and came to life. I knew it wasn't ours. It had to be the van's engine. I got my right eye open enough to look out and see the van moving away from us.

Though its rear end was smashed in, the crash hadn't disabled the van.

That's why White had *backed* into us – to prevent damage to his front end, where all the important stuff was located.

He bashed us to pieces, now he's leaving.

Maybe he was taking the van out of harm's way in case our car should explode.

But he didn't go far. He drove about twenty feet, then stopped.

Without moving my head at all, I turned my right eye and looked down at Peggy. She was slouched over the console, her left arm hanging between my legs, her head against my belly. I couldn't see her very well. The angle was bad, and I had to keep blinking blood out of my eye.

She wasn't moving.

'Sam?' My name sounded like a cross between a word and a moan. It came from behind me.

'Cat?'

'You okay?' she asked.

'Sure. You?'

'Rip-roaring.'

'Peggy's not so good.'

'She dead?'

'I don't know.'

'Ask.'

'Peggy?'

In the quiet as I listened for an answer I didn't expect to come, I heard the heavy crunch and scrape of footsteps approaching us. I raised my eye and looked out the windshield.

White marched past the rear corner of the van. He wore his motorcycle boots and jeans, but nothing above the waist. He was dark and sweaty and had thick, bulging muscles. His hunting knife was sheathed at his hip.

'He's coming,' I warned.

'Shit,' Cat murmured.

'Play dead.'

'Easy.'

I shut my eye.

And listened to his boots. He was coming toward us like another accident about to happen.

Unavoidable.

It hadn't *always* been unavoidable, but it was now. We could've done things differently earlier in the day or last night. Cat could've altered the course of events *before* last night: there were so many things she could've done differently, and we wouldn't have ended up this way.

I didn't blame her, though.

I loved her. If she hadn't gotten herself into the mess with Elliot, she wouldn't have brought me back into her life. I was glad to be with her, even now.

I just wished we weren't in such a mess.

If we'd done any of a thousand things differently since last midnight...

But we hadn't.

And now White had us completely.

My door swung open and I started to fall out. White caught me and pushed me the other way, so that I slumped over behind Peggy's back.

'What's the matter with you cocksuckers?' he roared. He sounded abundantly cheerful. 'Never been in a crash before?'

He seemed to be lingering at my open door, but I didn't

know why. Pretty soon, he gasped, 'Ah,' and shoved my legs out of the way. 'Got your tire iron, folks. Betcha were aiming to bash out my brains with it, huh?'

He slammed my door shut.

I heard a grunt. A few moments later, a ringing clank came from somewhere in front of the car. He must've thrown the tire iron.

The back door opened. 'Howdy, Cat,' he said. 'Under the weather?' He chuckled. 'Shit! Look at all these fucking *cans*!' He let out a wild laugh. 'No wonder you crashed, you damn bunch of drunks! Hope you saved me some.'

There were probably ten beer cans back there. I heard some of them click together, quiet background noise as wooden handles clacked and iron struck iron.

Though I could see nothing, the sounds told me that White was taking our pick and shovel out of the back seat. He stepped away from the car with them. Then he hurled them toward the rear of his van. First the shovel, then the pick. The pick landed with a heavy clang that I could almost feel.

Leaning into the car again, White said, 'Ah, these should come in handy.' Beer cans were knocked about as he rummaged. 'Thank you, thank you, thank you. Where'd this hammer come from? Didn't see it here before. Holding out on me, huh? What else you got? You can keep the flat.' He chuckled again.

He kept searching the back seat area, collecting goodies. Though he talked a lot and asked questions, he didn't seem to expect any answers. After a while, he climbed out.

I opened my eye to watch him.

For the first time, I noticed the white smoke and steam pouring out of our car. As it rose from under the buckled hood, it was whipped away, shredded and scattered by the wind. There was no sign of fire, so I turned my attention to White.

He was carrying the rope and hammer and Cat's laceless shoes. He put them on the ground behind the van. Then he came back.

'Here he comes again,' I whispered.

When he arrived, he pulled our two overnight bags out of the back. He took them to the van, dropped them on the ground, then started toward us.

'He's coming again,' I warned Cat.

'Terrific,' she muttered.

This time, White opened the passenger door.

'Hello, honey. Hmm. Look at all this. What've we got here?'

With my eye open just a slit, I saw that he was crouched in the V of the door. He seemed to be reaching in and picking things up off the floor around Peggy's feet. Whatever he found, he tossed into the sack from Lucky's. When he was done with the floor, he opened the glove compartment. Something from there went into the sack. Then he took his haul away.

The van had stopped at an angle so that I could see its right side. I was able to watch White carry his loot to the passenger door. He opened the door with one hand and climbed in.

'He's in the van,' I reported. 'Putting our stuff inside.'

'What'd he get?'

'Don't know. Everything, maybe.'

'Didn't ... leave much back here. Bastard. Even took my shoes. Left us the damn jack and ...'

'He's coming out.'

Cat moaned. 'Coming here?'

'Not ... No.' Instead of returning to our car, he stepped behind the van and picked up more of our things. He carried them to his passenger door and climbed in again. 'He's putting all our stuff in the van,' I said.

'God. What's he gonna do?'

'Don't know.'

He had disabled our car, then taken away nearly everything that we might eat, drink, or use as weapons.

'He must know we aren't dead,' I said. 'He's doing all this ... so we can't fight him.'

'Stupid.'

'Huh?'

'Why not just kill us?'

'I don't know.'

'Maybe he thinks we're ... already dead. So he's taking what he wants.'

'I don't know,' I said.

'You don't know much.'

Under different circumstances, I might've laughed at a crack like that. But we were both too badly hurt for me to laugh about anything. Also, I thought Peggy might be dead. And I was afraid of what White would do to us. He could do anything he wanted; we were in no shape to fight him, and I had major doubts that the cavalry would show up in time to save us.

Though I couldn't laugh or even smile, Cat's crack made me feel less awful. *You don't know much.* I wondered if she had smiled when she said it.

'He take your shoes?' she asked.

'No.'

'Took mine.'

'Yeah, I saw.'

'Still got your church key?'

'If my leg's still attached.' Concentrating hard, I made my right foot move. It worked. There was soreness, but no great pain. Rotating my foot, I was able to feel the stiffness of the church key above my ankle. It seemed to still be in place where Cat had slid it under my sock. 'Still got it,' I said.

'Good deal.'

'Yeah.'

'Lighter?'

'Huh?'

'You still got your lighter? You put it in your shirt pocket.'

'Can't get to my shirt,' I said. 'Guess it's under Peggy.'

'I've got mine.'

'Our luck runneth over.'

'Lighter fluid?'

'These're throw-aways, stupid.'

'Hardy har.'

'He probably took it,' I said. 'I don't know. And the WD-40. Maybe he missed them. If he didn't, they'd be down on the floor. I don't think I can get down there. Not right now.'

'What's he doing?' Cat asked.

'Still in the van.'

'Wish he'd leave.'

'He won't,' I said. 'Not till tonight.'

'He'd leave ... if he looked in the trunk.'

'He won't. Till after dark.'

'It could've popped open when he hit us.'

247

'Guess it didn't,' I said.

'He sure took a chance.'

'Paid off,' I said. 'He sure fixed us.'

'If you wanta call it that.'

37

With a sputter and cough, the engine of the van kicked into life. Gray smoke chugged out of its exhaust pipe.

'What's happening?' Cat asked.

'He started the van.'

'God, I hope he doesn't hit us again.'

'He's going forward.'

'Ah.'

'Now he's turning right. Going around the back of those rocks.' A few seconds later, the van disappeared behind the same house-sized mound where it had waited in ambush for us. 'He's gone,' I said.

'What the hell's he doing?'

'I don't know. Glad he's gone, though.' I forced my other eye to open, and had to squint. My head ached. The stark sunlight made it worse.

Grabbing Peggy by her neck and shoulder, I pushed her off me and sat up. Though I ached just about everywhere and a few sharp pains shot through me when I moved, my body seemed to be functioning all right.

'What're you doing?' Cat asked.

'Getting her off me.'

'He'll know we aren't dead.'

'He isn't here,' I pointed out.

'He'll be back.'

'Yeah. But I don't think we had him fooled. Anyway, we can't stay here.' Peggy didn't want to sit upright. She fell toward me a couple of times, so I pushed her until she slouched against the passenger door. Her arms hung by her sides. Her head drooped forward.

I hadn't watched Peggy during the accident, but she'd obviously hit the windshield. The safety glass in front of her seat looked like ice on a pond after being hit with a sledge hammer. Her head hadn't gone through it, but she'd clobbered it and knocked out a few chunks of glass.

The hair on top of her head was matted flat with blood. Blood sheeted her face. I watched a drip fall off the end of her nose. Another fell from her chin. Both landed on her bloody chest. Cat's shoe laces still held up the top of her dress. They were red with blood. The whole front of the dress was soaked most of the way down. It was gathered around her waist. The tops of her thighs were spattered with blood.

'Is she alive?' Cat asked.

'I don't know.'

'Find out.'

'Yeah.' I stared hard at her chest, figuring it should move up and down if she was breathing. I couldn't tell. My own vision wasn't entirely steady. So I leaned over, turning, and pressed my left hand against her chest. I put it on her bare skin just above the top of her dress. In spite of my own shaking, I thought I detected the rise and fall of her ribcage.

'She's breathing,' I said.

'Thank God,' Cat said.

With my hand still on Peggy's chest, my face was in front of the space between the seatbacks. I turned my head. For the first time since the crash, I saw Cat.

'Hi,' she said.

'Hi.'

She was sprawled across the back seat, face up, her left foot resting on the flat tire, her right leg hanging off the edge of the seat, bent at the knee, foot on the floor. Her arms were by her sides, hands resting on her hips. Her shirt, completely unbuttoned, was open a few inches wide down the middle of her chest. Lower, it had slipped off her right side just below the ribcage so half her belly was bare.

She might've simply been stretched out on the seat for a lazy nap – except for the blood.

She looked as if someone had wiped a handful or two of blood across her mouth and cheeks and neck. Maybe she'd done it, herself; both her hands were bright red.

'Bloody nose,' she explained.

'That's all?'

'Disappointed?'

'No! My God! You're lucky.'

'Lucky? That's a stretch. But the back seat's not the worst place to be. I hit Peggy's seat and ended up all over the floor. That's where I was when White came. All tangled on the floor. Hell, I probably *did* look dead. I feel like I got stomped by a herd of wildebeest, but . . . nothing much to show for it. Just a bloody nose. And maybe a million bruises later on. How about you? Just that cut on your forehead?'

'Not sure. Everything seems to work, though. Must have a knot . . .' I touched the left side of my head and found a bump near the top, about midway between my ear and my brow. It was about the size of a tennis ball that has been sliced in half. My hair felt stiff and sticky over it. When I touched my scalp on top of the bump, I winced. It felt tender and raw, so I apparently had a cut there. 'Guess I'm okay,' I said.

As I fingered the sore mound, Cat started trying to sit up. It looked like a struggle. She winced and groaned. The right side of her shirt fell open, then slipped off her shoulder. Even in my wrecked condition, the sight of Cat pushing herself up from the seat with one arm – naked on her right side from shoulder to waist – thrilled me, made me almost forget my aches and our dicey situation.

When she was sitting up, she lifted the shirt onto her shoulder again but didn't try to fasten its buttons. She spent a few seconds turning this way and that, squinting out the windows. Apparently, she'd been down below window level until now. This was her first chance to look outside. 'I don't see him anywhere,' she said.

'He's bound to come back.'

'Guess so.'

'We oughta get out of here before he shows up,' I told her.

'See if the car works.'

I was absolutely certain that the car would never start again, but I turned the ignition key a few times anyway. It made some quiet clicking sounds at first, then no sounds at all.

'Dead as hell,' Cat said.

'It's going nowhere. But we oughta take off, anyway. Maybe we can hide in the rocks.'

'What about Peggy?'

I shrugged.

'Let's see,' Cat said.

I got out of the way as she clutched the seatbacks with both hands and pulled herself forward. She put her head through the gap and studied Peggy.

'You sure she's alive?'

'Yeah. I felt her breathing.'

'PEGGY!' Cat shouted.

Peggy didn't even flinch.

'She's really out of it,' Cat said. 'Try shaking her.'

I grabbed the girl's bony shoulder and jostled it. Her head wobbled. She didn't wake up.

'Pinch her or something.'

I pinched her upper arm. It wasn't easy because my fingers were slick with blood. But I managed to catch some flesh between my thumb and forefinger and give it a nasty squeeze.

Peggy didn't react.

Cat said, 'She oughta be in a hospital.'

'That'd be a good trick.'

'What'll we do with her?'

'What'll we do with *us*?'

'You got a plan?' Cat asked.

'This car's gonna be like an oven.' Only a few minutes had gone by since the crash had killed the engine and air-conditioning, but the car was already stifling. 'We'll cook if we stay in here.'

'At least we've got shade. Maybe if we open the windows ...'

'I think we oughta get out. Are you okay enough?'

'Yeah. What about you?'

'Guess so. We could climb up those rocks ... pull a disappearing act. We can be gone when White gets back.'

'Why'd he leave? Where'd he go?'

'Who knows? But he still thinks we've got Elliot in the trunk, so he'll come back sooner or later. If he can't find us, he can't ... do anything to us.'

'Just to Donny,' Cat said. 'We're in the same boat as before. Except our boat's been scuttled. And it's hotter than hell.' Dropping backward away from the gap, she said, 'Let's at least get the windows open.'

'I think we oughta hightail it,' I told her, but started to crank

251

down the driver's window. Though I'd whacked it with the side of my head, the glass hadn't broken. It rolled down easily enough. 'We don't even know if Donny's ...'

'Shit!'

I stopped lowering my window. 'What?'

'I can't ... I can't get this thing down all the way. It's stuck or ...'

I turned my head to look over my left shoulder. My neck didn't really want to turn that way. Grimacing with the pain, I forced myself to turn more, and saw that the back window was only down about eight inches. It had at least that much to go. This puzzled me at first. Then I knew the problem. 'The car's probably *built* so it'll only go down that far,' I explained.

'Why the hell ...?'

'Child safety. So kids in the back seat can't climb out the windows.'

'Shit! You've gotta make halfass windows for that?'

'Government.'

'Shit!'

I almost smiled. 'They're just looking out for our safety.'

'Not *my* safety.'

'Kids.'

'That's what *parents* are supposed to be for.'

'It takes a village.'

'Fuck.'

I *did* smile.

'Windows that only go halfway down? Somebody's fucking nuts!'

'Yeah.'

'I didn't know they did that. Bet my ass *Bill* didn't know it, either. He wouldn't have *bought* the damn car.'

'They just don't want kids climbing out.'

'What about people who might wanta *breathe!*'

'Outa luck.'

Facing forward again, I cranked my window the rest of the way down. 'Anyway, what I was saying is – we're so worried about Donny, but we don't know whether or not he's still alive. For that matter, we don't know for sure that there even *is* a Donny.'

'Sure there is.'

252

'Have you ever seen him?'

'No. But he has to be real. Why would Peggy make up something like that?'

I thought about it for a moment, then said, 'So we'd go along with White?'

'Why would she *do* it?'

'Who knows?'

'I sure don't,' Cat said. Then she muttered, 'Hope the *other* window opens.'

'It won't. It'll be halfway.'

'Terrific.'

I looked back through the gap and saw Cat sweep by – coming up from her left and going down to her right. She planted her right elbow on the seat. That side of her shirt fell away. She was a smooth, bare curve from her hip to her armpit. She reached over with her left arm, but I could see under it. As she cranked the window down, the motion of her arm made her breast wobble. She cranked hard.

The window abruptly stopped midway down, and her breast lurched. She gasped, 'Shit!'

But when she sat up, her hair blew. She smiled and looked at me. 'Hey! There's a nice breeze.'

I could feel it myself. More than a breeze. A hot wind.

'You oughta get the other window down,' Cat told me. 'Yours go all the way, right?'

'Yeah. They don't care if people in the front seats climb out.'

'Lucky us.'

I leaned across Peggy and reached for the crank. It was an awkward position, my shoulder pushing against her ribs, but I managed to start the passenger window rolling down.

'Bill wasn't a complete waste,' Cat said.

'What do you mean?'

'At least he didn't have automatic windows on this heap. They'd be stuck shut and we'd *really* be outa luck. We wouldn't even get them *halfway* down.'

'A lot to be said for the old ways,' I said.

'Progress kills,' said Cat.

'And government loads the gun,' I added.

'Huh?'

'Somebody said that once.' When I pushed myself up, the

wind coming in through the passenger window flew hot against my face and bare shoulders and chest. It was *very* hot, but it felt much better than the dead, stifling air that had surrounded us earlier. 'Nice,' I said.

'At least we won't cook.'

I looked at Cat through the gap. She was sitting near the middle of the back seat, but slumped down low with her knees up in a way that reminded me of how kids sometimes sit in movie theaters. Her cut-off jeans didn't start until well below her belly button. Her shirt was fairly wide open, but still draped her breasts enough to cover her nipples. Her skin was dark and glossy. Her scars looked like tiny, pale nicks and specks. I noticed that most of the blood had vanished from her face and neck. Apparently, she'd cleaned herself. She'd missed a few places, though, and still had ruddy smudges here and there.

Even slumped down the way she was, the wind got to her. It stirred the hair on top of her head and swayed the hair that hung down her brow.

Her eyes were such a rich blue that the whites shared some of their color and looked the way that snow sometimes looks in shadows when the sky is clear and deep.

'This isn't so bad,' she said.

I said, 'We'd be better off in the rocks.'

'We've got shade here.'

'But White can get us.'

'If we leave, he'll nail Donny.' Cat narrowed her eyes at me. 'You don't *really* think Peggy made up that stuff about him, do you?'

'I don't know. It's possible. We've only got her word. Don't you think it's kind of funny that neither of us has even gotten a glimpse of the kid?'

'Why would Peggy lie? What's her motive?'

'Maybe White paid her.'

'That's crazy.'

'I don't know about that. He could've given her some money to play along . . . maybe a lot of money. Maybe he didn't even jack her car; maybe he *hired* it.'

'If that's how it went, everything she told us was a lie.'

'It's possible.'

254

'Unlikely, though.'

'Who knows?' I said. 'When we ditched White at breakfast, he had to get after us fast, or we'd be long gone. He didn't have time to be picky about rides. So he ended up with Peggy, either by force or by paying for her help. But maybe no one else was in the car. Suppose it was only Peggy? White probably didn't even realize he'd *need* another person till he was on his way. But then he figured out that he had to invent a brother for her. Or at least *somebody*. He needed a hostage. Otherwise, he'd have no leverage on us, nothing to make us cooperate. He had to have our cooperation. Without it, he couldn't do anything with us. He might be able to follow us for a while, but . . .'

'Run us off the road.'

'Your car had a lot more power than the van. We could've outrun him. What he needed to do was give us a reason to follow him and obey his orders. So he invented Donny.'

Frowning a little, Cat shook her head. 'I don't know. That's getting pretty tricky for a guy like White. He invents a hostage? I doubt it.'

'Maybe it was Peggy's idea.'

'I'm not sure *she's* that smart, either.'

'But what if Donny *doesn't* exist?'

'Then we've been had.'

I turned my eyes to the passenger seat and stared at Peggy. She still sat slumped against the door with her head down. Blood no longer dripped off her nose and chin. Now that my own condition had improved, I could see the slight rise and fall of her chest as she breathed.

'I wish she'd wake up,' I said. 'Maybe we could get the truth out of her.'

'I'm pretty sure we've already gotten it.'

Turning to face Cat again, I said, 'Donny or no Donny, we shouldn't stay here. We'll stand a much better chance up in those rocks.'

'Donny or no Donny, what about Peggy?'

'What?'

'Do we just leave her here?'

'I don't think we *can* take her with us. Not if she doesn't wake up. We'd have to carry her. We probably shouldn't even *try* it.'

'You're all right with leaving her behind?'

'I think she'll be okay with the windows open. Our leaving shouldn't make any difference as far as she's concerned, anyway. She'll be the same whether we're here or not.'

'I guess that's true.'

'And her chances are a hell of a lot better if we manage to get through this thing. If White nails us, she's as good as dead. Same with Donny.'

'If there is a Donny,' Cat added, and gave me half a smile.

'Right. You're catching on.' My shirt lay crumpled on the console. I picked it up, shook it open, and checked the pocket. 'The lighter's still here.'

'We'll set the world on fire. Or it'll set us.'

'We'll be fine,' I said, and put the shirt on. It seemed to trap the heat against my skin, made me feel hotter than ever. But I figured the sun would blister me without it, so I kept it on and fastened a few of the buttons. 'Are you ready?'

'Let's bail,' Cat said.

38

We climbed out opposite sides of the car, both of us moving slowly and stiffly. The heat from the direct sunlight felt like the breath of a forest fire.

'Why don't we leave the doors open?' Cat shouted through the wind. 'Give Peggy more air.'

I nodded, let my door stay open, then stepped to the back door. Its handle felt like a hot griddle, but I got it open. Then I walked to the rear of the car.

I glanced at the trunk.

'Hard to believe Elliot isn't in there,' Cat said.

'Yeah. *Nice* to know he isn't there.'

She came hobbling toward me, the wind blowing her hair, flapping her shirt behind her like a cape. Her hair was the color of hay in the sunlight. Her skin was the color of sand, and glistened as if she'd been rubbed with oil. Her hiking shoes were gone, but she still wore her white socks.

'Sure we don't wanta stay in the car?' she asked.

'This is pretty bad,' I admitted.

'I feel like I'm gonna combust.'

'But you *look* great.'

She laughed. 'That's the main thing.'

'How are your feet?'

'Burning.'

'Let's get Peggy's flip-flops. She doesn't need them.'

'She might need them if she comes to.'

'If or when that happens. Anyway, you need them now.'

Cat made a face as if she didn't like the idea, but she didn't raise any more protests. I hurried past her. At the passenger door, the handle flashed a blast of sunshine in my eyes. I turned my head away and muttered a curse.

'I'll open it,' Cat said. 'You get ready to catch Peggy. We don't wanta rob her *and* drop her.'

Careful to keep my eyes away from the glaring handle, I crouched slightly by the door and put out my arms. Cat used the front of her shirt as a glove and pulled the door open. Peggy, leaning against it, started to fall. I lunged forward, caught her and pushed until she slumped the other way.

Her dress had gotten rucked up so high that she wasn't even sitting on it. Her legs were bare all the way down to her feet. I couldn't see her sandals.

I crouched low inside the open door. The floor in front of Peggy's seat, shrouded by shadow, seemed very dark after so much blinding brightness. Not trusting my vision, I wrapped my hands around the bottoms of both her feet. The sandals weren't there, so I started to feel around. The carpet was warm and damp, probably from spilled beer. My hand encountered the carton that had held our twelve beers. I also found scattered nuts, the empty nut can, and a beer can.

'Aren't they there?' Cat asked.

'They probably came off in the accident.'

Though the beer can lay on its side, I picked it up and shook it. Empty.

'Maybe White took them,' Cat said.

'I didn't see ... He might've put 'em in the bag.'

'What did he leave down there?'

'Not much. Nothing worth ... *here's one*!' I snatched up the

257

sandal and passed it over my shoulder. Cat plucked it from my hand.

'Thank you.'

'If one's here, the other must be.' A few moments later, I found it underneath the beer carton. I grabbed it and stood up slowly, groaning with the effort and my soreness, then squinting my eyes almost shut as sunlight hit my face.

'What about her sunglasses?' Cat asked.

I shook my head.

'You could sure use them.'

'Well . . .' Shrugging, I turned around. Cat put a hand on my shoulder to hold herself steady, bent down and slipped the second sandal onto her foot without taking her sock off. She was already wearing the other one.

'Let me take a look,' she said.

I stepped out of the way, and she hunched down in the V of the open door. Leaning into the shadows, she put out her arms and seemed to be feeling around on the floor the way I'd done.

'Want some nuts?' she asked.

'No thanks.'

After a brief silence, she said, 'Not bad. A little moist.'

'They'll make you thirsty,' I warned.

'I think the salt's all washed off. The sunglasses don't seem to be here.'

'That's okay. We'd better get going.'

Cat started to rise, then stopped in a half crouch and patted Peggy on the thigh. 'Hang in there, girl. Okay? You'll be all right.' She stepped back and straightened up. 'I wonder if we should leave this door open, too,' she said.

'Maybe not. If she moves and tips over, she'll fall out.'

Nodding, Cat swung the door shut.

We turned away from the car and started to climb. I went first, figuring to lead the way. I quickly discovered, however, that Cat wasn't following me. She seemed to be breaking her own trail up the rough slope, a few yards off to my right. Doing a good job of it, too. In spite of the vicious heat and whatever injuries she might've suffered in the crash, she attacked the rocks as if she'd found herself in a race for the summit. I quickened my pace, but still lagged behind.

My head throbbed. My neck ached. My arms felt sore. My

back felt stiff. My legs hurt. I even had pains in my feet. Though my mouth was dry as sand, sweat poured down my body. I had to keep blinking it out of my eyes. My clothes were wet and glued to my skin.

As I struggled to climb, the sun felt like a two-hundred pound ape taking a free ride on my back.

Cat couldn't be feeling *much* better than I did. But she was climbing like crazy, anyway.

Soon, she was more than two body-lengths above me.

Taking a breather, I watched her leap from one boulder to a higher one, her arms out for balance, her shirt blowing behind her. Safely perched on that boulder, she tilted back her head and seemed to search the area above her. Then she turned around and looked down at me. 'You coming?' she called.

'Yeah.'

'Are you okay?'

'I was in a car crash.'

'Don't let that stop you.'

'I'm on my way,' I said.

'I'll wait here.'

Standing at the edge of the rock, she put her hands on her hips and waited for me. I took a route that angled me toward her. But I took my time. After all, we were safely away from the car. Even if White should suddenly show up, he would have a tough time getting to us.

My aches and pains aside, I didn't hurry because the view was so fine that I wanted it to last. I went slowly, climbing ever closer to Cat, savoring how she looked up there with her paint-splattered cut-off jeans slung low on her hips, her thumbs hooked in the belt loops, and her shirt flapping behind her.

Even in my miserable condition, I found myself wishing that I were a great artist, that I had canvas and paints and all the time in the world to capture how Cat looked as she stood on that desolate boulder.

Or if I could simply take a photograph . . .

I couldn't do either, but my disappointment suddenly vanished because I realized my mind would *always* hold a vivid picture of how she looked. And that image would be mine

259

alone. My private, secret portrait of Cat that nobody else could ever see or covet or steal, that could never be destroyed by flood or fire, that would be mine alone for all my life.

As I climbed closer, I saw that she was panting for air. In spite of the strong wind, her bare skin gleamed with sweat. When I was very close, I saw that her legs were powdered with dust. I saw dribbles of sweat running down her face and neck and chest.

Add all that to the portrait, I told myself. And the slanted, old-time scar on her cheekbone that she had even when we were kids.

Before I leaped onto her boulder, she took a couple of steps backward. Landing, I stumbled toward her. She braced herself and caught me by the upper arms, stopping me. Then she held me steady while my heart thundered and I gasped for air. Sweat kept pouring down my face. It made my eyes sting.

'You okay?' Cat asked.

I nodded. She let go of my arms. I lifted my shirt and used it to wipe my face.

'We're almost there,' she said.

'Almost where?'

'Look at this.' She turned around and stepped toward a vertical wall of rock the height of her shoulders. Sweeping her hand toward the area above it, she said, '*Voila!*'

'Shade!'

'Indeed!'

'All right!'

'Who wants to go first?' she asked.

'If you go first,' I said, 'I'll give you a boost.'

She smirked at me. 'Do you think I'll *require* a boost?'

'Probably not. But I'd be glad to give you one.'

'You would, huh?' She smiled. 'Okay.'

With my side to the wall, I crouched and made a stirrup of my hands. She planted a sandal in it, slapped her hands on top of the ledge, and flung herself up. I gave her some extra thrust. She nearly flew.

I watched her crawl away from the edge and stand up. Turning around, she said, 'Can you make it? Or should I come down and give you a boost?'

'You can just watch and admire my dexterity.'

'Okay.' She smiled. Bending over at the waist, she brushed the dust and grit off her knees. I was all set to go, but couldn't force my gaze away from her. Not until she quit slapping her knees.

Then I looked aside, jumped, and shoved at the ledge with both hands. Somehow, I got a knee onto the edge. And that was about as far as I could get. Sore and weak, momentum gone, I found myself sprawled half on the ledge, half off. I tried to squirm over and almost fell backward but Cat suddenly lurched forward and grabbed me with both hands and dragged me to safety.

After she let go, I stayed on the burning floor of rock, sprawled out and gasping.

'You okay?' she asked.

'Dandy.'

She started to stroke the back of my head. 'We're fine, now,' she said. 'White'll never find us up here. If he *does* find us, he won't be able to get us. We can drop rocks on him.'

'We're in business,' I said.

After a while, I raised my head. Cat was squatting in front of me. 'Feeling better?' she asked.

'Yeah. Except I'm cooking.'

'Can you get up?'

'Hope so.' I pushed myself to my hands and knees. Then Cat, unsquatting, clutched my upper left arm with both her hands and pulled me up. 'Thanks,' I gasped.

Our shaded nook was only a few paces away, but Cat turned me around by my arm.

We gazed down.

Still no sign of the van.

Our car was a pretty good distance below us, but close enough so that we could see it clearly. The view was about what you'd get if you were looking down from the roof of a two-story house at a car parked in the front yard – a car that had just been used for a getaway, three suspects bailing out and leaving their doors wide open.

The angle was pretty steep. Through the window of the passenger door, I could see the side of Peggy's right thigh but nothing else of her. Obviously, she was still slumped toward the driver's side.

'Doesn't look like Peggy's moved,' I said.

'We can check on her once in a while. If she wakes up, we might have to change plans.'

'Yeah.'

I took a few moments to scan the whole basin. It was just about the most desolate landscape I'd ever seen. Sun-blasted dry earth and stones. Cactus and stunted trees here and there. A scattering of rock formations – ours seemed to be the largest until you came to the surrounding bluffs.

And some ruins at the foot of the bluffs about half a mile to our right.

'Look at that,' I said.

'I see.'

What we saw were a few old shacks with tin roofs. The fallen remains of a wooden water tower. Some shambles that might've once been shacks, outhouses, stables, water troughs ... who knows? A lot of debris seemed to be spread around the area, most of it too small to identify at such a distance.

But poking out from behind the far corner of one of the shacks was the front of a vehicle. It had headlights, a dull chrome bumper and grill, gray paint or primer on the hood and fender.

'Is that a car?' Cat asked. 'Over to the right, just a little of it showing beside ...'

'I see it.'

'What do you think?'

'It's either a car or a small truck.'

'It's not the van.'

'No,' I said. 'But see its shape? That thing looks like it was built in the fifties, or something. It's ancient. Probably been here for years.'

'Too bad we can't see its tires,' Cat said.

'If it has any.'

'We'd be able to tell if it's a derelict or not.'

'Looks like one to me,' I told her.

'An old-timer might have a car like that.'

'Whoever had it, I bet he's long gone. That place looks like it's been abandoned for decades.'

'Looks like it. But you never know. There might be an old prospector ...'

'I doubt it. I bet there is a mine, though. Over there someplace.'

'A dark, cool mine,' Cat said.

'If we could find it.'

We both stood on the ledge, hands at our brows to shield our eyes from the sun and wind, and squinted into the distance. I was looking for a mine entrance on the slopes behind the ruins. I thought Cat was looking for the same thing. She wasn't.

'*That's* where White went,' she suddenly blurted. 'Look, you can see tire tracks. They kind of fade in and out.'

I shook my head.

Cat pointed and explained where to look. I finally spotted the tracks. They faded in and out, all right. But starting just beyond the point of our crash, twin parallel lines were visible now and then heading in the general direction of the ruins.

They were hard to keep an eye on. After ten feet or so of the tracks, there might be fifty feet of bare rock that showed no trace of the van's passage. If you looked on past where they vanished, though, you could pick them up again in the distance. Then you'd lose them again for a while.

Mostly, there weren't any tracks to see.

But they were visible just often enough to show that they led all the way to the shacks.

'Is he still there?' Cat asked.

'I don't see the van.'

'But there aren't any tracks coming back this way. He *could* still be there. Maybe he parked behind one of the shacks.'

'Or maybe he's on his way back.'

'How?'

'The tracks we can see?'

'Yeah.'

'They don't tell us which way the van was going. It might've made some of them heading *this* way.'

Cat scowled at me. 'Then where's the van?' she asked.

'I don't know. Maybe it *is* over there in the ruins. But it might be somewhere else. Maybe even circling around to come up behind us.'

'That's a cheerful thought.'

We both turned our heads and looked down to the left behind our car.

No sign of the van.

'Let's quit standing in the sun,' Cat said.

39

We sat down in a nook with rock walls on three sides. Overhanging rocks blocked out the sunlight. Though the hot wind still whipped against us, we had an area of shadow nearly the size of Cat's car.

'This is great,' I said.

'Not bad,' Cat said. 'Not bad at all. I wish we could see down, though. I'd like to keep my eye on the car.'

'It isn't going anywhere.'

'Peggy might.'

'I'll go out and check on her in a little while.'

'I can do it,' Cat said. 'And take a gander around for White while I'm at it. We don't want him sneaking up on us.'

'There's no hurry.'

'Nah. Let's relax and enjoy the shade.'

'It's still pretty hot,' I said.

'Hotter than hell. Take off your shirt and I'll clean you up a little. You're a mess.'

'Really?' I started to unbutton my shirt.

'Really. You look like you've been bobbing for apples in blood.'

'You'd think the sweat would've washed it off.'

'Mostly just smeared it.'

I handed my shirt to Cat. She took the lighter out of the pocket, set it nearby, then wadded my shirt and started to wipe my face with it. She took her time and was very gentle. Still, I flinched a couple of times when she got too close to the cut on my forehead.

Leaning very close, she peered at my wound. 'It's bleeding a little. Maybe you'd better lie down.'

I eased down onto my back. It felt very good to be stretched out. It would've felt even better, but the stone floor was pressing against my stake wound.

'Uh-oh,' I said. 'My back bandage is gone.'

Remembering the fang bites on my arm, I looked and saw that only two of the four bandages remained. Those on the underside of my arm were still securely attached. Somewhere along the line, however, I'd lost the other two. The exposed pair of fang holes on top of my forearm didn't appear to be bleeding.

'Sit up,' Cat said.

I sat up and leaned forward.

'It's gone, all right.'

'I must've lost it on the way up here. I was sweating like a hog. I lost a couple off my arm, too. Don't know where.'

'Doesn't really matter. You're not bleeding anymore. Not back here.'

'The arm's okay, too,' I reported. 'But I'd better climb down and look for that bandage. The big one off my back.'

'Forget it,' Cat said.

'White might find it.'

'So what? When he sees that we aren't in the car, he's gonna *know* we climbed up here. Where else *would* we go. He won't need your bandage to point the way. Just lie back down for a while, okay? We aren't done with you.'

I settled onto my back again.

Cat sat cross-legged by my shoulder, hunched forward and reached down with her right hand to continue cleaning my face. Apparently, she wanted to get all the blood off. After a while, she covered her forefinger with a layer of my shirt, moistened it in her mouth, then used it to clean around my eyes and lips. The sort of thing that mothers do to get chocolate off their kids.

'Lookin' good,' she murmured. 'Lookin' good.'

Then she shook open the shirt, nipped its hem with her teeth and tore it all the way up the front. After she'd jerked the upper end away from the collar, she had a strip of cloth two inches wide and nearly a yard long.

'You wrecked the shirt,' I pointed out.

'You did. You bled all over it.' She tore a large square of cloth off the front of the shirt. She folded that into a pad, pressed it gently against the cut on my brow, then tied it in place with the long strip. 'There you go,' she said.

'All patched up with no place to go.'

'All you need is a feather.'

'I'll be Big Chief Running Scared.'

Cat laughed softly and shook her head. Then, leaning forward again, she rubbed my chest and belly with the remains of the shirt. 'Seems like I'm always patching you up, cleaning blood off you...' She shook her head.

'I'm a high-maintenance kind of guy.'

She smiled, but only for a moment. Then she said, 'You'd still be in one piece if I'd stayed away from you last night.'

'I'm still in one piece. A few new rips and holes, that's all. I'm glad to have them.'

'You'll be singing a different tune after I get you killed.'

'My *silent* tune.'

'Ha ha.' She stopped rubbing me with the shirt. Frowning, she met my eyes. 'I wish I hadn't gotten you into this, Sammy.'

'There's no place I'd rather be.'

'Yeah, sure.'

'It's a fact.'

'I just never thought it would get this bad,' Cat said. 'I thought we'd kill Elliot and dump him out in the boonies somewhere, and that'd be it. I never would've dragged you into a mess like this.'

'Thank God you did.'

'No. I never should've...'

'You've got no idea, Cat. It's so good... Till last night, I thought I would never seen you again. I'd resigned myself to it. So... I don't know... This has been great. Having this chance to be with you...'

'Yeah, I'm such a prize.'

'You're the *only* prize that matters to me.'

Even as I said that, I knew how cornball and pathetic it probably sounded. But I went ahead and spoke the words, anyway. After what we'd gone through, I saw no real point in holding back.

Cat said, 'Jesus, Sam,' her voice breaking a little. She wiped her eyes. 'Why didn't I come running back to you *years* ago?'

'Big mistake,' I said.

'I'll say.' She sniffed and wiped her eyes again. 'You were such a sweet guy. And I just threw you away.'

'Well, your folks moved.'

'That was no excuse. And it wasn't why. You just weren't the kind of guy I thought I wanted.'

'What kind did you want?'

'Sadistic bastards, apparently.' She patted my chest and made a single laugh that sounded a little like a sob. 'Too bad you didn't know that, huh? You might've hung onto me. Forget the poetry, make me scream.'

'If only I'd known,' I said.

'That's right. It's like they say; nice guys finish last.'

'But I'm with you now.'

'That's right. You are.' She reached down to my waist with one hand and tugged at my belt.

'I hope you don't want me to whip you with that,' I said as she unfastened it. 'I don't think I'm up to it. I was in a crash, just climbed a mountain . . .'

'You don't have to whip me.'

She unbuttoned my jeans and lowered the zipper. My heart suddenly found itself pounding much harder than before.

'You'll be a lot more comfortable without these jeans on,' she said.

'Well. Yeah. They're pretty hot.'

She uncrossed her legs and crawled away. Staying on my back, I raised my head off the stone floor and watched her. She knelt down beyond my feet and took my shoes off. Then she leaned forward, grabbed the legs of my jeans and started to pull.

I lifted my hips and held on to my shorts.

A few seconds later, the shorts were all I had on. Except for my socks and a few bandages.

Cat rolled my jeans. Then she stood up and brought them to me. Crouching, she stuffed them under the back of my head like a pillow. 'I'll be right back,' she said.

'Where are you going?'

'I just want to see how things look down below.'

I thought about warning her to be careful; White might be around. It'd be bad news if he spotted her. But she was well aware of the danger, so I kept my mouth shut and watched her.

Bent over slightly, she stepped into the glaring sunlight. She took a few slow strides, then halted. As she scanned the basin, the wind tore at her shirt, sometimes lifting it so high that I

267

caught glimpses of her bare back. Finally, she went down on her hands and knees and crawled the rest of the way to the edge.

She spent a minute or two looking down, then crawled backward. Clear of the edge, she stood up and turned around. She shook her head as she came into the shadow. 'No sign of White. Peggy's the same.' She bent over and brushed the grit off her knees. Her knees were red. 'Nothing going on.'

'I wish we knew where White is.'

'Well, at least he's not here.' She took off her sandals, then sat down near my shoulder and crossed her legs. And stared me in the eyes. Her face looked solemn. Raising a corner of her mouth, she said, 'So what's the plan, Sammy?'

'I don't know.'

'You don't know much.'

'It's hard to think with my jeans off.'

'And you without clean underwear. Didn't your mother warn you about such things?'

'Sure she did. But people keep bleeding all over them. I've got a clean pair in the car.'

She grinned. 'Maybe you *did*. White took our luggage, remember?'

'Oh. That's right.'

'He didn't *want* you to have a clean pair.'

'That must be it.'

'So anyway, what'll we do now?'

'Stay here, I guess. Keep out of the sun.'

'That's what I was thinking.'

'Just lay low and see what develops. Maybe we can make it till dark without White finding us.'

'What then?' Cat asked.

'Good question. Sneak down, I guess. Deal with him.'

'*Deal* with him?'

'He'll be wanting to pull the stake on Elliot.'

'Soon as the sun goes down,' Cat said, nodding. 'But of course, Elliot ain't in the trunk.'

'We'll just have to play everything by ear. One way or another, we've gotta put White out of commission and take the van.'

'Don't forget rescuing Donny.'

'Right. Donny. The fly in the ointment. If he even exists.'

'He does,' Cat said. 'It would be nice if he didn't, but I bet he does.'

'God, what I'd give for a rifle.'

'At least we've got each other.' Smiling, she reached down and patted my chest.

'That's the main thing,' I said.

'What do you say we get some shut-eye?'

'Good plan,' I said.

'I'm full of good plans.'

'One of us should keep watch.'

'Let's not, and say we did.'

'White . . .'

'The hell with him.' She gave my chest a couple of gentle pats, then eased down and lay on her back. I turned my head. We were almost face to face, mine slightly higher than hers because of my jeans pillow. 'If he finds us,' she said, 'he finds us. But I don't really think he'll abandon Donny . . . or the nice shade he's got inside the van . . . to start climbing around on this rock pile in the noonday sun.'

'You're probably right,' I said.

'Hope so. All I know for sure is, I've gotta sleep. You do, too.'

'Yeah.'

'I'm all done in.'

'Me, too.'

Cat raised her arms from her sides and put her hands underneath her head for a pillow – the backs of her hands against the rough stone floor.

'Why don't you take my jeans?' I said. I started to pull the rolled bundle out from under my head.

'No. You keep them. This is fine.'

'It's gotta be tough on your hands.'

'A little.'

'Here. I insist.'

'They're yours. Anyway, I don't need them.' She sat up, took off her shirt, and rolled it into a neat little bundle. Then, holding it with both hands to the back of her head, she eased herself down again. 'See?'

'Yeah.'

269

'I bet it's softer than your jeans, too.'

'I'm sure it is.'

With the tiny pillow of her shirt beneath her head, she turned her face upward, rested her hands on her bare belly, yawned, and shut her eyes. 'This isn't bad,' she said.

'Not bad at all.'

Cat soon drifted off.

Not me.

I kept watch.

40

I lay there on my back, watching Cat.

Later, I stood up slowly and quietly. Not bothering to put my shoes on, I walked out into the sunlight. I was wearing only my shorts and socks. The sun felt blistering on my bare skin, but the wind helped. The rocks scorched my feet through the bottoms of my socks.

Trying to ignore the pain, I scanned the area. There was no sign of the van. Nor could I see any new tire tracks on the floor of the basin. Nothing looked different over at the distant ruins.

I crawled to the edge, just as Cat had done. The hot surface of the boulder stung my hands and knees, but I didn't let it stop me. I gazed down. No van. Our car still sat at the bottom of the slope with three of its doors open, nothing visible of Peggy except for a pale strip of thigh. I spent a few minutes studying the slope, trying to spot the bandage that had fallen off my back. Couldn't find it, though.

So I crawled backward, then stood up and hurried into our shaded nook.

I stood there, dripping sweat, and gazed at Cat.

She appeared to be asleep. She looked as if she hadn't moved at all since the last time I'd seen her: she was still lying on her back, face up, eyes shut, mouth open slightly, her hands curled on her belly, her legs stretched out and parted like a long, narrow V. She still wore only her cut-off jeans and her socks. But something had changed.

Her cut-offs were unbuttoned at the waist.

And unzipped.

And spread open enough to reveal a narrow blade of skin that seemed to be pointing at me. About three inches of bare skin, then a sheath of black panties for a couple more inches.

What's going on?

She must've *done it herself*, I thought. But why?

Maybe just because of the heat.

Or maybe she'd done it to tease me.

I remembered the magic breast creeping out of her blouse that morning in the car.

No matter the reason for her open fly, the view was getting to me . . . in a way that Cat would see for herself if she opened her eyes.

She can't possibly be asleep. She has to be faking it. Nobody unzips their jeans in their sleep.

I said quietly, 'Your barn door's open.'

And she cracked up. You'd think she had never heard anything so funny. She looked as if she'd been struck by a fit. While she shook her head, her shoulders and chest and belly jerked with convulsions. Her breasts bounced and jiggled. 'My *barn door*!' she gasped.

I noticed cringes mixed in with her laughter. A couple of times, she said, 'Ooooo.' And she took deep breaths and tried to calm down. 'Oh, it hurts. Don't make me laugh again. Don't say "barn door."'

Which set her off again.

She giggled and writhed and moaned and wiped tears from her eyes and finally regained control of herself. She shut her eyes. She seemed to concentrate on taking deep breaths and letting them out slowly. She murmured, 'Okay.'

'You okay?'

'I'm okay.' She sighed, wiped away her tears, and opened her eyes. 'Don't laugh. It hurts.'

'Sorry I did that to you. I wasn't trying to be funny.'

'It's just . . . I haven't heard that expression in years. It struck me.'

'Apparently so.'

'"Your barn door's open."' She shook her head and didn't even crack a smile. 'Lordy,' she said. 'Anyway, thanks for pointing it out.'

271

'You're welcome.'

'Is it *still* open?'

I glanced at the bare strip of skin, the wisp of black panties.

A grin stretched itself across Cat's face. 'Made ya look, made ya look.'

'Very funny,' I said.

Her gaze flicked downward. 'Is that your funny bone?'

'Jeez, Cat.'

She propped herself up on her elbows and said, 'Why don't you take your shorts off?'

The request made my heart pound like a mallet. 'You're kidding.'

'It's too hot for clothes.'

'Maybe so, but . . .'

'I'll take off mine.'

I tried to swallow.

'Would you like me to go first?' she asked.

'If you'd like.'

She grinned and shook her head. 'Huh-uh. *You* go first.'

'Me?'

'Come on, come on. Please. Pretty please.'

'I don't know.'

'Nothing to be scared of.'

'I know, but . . .'

'Pretty please with sugar,' she said.

'Okay.'

I pulled down my shorts, stepped out of them and stood up straight in front of Cat. She looked me up and down. I didn't know what to do with my hands, but I wanted to keep them out of the way so I patted the sides of my thighs. The hot wind felt good gusting against my body.

'Don't you feel a lot better now?' she asked.

'I feel like a dork.'

Grinning, she said, 'You should be feeling liberated.'

'Liberated, all right.'

'Turn around?'

I turned around slowly until I faced her again.

'Thank you,' she said. 'Now, come over here and lie down and try to get some sleep.' She patted the stone floor beside her.

'What about you?' I asked.

'We both need some sleep.'

'Aren't you . . . ? I took *mine* off.'

'So I see. And don't think I don't appreciate it.'

Her remark made me grin. 'Isn't it supposed to be your turn, now?'

'Nah.'

'You said you'd do it.'

'Maybe I'm a liar.'

'What're you up to?' I asked.

'Nothing. Not a thing. You looked hot, that's all.'

'*You* look hot.'

'I *feel* just fine.'

I crouched down for my shorts.

'No no no. Leave them there.'

'I'm getting cold.'

'Liar.'

'Now we're both liars,' I said.

'Just leave them off, okay?'

'They might blow away.'

'Pin them down with a shoe.'

I felt too vulnerable and excited and curious to put up any real argument, so I weighted my shorts down with a shoe. Then I returned to my place and lay down on my back beside Cat, my head on my rolled jeans.

'Doesn't that feel a lot better now?' Cat asked.

'It feels pretty good.'

'The wind.'

'Yeah.'

'Close your eyes.'

I shut my eyes.

'Now it's time to sleep.'

'How am I supposed to sleep?'

'Too keyed up?' she asked.

'I'd say so.'

'Worried about White?'

'Not at the moment.'

'Worried about me?'

'Not exactly worried.'

'I'll help you sleep,' she said.

273

'You will? How?'

'Through the magic of hypnotism.'

'Sure thing.'

'Mock me not. I have powers beyond your wildest dreams.'

'More than likely.'

'Lie still, and keep your eyes shut.'

'Whatever you say, Catherine.'

'Ready?'

'Ready.'

'Youuuu are in my powwwwer,' she said, her voice a low, droning mockery of a stage hypnotist. 'I am in controlll of your every moooovement, your every thought. Only mmmeeee. Allll you hear is my voice. It is making you verrry sleeeepy.'

'You've got a wonderful voice,' I whispered.

'Shhhh. You shaaaalll not speak.'

'Sorry.'

'You're feeeeling verrry sleeeepy. Verrry, verrry sleeeeepy.'

I felt anything but sleepy.

'Verrrry sleeeeeeeeeepy,' Cat intoned.

'Verrrry horrrrrrrrrrny,' I mimicked her.

'Wiiiiise-aaaass.'

'Screwwww youuuu,' I said.

'Okaaaaaaaay.'

My eyes leaped open. I turned my head and found Cat grinning in my face. She was lying on her side. Her cut-off jeans were gone, and so were her panties. She was bare all the way down – at least as far down as I could see. Her legs were bent at the knees, so that's where my view ended.

'Guess I'm not much of a hypnotist,' Cat whispered.

'You mean I'm not asleep?'

'I don't think so.'

'I was afraid I might be dreaming this.'

'Fear not.'

We were only a few inches apart. It took some effort and aches, but we squirmed closer to each other. Our mouths met. Her breasts touched my chest. My penis pushed against her belly. Her knees pressed my thighs.

We kissed.

Cat's lips felt dry and cracked. Her breath smelled like beer, not spearmint or cotton candy. My head ached. I felt sore all the way down to my toes. We were lying on a rough, gritty mattress of rock.

But this was it.

The best kiss ever.

It started with just our mouths and the small places where our bodies met. For a long while, it was only that. Lips and teeth and tongues ... sharing breath, sharing saliva ... gasping and sucking. Then were caresses. Hands stroking damp hair, gliding over wet, slick skin.

We were careful to be gentle because of our wounds.

I was timid about touching her, at first. She seemed timid, too, her hand roaming my back and side and never straying below my waist. But then I dared to reach lower and fill my hand with one of her buttocks. As my fingertips slipped into the heat of her crease, she lifted her leg and swung it over me. She rolled me onto my back and came down on top of me. All her weight was on me. I felt her heat and bones and softness.

While we'd been on our sides, we'd each had one arm pinned to the stone floor. Now our arms were free. I ran my hands up and down her slippery back and rump.

Soon, she pushed herself up. She held herself over me on her hands and knees, her face above mine. Wet curls clung to her forehead. Sweat dripped off the tip of her nose and chin and splashed onto my face. She was breathing hard.

I reached up underneath her and took her breasts in my hands. They felt as if they'd been dipped in hot water. Her nipples were erect and rubbery. I squeezed them. She moaned and arched her back.

Somehow, she must've known that I couldn't take much more of this.

So she waited no longer.

She didn't look, didn't hesitate. She seemed to know just where to go, and eased herself down. I felt her spread open. She took me slowly in, slowly and deeply. I felt myself sliding up her as if being sucked into a snug, juicy tunnel. It was more than I could take. Way more. Suddenly her mouth was on mine, sucking my tongue in as I thrust the rest of the way up, erupting.

For a long time after that, we stayed as we were, dripping sweat and panting for air. Then Cat kissed me many times, slowly and tenderly, on the eyes and cheeks and mouth. Then she lifted herself. I slid out of her. She climbed off and lay down beside me on her back. She put a hand on my hip, and sighed.

'Think you can sleep now?' she asked.

'Probably.'

I took hold of her hand and closed my eyes. The hot wind blew against me and seemed to cool the moisture on my body. I could hardly believe that, here in a forlorn corner of desert wasteland, hiding in the rocks from a man who probably intended to murder us, I had finally made love with Cat.

It was what I'd always wanted to do.

And I'd pretty much given up all hope.

I'd thought it would never happen, that I would pass my entire life without her, without ever finding out how it is to plunge so deeply into the body and soul of a woman you love.

It was like nothing that had ever happened to me before.

And better.

41

I think we slept for a long time.

Cat woke me up with her mouth.

My headache was gone.

'Hi,' I said.

'Urrrr,' she said. Then she raised her head until her mouth was empty. She grinned and said, 'Time to wake up.'

'You're a great alarm clock.'

'Hope I haven't alarmed you.'

'Did White come back?'

'Nope. Already checked. Everything looks the same down there.' She slid her tongue up me and I squirmed. Then she said, 'How are you feeling?'

'A lot better.'

'Me, too. I probably should've let you sleep longer.'

'No, that's fine.'

'I just got tired of waiting, that's all.'

'Waiting for what?' I asked.

'A refill.'

* * *

This time, nothing ended quickly. We lingered over each other. She explored me, played with me. I touched her in ways that I'd never touched a woman before. I delved into her with my fingers, with my tongue, with my penis. I kissed and licked and sucked her in many wonderful places, and she did much the same to me.

We worked each other into mindless, thrashing frenzies.

We wore each other out.

By the time we finished, we were limp ruins, sweaty and breathless. We had abrasions on our elbows and knees, even on our hips and buttocks from too much contact with the stone floor. We were red around our lips. Cat's cheeks were ruddy from my whiskers. We both had several red blotches from being sucked on.

And we both bled.

All our bandages were gone. Some, we'd lost earlier. Those that remained, we'd pulled off each other – picked off, nibbled off with our teeth.

I bled from my cut brow, the stake wound in my back and the fang holes in my forearm. Cat bled from the fang holes in her neck and foot and groin. We'd gotten a little carried away with the sucking.

When we finally finished, we lay exhausted on our backs, drenched with sweat, gasping for air.

For a long time, we couldn't talk.

Then Cat said, 'Are you okay?'

'Wrecked for life.'

'Me, too.'

'I don't think I can move.'

'Too much loss of precious bodily fluids,' Cat said.

'At least.'

'Not that much was lost. Mostly exchanged. You taste great, by the way.'

'You, too.'

'Lip-smackin' good.'

'Thanks.'

She was silent for a few moments, then said, 'Have you ever done that before?'

'What in particular?'

277

'Tasted somebody else's blood?'

'I don't think so. Have you?'

'Yeah.' She turned her head and looked at me. 'A few times. But this was the first time without Elliot forcing me to do it. I liked it.'

'Me, too.'

'The sucking.'

'Yeah.'

'And how it squirted and filled my mouth.'

'It was pretty damn exciting,' I said.

'And knowing I've got your blood inside me. Your blood *and* your semen.'

'Not to mention sweat and spit,' I added.

She smiled. 'We're all mixed together now, you and I. We're each other.'

She slid her hand toward me. I took hold of it and squeezed it. 'We're each other,' I said.

'The question is, are we vampires now?'

'Because we sucked each other's blood?'

'Right,' Cat said. 'What do you think?'

'Nah.'

'If not, why not?'

'Me, I'm just a guy who went overboard sucking your neck and happened to hit the place where Elliot put those holes.'

'A freak accident?' Cat suggested.

'Right. But then you wouldn't let me stop.'

'You didn't *want* to stop, did you?'

'Not exactly. But it doesn't make me a vampire.'

'You seemed to like it *a lot*.'

'Only because it was you,' I said.

'Really?'

'Absolutely. I've got no interest at all in sucking anyone but you.'

'Does that mean I'm your gal?'

'You've always been my gal.'

' "And you, in the dark, suck sweetly my heart's core down the secret corridors of my veins." It's almost like you had a premonition about all this.'

'It was just wishful thinking,' I explained.

'Being the sucker or the suckee?'

'Maybe both.'

'Now you've got me inside you. How do you like that?'

'I love it.'

'I love having you in me, too.' Her hand tightened its grip. 'If we get out of this alive...'

'We will.'

'If we do, Sammy, I don't want to lose you again. I feel so good when we're together. I guess I love you. I guess I've always loved you.'

She came to me. She put a leg and an arm across me, and gently kissed me on the mouth. There was no urgency to it, no lust. After we kissed, she rested her head on my chest. I stroked her short, damp hair.

Soon, I fell asleep.

When I woke up, I found Cat still sprawled half on top of me, asleep and breathing slowly. The wind had died down. Though we were still lying in shadows, the air felt hot and suffocating. I felt Cat's breath on the skin of my chest. And an odd wetness. Looking down, I saw a small, clear pool where the corner of her mouth rested on my chest. She was drooling on me.

I smiled.

Then heard the blare of a car horn.

Cat still dozed.

The horn honked again.

Gently, I jostled Cat's shoulder. She moaned. Her head moved, and the drool vanished under her face. When she raised her head, the fluid ran down her ruddy cheek and dripped off her jaw onto me. 'Wha's...?' she asked.

'Somebody honked a horn.'

'Huh?' She twisted her head around and peered up at me, blinking.

'A horn honked.'

She grimaced. 'White?'

'I don't know. Maybe it's Peggy.'

Frowning, Cat slowly shook her head. She looked as if she hadn't quite finished waking up. 'The way my car's wrecked, I don't think...'

It honked again.

'My horn doesn't sound like that.'

'I'll go and take a look,' I told her.

'Me, too.'

We both got to our feet, groaning and wincing. Our clothes were scattered all over the place. We weren't even wearing our socks anymore. Cat snatched up her shirt and put it on. I stepped into my shorts. We both struggled into our socks as fast as we could, hopping from foot to foot.

'It hasn't honked in a while,' Cat said.

'Maybe it went away.'

'Fat chance.'

I slipped the church key down the side of my sock. Cat stepped into her sandals, then started toward the sunlight.

'No, wait,' I said.

Ignoring me, she left the shadow behind and hurried forward, crouching low. I went after her. I caught up to her as she sank to her knees.

Side by side, we crawled toward the edge. It was tough on the hands and knees. But not nearly as tough as what we saw.

White had returned.

Donny was real.

They stood together on top of the van, which was stopped behind the wreck of Cat's car.

All four doors of the car stood open.

Peggy looked as if she'd tumbled out – or been shoved. She lay sprawled on her back, her legs propped up on the door sill, her feet still inside the car. She seemed to be unconscious or dead.

Donny was very much alive.

Like his sister, he was skinny and blonde. He had very long hair. White was clutching it, tugging it upward to keep the boy standing and under control. Donny's arms were behind his back. Though I couldn't see them, I figured they must be bound together with something.

He wore Cat's high-top leather hiking shoes. Without the laces, they looked big and floppy on him.

He wore nothing else.

His skin was red and shiny, but he didn't appear to be injured.

White, slightly to the rear of Donny, held his knife close to the boy's throat. His eyes seemed to be searching our hillside.

Afraid he might spot us, I gave Cat's shirt a tug. We both crept backward a few inches to where the edge cut off our view of White. If we couldn't see him, he couldn't see us.

'We've gotta do something,' Cat muttered.

'I know. I know. Good God.'

'Did you see Peggy?'

'Yeah.'

'Think he killed her?'

'I think the crash did,' I said. 'Or she might be alive.'

'She didn't look alive.'

'The kid looks okay.'

'Shit. The poor . . .' She clamped her lower lip between her teeth.

I rubbed her back gently through her shirt.

'We've gotta save him,' she said.

'How'll we do that?'

'Any ideas?' she asked.

'You're the tricky one,' I reminded her.

She had a frantic look in her eyes. She shook her head. Then she said, 'Just . . . We've gotta separate them, you know? It's the same as before. As long as White's got Donny, we can't touch him.'

'I don't *wanta* touch him.'

'You and me both.'

'But I guess we have to take him down,' I said.

'We'd better.'

'Let's go back and get dressed,' I said. 'I want to have my clothes on before we try anything.'

'Same here.'

We crawled backward until we were well clear of the edge, then turned around and scurried into our shaded nook. We hurried into our clothes. My jeans felt heavy and stiff. They seemed to trap the heat of my legs. My shirt was a ruin, but I put it on anyway and dropped the lighter into the pocket.

I watched Cat try to button up her shirt. Her hands were trembling badly. The buttons kept slipping out of their holes. She finally managed to fasten two of them. Then she picked up my headband and bandage.

Standing in front of me, she gently pressed the bandage against the wound on my brow. Then she tied it in place with the long strip of cloth. Resting her hands on my shoulders, she stared into my eyes.

'I hope I haven't gotten you killed,' she said.

'Same here.'

She smiled. 'Tough cookie.'

'*You're* the tough cookie.'

'I just hope we're tough enough for this.'

'Whatever happens,' I said, 'I'm glad I got to be here with you.'

'I'm not worth dying for.'

'The hell you're not. If I die today, my life had a happy ending.'

Her eyes watered up. 'That's so corny.'

'I know. I try not to be.'

'I love you, Sammy.'

'And I love you, Cat Lorimer.'

She came in close against me. We put our arms around each other and kissed. We both knew this might be our last kiss, that these might be our final minutes of being alone together. We were in no hurry for it to end.

We kissed gently, clinging to each other as if letting go would destroy us.

Then the boy let out a quick, sharp cry.

Cat hugged me fiercely and said, 'Let's do it.'

42

I glanced back to see if we were leaving anything behind.

A few plastic bandage strips and dots, that's all.

If I'd had time, I would've picked them up. But the kid had cried out, so I couldn't be bothered about clean-up.

I knew we were leaving behind a lot more than just those bandages. I hated to go. I wondered if we would be able to find this place again, this shadowed nook that would always remain a most special place to me. It would be nice to come back, someday.

I just hoped to God there would *be* a someday for us.

A future.

If we can just make it through tonight...

The kid shouted, 'Cat! Sam! Help me!'

We sank to our hands and knees, and crept forward until we could see him and White on the roof of the van. White still held him by the hair.

Only one thing had changed.

Blood now spilled out of a three-inch, diagonal slash above Donny's left nipple. He looked as if somebody had painted a bright red stripe down his body. It started at the slash and traveled downward, wavering a little here and there but always descending. It had already made its way past his waist and halfway down his left thigh.

'I reckon you're up there someplace!' White called out. 'You better come on down, 'fore I lose my patience. Can you see what I done to this boy? Your fault! You should've stayed put. Try and run out on me, bad shit flies. *Blood* flies. You hear me?'

Cat eased herself backward, and I did the same. We faced each other.

'I've got a plan,' Cat said.

I gave her a quick nod.

'I'll go down,' she said.

'No.'

'I'm gonna count to ten,' White called. We stayed out of sight and stared at each other. 'That'll give you time to think about it. Figure out if you wanta hide up there and watch me whittle this boy down to shreds. 'Cause that's what I aim to do, right here in front of your eyes, if you don't come on down and give yourselves up. If you gone off somewhere and can't hear me, tough titty. The kid gets it anyway. You should've stayed in the fuckin' car. *One!*'

'I'll go down and tell him you're dead,' Cat said, speaking softly and quickly. 'I'll say we crawled up here, but you were really badly injured in the crash and you bled to death.'

I shook my head.

'*Two!*'

'You can't go down there,' I said.

'Sure I can.'

'He'll know you're lying.'

'*Three!*'

283

'No, he won't. The only way he can find out is by climbing up here. He won't do that. Not in this heat.'

'If you go down, you'll just...'

'*Four!*'

'...be giving him another hostage.'

'But you'll be free to sneak around. Maybe you can sneak up close enough to jump him.'

'What'll he be doing to *you* while I sneak around?'

'I'll be...'

'*Five!*'

'...all right.'

'*Gonna cut this boy, make him squeal for his momma!*'

'Like Donny's all right?' I asked.

'That's just it,' Cat said. 'He doesn't want me, he wants you.'

'He wants us both.'

'Yeah. Sure he does. He...'

'*Seven-eight, cut him straight!*'

'Shit, did you hear that?'

Cat nodded and said, 'He can't let us get away. But *you're* the one he's really interested in. He likes guys.'

'He was messing around with Peggy, remember?'

'So she said. But she was...'

'*Niiiine!*'

'She was the one he sent on errands,' Cat continued. 'Not the boy. He always kept Donny with him. Peggy was the expendable one. He used her as a helper, and meanwhile he was playing games with Donny in the back of the van.'

'If you're right...'

'I'm right.'

'*Nine and a half!*'

'Then shouldn't *I* be the one to go down?' I blurted. 'I'd be a better distraction than you.'

'Maybe so.'

That wasn't what I'd really hoped to hear. I'd only wanted to talk her *out* of going down to White, not talk myself *into* it.

'Only one problem,' Cat said. 'You're...'

'*Nine and three quarters! You gonna let me carve this kid? Ain't you got a decent bone in your bodies?*'

'You're bigger and stronger than me,' Cat said. 'We'd stand

a better chance if I'm his captive and *you're* the one who jumps him from behind.'

'I'll go down and give myself up,' I said, 'and try to jump him from the front.'

She grimaced as if the idea caused her pain. 'I don't know,' she muttered.

'Time's up!'

'I'm coming down!' I shouted.

'Ha! I knew you fucks were up there! Knew it! Get on down here.'

I said quickly to Cat, 'I don't want you to start playing commando. I'll do whatever I can to take care of White, but you stay out of it.'

'That defeats the whole purpose, dummy.'

'The purpose is for you to survive.'

'It's for *all* of us to survive. Except him.'

'Let's see you! Show yourselves! Now!'

'You can get away,' I told Cat. 'If I run out of luck, you can still make it out of here. Hide till after dark, and...'

'Don't insult me.'

We gazed into each other's eyes.

'I'm gonna start cuttin'!'

'Wait a minute!' I yelled.

'I just want you to make it,' I told Cat. 'That's all.'

'Hey. There's an old saying. "We must all hang together, or we'll surely hang separately." I think Dylan Thomas said it.'

'I think it was Winston Churchill,' I told her. 'Or maybe Benjamin Franklin.'

'They'll do,' she said.

'That's it!' White shouted. *'The kid...'*

'Okay okay! Here I come.'

'We'll hang together,' Cat said. 'Go on down, honey.' She leaned toward me and kissed me gently, briefly on the lips.

I stood up.

White latched his eyes on me. 'Where's the bitch?'

'I don't know any bitches,' I said, and sat on the ledge.

He sneered. 'Same wiseass fuckhead punk, aren't you?'

'That's me.' I scooted off, dropped, and landed on my feet.

'So where is she?'

'Who?'

He slashed the boy. I cringed as if the blade had sliced my own skin. Donny squealed, his whole body jerking. This time, White had cut him above his right nipple. Blood started sliding down from the gash.

'Don't!' I shouted.

'Where *is* she!'

'She's dead.'

'The fuck she is.'

'She *is*!' I hurried downward, leaping from boulder to boulder.

'Stop!' He pressed the blade to Donny's throat.

I stumbled to a halt.

'Cat's dead, huh?'

'It was the crash. She . . . She seemed okay, but . . . Must've been something inside her. Some kind of internal bleeding, maybe, or . . . We laid down to rest, up there.' I turned my head and pointed at the slope above me. 'And she just . . . just *died*.' I shook my head, trying to show how upset I was. Then I shouted, '*You killed her, you bastard! You did it!*'

'Yeah, sure I did.'

'*Why did you have to crash into us like that?*'

He grinned and said, 'Nailed you good, huh?'

'*Why'd you do it!*'

'Felt like fuckin' you up, that's why.'

'*You killed Cat!*'

'Sure I did. Tell you what . . . Go on up wherever it is you say she croaked and get her body. Bring it on down here.'

I gaped at him.

'Got a problem with that?' he asked.

'I can't carry her. I'm too wrecked.'

'Well, then, just throw her down. I don't care how you do it, but get her ass down here. And guess what. She better be dead, or I'll slash Donny's throat from ear to ear. *Now go get her!*'

43

I turned away and started to climb. I felt sick.

He was too smart for us; he'd seen through our trick.

Now what?

I thought about taking a fall. I might pretend to be knocked out cold. Maybe I could take a really *bad* fall and knock myself out for real, or break a leg. That would at least stop me from climbing up to fetch Cat's 'body'.

But I had no idea about how to stop him from slitting Donny's throat. He'd already cut the boy twice. He probably wouldn't need much of an excuse to finish the job.

The old reasoning didn't work anymore; as far as I could see, he no longer needed Donny. He'd stopped needing him the moment he crashed into our car: we'd apparently reached our destination; we couldn't drive away; Peggy, in a coma or dead, no longer had to be controlled. He probably had little more use for Donny sexually, either, since they'd been together the whole time Cat and I were up in the rocks. Anything he'd wanted to do to the kid, he'd probably already done. Except kill him.

We oughta just let him do it. Hell, let him do whatever he wants to them.

But I knew Cat would never go for that.

I suddenly hoped that she had already disappeared.

But when I climbed high enough to see over the top of our ledge, I found her sitting cross-legged, staring at me.

I said, 'We're screwed.'

I boosted myself up and struggled to swing my leg over the top. Last time, Cat had lent a hand. Now she sat a few feet away, where White couldn't see her, and watched me. She seemed calm.

'We have to do what he wants,' she said, speaking barely loud enough for me to hear her.

I squirmed and clawed my way over the edge, and rolled onto my back. Turning my head, I looked at Cat. 'Are you nuts?' I asked. 'He wants your *body*.'

'Doesn't everyone?'

'Your *dead* body. I told him you're *dead*. Now I'm supposed to . . .'

'I know, I heard.'

'And you think we should give him what he *wants*? Am I supposed to *kill* you?'

287

'I'm already dead. See?' She flopped onto her back.

'Oh, God.'

Scooting herself farther away from the edge, she said, 'Take me down to him.'

I pushed myself to my hands and knees, and crawled to her. 'This won't fool him,' I said.

'It might for a while. As long as he doesn't get a close look at me. Maybe it'll give us a chance.'

'How the hell do I get you *down* there?'

'Carry me. I'm dead.'

'What if I *drop* you?'

'It'll add to the authenticity.'

'Oh, terrific.'

'Just be careful.'

'Why don't we stay here? He won't be able to get us up here. After dark, we'll . . .'

'We can't do that.'

'I don't want to lose you.'

'This could be our best chance,' Cat said. 'Now, pick me up before he starts getting suspicious.'

'Hell, he knows you aren't dead.'

'He doesn't *know* it. He just *thinks* it. We'll change his mind. Now, come on.'

As I squatted beside her, she hooked her left hand behind my neck and sat up slightly. I slipped one arm under her back, the other behind her legs.

'Up we go,' she said.

'You can't hold on to me.'

'I know that.' She lowered her arm and draped it across her body. She rested her right arm on the ground by her side. 'I'll let this one dangle lifelessly,' she said.

I had to smile.

'Okay,' I said. 'Here we go.'

I stood up straight, lifting her, and held her cradled in my arms like a guy about to carry his bride over the threshold. Like that, but also like the peasant in *Frankenstein* bringing his dead daughter into the village.

Too bad Cat wasn't the *size* of that girl.

Even though she was thin, she wasn't small.

She wasn't light.

I turned around with her, staggered by her weight.

'Howdy, Cat!' White called from below.

She didn't respond.

'Can't I just leave her up here?' I called. 'She's awfully heavy.'

'If she's too heavy for you, throw her down.'

Shaking my head, I took a couple of steps in the direction of the edge. As I neared it, Cat's body blocked it from my view. And I realized that I couldn't possibly carry her down like this. For one thing, I wouldn't be able to see where we were going. For another, all her weight was in front of me; it was too much strain on my arms and back, and made my balance precarious.

We'd been stopped by the very first obstacle: the five-foot drop from our ledge to the boulder below it.

I turned around, putting my back to White, then whispered, 'Stay loose,' and sank to a crouch. I tried to be careful, setting her down, but the back of her head bumped the rock surface. Her face flinched slightly, but White had no way of seeing that. Mostly, she did a good job of looking dead.

Leaving her sprawled on her back, I scurried down over the edge. Then I leaned against the wall and reached for her. I clutched her upper left arm with one hand, grabbed the leg hole of her cut-offs with the other. And pulled. Dragged her to the edge and off it.

She tumbled against me, knocking me backward. I planted a foot behind us and shoved, propelling us forward – saving us, but ramming Cat against the wall. She grunted. White didn't stand a chance of hearing it, though; he was laughing too hard.

I pinned Cat to the wall and struggled with her, trying to lower her legs and stand her upright.

She did a good job of staying limp.

After wrestling with her for a while, I managed to flop her over my shoulder. I stepped away from the wall, lifting her and hugging her thighs to my chest. This was much better. She felt half as heavy as before, and didn't ruin my balance.

'You okay?' I asked.

She didn't answer, but maybe she hadn't heard me. I'd spoken softly, and her head was down behind my back, probably near my waist.

I didn't risk saying anything else to her. But I gave her rump a pat through the seat of her cut-offs before turning around.

White, on top of the van, still clutched Donny by the hair. But he'd lowered the knife and held it by his side. He had stopped laughing. He was grinning, though, and shaking his head as he watched me lug Cat down the rocky slope.

Donny was watching, too. The way his lips were peeled back, he almost looked as if he were grinning. But I figured it must be a grimace. He had a pair of broad, red stripes down the front of his body. They ran from the gashes on his chest, leaving a median strip of bare skin down to his groin. The twin paths of blood continued down both his thighs. They turned his knees and shins crimson, then vanished into the open tops of his shoes ... Cat's shoes.

So it probably wasn't a grin on his face.

On my way down, I also looked at Peggy. She was still sprawled on her back beside the car, her legs propped up by the door sill, her dress shoved up so that she was bare below the waist. The blood on her head and face looked as if it had dried out and turned maroon.

She looked mighty damn dead.

I wondered if Donny had seen her. *Could* he see her from up there on top of the van? Maybe not. Hard to tell. She was very close to the car and down on the ground; maybe the car blocked Donny's view. I hoped so. It'd be awful for him to see his sister that way.

'Hold it there,' White said.

I couldn't stop right away; momentum seemed to be shoving me down from boulder to boulder. But I staggered to a halt at the rim of the next drop-off. I stood there, struggling to breathe, shaking all over from the exertion and the heat and my fears. We were nearly to the ground. Why had he ordered me to stop? Had he noticed something?

'Don't move,' he said.

I raised my head and blinked sweat out of my eyes.

And found myself face to face with him.

He'd stopped our descent when I was level with the roof of the van. He and Donny stood on the other side of a fifteen-foot gap.

I said, 'Wha' y'wah?' It was the best I could do. I couldn't get enough breath. My heart pounded so hard and fast that I thought it might crash its way out through my ribs.

'Hate to tell you this, scout,' White said, 'but I've got me a gut feeling you and the bitch are trying to pull a fast one.'

I shook my head.

'She's no deader than you are.'

I shook my head some more. It felt drenched and baked.

'Do *you* think she's dead, Donny boy?'

The kid's head twitched up and down a couple of times. He muttered, 'Sure.'

'Bet you're only just saying that, on account of how I'm aiming to slit your throat if she ain't.'

'She's dead,' I gasped out.

'Well, I got me some doubts. Why don't we make sure?'

'Just ... I can't keep ... I wanna get down.'

'Put her on her feet. Stand her up for me. Right there where you are.'

I took a couple of strides backward.

'Right there!'

With shuddering muscles, I crouched until Cat's feet touched down in front of my own feet. Then I hugged her like a kid clinging to a tree trunk and worked my way up her body, my shoulder shoving up against her belly, unbending her, sliding up her chest. She was bare and hot and wet all the way to her neck.

She felt completely limp.

When I had her upright against me – my arms beneath her armpits and wrapped tightly around her back – I could feel her heartbeat and her breathing. I could also feel her shirt. Though it was no longer buttoned, it had stayed on while she'd been hanging upside down behind me. As I straightened her up, it fell down over my arms.

Her head hung backward and off to the side. Her eyes were shut, her mouth open.

I wished her eyes were open. I wished she'd give me a wink. Nothing.

You're damn good at this, I thought.

'Real good,' White said. 'Real good. Now turn her around so we can take a good look at her.'

I clutched her against me and shook my head.

'Hey, now, this ain't no time to quit. You hauled her all the way down this far. You're damn near home free. Just turn her on around.'

'She'll fall!'

'So what? She's dead, ain't she?'

'I don't wanta drop her.'

'Just turn her around and hold on tight.'

And that's what I did. It wasn't easy. My muscles were almost too weak and shaky to work at all; Cat was heavy and limp and slippery. I had to do it, though. She would've told me to do it, if she'd been able.

Finally, I had her facing White and Donny.

I stood behind her, my arms underneath her shirt and arms, hugging her tightly around the chest, holding her up.

'What do you think, Donny boy? She dead or alive?'

Donny shook his head slightly. His eyes seemed to be fixed on Cat's chest.

'I asked you something, kid. What's the answer?'

'Dead,' Donny said.

'You better hope so.' White grinned at me. 'Let go of her.'

'No!'

'Well then, sorry about this, Donny, but looks like . . .'

Cat suddenly jerked and twisted in my arms, her head coming up, her right arm rearing back. I thought for a moment that she'd been struck by a convulsion.

Then her arm whipped forward and a stone streaked toward White.

44

Instead of slashing Donny's throat, White tried to duck. He also flung up his knife-hand as if he hoped to knock the stone aside.

His hand wasn't quick enough to intercept it.

His duck, not Cat's aim, lined it up with his right eye.

The chunk of rock was about the size of a golf ball. I'd never seen it before. Cat must've kept it hidden in her hand, waiting for just the right moment.

It hit White in the eye. But it hit his socket, too. I heard a thump like a knuckle striking wood. As the stone bounced off him, he cried out, '*Yahhh!*' His red face was pinched with sudden pain. His hand lurched up. I thought he might put the knife through his eye, but he stopped himself just in time. Blood began spilling down his face.

Apparently, he *had* to grab the wound. So he let go of Donny's hair and did it.

That hand must've been White's anchor. The moment he let go of the hair, he started staggering backward.

Cat grabbed my arms with both her hands and wrenched them open, setting herself free.

Donny turned and saw White stumbling backward.

Cat leaped off the boulder, arms out, shirt catching the air and rising behind her.

Donny, hands tied behind his back, ran at White with his head down.

White teetered on the edge of the van's roof.

Donny rammed him in the belly and knocked him off.

Squealing and waving his arms, White fell out of sight.

'Let's nail him!' Cat shouted as she charged full-tilt down the slope.

I rushed after her.

In just a few seconds, she reached the bottom. She cut hard to the left and raced for the rear of the van, her feet kicking up behind her. I noticed that she'd lost both sandals somewhere along the way.

'Wait up!' I shouted, though I don't know where I found the breath for it.

Cat dashed out of sight around the van's rear corner just as I sprang to the ground.

'*Wait!*' I shouted again.

Don't go after him alone! I wanted to yell, but couldn't.

I raced around the rear of the van.

And found them on the other side.

White lay spread-eagled on the ground, looking dazed. He still had the knife in his right hand. But he seemed incapable of lifting it.

Cat, standing between his spread legs, kicked him in the groin. His eyes bugged out and he made an awful noise – a cross between a grunt and a scream. Then Cat took a big hop and landed with both feet on his belly. Air blasted out of him. His head, hands and feet jumped off the ground and dropped back down. He had his mouth wide open like someone on the verge of throwing up.

As Cat stumbled off him, I hurried over and took the knife out of his hand.

Then she came into my arms. We held each other – held each other *up* – while I kept an eye on White. For a few minutes, I thought that neither of us would be able to move again.

White seemed to be worse off than we were.

Finally, we let go of each other. We both leaned back against the side of the van. The metal felt hot, but not seering, and the sun had traveled across the sky enough to give us a few feet of shade.

'What'll we do with him?' Cat asked.

'I don't know. We'd better do something, though.'

'Kill him?'

'I don't know,' I said.

'You don't know much.'

We looked at each other and smiled.

'God, Cat.'

'Yeah.'

'We did it. *You* did it. I ... I couldn't believe my eyes. Where'd you get that stone?'

'Duh.'

I actually laughed. 'Did you see Donny knock him off the van?' I asked.

'No. Did he?'

'Butted him with his head.'

'Jeez. That's cool.'

'Where'd he go?' I asked. Then I called out, '*Donny! We've got him, Donny! Over here. We're beside the van!*'

He didn't answer.

Cat yelled, '*Yo! Donny! Hey!*'

Nothing.

'Maybe he's over with Peggy,' I said.

'He could at least answer us,' Cat said.

'*DONNY!*' I shouted.

Still nothing.

'I'll go and see what's up,' Cat said. 'You keep an eye on our friend.'

She hurried away.

I watched White. His right eye had already swollen up. It look like a peeled egg with a gash across the front. But I'd never seen a peeled egg that was drenched with blood. His other eye was open and seemed to be staring vacantly at the sky. His mouth gaped, lips peeled back to bare his teeth. I could see his chest rise and fall. I could also see that he'd peed the front of his jeans.

'If you decide to get up,' I told him, 'change your mind. I've had enough action for one day.'

He looked as if he hadn't even heard me.

The van rocked slightly against my back. I didn't move, though. Just kept leaning against it, watching White.

A couple of minutes later, Cat muttered, 'Well, shit.' Her voice seemed to be coming from the roof of the van. She shouted, '*DONNY! HEY! COME BACK HERE!*'

'What?' I called.

'He's running away.' She shouted for him a few more times. Then she said, 'I don't know if he heard me, but he isn't turning around. Running like a bat outa hell. In *my* shoes.'

'How'd he get down?'

'I don't know,' Cat said. 'Jumped? He sure didn't climb down the ladder, not with his hands tied behind his back.' A few moments later, she said, 'Looks like he's heading for those old mining ruins.'

'Damn it, we won! What's the matter with him?'

'Maybe he saw Peggy and freaked out. Who knows? He's just a kid. God knows what White put him through. Maybe he just wants to get *away* from everyone. Anyway, I'm coming down.'

The van shook a little more. I heard a quiet 'Ooomph,' which must've been Cat hitting the ground after jumping off the bottom of the van's ladder. After that, I heard a door open on the passenger side.

When Cat came along a few minutes later, she had a plastic bottle of water in each hand. Our rope hung in coils off her right shoulder. 'Here you go,' she said, and handed a bottle to me. Then she stepped in beside me and leaned back against the van.

I still had the knife in one hand, so I slipped its blade down behind my belt. I used both hands to twist off the bottle cap. Then I drank.

The water was warm, but tasted great.

We both spent a while drinking.

As we drank, we watched White.

'Most of our stuff's in there,' she said. 'The tools and lighter fluid and things. Not the food and drinks. I don't know what they did with it all.'

'Are there empties?'

'A few. Most of it's just gone . . . Like maybe they threw it out.'

'Or unloaded it,' I suggested.

'Where would . . . over at the ruins?'

'Maybe.'

'Had themselves a party in one of those shacks, maybe.'

'They might've,' I said. 'They were apparently over in that direction.'

'And they sure wouldn't have wanted to stay in the van. Hotter than blue hell in there.'

'Nice of them to leave the water behind.'

'I guess they don't drink the stuff.'

'Some people don't.'

'Why drink water when you've got Pepsi or beer?'

'No calories,' I pointed out.

'Kids and psychos don't worry about calories.'

'Think not?'

'I'm positive,' Cat assured me. 'It's a well-known fact.' She took another drink, then lowered her bottle and said, 'So what'll we do about *our* psycho? I've got the rope and you've got the knife. Should we tie him up or butcher him?'

If he could hear us, he gave no sign.

'I don't think we should kill him in cold blood,' I said.

'Probably not.'

'Let's compromise,' I said.

'How?'

'You tie him up, and I'll kill him if he resists.'

'That sounds fair,' Cat said. 'Did you hear that, White?'

He didn't respond.

'I must've hurt him pretty good,' Cat said.

'Unless he's faking.'

'Faking does happen.'

'Let's go ahead and get him tied. Then it won't matter.'

We finished our bottles of water. While Cat tossed the empties into the van, I pulled the knife out of my belt, stepped around White and stood over his head.

Cat slung the coiled rope off her shoulder. She squatted by White's right hand, knotted one end of the rope around it, then stood up. Pulling the rope, she stepped over his body. She dragged his hand to the center of his belly, then gathered in his other hand, holding it by the wrist, and bound the two hands together. She wrapped them with several figure-eights and loops, drawing the rope so tight that she must've cut off the circulation in his hands. By the time she was finished, it would've taken Houdini to get loose.

She had plenty of rope left over.

'Now what?' she asked. She stood up, paying out rope as she stepped clear of him. 'Tie his feet?'

'Maybe not yet. We've gotta figure out what to do, first.'

'What're you thinking?'

'I guess what we need to do is load Peggy into the van, go find Donny, and get the hell out of here.'

'Right.'

'So we have a choice about White. Either take him with us or leave him behind.'

'By 'behind,' you mean alive and tied up right here on the ground?'

'Yeah.'

'No,' Cat said. 'Bad idea. We can't leave him anywhere alive. If we don't kill him, he has to stay with us so we can keep our eyes on him.'

'Yeah, you're probably right about that.'

'So I guess we load him in the van and take him along.'

'Turn him in to the cops?' I asked.

'Who said anything about that?'

'If we're not going to kill him...'

'We sure as hell aren't turning him in. He'll tell the cops about Elliot.'

'What'll we do with him?'

'We'll think of something. For now, let's worry about getting him into the van.'

'I don't think we can pick him up,' I said.

Cat gave the rope a tug, jerking his bound hands. Then she said, 'White, you wanta stand on your feet?'

'He seems pretty well out of it,' I said.

'Let's both pull.'

I slipped the knife into my belt. Then the two of us lined up, me behind Cat. Using all four of our hands, we had a tug-o-war with the rope and brought White into a sitting position. Even then, he seemed barely aware of what was going on. He slumped forward, head drooping toward the ground between his knees.

'I think this is about as far as we'll get him,' I said.

'Stand up,' Cat commanded. 'Get on your feet, White. We want you in the van.'

He just sat there, not even looking up.

'Hold the rope,' Cat told me.

I kept it taut, stretching White's arms toward me, while Cat pulled the knife out of my belt and walked over to him.

He paid no attention to her approach.

'What're you going to do?' I asked.

She didn't answer until she was standing behind him. Then she said, 'I'm going to hurt him if he doesn't stand up.'

'You'd better stand up, Mr White,' I said.

He still just sat there.

'Should I give him a count of ten?' Cat asked.

'Sure, why not.'

She said, 'One.'

White didn't move.

'I think it'll be a waste of words,' she said.

'What?'

'Counting to ten. Did I just say "ten"?'

'Yeah.'

'I thought so,' she said, and suddenly bent down, pounding the knife's blade hard into the top of his right shoulder.

45

It got his attention.

He threw back his head, squealing at the sky.

Cat pulled the knife out and took a side-step, stopping behind his left shoulder. She raised the knife. Holding it ready, she waited for White to quiet down.

After the squeal ended, he gasped and whimpered.

Blood ran off his shoulder and down the slopes of his upper arm, his chest and back.

'Do you want to stand up?' Cat asked him.

Instead of speaking, he gasped, '*Eeeee!*' and started trying to get up. It wasn't easy with his hands tied together. I helped him by pulling the rope.

On his feet, he twisted his head sideways as if he had to see what Cat was doing behind him. He only had one working eye. It was his left. Cat stayed over to his right. He couldn't turn his head far enough to see her back there. He whimpered . . . either in frustration or fear.

It amazed me to see him acting so pathetic.

While he kept trying to spot Cat, I towed him around the rear of the van and up its other side to the open passenger door. There, I stepped out of the way. 'Climb on in,' I said.

'No, wait,' Cat said. 'It might get tricky, having him inside with us. He's a big, strong guy. Why don't we tie the rope to the back of the van and make him walk? It'll keep him a safe distance from us.

'Excellent plan,' I said.

So I led White away from the passenger door and back to the rear of the van. Cat stayed behind him, which seemed to keep him very nervous so he hardly paid any attention to me.

I tied the rope to the smashed rear bumper of the van, giving White about eight or ten feet of leash. Then I tugged the rope a few times to make sure it was secure.

He looked miserable and scared. He kept jerking his head from side to side, trying to see Cat. And not being able to.

Not until she stepped in front of him.

When he saw her, he tried to back away but the rope wouldn't let him.

'What're you afraid of?' she asked.

'Don't hurt me.'

'You don't like pain? You seem to enjoy dishing it out.'

He shook his head.

'What about Donny? Does *he* like pain?'

He shook his head some more.

'Tell you what, I won't stab you again if you behave. But if you cause any trouble...' She gave the knife a somewhat jaunty twirl. 'You gonna be good?'

He bobbed his head up and down.

Cat turned away from him and stepped toward me, holding out the knife. 'Why don't you take this?'

I accepted it, and slid the blade down under my belt.

As we walked alongside the van, she said in a quiet voice, 'We'd better watch him.'

'You've got him terrified.'

'It might be an act.'

'You should've seen the look on his face when you stabbed his shoulder. I don't think he's faking.'

'I don't either. But you never know. If he gets loose, we could be in for some real trouble.'

We left the van behind, and walked up to the open passenger door of Cat's car. Peggy still lay on her back with her legs on the door sill. She looked no different from the last time I'd seen her.

Cat crouched beside her and picked up her hand.

I tried not to stare at Peggy's groin, but it isn't easy to look away from something like that. Even though I didn't feel aroused by the sight, it kept pulling at my eyes.

'She's alive,' Cat said.

'I guess we'll have to carry her.'

'Maybe we can wake her up.'

'Stab her in the shoulder?'

Cat looked over her shoulder at me and grinned. 'Would I do that?'

300

'Maybe not to her,' I said.

'I'll run back to the van and get some water for her.'

'I could go.'

'I know right where it is.' With that, Cat stood up and jogged to the van. The passenger door was ajar. She stepped past it, swung it open, and climbed inside.

While she was in the van, I squatted over Peggy and grabbed the hem of her dress. I pulled. The dress seemed to be trapped under her back, but I tugged until it came down far enough to cover her pubic area.

Then I stepped around behind her head. I shoved my hands under her shoulders, hooked her by the armpits and waddled backward, dragging her until her feet dropped off the door sill.

Her heels struck the ground fairly hard. It must've hurt, but the pain didn't seem to disturb her.

Cat hopped out of the van. She held a clear plastic bottle of water in one hand.

She walked toward the rear of the van.

From where I crouched, I couldn't see White.

Cat only went far enough to glance behind the van. Then she turned around and hurried toward Peggy and me. 'He's fine,' she said. 'Sitting down back there. You moved her?'

'Figured I might as well.'

'Should've shown some *real* initiative and lugged her over to the van.'

'I guess it'll come to that.'

'Not if we can wake her up.'

Cat squatted beside Peggy and twisted off the cap of the water bottle. 'Hold her head up a little, would you?'

As I lifted Peggy's head off the ground, her mouth closed. Cat used one hand to open it a little. With her other hand, she dribbled water onto the girl's parched, cracked lips. Then she poured some slowly between them.

'I think it's going down,' Cat said.

'Is she swallowing?'

'Her mouth isn't filling up.'

'I guess that's a good sign.'

'It doesn't go into her lungs, does it?'

'I don't know,' I said.

'I'd hate to drown her.' She took the bottle away and started

301

twisting the cap onto it. 'Maybe we'll try some more later. I mean, we don't want to do anything to make matters worse.'

She set the bottle aside. Then, while I continued to hold Peggy's head elevated, Cat gave her cheek a fairly mild slap.

'Peggy!' she said. 'Peggy? Wake up.' She slapped the girl's face again, a little harder than before.

Peggy didn't stir.

'I don't think she's coming around,' I said.

'I'll give her one more.' Cat smacked the other side of Peggy's face, this time hard. It sounded like clapping hands.

But Peggy didn't even flinch.

'She's out. We'll have to carry her.'

'I can do it.'

'I'll help. I'll take her feet.'

'Okay.'

She stepped between Peggy's feet, crouched, and picked them up. I hoisted the girl's back off the ground, got my hands under her armpits, and stood up with the back of her head pressed against my belly. My shirt was open. Her hair, caked with blood, felt hot and sticky.

I took the lead, turning her toward the van, then walking backward. Cat followed, a foot clutched against each of her hips.

'She's a lot lighter than you,' I said.

'I'm such a fatso.'

'You're gorgeous.'

She grinned. 'Sure.'

'I'm just saying she's easier to carry than you were.'

'You made those cracks to White about my weight.'

'They weren't cracks.'

'Sounded like cracks to me.'

'You just *felt* heavy. You feel a lot heavier than you look.'

'So you're saying I need to lose weight?'

'If anything, you need to *gain* some. You're sort of skinny.'

'I thought I was supposed to be gorgeous.'

'You are.'

'Gorgeous, but cadaverous.'

'Mostly, you're a wise-ass.'

'*That's* a crack.'

'There's a crack in there somewhere,' I admitted.

'Watch out, the door.'

I looked over my shoulder. The van's passenger door stood wide open, and I was about to bump into it. I nudged it with my back, knocking it shut. With the door out of the way, I saw White standing behind the van, staring at us with his left eye. His hands were still tied, the rope hanging slack on its way to the bumper.

He didn't say anything, just stared.

With his hands bound in front of him, his powerful body bare to the waist, his flowing white hair and his gory wounds, our prisoner could've been a Viking warrior.

It was hard to believe that we'd beaten such a man.

He looked ruined, defeated.

I moved backward until Cat stepped past the door. Then I stopped. She backed up carefully and worked the door open with her elbow.

'Maybe I'd better go up first,' she said. 'Unless we want to turn her around.'

'No, that's okay. Go on.'

Cat stepped backward onto the running board, raising Peggy's legs. I swung the rest of the body away from the side of the van to give her a straight shot, and Cat climbed up into the space in front of the passenger seat. I went up after her.

With a lot of lifting, twisting and bending of Peggy's body, we finally maneuvered it between the seats, through the open curtains, and into the rear of the van. As Cat had warned, the air inside was furiously hot.

The rear area of the van looked like a sloppy kid's bedroom. The two beds were rumpled messes with stained sheets. Clothes were scattered everywhere. Including mine and Cat's; someone had dumped our overnight bags.

We lowered Peggy onto one of the beds.

Cat stepped past me, apparently in a hurry to get outside. I stayed behind long enough to look around. Our shovel and pick lay on the floor between the beds. Our tire tool, too. And the hammer. Our first aid kit was also there. So were the cans of WD-40 and lighter fluid, the rubber gloves and wet wipes . . . just about everything that White had taken from Cat's car.

Except for a couple of water bottles, however, there was no trace of the food and drinks taken by Peggy.

I hurried outside into the glare of sunlight.

White still stood behind the van, watching us like a vanquished Viking, a dull look in his eye.

I turned away from him. Cat, up ahead by the passenger door of her car, was bending down to pick up the water bottle that she'd left there. She stood and turned around as I approached. 'Can you hold this?' she asked.

'Sure.'

'I suppose my car's a total loss.'

'I'd say so.'

She handed the plastic bottle to me, then ducked inside her car and opened the glove compartment. She removed a handful of maps and other papers – probably including her registration certificate. Then she opened the console and took out a few things. 'That should about do it,' she said, climbing out. 'I guess I'll have to get someone to tow it out of here, but...' She shrugged. 'Might as well take what I can.'

'Anything you don't want to lose,' I told her. 'No telling what might happen to the car after we leave this place. It'll probably end up in someone's front yard.'

'Think so?'

'It's more than likely. Desert rats love nothing better than to decorate their property with broken-down cars.'

We started walking toward the van.

'Okay if I do the driving?' she asked.

'Fine with me. Do we leave White tied to the back?'

'Sure.' She called out, 'That okay with you, White-ass? You don't mind if I drive, do you?'

He didn't answer, just stared.

'I'll try to go nice and slow,' she called to him. Then she climbed up, entered the passenger side, and made her way to the rear.

I sat in the passenger seat and shut the door. Leaning over, I looked back and saw Cat filling a paper sack with all that she'd rescued from her car. She crumpled the top of the sack so nothing would fall out.

Peggy lay motionless on the nearby bed. In the shadows back there, she looked like someone taking a nap.

Cat came forward and swung herself into the driver's seat.

The key waited for her, still plugged into the ignition. She twisted it. The engine came to life, making a grumbly rumble and sending vibrations through the van.

She put her hand on the shift, then grinned at me.

'What?'

'Look what's in front of us.'

Her wrecked car, of course.

'We'll have to back up,' she said, and shifted to reverse.

'White's back there.'

'Hope he's quick on his feet.'

46

Cat stepped on the gas.

The van lurched backward.

White shouted, '*Yaaaaa!*'

Leaning against the door, I stuck my head out the window and twisted it around. White was over to the side far enough for me to see him.

Caught by surprise, he hadn't even taken the time to turn around. He ran backward, yelling as the van bore down on him.

'*Stop! Stop!*' he cried out.

'What's he doing?' Cat asked me.

'Running backward.'

'Right behind us?'

'Pretty much.'

'I wish I could see him.'

'He just fell! Stop!'

Cat hit the brakes.

She stopped with two or three feet to spare.

Behind us, White struggled to get up. He couldn't do much with his bound hands, so he rolled over and used his knees and elbows. The moment he was standing, he whirled around and yelled, '*Fucking bitch! You're dead! You're both dead! Deader than shit!*'

Cat eased down on the gas pedal.

White stopped yelling and started hurrying backward as the van crept toward him.

I kept an eye on him in the side mirror.

'He perked up,' Cat said.

'Sure did. Looks like he *was* hoping we'd let our guard down.'

'Can't trick the tricker,' Cat said.

We continued the slow, backward chase until we were clear of the alley-like passage. Then Cat started forward, steering to the right. In the mirror, I saw White follow us with brisk strides.

Cat started to circle around our rock pile.

Even though she kept our speed down, the van kicked up plenty of dust. The cloud drifted up in front of White. It surrounded him like a pale aura.

I could see him coughing back there.

When Cat steered to the left, I couldn't see him any more – but she could.

'There he is,' she said, sounding pleased as she gazed at her mirror. 'He'll need a bath when he gets home.'

A few minutes later, she said, 'Oops, he disappeared.'

'Where?'

'Is he over on your side?'

I checked my mirror. 'Nope.'

'Must be in the blind spot.'

'He might try to jump aboard and ride us.'

'I wonder,' Cat said.

She floored the gas pedal. As we jolted forward, White yelped. Cat immediately slammed on the brakes.

Then she shifted to 'park' and we leaped out and hurried to the rear. We found White sprawled belly down, arms overhead. He looked as if he'd taken a fall. Maybe he'd been dragged, too. But not far. He probably hadn't been dragged more than a couple of feet.

As we approached him, he pushed himself to his knees. He was gasping for air, sobbing. His chest and belly had gotten torn up a little. He was powdered with dust. It was caked on his sweat and blood.

'You all right?' Cat asked. 'I'd tell you my foot slipped on the accelerator, but that'd be a lie. I cannot tell a lie.'

'Fucking cunt.'

'Hey,' I said. 'Watch your...'

The puttering mutter of the idling engine suddenly swelled to a *VVVRRRRRMMMMMMM!!!*

White's mouth jumped open.

Cat and I jerked our heads sideways to see what was going on.

Dust flew up from the van's rear tires.

I yelled, '*Shit!*'

Cat yelled, '*No!*'

White yelled no words at all, but let out a shriek of disbelief and horror as the van shot forward.

The rope banged taut.

White's arms sprang up.

His shriek changed pitch.

He suddenly rocketed off his knees, diving into the dusty air behind the van.

He must've been airborne for ten or fifteen feet. He screamed the whole time. But the scream stopped the moment he struck the desert floor.

The van raced on, dragging him.

We chased it. We chased the van *and* White, both of us shouting for Peggy to stop.

It had to be Peggy, we both knew that.

She'd made a hell of a recovery.

White bounced and twisted and tumbled behind the van like a crazed water skier doing tricks without benefit of skis or water. He even crossed the wake a couple of times.

Peggy towed him all the way around the backside of our hill – and then some – before she stopped.

By the time she stopped, she'd probably dragged White a quarter of a mile.

We must've been a couple of hundred yards behind them. We'd already quit running. Baked and breathless and pouring sweat, we trudged toward them.

In the distance, a motionless heap of rags and flesh lay in the dirt behind the van. It was all two colors: the pale gray of dust and the red of blood.

The driver's door swung open.

Peggy leaped down. She stumbled forward in a bizarre little dance, then fell to her hands and knees. After crawling a short distance, she managed to rise again.

She staggered toward the rear of the van.

Her stiff, awkward shamble reminded me of those zombies in *The Night of the Living Dead*. So did the way her head looked – hair matted down and face streaked with old blood.

'What's she ... gonna do?' Cat said.

'Kill him?'

'Can't be ... much left to kill.'

'*Peggy!*' I shouted. There wasn't a lot of breath behind it, but my voice must've been loud enough for her to hear.

She didn't even glance at us, just kept shambling toward White.

I looked at Cat and said, 'I guess I might ... run on ahead. Try and stop her.'

Cat shook her head. Reaching out, she took hold of my wrist. 'Don't bother. He's already dead.'

'I guess.'

'Anyway, let her do what she wants.'

'Yeah.'

'After what he did ...'

I nodded.

'To her. And Donny.'

'You're right.'

Up ahead of us, Peggy stumbled to a halt over White's motionless, sprawled body. I thought at first that he was on his back. Then I changed my mind. Then I realized that I simply couldn't tell his front from his back; he was too twisted and messy.

Peggy stared down at him.

Then she dropped to her knees and bit his neck.

He screamed.

47

I'm not sure why Cat and I suddenly started running. It was too late to stop Peggy or rescue White. Maybe we just wanted to be there, to get a good close look at the madness and slaughter.

White was on his back, after all.

Peggy, hunkered down over him, had already ripped open the right side of his neck. The way the blood shot up, she must've taken out the jugular or carotid or both. It was hosing her face and neck and chest.

As we stumbled to a halt near White's feet, Peggy swiveled his head. He had already stopped screaming and twitching, but his blood still spurted.

Peggy ducked down and chomped the left side of his neck.

I heard wet ripping sounds.

She shook her head roughly like a dog, then came up with flesh hanging out of her mouth.

Turning her head, she looked at us.

She blinked a few times. Her eyes, stark blue and white, seemed like they didn't belong in a face so drenched with blood. What belonged in a face like hers were empty, oozing sockets.

With her teeth clamped tight on the gore from White's neck, she seemed to have a hard time breathing.

Air hissed in and out her nostrils.

I watched a bubble of blood form under one nostril and pop.

She spit out her mouthful, opened up wide and breathed deeply.

White still squirted from both sides of his neck.

He didn't move, though.

Cat said, 'My God, Peggy.'

Peggy just knelt there, her back straight, taking deep breaths and blinking at us.

'Sammy, we need to clean her off and get her something to wear. Why don't you hop in the van and see what you can find? I'll stay with her.'

I felt a little sick to my stomach, so I was glad to leave. I went to the passenger door, swung it open, and climbed into the van. The moment I entered, I felt the vibrations and realized that Peggy had left the engine running. I reached over to the ignition key and shut it off.

In the rear of the van, I picked up the plastic container of wet wipes and an old beach towel that apparently belonged to Peggy and Donny. They'd get most of the mess off her. But certainly not all of it. She would wreck whatever she put on.

Clothes were scattered all over the place. They included everything from our overnight bags.

I didn't want Peggy to wear any of Cat's garments.

After searching for a while, I ended up with a green tube top and a very short denim skirt that were probably Peggy's, and a pair of my own white socks. The only underwear I found were mine and Cat's. I recognized Cat's panties because I'd watched her pack them. Peggy and Donny didn't seem to have any underwear of their own. I couldn't find any shoes, either.

I carried everything to the front of the van, climbed down into the sunlight, and hurried around to the back. Cat and Peggy weren't there.

White was, though. Still roped to the bumper, and no longer bleeding.

Flies buzzed around his carcass.

I made a detour around him and found the girls standing at the other side of the van where it was shady. Peggy was bent over at the waist with her hands on her knees, her head drooping. Cat stood beside her, gently rubbing her back.

'Here he is,' Cat said as I approached them. 'Let's get this off you.'

Peggy nodded, but didn't move.

'It's all right,' Cat said. She lifted the dress up Peggy's back, then stepped around her and drew it forward over her head.

I stopped near Peggy's side, but half a step behind her.

She didn't look at me.

When she raised her arms, Cat stepped backward, slipped the dress the rest of the way off, and tossed it to the ground.

'What've you got?' Cat asked me.

'Wet wipes, a towel and some clothes.'

'Let's start with the towel.'

I handed it to her. Then I set the package of wet wipes on the ground near Peggy's feet and stacked the clothes beside it. 'I'll go and cut White loose,' I said.

It was something that needed to be done. Also, I figured Peggy didn't want me hanging around while she was naked.

Cutting White loose turned out to be a nasty chore. I'd planned just to slice the rope off the bumper, and that's what I did. White's knife made it easy.

After I'd done that, however, it occurred to me that we shouldn't leave the rope behind. For one thing, we might need it. For another, someone would probably find White's body sooner or later. There might not be much left of it by then, but I don't know of any scavengers that eat rope. Tied hands would point to foul play.

I crouched beside White's arms.

They were lying on the ground above his head, wrists roped together, elbows bent and pointing at the sky.

I pressed the blade against one of the loops between his wrists and sawed it back and forth. I didn't let myself look at his face. Or his neck. But I heard the flies. Their lazy buzzing sounds reminded me of summer days when I was a kid.

'I'd rather be fishing,' I called out, and heard Cat laugh.

She called back, 'You don't fish, do you?'

'Not anymore, but it'd be better than this.'

'It would be very nice to be on a boat,' she said. 'A little rowboat or canoe on a river.'

'That'd be nice, all right.'

'I'd jump in,' she said.

'Me, too.'

I severed the rope in just one place, then started to unwind it from around White's wrists.

'We could throw Peggy in,' Cat said, 'and get her really clean.'

'Nobody's gotta throw me in,' Peggy said. She sounded groggy. 'I can jump in all by myself. Reckon I'd do it, too.'

'Hey, you're talking!' I called out.

'Who says I couldn't?'

She sounded about as sour as she used to.

'How are you feeling?' Cat asked.

'Rotten. Got me a headache.'

'Surprising,' Cat said.

'I'm all itchy and I got a bad taste in my mouth and I feel like I wanta pitch.'

'Join the crowd,' I called.

'You're real funny.'

Done removing the rope, I stood up and slid the knife under my belt. As I gathered the rope into a coil, Peggy said, 'Reckon I put one over on Snow White, huh? He figured it'd be that

Elliot of yours that'd bite him in the neck. Only it wasn't that Elliot, it was me. See if *that* makes him into a vampire.' She let out a harsh laugh. 'Me, I don't figure it's likely.'

'I don't, either,' Cat said.

'Fuck him and the horse he rode in on.'

'You did,' I said.

'Well, he got what he had coming. Where's Donny at? He okay?'

'He's fine,' Cat said.

'He ain't *fine*. Neither of us is *fine*.'

I took a couple of steps and peered around the corner of the van. The towel lay on the ground. Peggy stood with her back to me, Cat facing her. They were both busy with the moist, scented paper towelettes. Cat worked on her face while Peggy rubbed the lower stains.

'Donny was fine enough to run away,' Cat said. 'White had him up on the van's roof. I hit White with a rock, and Donny knocked him over the edge. That's how we got him. But after that, Donny took off. He looked like he might be heading for some old mine ruins. We were driving over to look for him when you ... took care of White.' Cat stopped dabbing at Peggy's face. Stepping back, she cocked her head to one side, then the other. 'Looks like that's most of it,' she said.

'We gotta go after him,' Peggy said.

'No big hurry.'

As Peggy slid one of the little wipes up and down her arm, she twisted sideways and looked over her shoulder and saw me. 'What're *you* looking at?'

'Nothing,' I said, and started to turn away.

'Keep your eyes to yourself.'

'Take it easy,' Cat told her.

'Well, he's *gawping* at me.'

'Big deal. He risked his life for you and Donny.'

'That don't mean he gets to gawp at me.'

'It means you should try to be nice.'

I liked hearing Cat stick up for me that way.

'I'm not so sure you're the one he was gawping at, anyway,' Cat added.

I laughed and called out, 'Exactly!'

'You'll never get all that off you,' Cat told her. 'Not with these things. Why don't you go ahead and get dressed? We'll find Donny and head on out of here.'

'What about White?' I asked, keeping my back to the women.

'What do *you* think we should do?' Cat asked me.

'I don't know. Any reason not to leave him where he fell?'

'Somebody's bound to find him,' Cat said. 'That's the only thing.'

'If they don't find him quick, there won't be much left.'

'Bones and stuff, anyway.'

'That's true,' I said.

'Hey, he brought us here to show us a hole. Brock's hole.'

'That's right.'

'Maybe we oughta return the favor and show it to *him*.'

'If we can find it.'

'I'd rather leave him down at the bottom of a hole than out here in plain sight.'

'Well, we'd have to load him in the van to get him there. And then *unload* him and *carry* him to the hole.'

'You don't sound too thrilled,' Cat said.

I turned around and grinned at her.

Peggy was bent over, pulling the faded, denim skirt up her legs. I glanced at her ass, but it didn't interest me much. Cat was smiling at me.

'It just seems like we're always hauling bodies around,' I explained.

Her grin widened. 'Not always.'

'Not always. But more often than not. Ever since midnight, it's been one body after another. Pick them up, lug them around, shove them in the trunk, take them *out* of the trunk, carry them to the *van* ... It's too damn hot for that kind of stuff. And I'm no muscle man, either. I'm worn out.'

'Not sure it was lugging the bodies that wore you out,' Cat said.

'Yeah, I know, I know. But that was a big part of it. And we're always getting so damn *bloody*! Everybody's *bloody* all the time. I never cared much for blood in the first place...'

'It's not all bad.'

I couldn't hold back a smile. 'I don't mind *yours* so much,' I admitted.

'Why, thank you.' She crouched down, picked up Peggy's tube top, and handed it to her.

The top wasn't much more than a broad circle of green elastic. Peggy put her arms through its middle, then pulled it over her head and about halfway down her back.

'Does this mean you don't want to throw White down a hole?' Cat asked.

I shrugged. 'I guess it *would* be a good idea. If we can find a good hole.'

'You want *me* to carry him?'

'Let's have Peggy do it,' I suggested. 'She's the one who killed him.'

'Ha ha, very funny,' Peggy said. Now that she had clothes on, she turned around and scowled at me.

Her face looked clean, but the ropy hair hanging down her brow had a reddish tint.

The snug tube top left her bare to the tops of her breasts, covered about six or eight inches of her chest, and stopped just below her ribcage. From there, she was bare down to the waistband of her denim skirt. Plenty of skin showed. Much of it was scratched and bruised.

She'd managed to wipe off the worst of the blood, but not all of it. I saw ruddy stains and smudges on her shoulders, chest, arms and belly.

'You want me to carry him, I'll do it,' she said.

'I was just kidding,' I told her. 'I'll do it.'

'You oughta be happy I killed him for you.'

'You didn't kill him for *me*.'

Cat picked up the socks and handed them to her.

Peggy took them without a comment or gesture of gratitude. She almost fell over when she tried to put one on, so Cat grabbed her and held her steady.

'How long were you conscious?' Cat asked her.

'Huh?'

'You were knocked out cold by the crash, weren't you?'

'Yeah, I reckon.'

'So when did you wake up?'

Now, Peggy actually smiled. It was a rare thing to see, and not pleasant. 'Had you fooled, huh?'

'Apparently,' Cat said.

'I come to when you smacked me in the face.'

'But you didn't let on,' Cat pointed out.

'Nope.'

'So you were conscious when we picked you up and carried you into the van.'

'Sure was.'

'Very cute,' Cat said, and let go of her.

Peggy had one foot on the ground, one crossed over her knee as she struggled to pull on a sock.

She hopped, trying to stay up. She might've succeeded, but Cat gave her a small shove backward.

As Peggy fell, Cat said, 'Oops.'

48

Peggy let out a yelp. She landed on her butt and tumbled onto her back, her feet flying into the air. Then she lay there with her knees up. Lifting her head, she glared at Cat and said, 'What'd you do that for?'

'That was for making us carry you. Don't ever mess with us.'

'Fuck you.'

'Come on,' Cat said to me. 'I'll give you a hand with White.'

We walked behind the van and looked down at him.

Even more flies were buzzing around him. A line of ants was marching into the gash of his swollen eye.

'What a mess,' Cat said.

'Maybe I should get the rubber gloves. They're just in the van.'

'I'm wondering if there's some easier way . . .'

'I know an easier way – leave him right here.'

'We should at least put him out of sight,' Cat said. 'I'd feel a lot better about things. Somebody might show up any time. I'd like to be long gone before the body gets found.'

'Anybody coming up here is gonna run into Elliot's body first.'

She grimaced and nodded.

'What'll we do about *him*?' I asked.

'Elliot? I guess we'd better drive back to the pass and pick him up. We can throw him and White in the same hole.'

'So we've gotta haul around *both* of them.'

'Looks that way. Should've left Elliot in the damn trunk.'

'In retrospect.'

'Yeah,' Cat said. 'I didn't exactly count on things going this way. I underestimated us.'

'You and me, both.'

'I figured we barely stood a chance against the bastard, you know?'

'I know. I figured the same thing. I had our chances of survival at slim-to-none.'

'Same here. Ditching Elliot was just a way to screw White up. Throw him off balance.'

Nodding, I added, 'He'd have to keep us alive so we could lead him to the body.'

'It would've bought us time. Given us a chance.'

'It was a fine plan,' I told her. 'It might've saved us.'

'You haven't even heard the best part.'

'Really?'

She laughed softly and said, 'Not that I thought it would actually *accomplish* anything. I mean, I don't...'

The engine suddenly grumbled to life.

'NO!' I shouted.

Cat cried out, '*Peggy!*'

The van hadn't even started to move before we both raced around its corner. Peggy no longer lay sprawled on the ground. The driver's door stood open.

As we raced for it, the van sprang forward.

'*Damn you. Peggy!*' Cat shouted. '*Stop the van!*'

It started to gain speed.

But so did Cat. She suddenly exploded forward, long legs flying out, arms pumping, shirt afloat behind her back, head tucked down. I couldn't believe my eyes.

She didn't stand a chance of reaching the door, but I sure admired the try.

Peggy must've spotted her; she reached out to pull the door shut.

Cat, leaping, caught hold of her arm. In a diving fall, she

kept her grip on Peggy's arm and wrenched her out of the driver's seat.

They landed in the dirt. The van kept going, driverless.

I quit running, and watched the action. After tumbling and rolling in a tangle of arms and legs, Peggy found herself on her back. She flung her arms up to protect her face.

Cat, straddling her, didn't let the arms stop her. She laid into Peggy, pounding the side of her face.

I was tempted to join in.

But Cat didn't seem to need any help, so I went racing after the van.

It had a healthy headstart on me. With no foot on the gas pedal, though, its speed gradually drained away. It also seemed to be following a wobbly course, veering one way then the other as if wandering out of its way to investigate odd sights.

After chasing it too far for my own good, I finally closed in on the driver's door. It was swinging back and forth on its hinges. Though I wanted more than anything to leap into the seat and stomp on the brakes and put an end to the pursuit, I needed to time things so the door would be wide open for my jump.

It swung wide.

I dashed into the V and reached for the steering wheel.

And the van slammed into a boulder.

It stopped fast. I ran myself against the inside of the door, which bashed my wind out and knocked me sideways. I bounced off the edge of the driver's seat. As I did a spin, the door swung back and pounded me. I ended up on the ground.

I didn't try to get up.

I just stayed down, exhausted and sweaty and breathless, my heart slamming, my body hurting just about everywhere.

When I finally moved, I moved fast.

Because something burnt my arm.

I yelped and scurried up, my arm dripping.

And saw a pool of reddish fluid creeping out from under the van. It steamed as it spread toward me over the rocky ground.

I took a few steps backward, dropped to my hands and knees and peered into the shadow beneath the undercarriage. Near the front, fluid dribbled and splashed as if the van was having a rain storm under its hood.

But this rain wasn't water.

It was coolant.

I groaned and pushed myself up and staggered toward the front of the van. Steam was rushing out from under the edges of its hood. There wasn't much wind just then – but enough to whip the steam sideways. Something smelled like bad eggs.

The grill was caved in and tight against the boulder.

Hissing sounds came from under the hood. And I still heard the splash of coolant spilling onto the ground.

Coolant, the blood of the vehicle.

'Oh, man,' I muttered.

Just for the hell of it, I climbed up and sat in the driver's seat. The crash had snuffed out the engine. I tried the ignition key a few times. The engine wheezed and died, wheezed and died. Then it wouldn't even wheeze anymore. Twists of the key caused a few clicks, but nothing else.

I climbed down. Standing in the shade by the side of the van, I took off my shirt and mopped my face. Then I scanned the distance for Cat and Peggy.

They weren't easy to spot.

That's because they were both sprawled on the ground.

When I first saw them, a surge of alarm crashed through my chest. I thought they'd been killed.

White got them! He wasn't really dead!

But it only took a moment for me to realize that Cat and Peggy hadn't been butchered by White or by anyone else. They were sprawled on the ground because Peggy had gotten the crap beat out of her, and Cat had worn herself out by doing it.

It would be a long walk back to them.

I was fairly close to the ruins, though. If Donny would just come out, we could both head over to the gals and none of us would have to come back this way again.

Turning away from them, I called out, '*Donny! Everything's fine! Come on out! It's all over! White's dead! Peggy's fine! She's waiting for you! Donny! Hey! Come on out! There's no more reason to hide! It's all over! Come out, okay! Come on! We all want to get out of here. Donnnnnnnyyyy!*'

318

I waited.

I yelled some more.

No answer came. I scanned the ruins, hoping to see him walk out of a doorway or step around the corner of a shack. No sign of him, though.

Turning the other way, I saw that Cat was standing up. She seemed to be gazing in my direction.

'*What's going on?*' she called.

'*Van's dead!*'

She seemed to slump a little, as if the news had stolen what strength it took to keep her back straight. She shook her head from side to side. Then her head turned and tilted downward. She spoke to Peggy, who was still sprawled on the ground. I couldn't hear what she said, but Peggy pushed herself up.

Cat called to me, '*Any sign of Donny?*'

'*No!*'

Peggy made it to her feet, then bent over and held on to her knees.

'*Stay there, Sammy!*' Cat yelled. '*We're on our way!*'

Glad to hear it, I leaned back against the side of the van to wait for them.

They walked side by side, slowly and stiffly, both of them limping. They both wore white socks, but no shoes. The sun-blasted earth must've been burning their feet. But their shambling gait came from more than hot feet; it also came from the punishment of crashes and falls and fights – and maybe, in Cat's case, from her time with me on our bed of rocks.

The waves of heat made their bodies wobble and undulate as they came toward me.

Cat's cut-off jeans rode low on her hips. Her shirt hung open, more on one side than the other. Her right breast showed, her left didn't. There wasn't enough wind to whip the shirt out behind her.

The way she looked reminded me of a gunslinger, beaten but unstoppable, stumbling toward a showdown. She had no gun, of course. And she was a half-naked girl, not a cowpoke. But she reminded me of that, all the same. It had to do with the low-slung jeans and her battered stride and a kind of strength she showed. And the way she looked ready for a grim fight.

Peggy, shambling along by her side, might've been her sidekick or her deputy.

But she reminded me of no such thing.

She still reminded me of a zombie from *The Night of the Living Dead*.

More so than ever, now that I'd seen her rip the throat out of White.

I suddenly didn't like the idea of Cat walking beside her out there. I suddenly didn't like it at all.

So I abandoned my shade and started walking toward them.

The heat of the sun pressed down on me.

'*Stay there!*' Cat yelled.

This is stupid, I thought. Peggy might be a monster, but she's a *weak* monster. White was half dead when she chomped his neck. Cat had already subdued her *twice*, so there was no reason to doubt that she could do it a third time.

But if the bitch takes her by surprise . . .

'*You oughta wait in the shade!*'

'That's okay,' I called. 'I need the exercise.'

Cat smiled. Her teeth looked very white in the bronze of her face. 'Do you feel the burn?' she asked.

'You bet. Every which way.'

'You're nuts. You had it made in the shade.'

'I don't trust her,' I said, and nodded toward Peggy.

Who glared at me.

'I don't trust her, either,' Cat admitted.

'I was afraid she might try something.'

'You came out to save me?'

'Something like that.'

'That's sweet,' she said.

'Not that you'd need saving.'

'Right. I'm one tough cookie.'

'And a tricky cookie.'

Face to face with Cat, I stopped walking. But she didn't stop. She walked straight up to me and put her arms around me and kissed me on the mouth. We were hot and sweaty and slippery.

In Cat's embrace, I couldn't see Peggy.

I wanted to tune Peggy out and focus completely on Cat. On

the surprise and delight of having her embrace me, kiss me so unexpectedly and fervently here in the wasteland. On the good solid feel of her, and how I could feel her heartbeat and the slippery push of her single naked breast.

But I couldn't forget about Peggy. I had to stay on guard against her to protect Cat and myself.

So I turned Cat until I could look over her shoulder and watch the girl.

She stared at us with strange intensity.

At first, the look in her eyes only seemed peculiar. Then it started to give me the creeps.

I couldn't tell whether her eyes were filled with hatred or lust.

Maybe neither.

Maybe both.

49

'What happened to the van?' Cat asked as the three of us walked toward it.

'It hit a boulder,' I said. 'There's coolant all over the place. The radiator must've sprung a leak, or something. And the engine doesn't start.'

'Swift,' Cat said.

'How're we gonna get out of here?' Peggy asked.

'It'd be a cinch if we had a time machine,' Cat said, looking at her. 'All we'd have to do is go back about ten minutes and break your neck.'

'Real funny.'

'What the hell did you think you were doing?' Cat asked.

'I was just gonna drive over and look for Donny.'

'Without us,' Cat said.

'I would've stopped for you.'

'It sure looked that way.'

'Well, you *scared* me when you both came running like that. I was all set to stop, but you had to go and *chase* me. It's not my fault the van crashed. I was driving it just dandy till you pulled me out and made me fall.'

'You really screwed us,' Cat told her.

'Did not. Wasn't my fault.'

'The hell it wasn't,' I said.

'But you're in the same jam we are,' Cat told her. 'So enjoy it.'

When we reached the van, it was no longer steaming and hissing. Its reddish fluid stained the ground.

We walked slowly, making a circle around the van, staring at it as if the thing were a rare and wonderful beast that had been dropped in its tracks by a poacher.

Cat climbed in and tried to start it.

Shaking her head, she climbed out. 'I guess we're going noplace in that.'

'What're we gonna do?' Peggy asked.

'Walk,' Cat said.

As we started toward the ruins, she said to Peggy, 'Call your brother. Get him out here.'

'*DONNNNNYYYY!*' she shouted. '*Hey! It's me! Come out, come out, wherever you are!*'

He didn't.

'Why doesn't he come out for you?' Cat asked her.

'How should I know?'

'You're his sister,' I said.

'So what? That don't mean nothing.'

'Means plenty to *my* sister,' I pointed out.

'Goody for her.'

'Keep calling him,' Cat said.

'Won't do no good.'

'Why not?'

'If he was gonna come, he'd come.'

'He might be out of earshot,' I said.

'Maybe he just wants to hide from everyone,' Cat suggested. 'I've felt that way, sometimes. Especially after the really bad stuff. You just want to find a dark corner and never come out.'

'We'll find him if he's here,' I said.

'He *has* to be here,' Cat said. Halting only a few yards from the nearest shack, she shouted, '*Donny! Where are you? We're your friends! Nobody's going to hurt you! Donnnnnyyyyy! Don't you want to get out of here?*'

'*We do!*' I yelled.

'*We aren't going to leave without you. Donny. Please! Come on out.*'

We waited, but he didn't answer or show himself.

Cat met my eyes and shook her head. Then she turned to Peggy.

'Don't look at me,' Peggy said. 'It ain't *my* fault.'

'Nobody says it is.'

'You're *looking* at me.'

'*Do* you know something about this?' Cat asked.

'No!'

To me, Cat said, 'Let's see what we can find.'

I nodded.

Staying together, we walked to the nearest shack. Its windows were boarded shut, but the door hung loose. The wooden walls and tin roof were punctured with bullet holes. Cat swung the door open and stepped inside. I followed her. The room was streaked with dusty, bright rods of sunlight that came in through the holes.

We wandered slowly through the place.

Someone had lived there, once.

But not recently.

The shack was cluttered with garbage such as empty beer cans and cigarette packs, rags and old boards. There was a bucket pocked with bullet holes, a sofa cushion, a cardboard box with nothing in it except an old bent nail, and an overturned, three-legged wicker chair.

Donny wasn't there.

It didn't look like *anyone* had been inside the shack for months, maybe years.

'Notice anything funny?' Cat asked.

'What?'

'No graffiti.'

She was right. The weathered wooden walls were unmarked by spray paint or marking pens. 'The gang-taggers never made it out this far,' I said.

'Somebody with guns did. Look how everything's shot up.'

'Just part of the desert landscape,' I said. 'Out in the boonies like this, some people go around taking pot-shots at anything that looks like junk.'

323

'Which is pretty near everything,' Cat said.

'It'd be nice if some of those pot-shooter's would show up about *now*,' I said. 'In a nice big Jeep or Range Rover.'

'They might shoot us.'

'Do we look like junk?'

'Pretty near,' she said, and laughed.

'They'd give us a ride out of here,' I said. 'That's what they'd do.'

'They'd also find the bodies.'

'Ooo. You're right. Maybe just as well if they *don't* show up.'

We stepped out into the glaring sunlight. As I squinted and lowered my head, Cat said, 'Where'd Peggy go?'

'Huh?'

'She's not here.'

'She's probably around.'

We walked away from the front of the shack and scanned the area. There were a couple more shacks and an outhouse that seemed to be pretty much intact, but most of the other structures lay in ruins as if they'd been smashed by a rampaging army tank.

The water tower leaned at an angle, ready to fall and crush the next person to venture near it.

I saw nobody. No Peggy, no Donny, nobody except Cat standing by my side.

'This is just what we need,' she muttered. 'Now we've lost them both.'

'Maybe she's just looking for Donny,' I said.

'*Peggy!*' Cat shouted. '*Where are you? Peggyyyy!*'

Peggy didn't answer or show herself.

Cat said, 'Shit.'

'It's a lot more pleasant without her,' I pointed out.

'That's a fact. But I'd really like to get the hell out of here. We've got a long hike ahead of us.'

'Maybe we oughta take a look at that car or truck we saw when we were up in the rocks.'

'Can't hurt to look,' Cat said.

I led us toward the last shack on the left. If nobody'd moved the vehicle, we should find it there.

'The way our luck's been going,' Cat said, 'it'll probably have four flat tires and a missing engine.'

'More than likely.'

'Or it'll blow up when we look at it.'

'Our luck hasn't been *that* bad,' I told her. 'We're still alive and kicking.'

'For the time being. But we ain't yet outa the woods, as they say.'

As we neared the shack, the headlights, chrome bumper and grill came into view. The headlights were smashed.

'Doesn't look good,' Cat said.

It had no front license plate.

Walking closer, I saw that it was a Ford pickup truck. An old one, probably from the fifties.

Both front tires were flat. The windshield had been bashed in .

'I don't think we're going anywhere in this,' I said.

'Elliot's curse strikes again,' said Cat. 'I *knew* we wouldn't be driving out of this place. They don't bust your car and your van, then hand you a perfectly good pickup truck.'

'I don't suppose so. Whoever *they* are.'

'If I knew who they are, I'd have a few words with them.'

'Give them a piece of your mind.'

'Darn tootin'.'

We wandered toward the rear of the pickup, looking it over. The seats were torn and leaked their stuffing. The steering wheel was gone. The side was dotted with bullet holes of several different sizes. The right rear tire was missing completely, and the left rear tire was flat.

In the bed of the pickup, we found an overturned wheelbarrow and a ball of tumbleweed. The tumbleweed, a pale brown sphere of dry twigs about twice the size of a beachball, must've been tossed in by the wind and left behind.

'Too bad there isn't something useful,' I said.

'Like a cell phone?' Cat asked, staring at the tumbleweed.

'I don't know who we'd call, anyway.'

'The auto club? Maybe we could get them to tow my car out.'

'That's an idea. But we'd have to hide the bodies, first.'

'Just as well we don't have a phone,' Cat said. Leaning forward against the side panel of the pickup, she reached in with both hands and picked up the tumbleweed.

325

'What're you doing?'

She shrugged. 'Setting it free,' she said. 'It looked trapped.'

'It's a dead weed.'

'I know. And don't think I don't feel foolish about this.' With a big smile, she lowered it to the ground and let go. The tumbleweed started rolling away, nudged along by the mild wind. She waved at it and said, 'Bye-bye, little fellow.'

'The heat's gotten to you,' I said.

'Something has, I guess.' She came to me and leaned against me, putting a hand low on my back and resting her forehead against the side of my neck. 'I did something kind of stupid, Sammy,' she said.

'But I'm sure the tumbleweed is grateful.'

'Not that.'

I'd already realized it wasn't that. I didn't know *what* she'd done, but I realized it must be something serious. I found myself afraid to hear it. I caressed her back gently through her shirt, and waited.

'You know when we stopped in the pass and unloaded Elliot?'

'Yeah.'

I began to get a cold, crawly feeling in my stomach.

'You know how you got back into the car and I stayed behind to look for the hammer?'

'Yeah.'

'I did something else. I did something *before* I searched for the hammer.'

'You did?'

I felt so cold and twisted inside that I wanted to bend over and hug my guts. But I just stood there and kept on caressing Cat's back.

'I pulled the stake out of Elliot.'

50

When Cat said that, I felt as if the trap door of a gallows had just banged open under my feet. I plunged down, terrified. On my way down, though, I realized that the noose was imaginary.

'I was trying to be tricky,' Cat explained. She shook her head slowly, rubbing her brow against the side of my neck. 'It seemed like a great idea at the time. Like pulling the pin on a hand grenade. It was hard to do, though. You really had it taped down.'

'That was to keep it in him,' I said. But not harshly. I didn't *feel* harsh, just disoriented and even slightly amused.

'I know,' Cat said. 'I know. I'm sorry. But I figured . . .' She shook her head again. 'I never thought we'd be able to get the upper hand on White. Much less kill him. Anyway, *he* was planning to pull the stake, so I figured it was going to happen sooner or later anyway. Why not beat him to it and throw him another curve, you know? Come sundown, we'd have a wild vampire thrown into the works.'

'Wouldn't he attack *us*?'

Raising her face, she stepped back a little and looked me in the eyes. 'I figured there was nothing much to lose. For one thing, I didn't really believe Elliot *would* come back to life. Stake or no stake, he'd be staying down. But if it *did* work, he might go on a rampage and take White out of the picture.'

'Along with the rest of us,' I said.

'*White* was going to kill us tonight, anyway. He probably planned to wait and do it after Elliot had changed him into a vampire, and we'd be his first victims. I think that's one of the reasons he didn't kill any of us – he wanted us to be alive tonight when he sucked our blood. But even if he *didn't* get changed into a vampire, he'd have had to kill us. There was no way he would've let us out of here alive.' Staring into my eyes, she grimaced and said, 'I really figured we stood a better chance if Elliot popped in. And you never know – they might've killed each other and we'd be home free.'

I nodded. I understood.

'It wasn't really such a bad idea,' I admitted.

'Not such a good one, either.'

'You get points for trickiness.'

She almost smiled. 'I'm a very tricky girl. But you have to take points off for stupidity.'

'It wasn't all that stupid. I might've pulled the stake, myself, if I'd thought of it. And if I'd had the guts. I don't think I would've had the guts to do it, though.'

'It helped, being a little tipsy.'

'The beer made you do it?'

'Exactly. Let's blame the beer.' She smiled. 'Maybe I *wouldn't* have pulled the stake if I'd been completely sober. A few beers, and sometimes lousy ideas start looking brilliant.'

'It wasn't a lousy idea.'

'Looks lousy from here.'

'Hindsight. Now that White's not a threat anymore.'

'And now that we're still gonna be in the neighborhood when the sun goes down.'

'Shouldn't matter,' I said. 'We both know Elliot's dead. And he'll still be dead after the sun goes down. We both *know* it. This is real life. In real life, nobody gets up and goes on a rampage after he's had a stake through his chest like that. It just can't happen.'

'Then why have I got a knot in my stomach?'

'We're just spooked by our imaginations.'

'You've got a knot, too?'

'A big, icy one. An iceberg of a knot. But there's no logical reason for it. He's *not* gonna get up and come after us.'

'Hope not.'

'You *know* he won't. We both know he won't.'

'If we're both so sure he'll stay down, then how come I pulled the stake out of him in the first place?'

'Desperation. Hope.'

'Budweiser,' she added. Then she shrugged and said, 'He probably *will* stay down.'

'It's a virtual certainty.'

'How come only "virtual"?'

'Almost nothing's absolutely certain. But I'd say this is about as close as it comes.'

'You think it's . . . what, maybe ninety-nine percent certain?'

'Maybe.'

'That's a comfort. Would you go up in an airplane if it had a one percent chance of crashing?'

'Those aren't such bad odds.'

'They only look that way till you think about them. Ninety-nine percent? Out of every hundred flights, one goes down. Those are horrible odds. You'd have *hundreds* of airplanes crashing every day. If the odds are *one in a thousand*, you'd have

328

so many crashes each day that you'd have to be nuts to step foot on a plane.'

'You may be right.'

'And I guess I *must* believe there's at least one chance in a thousand that Elliot'll come back to life tonight. Otherwise, why did I bother to pull the stake out of him?'

'Well, there's a way to take care of the problem. All we have to do is put the stake back into him before sundown.'

'I know,' Cat said, a smile spreading across her face. 'I already thought of that. It's why I . . . had to tell you what I'd done. So we wouldn't end up waiting too long. I mean, we've got no transportation anymore. And we still need to find Donny. And now Peggy. And Elliot's probably about two miles away.'

'That's not so far,' I said.

'It's pretty far in this heat. And in the shape we're in. We need to give ourselves plenty of time.'

'You could've told me about all this before, you know. What were you afraid of?'

'Nothing. I wasn't *afraid* to tell you. I just . . .' She shrugged. 'I never really planned to pull it out, for one thing. I didn't even think of it till after you threw Elliot out of the trunk. I didn't *know* I'd do it until I actually got down and started ripping at the tape. By then, you were already back inside the car waiting for me. And after that, I didn't want to talk about it in front of Peggy. I mean, she would've gotten smart about it, given me some kind of crap. Who needed that? And then we had the crash. Things just kept happening. The next time I thought about telling you, I decided it'd be better to keep it a secret. It'd make a nice surprise for you if Elliot suddenly showed up just in the nick of time to save us. And if he *didn't*, you wouldn't be expecting him anyway, so you wouldn't be disappointed.'

I smiled and said, 'That was very thoughtful of you.'

'I thought so. I thought I'd just keep the trick to myself and see what happened. But now we don't *need* Elliot's help . . . and we can't just drive over to him and put the stake back in. It seemed like I'd better tell. Now or never.'

'Well,' I said, 'I don't see where there's any real problem.'

'Not as long as we get to Elliot before dark.'

'Even if we don't.'

'I think we'd better,' she said. 'Just to be on the safe side.'

'Okay.' I pulled her against me and kissed her on the mouth. She slipped her hands under my shirt and ran them up and down my back, staying away from the stake wound. She pushed her tongue into my mouth. With both our shirts open, I felt her bare skin all the way down to my waist. She rubbed her breasts against me. Then she squeezed me so tightly that I felt the beating of her heart.

Relaxing her fierce hug, she whispered, 'That makes me feel a whole lot better.'

'What does?'

'This.' She hugged me and kissed me again, sliding her body against mine, moaning. Then she looked up into my eyes and said, 'That.'

'Ah. Makes me feel a lot better, too.'

'Glad to hear it.' She lifted her eyebrows and asked, 'You're not mad at me, are you?'

'For what?'

'Pulling out the stake.'

'No, huh-uh. It *wasn't* a bad idea. And so damned gutsy ... You know how you said it was like pulling the pin on a hand grenade?'

She smiled. 'Probably a dud.'

'I think it was more like calling in an artillery strike on your own position when you're being overrun.'

'Suicidal?'

'A little of that, but mostly just damn brave. You don't know who's gonna get creamed, but you're willing to take the risk just in order to give your own bunch a tiny little chance at surviving.'

'And to screw the enemy,' Cat said. 'I'm just glad we've got plenty of time to call it off.'

Though I didn't want to stop looking at Cat, I forced my gaze away from her and studied the shadows around us. They had grown fairly long.

Late afternoon long.

'We've probably got a few hours before sundown,' I said.

'What makes you think so?'

'The shadows.'

'The shadows? What time is it according to the shadows, Big Chief Running Scared?'

'Three or four o'clock.'

'Gonna have to send you back to nature school.'

'Huh?'

'Remember when I was tying White's hands together right after he went off the roof of the van?'

'Sure.'

'Remember how he wore two wristwatches?'

I vaguely remembered some mention, a long time ago, of White's two watches. But I couldn't recall paying any attention to them, or even noticing them.

'I sort of remember that,' I said.

'Well, one was gone. I don't know what happened to it. Doesn't matter. He had one on, and I looked at it and noticed the time. Five minutes past four.'

'*Five after four?*'

'Yeah.'

'That late? I can't believe it.'

'It surprised me, too,' Cat said. 'We must've been up in those rocks for *hours*.'

'But *five* hours?'

'Something like that. Time really flies when you're having fun.'

'Flies when you're asleep, too,' I pointed out.

'Yeah. I think we must've slept a lot longer than we thought.'

'If his watch said four o'clock when you were tying his hands...'

Nodding, Cat said, 'It must be five by now.'

'At least. Maybe five-thirty.' I was starting to feel squirmy inside again. 'But we oughta have till eight-thirty or nine before the sun goes down. That'd be about three hours. Plenty of time.'

'I've got a technical question for you, Sammy.'

'Shoot.'

'Do vampires rise *after dark* or as soon as the sun drops below the horizon?'

'After dark?'

'You don't sound very sure.'

'I'm not.'

'There's a big difference, you know.'

'I suppose so.'

'I'm no meteorologist, but I've noticed over the years that sunset comes quite a while before actual darkness. Maybe an hour, an hour and a half. So if vampires rise at *sunset*, we might only have until seven, seven-thirty, something like that.'

'Of course,' I said, 'we both know that they don't rise *at all* because there ain't no such thing. Elliot's dead and he's going to stay dead.'

'Sure. We both know that.'

'We'd better get a move on,' I said.

'The sooner, the better.'

'Do we have to find Peggy and Donny first?'

'We don't have to, but I think we'd better give it a good try. I got them into this.'

'You didn't make them run away from us.'

'No, but we owe them, anyway. They took care of White for us.'

'*You* took care of White.'

'I hit him with the rock, but Donny knocked him off the roof. If he'd stayed on top of the van, no telling what might've happened. And then Peggy finished him off. We owe her *big* for that.'

'She's still a pain in the ass.'

'But maybe she saved our lives, killing him. If she hadn't done it, he might've gotten us sooner or later.'

'I guess it won't hurt to spend a while looking for them,' I said. 'Hell, they can't be that far away.'

51

We shouted for Peggy and Donny again and again as we searched the ruins. They never answered. We crisscrossed the area, looking inside every structure, behind every boulder and tumbled wall and pile of rubble large enough to hide a person.

We couldn't find them.

'They've gotta be around here someplace,' Cat said.

'Maybe at the mine.'

'What mine?'

'There's gotta be a mine. People didn't come here for the fishing.'

'Why can't we see it?'

'It must be over there someplace,' I said, nodding toward the craggy walls of rock that rose from the basin floor a short distance beyond the ruins. They seemed to climb into the sky, forming a ridge hundreds of feet above us.

'Let's go look,' Cat said.

We started walking in that direction.

Very soon, I noticed that there appeared to be a distance between the nearest outcropping and the rocks that towered behind it. Cat seemed to notice it, too; she picked up her pace.

We rounded the side of the outcropping and went in behind it and found the mine.

Its entrance looked like a doorway chipped in granite.

We walked over to it, keeping silence.

And peered inside.

Into a narrow, black tunnel.

I motioned to Cat, and we stepped away from it.

'What do you think?' I whispered.

'My guess, they're probably in there. Where else *could* they be?'

'I don't know. But I'll bet this is where White took Donny this afternoon. He might've parked the van right here. That'd explain why we couldn't see it from our place in the rocks. It was hidden behind that.' I nodded toward the bulky stand of rocks that had done such a good job concealing the mine entrance from us.

'Think this is Brock's hole?' Cat asked.

Shrugging, I whispered, 'I had a *vertical* hole pictured in my head. I don't know.'

'Anyway, you're probably right about him bringing Donny here. They didn't spend the afternoon in any of those shacks. We would've found some of our stuff, you know? Where's all our *stuff*?'

'In there?' I nodded toward the mine entrance.

'Maybe that's why Donny hightailed it back the minute he got away from White.' She met my eyes and smiled. 'Wanted another Pepsi.'

Smiling myself, I said, 'Sure.'

'Or an Oreo cookie.'

'Think so?'

She shook her head, her smile dying. 'No. Not really. I think he came back here to hide in the dark. To disappear. To make himself part of the darkness so he'd be safe. And maybe never come out.'

She had pain in her eyes. I could feel her kinship with Donny. Like him, she'd been brutalized. She knew how it was to be hurt and humiliated and raped. She knew about wanting to hide in the darkness.

'You came out,' I reminded her.

'But it was so hard. I didn't *want* to.' Tears shimmered in her eyes. 'So many times, I wanted to curl up in a corner and . . . vanish.'

'I'm sure damn glad you didn't.'

'Me, too.'

'You're a tough cookie.'

'That's me.' She sniffed and wiped her eyes. 'Anyway, he's just a kid and he got it bad. He might give us a hard time . . . try to hide if he knows we're coming . . .'

'Don't you think Peggy's probably in there, too?'

'Maybe. Who knows?'

'She must be,' I whispered.

'I hope so,' Cat said. She wiped her eyes again, then said, 'Ready to go in?'

'Guess so.'

'Let's be real quiet and maybe we can sneak up on them.'

We stepped back to the entrance. The tunnel was probably wide enough to let us walk side by side, but we would've had a tight squeeze. So I went in first, ducking slightly to save my head from the rock ceiling. Cat put a hand on my back. I felt its gentle pressure just above my belt.

With every step we took, the light from outside faded.

And so did the heat. The air stirring around our bodies felt less and less like the breath of a furnace.

Before we'd walked very far, the gray darkened to black. Total black.

I could see nothing at all.

But the air felt almost cool. It felt great.

'Can you see where you're going?' Cat whispered.

'Are you kidding?'

'Still got your lighter?'

'I thought we wanted to *sneak* in.'

'I'd rather lose the element of surprise than step on a snake or fall in a pit.'

'I'd be the first to go,' I pointed out.

'Even worse.'

I didn't know what to say to that, so I said nothing. I pulled the lighter out of my pocket and lit it. The small spurt of flame surrounded us with a wavering, yellowish glow. It illuminated the fairly smooth rock floor of the mine, and the rough walls and ceiling that looked as if they'd been carved out with a chisel or jackhammer.

Ahead of us, I saw nothing except more tunnel. And not much of that – maybe ten feet of it before the glow of our tiny flame was eaten by the darkness.

I saw no trace of Donny or Peggy or snakes or pits.

'Looks all right,' I whispered.

'Where *are* they?'

'I don't know.'

'Maybe they're not in here, after all.'

'Want to turn back?' I asked.

'Not yet. Let's keep going for a while, anyway.'

We kept walking.

My brand new lighter was burning strong. But I wondered if I should shut it off to conserve fuel.

'Do you still have your lighter?' I asked.

'Yeah. Want it?'

'Not yet.'

'Lost my matches, by the way.'

'Matches?'

'Yeah. I had a matchbook from home. It was in my shirt pocket, but it must've fallen out somewhere.'

'Can't imagine how that could've happened.'

She laughed softly behind me.

Since we both had lighters, I saw no reason to spare fuel and walk in darkness. So I kept my lighter ablaze.

Cat's hand moved lower down my back. It went under my shirttail. I felt her fingers push inside the waistband of my jeans. She seemed to make a fist, clutching the back of my jeans and belt. I felt it against my bare skin.

I also felt the heat of the lighter's flame against the side of my thumb.

'I'm gonna burn my thumb,' I whispered.

'Wouldn't want that.'

'I'll switch hands.'

The lighter died when I released its gas lever. Darkness clamped down on us. I changed the lighter to my right hand, thumbed it to life and squinted as a new blaze sprang from its top.

'I sure hope nobody else is in here,' Cat whispered.

'If nobody else is in here, we might as well leave.'

'I don't mean *them*.'

'Oh.'

'I mean, like a stranger. Like a hermit, or something.'

'A mine-dwelling maniac?' I suggested.

'Right. I hope there aren't any of those.'

'You and me, both.'

'What do you think the chances are?'

'Let's not get into that again.'

I heard a quiet chuckle and felt a slight downward tug on my jeans.

'Hey,' I said.

'Hey yourself.'

And then, at the dim reaches of my lighter's glow, I saw what looked like the remains of a picnic on the mine's rock floor. 'Here we go,' I said. I walked closer, then stopped and stood up straight. The top of my head didn't quite touch the ceiling.

Cat took her hand out of my jeans. She stepped over beside me. 'Well, now,' she whispered.

The package of double-stuffed Oreo cookies was open and half empty. Pepsi cans lay here and there. The potato chip bag gaped open. Broken chips were scattered about as if someone had been playing with them – throwing them. The salami lay near the potato chip bag. Though White could've used his sheath knife on the salami, he must've used his teeth instead. Maybe Donny had, too. Much of it was gone, and it had teeth-marks at one end.

'This was the place,' Cat said.

'Yeah.'

'While we were up in the rocks...'

'Yeah.'

'White had him in here. My God. Doing God-knows-what to him.'

'Yeah.'

'The poor little bastard.'

'White won't do it to anyone again,' I said. 'That's something, anyway.'

'Won't make it un-happen to Donny.'

'So where the hell is he *now*?'

My thumb hurt from the flame, so I released the gas lever. Everything went black. I switched the lighter to my left hand. Then I thumbed it back to life just in time to see a chunk of rock flying out of the darkness straight at my face.

I yelled, 'Shit!' and ducked.

The rock puffed my left ear with a breeze.

Then came two more, one slightly ahead of the other and a little higher.

Cat shouted, 'Hey!'

I jerked my thumb off the gas lever. In the sudden darkness, I lunged in front of Cat, twisting, trying to put my back to the oncoming rocks. One struck the back of my right shoulder. The other missed. I wrapped my arms around Cat and took her down.

When we were curled on our sides, I pulled her face close against my chest and covered her head with my arm.

The rocks kept coming.

They came fast.

Peggy and Donny must've both been throwing. Apparently, they'd gathered plenty of ammo in advance.

I don't know how many rocks flew by. Maybe twenty. More likely thirty.

Since they were being hurled into total blackness, most missed us. I heard them bounce off the walls and ceiling and floor on both sides of us, in front of us, behind us. They clacked. They thunked. Their sounds varied, depending on their size and what they hit and where.

A few struck me.

I took hits in the back and rump and legs, but none in the head. Some hurt more than others. Though I flinched, I gritted my teeth and kept silent, afraid the kids might home in on any noises from our direction.

At last, the barrage stopped.

We stayed down, motionless and quiet. I could feel Cat's warm breath on my chest.

Except for the hushed sounds of our breathing and heart-beats, there was an absence of sound – a silence as deep and heavy and oppressive as the darkness.

52

If we moved, if we spoke, we might trigger a new wave of flying rocks.

But maybe they'd used up their arsenal.

Maybe they'd crept away.

Maybe that's what we'd better do. The hell with them. They want to throw rocks at us, they can stay in this damn mine till they rot.

I doubted, though, that Cat would be willing to abandon them.

'Are you okay?' she whispered.

'Shhhh. They'll start throwing again.'

She stayed silent for a few seconds.

No rocks came.

'Maybe they left,' she said.

'Maybe.'

'Are you okay?' she asked again. 'They got you pretty good.'

'I'll live. You weren't hit, were you?'

'Not even once. Thanks.' She gave my chest a gentle, moist kiss. Then she said, 'Think it was Peg and Donny?'

'It had to be. And they knew it was us. They did it on purpose.'

'What'll we do?'

'Leave. Make a run for it. Get outside where we can see what's going on.'

'Okay. Yeah. That's probably a good . . .'

From behind me came a clank and a clinking metallic scurry. I knew what it had to be; someone sneaking through the dark had kicked an empty Pepsi can and sent it rolling.

It rolled over the rock floor, coming toward my back.

I lifted my arm off Cat's face, dropped onto my back and thumbed my lighter.

Its flame bloomed.

Shocked by the sight of them, I cried out, '*Yaaaaah!*'

Donny jumped. Peggy, by his side, raised her knife.

It looked like Cat's steak knife.

They looked like a couple of demented savages.

In the glow of the lighter, I saw that Peggy was naked down to the waistband of her denim skirt. Skinny and almost breastless, she might've been mistaken for a boy except for her big, stiff nipples.

Little Donny wore her tube top around his chest – probably as a makeshift bandage for his twin gashes. It wrapped him snugly from his armpits down to his waist. Below it, he was naked. He didn't even have Cat's shoes on, anymore. He held a dark flashlight in one hand, a corkscrew in the other.

Cat's corkscrew? Had to be. White must've taken it from the glove compartment after the crash, just as he'd taken nearly everything else.

Donny had Cat's corkscrew and Peggy had Cat's knife.

I had about one second to gape at them before they rushed us.

I jerked Snow White's hunting knife out of my belt. '*GET BACK!*' I shouted.

They both flinched and seemed to freeze in mid-stride.

'*DROP YOUR WEAPONS!*'

Donny, gaping at me, dropped his corkscrew and flashlight. Peggy shook her head and held on to her knife. 'No way,' she said. 'Fuck you. You drop yours.'

While she spoke, I sat up. But both my hands were full, so I knew I'd have a tough time getting to my feet.

The amount of light suddenly doubled.

Behind me, Cat said, 'Nobody has to drop anything. But let's just calm down, okay? We're not your enemy.'

'Fuck you aren't,' Peggy said.

Now that Cat had her lighter going, I let mine die and used my left hand to push myself off the floor. As I struggled to stand up, I watched Peggy closely. I remembered what she'd done to White.

On my feet, I stepped to one side and turned slightly so that I could see everyone. I ignited my lighter.

Peggy, lips peeled back, glared at me with fierce hatred. She looked as if she *ached* to rip me apart with her knife – or teeth. Donny, near her side, stared at Cat with a strange, frantic look in his eyes. He was breathing hard, his small shoulders rising and falling.

Cat, still down, was braced up with her left elbow, her right hand holding her lighter high. Her open shirt drooped off her left shoulder, leaving her whole left side bare all the way to her cut-off jeans.

Donny's eyes were glued to her.

As she pushed herself up, Peggy flung out a hand and punched Donny's shoulder. 'Quit gawping at her.'

'Don't hit him,' Cat said.

'Fuck you.'

'I mean it,' Cat said, getting to her feet. 'He's been hurt too much already. You have, too.'

'Thanks to you. And him.' She glowered at me.

Cat shut off her lighter. Mine gave the only flame as she lifted the shirt onto her shoulder. The front slid over, draping her breast. Donny raised his eyes to her face. 'Some things went wrong,' she said. 'I'm sorry about that. I'm *awfully* sorry you two got mixed up in all this. It is my fault, but it wasn't on purpose. The thing to do now is get out of here.'

'Nobody's going nowhere,' Peggy said.

'*We* are,' I told her. 'We're leaving. You and Donny can come with us if you want. Or you can stay. Makes no difference to me.'

'I think we should all leave together,' Cat said. 'You two can't stay here. You'll die. You've got nothing to drink ... maybe a few Pepsis.'

Peggy smirked and said, 'Maybe we'll drink your blood. That'll keep us going a while.'

'Sure thing,' Cat said, and thumbed her lighter to life.

340

I was glad to see her do that; my thumb was getting scorched. I released the gas lever and my lighter went out.

'I kinda like blood,' Peggy said. 'I liked White's.'

'Good for you. Now, get serious. Maybe *you* want to die out here in the middle of the desert, but you've got no right to take Donny with you.'

'He stays, too.'

Cat turned her eyes to the boy. 'You don't want to stay here, do you?'

'I've got to,' he said in a small, trembly voice. 'I have to do what Peggy says.'

'Not if it's something bad for you,' Cat told him. 'And staying here would be *very* bad.'

'Maybe he likes it here,' I said.

Donny frowned at me as if he were either confused or angry.

'I mean, you ran straight back here the minute you got away from White. You must *love* this mine.'

'It's good for hiding,' he said.

'You didn't have to hide anymore,' Cat told him. 'White's dead.'

'He ran away to hide from *you*,' Peggy said. 'So you wouldn't kill him like you'd killed me.'

'We didn't kill you,' I pointed out.

'Sure looked like it to Donny. That's how come he run off.'

Meeting the boy's eyes, Cat said, 'That was a natural mistake to make. She looked pretty dead to us, too. But we didn't do that to her.' Cat switched the lighter to her other hand without letting its flame die. I kept mine off. 'She got hurt that way when White crashed into our car.'

'I know,' he said. He glanced at Peggy.

She glared at him.

He cast a sheepish glance at Cat, mumbled, 'I'd better stay here,' and lowered his eyes.

'No,' Cat said. 'You'd better *not*. We're not going to let you.'

'Didn't you hear me?' Peggy asked. 'Nobody's going anywhere.'

'We are,' I told her again.

341

'And Donny's coming with us,' Cat added.

'The fuck he is.'

'Being his sister doesn't give you any right to . . .'

'*She's not my sister!*' Donny blurted.

Peggy let out a squeal and leaped at me, raising her knife overhead.

Cat's light went out.

In the sudden black void, I held the image in my head of Peggy coming at me like a madwoman in a movie. I knew where she was and where her knife was.

Maybe.

In the total darkness, I probably could've dodged clear.

But I didn't want to get away from her; I wanted to stop her. If I dodged her knife, it might find Cat.

So I stayed put and flung my left arm up to block her overhead strike.

My arm got hit. Not by the knife, though. I felt a blow, but no cutting.

As the impact jolted my arm, I drove my right hand forward. It held White's hunting knife.

But I kept the blade sideways and drove the flat of my fist into her. It smacked bare skin. Peggy gasped, '*Oooomp!*'

Light returned.

In the fluttery glow, I saw the serrated blade of Peggy's knife drag across the top of my forearm as my blow sent her stumbling backward, folding at the waist. Her right foot knocked one of the cans skittering away. The heel of her left foot stomped the potato chip bag. Some chips exploded out. Before she could fall flat on her back, she went crooked. Her left shoulder hit the wall of the mine. The wall seemed to swat her away. She flipped over and struck the floor chest first and grunted.

I hurried toward her sprawled body, planning to take the knife out of her hand.

Donny beat me to it. Straddling her back, he squatted and reached down to her right arm. He unwrapped her fingers from around the knife. Then he stood up with it and stepped away from her.

'Why don't you give that to me?' I said.

Frowning, he shook his head.

'No. But *Cat* can have it.'

53

Donny clamped the knife in his teeth. Then he used both hands to slide the tube top down his body, down past his waist, down until it wrapped him like a miniskirt. Only after that did he turn toward Cat. Taking the knife from his teeth, he walked over to her. He offered her the knife, handle first.

'Thanks,' she said. She took it and slipped it into the right front pocket of her cut-offs.

'I knew you were the good guys,' Donny told her. 'I'm sorry I threw rocks at you. She ... she told me to, and ...'

'It's all right.' Looking past him, Cat said to me, 'How's your arm?'

'What's one more wound, more or less?'

'Let's get into some light and we'll take care of it. Can you handle Peg?'

'Sure.'

She was still sprawled face down. 'Get up,' I said.

'Fuck you,' she muttered.

So I dropped the lighter into my pocket, switched the knife to my left hand, bent down and jammed my right hand under the waistband at the back of her denim skirt. I hauled her up by it. She squirmed and kicked.

'Let go! I'll kill you!'

While she struggled and yelled, I heard Cat say to Donny, 'Bring any Pepsis that're left.' Then she said to me, 'You bring her,' and started striding through the mine, holding her lighter out in front of her.

As I lugged Peggy along, I looked over my shoulder. Donny, a distance behind us, had a flashlight on. By its dim yellow light, I saw him crouch to pick up something. I hoped it was a Pepsi, not a rock.

I also noticed that he was at a somewhat lower level than me; the mine apparently angled downward from its entrance. I hadn't noticed that before. Now that I knew it, though, I felt the uphill grade as I trudged along with Peggy.

She swung by my side like a kicking, thrashing suitcase.

Donny caught up. By the scuffing sounds he made, I guessed that he was again wearing Cat's shoes. He walked quickly until he was a few paces away from me, then hung back as if afraid of getting too close.

Soon, daylight appeared in the distance above Cat's head. We walked closer and closer to it. The darkness all around us faded to gray. More and more warmth seeped into the air.

I thought that Cat might go all the way outside, but she halted in dusky light about twenty feet short of the opening and shut off her lighter. Turning around, she asked, 'How's this?'

'Fine,' I said.

'Nice to have some light again. Pretty warm, though.'

'Not as bad as outside. What should we do about her?'

'Just put her down.'

As I lowered her, she found the rock floor with her hands and feet and tried to scurry free. I kept hold of her skirt. Cat grabbed the nape of her neck and said, 'Lie down and don't move, Peggy.'

Peggy didn't have much choice at the moment.

When she was flat on the ground, we both let go of her. I planted a foot in the middle of her back to stop her from rising.

'I'll watch her,' Donny said.

Sure enough, he had Cat's shoes on. He was clutching two Pepsi cans against his stomach, and held the flashlight in his right hand. The flashlight was off.

'Okay,' Cat told him. 'Make sure she stays down.'

I took my foot off Peggy and stepped out of the way.

Donny sat down on her back as if she were a cushion. He stretched out his legs. 'I'll brain her with the flashlight if she tries to pull something,' he said.

'Very good,' Cat said. She led me a few steps closer to the mine entrance. 'Let's see that arm.'

'It's not too bad.' I held it out for her. Blood was still coming out of the straight line across the top of my forearm, but not in great amounts. 'She just sort of *dragged* the knife across. It's not very deep.'

'Does it hurt?'

'*Everything* hurts.'

'I'll make it all better.' She lifted my arm to her mouth, gently kissed the cut, then licked the blood off it. 'That's just so I can see your wound,' she said.

With her head down, 1 couldn't see her smile. I knew the smile was there, though.

'I've got cuts,' Donny said, watching us from his seat on Peggy.

'I'll take a look at them in a minute,' Cat told him. 'Let's have your shirt,' she said to me.

I took it off. She tore a strip up its front and bound my arm. When she was done, I put my shirt back on. What was left of it. Then we both stepped over to Donny.

He touched the back of Peggy's head with the flashlight. 'Don't move,' he said, 'or you'll be sorry.'

'Fuck you,' she muttered.

'She likes to say that a lot,' Donny explained as he stood up. 'She says it *all* the time. I don't think she's got much of a vocabulary.'

'Who *is* she?' Cat asked. 'Who are you? You're *not* really her brother?'

'Keep your trap shut, Donny,' Peggy said. 'I'm warning you.'

'You be quiet,' I told her.

'I'm not her brother,' Donny said. 'She's not my sister.'

'She told us she was.'

'That's what she tells everybody. Did she say I'm twelve?'

'Yeah.'

'I'm sixteen. I'm small for my age, that's all. But she likes to tell everybody I'm only twelve.'

'What're you doing with her?' Cat asked.

'We just . . . she sort of like kidnapped me.'

'You better shut the fuck up!' Peggy snapped.

'Knock it off down there,' I told her.

'What do you mean, she kidnapped you?'

'Well, she used to park near my school. And I'd see her sometimes when I'd walk by. She'd be inside her van, and . . .'

'You *walked* to school?' Cat asked.

'Back and forth. Yeah. But it wasn't very far.'

'Your parents *let* you walk to school?'

'I only had my mom,' Donny said, his voice soft.

'What about your father?'

'Don't have one.'

'Everybody has one,' Cat told him.

'Mine went away when I was little.'

'And your mom made you walk to school?'

'She had to go to work.'

'Terrific,' Cat muttered. 'No wonder you got kidnapped.'

'I didn't kidnap him,' Peggy muttered from down on the ground. 'He's lying through his teeth.'

'So how did you wind up with her, Donny?' Cat asked.

'Well, I used to see her by the school, like I told you. She'd be in her van, and smile at me. Then one day *after* school her van turned up in front of where I lived. And she came up to the door and rang the doorbell.'

'You let her in?' Cat asked.

'Sure.'

'Where was your mother when *that* happened?'

'At work.'

'Great. So you were alone and you opened the door for a stranger?'

'Yeah. But she wasn't exactly a stranger. Anyway, she was a *girl*. I wasn't scared of her.'

'Why *did* you let her in?'

'I don't know. She asked me if she could use the bathroom. I didn't see any harm in it. Sometimes, you've gotta go. So she came in and I showed her where the bathroom was.'

'You shouldn't have let her in,' Cat said. 'You should never let *anyone* in when you're alone like that.'

'I guess not,' he said. 'She seemed nice, though. Anyway, after she got done in the bathroom, she asked me if she could have something to drink. So then I took a couple of Cokes out of the refrigerator. Then we got to talking and she asked me if I'd like to take a look inside her van.'

'You *begged* me to show it to you, you little liar.'

'Did not.'

'Did, too.'

'Let Donny tell his story,' I warned Peggy.

'Well, he ain't telling the truth.'

'Let him talk,' Cat said.

'So, anyway, we went out and got in her van. It was sort of

dark in the back of it. All of a sudden, she ... she took off all her clothes right in front of me. She told me to touch her ... you know, down there.'

'You dirty little...'

'Knock it off, Peggy,' I said.

'He's lying! I stripped, okay, but he wanted me to. He *asked* me to.'

'She's the one who's lying,' Donny said.

'Someone sure is,' I said.

'How did she *kidnap* you?' Cat asked. From her tone of voice, I figured she was starting to have doubts about Donny. 'Just skip to there,' she told him. 'We don't need a debate about this other stuff. Okay? How did you end up leaving with Peggy in her van?'

'She said she'd tell on me. If I didn't go away with her, she'd tell my mom all about how we took off our clothes and did things to each other. But I hadn't done anything – just what she *made* me do.'

'You're really gonna get it, Donny.'

'Not from you,' I told her.

Donny continued, 'I said I hadn't done anything wrong and she could tell on me to anybody she wanted. I just wanted to get out. So then she threatened to *kill* my mom if I didn't go with her. I didn't want her to do that, kill my mom. So I stayed in the van and Peggy drove off with me.'

'When was that?' Cat asked him.

'A couple of months ago.'

'May seventh,' Peggy muttered.

'That's *more* than two months. You've been driving around all that time ...?'

'Yeah,' Donny said.

'Does your mother know you're all right?' Cat asked.

'Yeah. Not that she cares. But Peggy let me call her on the phone.'

'Are the cops looking for you?' I asked.

He shook his head. 'Peggy made me say that I ran away on purpose.'

'You *did* run away on purpose, you little bastard. You loved it. You loved every minute of it.'

'Did not.'

'What've you been doing for money?' I asked.

'Peggy . . .'

'You better just shut the fuck up right now if you know what's good for you. You start in blaming me with more lies, I'm gonna tell 'em what we *really* did.'

Donny shook his head. 'Peggy drove me to the bank. She made me go to the automated teller machine and take money out of my mom's account. We've been using that.'

'Is that right, Peggy?' Cat asked.

'Yeah,' she muttered. 'That's what we did.'

Cat said, 'Uh-huh.'

She knew it was a lie. We both did. Peggy wouldn't have made such threats over the crime of withdrawing funds from the mother's bank account.

Lifting his gaze to Cat's face, Donny said, 'Will you look at my cuts, now?'

'I guess so. Let me have the flashlight.'

He gave it to her. She switched it on. The murky yellow light came out.

'That guy had it on a long time,' Donny explained. 'When he had me in here. The batteries are awfully weak.'

'This is fine,' Cat said, and shined the dim light on his chest. The two gashes, one above each nipple, looked shiny and raw. They were no longer bleeding, though.

'Must've hurt,' Cat said.

'Yeah.'

'They aren't bleeding any more. Do they hurt now?'

'A little bit.'

'Do you want me to kiss them and make them better?'

'Only if you want to.'

'You saw me kiss the cut on Sammy's arm, didn't you?'

'Yeah.'

'And you figured it would be nice if I did the same for these cuts on your chest?'

'It'd be nice.' Donny sounded hopeful.

'Maybe it would, and maybe it wouldn't.'

'What do you mean?'

'Do you want to know a little secret about my mouth?'

'I guess so.'

'It's a lie detector.'

348

'Huh?'

'My mouth. It *kisses* people who are upright and honest. But if it goes to kiss a liar, it *bites*.'

Donny made a soft, uneasy laugh. He said, 'Yeah, sure.'

'Do you *still* want me to kiss your cuts?'

He hesitated for just a moment. Then he said, 'Your mouth isn't any *lie detector*.'

'You aren't calling *me* a liar, are you?' Cat·asked.

'No.'

I suddenly smiled, but Donny couldn't see it.

'Doesn't matter,' Cat said. 'You don't have to believe me. Do you still want me to kiss your cuts?'

He hesitated again. Then he said, 'Sure.'

'Do you want to change any of your story first?'

'Why should I? I was telling the truth.'

'Okay, then.'

She put a hand on his back – the hand with the flashlight. She switched the light off, then bent her knees. In the gray gloom from outside, I saw her head stop at the boy's chest. I heard a soft, kissing sound.

Then Cat murmured, 'Uh-oh.'

Donny squealed.

54

Donny tried to shove Cat away, but she held onto him and kept her mouth to his chest. He cried out, '*No! Stop it! Please! It hurts!*'

But she didn't stop.

Donny squirmed and thrashed and struggled and sobbed. He blurted, '*I lied! I lied! Stop it! Stop biting me! Please!*'

Cat's mouth was busy, so I asked, 'Lied about what?'

'*Everything! Make her stop! Please! Please!*'

She stopped and let go of him.

He backed away, hunching over and pressing a hand against his chest. 'You *bit* me!' he gasped.

'Sorry,' Cat said. 'My mouth has a mind of its own. But I warned you, didn't I?'

'It isn't . . . any lie detector.'

'I beg to disagree.'

'Fucking bitch,' Donny said.

'Hey,' I said. 'Watch it.'

'That's okay,' Cat said. 'Maybe he's right.' With that, she turned and handed the flashlight to me. I saw her face. Her lips and cheeks and even her nose were smeared with Donny's blood. 'Make sure Peggy stays put,' she told me. Then, turning to Donny again, she said, 'Tell me about the lies.'

'Why should I?' he gasped, his voice hitching.

'A couple of reasons. For one, Sammy and I risked our lives to save you. To save you *and* Peggy. You owe us the truth. For another, all I've done so far is nibble on you a little bit. Tell me the truth, or I'll *really* hurt you.'

'Okay,' Donny mumbled.

'You better keep your trap shut,' Peggy warned.

'Sammy, would you like to shut her up?'

'Sure.' I sat down on her back, just as Donny had done a few minutes earlier. 'Next time a word comes out of your mouth,' I said, 'I'll bop you on the head with the flashlight.'

'Fuck you,' she said.

I bounced the flashlight off her head. Not hard enough to do any real damage to her, but hard enough to kill the bulb. She flinched under me and made a quiet squeaky noise.

'Much better,' I told her.

She said nothing.

'Okay, Donny,' Cat said. 'You ready to tell the truth?'

'Yeah.'

'Is Peggy your sister?'

'No. It was like I said. She came over in the van.'

'Did she kidnap you?'

He didn't answer.

'Talk,' Cat said. 'And it better be the truth.' She clicked her teeth together.

'No,' Donny said. 'It wasn't . . . she didn't really kidnap me.'

'Why did you go with her?'

'Wanted to.'

'Why?'

'I don't know.'

'Yes you do.'

350

'We did stuff. We took off our clothes and ... you know, did stuff. I didn't have any girl friends. I'd never done anything like that before. Anyway, why *shouldn't* I go with her? I hated my mom and school and everything. Everything sucked. But I thought Peggy was pretty cool. And she was *nice* to me. So we just did it. We drove off and never went back.'

'You drove off and lived in the van?'

'Yeah. Except sometimes we camped out. And sometimes we stayed in motels, when we had a lot of money.'

'Where did you get a lot of money?' Cat asked.

'From the ATM. Like I said.'

Cat slipped her shirt off her shoulders. It drifted down her back and fell to the ground. She stood straight up in front of Donny, dressed only in her cut-offs and white socks, her arms at her sides.

'Do you want to tell me the truth?' she asked.

'About what?' His voice trembled.

'About where you got your money.'

'Do I get to ... touch you?'

'Is that what you want?'

'Sure. Yeah. I mean, who wouldn't?'

'Tell me the truth.'

'We ... we didn't do the ATM. That was a lie. We...'

'Donny!' Peggy blurted.

I struck her hard on the head with the flashlight. Her body jerked and she cried out, '*OW!*'

'We stole it from people.' He was silent for a moment. Then he said in a quiet, trembling voice, 'Can I touch you now?'

'Try it and I'll cut your hands off.'

'But...'

She dug a hand into the front pocket of her cut-offs and pulled out the steak knife. 'I didn't take off my shirt to give you an eyefull, Donny. I did it so my shirt won't get bloody...'

'Huh?'

'...when I start *carving* you.'

'Hey, no.'

'Tell me about robbing people.'

351

'We ... we just *did* it.'

'How?'

'We'd get somebody into the van. One of us would be the bait. We'd like ... you know, pretend we wanted to have sex with him. Or her. It was mostly guys, but sometimes women. Guys really go for me. A lot more than gals do. Anyway, I'd bring them into the van and we'd start messing around on one of the beds in the back. Then Peggy would sneak in and bash them on the head.'

'With what?' Cat asked.

'It was usually a big old rock. She'd knock them out with it. Or I would, if she was the one on the bed. Anyway, they'd get knocked out by one or the other of us. Then we'd drive off somewhere deserted and take all their money and throw them out by the side of the road.'

'Alive?' Cat asked.

'I don't know. Maybe some weren't. Who cares? They were all a bunch of perverts. They got what they had coming.'

I muttered, 'And we thought Snow White was bad.'

'Tell us about White,' Cat said. 'Is that how *he* ended up in your van? Did you lure him in?'

'No. Huh-uh. We never would've tried it on a guy like him. He was too big and tough. What happened there, he caught us off guard. We were about to go in and have some breakfast, and he all of a sudden barged into the van and told us to go after you guys. We couldn't do anything about it. Peggy was driving, and I was in the passenger seat. He stayed behind us, so there wasn't any way for us to sneak up and knock him out. That's what we *wanted* to do, though. Bash his brains out. We couldn't talk it over or anything, but both of us started coming on to him.'

'Coming on to him?' Cat asked.

'You know, flirting.'

'I get it.'

'Anyway, he didn't pay any attention to Peggy. He sure liked me, though. I got him to take me back to one of the beds. The only problem was, Peggy had to keep driving. There wasn't any way for her to sneak back and brain him.'

'Tough luck,' Cat muttered.

'Yeah.'

'Or was it?' I asked from my seat on Peggy's back.

'He wasn't so bad,' Donny admitted. 'He was rough, but . . . he liked me. I thought he really liked me a lot. Sure acted that way. We were going to be partners. He said Peggy'd gotten killed in the car crash, and it'd just be him and me from now on. I told him fine. It *was* fine. I'd gotten kind of sick of Peggy. She's so bossy. She has to always run everything and tell me what to do. And she's not exactly a *babe*, if you know what I mean. She's skinny and ugly and mean, and . . .'

I could feel Peggy breathing hard underneath me.

'I'd gotten to where I could hardly even stand her.'

She suddenly blurted, 'You dirty rotten cocksucker, I'm gonna rip your dick off and . . .'

I bonked her on the head again.

She let out a little cry and went silent.

'You're quite a fellow, Donny,' Cat told him.

'She makes me sick. I was *glad* when White said she'd gotten killed. I mean, who needs her? And I liked the idea of being partners with White. I figured I could be the bait, and he'd be even better than Peggy when it came to . . . you know, *taking care of business*.'

'So what went wrong?' Cat asked.

'Nothing. I mean, everything was cool. After the crash, we came over here to the mine and had snacks and Pepsis. And we spent most of the afternoon messing around. We had a good time, you know?'

'Sure,' Cat said.

'I wish he'd been you, though.'

'Yeah?'

'Guys are okay, but . . . I mean, you're . . . You're the most beautiful woman I've ever . . .'

Her hand darted forward. She flicked the knife. Its point nicked his side, just above his hip.

'*Hey!*' he gasped, and clapped a hand against the tiny cut.

'Shut up about me.'

'I'm sorry. Shit!'

'Ha ha,' Peggy said.

'Tell us about White,' Cat said. 'You spent the whole afternoon fooling around with each other?'

'Mostly. We also took a nap. And then we went walking and

he showed me the hole where he was planning to throw all your bodies.'

'A hole?' Cat asked.

'Yeah. A deep one. You have to go through all these side-tunnels, and it's way at the back. It's really neat, though.'

'Brock's hole,' I said.

'Huh?'

'Did he call it Brock's hole?'

'No. I don't think so.'

'What about the hole?' Cat asked.

'Well, he shined the flashlight down it, and there were some bodies way down at the bottom.'

'*Some* bodies?'

Donny nodded. 'Four or five, I guess.'

'I thought there was only supposed to be Brock,' I said.

'One of them *might've* been a guy named Brock, I think. He told me who they were, but I didn't pay a lot of attention to their names. He told me stories about all of them. What was really neat, he put some of them down there alive. He lowered them with ropes, then threw the ropes in after them. They didn't have any way out and just had to stay down there till they croaked. But he gave them water and stuff, so it wouldn't be too quick.'

'Charming,' Cat muttered.

'It was pretty cool, all right.'

'He planned to throw *us* down there?' she asked.

'Yeah. After we were done in the mine, we got in the van and drove over to pick up all your bodies and bring you back.'

'White knew we weren't dead,' I said.

'Well, he thought *Peggy* was dead. With you and Cat, he figured it was a toss up. He said you were alive right after the crash, but you might've croaked later. Or if you hadn't, you were too badly hurt to get away. One of the reasons we stayed in the mine so long, it was to give you guys a chance to bite it.'

'Sorry to disappoint you,' I said.

'You didn't disappoint *me*. I didn't want you to be dead. I didn't even know you. But White was *awfully* upset when we got there and he couldn't find you. He looked all over the place. Then he figured you must be up in those rocks. He didn't want to go climbing to look for you, so that's when we went up on the roof of the van. He took a stick with him so he could reach down into the cab and honk the horn.'

'Tricky fellow,' Cat said.

'It was my idea,' Donny explained. 'The whole thing was my idea. I figured you'd want to save me.'

'Well, you figured right. We *did* want to save you.'

'At that time,' I added.

'He wasn't supposed to cut me, though.'

'How'd you get up there with your hands tied behind your back?' I asked.

'I climbed the ladder. He didn't tie me till after we were up on top.'

'So you weren't really his hostage,' I said.

'I didn't think so. But then he started hurting me. Making me yell and scream. That wasn't in the plan.'

'Not in *your* plan, anyway,' Cat said.

'Sure wasn't. So I guess I really was like his hostage, after all. I guess he never *really* cared about me. He just wanted to ... have his fun with me and use me to get you guys back.'

'Tough luck,' I said.

'Yeah.'

'What'd he tell you about Elliot?' Cat asked.

'Who?'

'The vampire.'

'*Vampire?*'

'The vampire in our trunk.'

'He never said anything about any vampire. What're you talking about?'

'Sounds like he left Donny out of the loop,' I said.

Nodding, Cat said to the boy, 'This has always been about the vampire in our trunk.'

'Huh?'

'Why do you think he made us follow your van to this godforsaken place?'

'So he could, you know, *do* things to you. Take all your stuff and fool around with you and throw you down the hole. That's why.'

'It might've come to that,' I said.

'But it wasn't the real reason,' Cat explained. 'We had a vampire in the trunk of my car. White found out all about it.

355

He made us come here so that he would have a nice, desolate place for carrying out his big plan – to wait until after dark, then pull the stake out of the vampire's heart.'

'Why would he do that?' Donny asked.

'So the vampire would come back to life.'

'And attack him,' I said.

'And kill him,' Cat added.

'So that he would become a vampire,' I said.

'And have life everlasting.'

'A deathless creature of the night.'

'Like in the movies.'

'*Dracula*.'

'*Nosferatu*.'

'*Interview with the Vampire*.'

'*Salem's Lot*.'

'*Near Dark*.'

'And so on.'

'And so forth.'

Donny looked from Cat to me, then frowned at Cat and said, 'What a crock of shit.'

55

'Maybe, maybe not,' Cat said.

Donny made a snorty sound of scornful disbelief. 'There's no such thing as vampires.'

'I beg to differ,' Cat said. 'Looks to me like we've got vampires up the wazoo.'

'Huh?'

Instead of answering, she turned, crouched, and picked up her shirt. 'I guess I could've kept it on.'

'Glad you didn't,' Donny said.

When he said that, I felt like getting up from Peggy's back and slamming *him* with the flashlight. But I stayed put.

'You're just lucky you told the truth,' Cat told him. With the shirt in one hand, the steak knife in the other, she turned to me and said, 'Let's get going. Sundown's on the way.'

'What about these two?' I asked.

'The truth shall set them free.'

'What do you mean?'

'We did our job,' Cat said. 'We saved them from White. Donny obviously *wasn't* kidnapped by Peggy, so we don't need to save *him*. We've got no reason to save either of them. They aren't victims, they're criminals. So we walk out of here, you and I – and they do whatever they want.'

'We're just going to *leave* them?'

'Why not?'

'They're *killers*.'

'So are we. And they know it.'

'Fucking-A right, we know it,' Peggy said from under me. I hit her with the flashlight.

She flinched and gasped, '*Hey!*'

'Keep your mouth shut,' I told her.

'I don't like the idea of just letting them go, either,' Cat said. 'But what choice do we have? We can't turn them in to the cops; they'd squeal on us and we'd end up getting nailed for Elliot.'

'You mean he *isn't* going to rise at sundown?' I asked.

'He might, but I wouldn't want to bet my life on it. If we try to put these two behind bars, we'll probably end up there, too. So turning them in isn't an option. Not as far as I'm concerned.'

'No. You're right.'

'Of course, we could kill them.' Cat said. 'That's an option.'

'Well, yeah. But . . .'

'No, it's not,' Donny blurted. 'Hey, come on. You can't *kill* us. Shit!'

'You tried to kill us,' Cat pointed out.

'No, we didn't!'

'You came sneaking toward us in the dark after the rock attack. Peggy had a knife and you had a corkscrew. You were on your way to finish us off.'

'No, we weren't!' Donny cried out. 'That's bullshit!'

'Shut the fuck up,' Peggy said.

This time, I didn't hit her.

She kept talking. 'We were gonna kill 'em, and you know it, so stop lying. Haven't you got ears? They might let us go if you don't piss 'em off. So shut your fucking trap for once.'

Donny shut his mouth.

'So, will you let us go?' Peggy asked.

'What do you think about it?' Cat asked me.

'I don't know. If these two get back into action . . .'

'We won't,' Peggy said. 'Never. I'm done with him.'

'I've learned *my* lesson,' Donny said. 'I promise. I'll never do anything bad again.'

'I hope you mean that,' Cat told him.

'I do. Honest. I'll go back home to my mom and go back to school . . .'

'I'll go to Los Angeles and get a job,' Peggy said.

'Not Los Angeles,' Cat said. 'We're there. Pick another city.'

'San Francisco?'

'Good choice.'

'So we're going to do it?' I asked Cat.

'Unless you have a better plan.'

'I guess we can't just . . . kill them.'

'I wouldn't want to. Would you?'

I shook my head. 'It wouldn't exactly be *wrong*. I mean, I don't feel it was wrong to kill Elliot.'

'He's a vampire,' Cat said. 'Of course, so are these two.'

'Yeah. But Elliot was busy attacking you when we did it to him. This'd be different. This'd be in cold . . .'

'*We* aren't vampires,' Donny broke in.

'Shut the fuck up,' Peggy told him.

'Well, we aren't. What the hell is she . . . ?'

'You're just a different kind,' Cat said. 'That's all. You're the kind that can walk in sunlight.'

56

'Take my shoes off, Donny.'

While he removed them, Cat put her shirt back on. I stood up and stepped away from Peggy. I picked up the two Pepsi cans as Cat stepped into her shoes. I stuffed one can into each front pocket of my jeans.

'You're taking *everything!*' Donny whined.

'You can keep the flashlight,' Cat told him.

'Oh, thanks a heap.'

'You don't want it?'

'Yes! But you're taking all our *stuff!*'

'Just what was stolen from us,' Cat said.

'What're *we* going to do?'

'Shut up,' Peggy said. She pushed herself up to her hands and knees.

'You can do anything you want,' Cat told Donny. 'Except that you can't have our stuff and you can't come with us.'

'But we'll *die* if we stay here. You said so.'

'Then don't stay,' Cat told him.

'Just wait till after dark,' I suggested. 'Then start walking. Go back the way we came in. Go through the pass and down to the desert floor and just keep walking. You'll run into a road, sooner or later.'

'But...'

'It can't be more than ten or fifteen miles from here. You can get there overnight.'

'And then,' Cat said, 'I'm sure some nice person will give you a ride.'

'And wish he hadn't,' I said.

'We're done with that stuff,' Peggy said. 'We are. I promise. We learned our lesson.'

'Well, good,' Cat said. 'Come on, Sammy. Let's move it.'

I followed her outside. The area in front of the mine was draped in shadows, but still seemed very bright after the gloom inside. The wind had kicked up again. It made a lot of noise, and gusted against us, but didn't blow the heat away. In spite of the wind and shadows, the heat was bad.

I kept an eye on the mine entrance as we walked.

Nobody came out.

After we rounded the end of the outcropping, we could no longer see the mine. I kept glancing back, anyway, as we made our way through the ruins.

No Peggy. No Donny.

Nobody at all.

The evening sun cast a ruddy glow over the broken-down, abandoned remains of the mining camp. In that gawdy light, the place no longer looked dry and dead. It looked as if it had a secret life more strange than anyone might guess – more wonderful but maybe more frightening. The pickup truck seemed to be lurking like a stealthy beast, watching us from around the corner of the shack.

The shadows of the ruins were long and dark. They looked like hiding places.

'It's beautiful, isn't it?' Cat said. 'In this light?'

'Yeah.'

'Haunting.'

'That's for sure,' I said. 'I wouldn't want to be here at night.'

'We won't be.'

'Hope not.'

'I just wish I had my shoe laces,' she said.

I looked down at her feet. The big, high-top leather shoes were open down the front. Their bulging tongues flopped and wobbled as she walked.

It took me a moment to remember why the laces were missing; she'd used them to tie up the top of Peggy's dress after breaking the shoulder straps with a flying tackle. Later, the dress had been drenched in White's blood, ruined. So Peggy had changed into the tube top and denim skirt.

'If we go back the way we came,' I said, 'we can stop by Peggy's dress and take your laces back.'

She frowned at me. 'Over by White's body,' she said, as if not completely sure.

'That's where it oughta be, I think.'

'Yeah. Where the van was – before she tried to take off and ditch us.'

'Right.'

'The rope oughta be there, too,' she said. 'Let's get the laces and the rope. But we'll stop off at the van, first.'

We were nearly to the place where it had ended its driverless run, crashing and dying against a boulder. When we got there, we stopped beside its open door. We stared back at the ruins.

'Do you see them?' Cat asked.

'No. Do you?'

'Nope.'

'Maybe they're planning to spend the night.'

'Not real likely,' Cat said. 'Do you want anything from the van?'

360

I thought about my overnight bag. And Cat's. The clothes and toilet articles we'd packed. 'Nothing of mine that I want to be carrying all night,' I told her.

'Wait here,' she said, and climbed in.

She returned a couple of minutes later with the pick and shovel.

'You're kidding,' I said.

'We came out here in the first place to dispose of Elliot's body, didn't we?'

'It started out that way.'

'Don't you think we oughta go ahead and do it? We'll put the stake back into him, then bury him right where he is.'

'Well . . .'

'I'll help you carry the stuff,' she said, and climbed into the van again. This time, she came out hauling her overnight bag.

I said, 'Huh?'

'Don't worry, I'll carry it. I could take the shovel, too,' she offered.

'No, that's fine. I've got it.'

We looked back at the ruins again, but still saw no sign of Donny or Peggy.

'Ready to go?' Cat asked.

'All set.'

She carried her overnight bag. I carried the pick and shovel. Her bag rattled and clanked.

After a while, I asked, 'What've you got in there?'

'Everything.'

'Huh?'

'Most of my stuff and your stuff.'

'I could've done without . . .'

'Why leave it behind?'

'We've got a long walk.'

'It's not heavy.'

'Looks heavy.'

'That's mostly the *other* stuff.'

'What other stuff?'

'Well, I've got all the identification papers and maps and things that I took out of my car this afternoon.'

'The registration?'

'That, the insurance papers . . .'

'Maybe we oughta go over to your car and take off its license plates.'

'Nah. It's too far out of the way. Anyway, I don't think it would do any good. If there's an investigation, I'm sure they won't need the license plates to trace it back to me. What I thought I'd do is call the cops when we get home and report it stolen. Good plan?'

'Good plan. Can't hurt. So what else is in your bag? Papers don't clank.'

'I've got the lighter fluid, the WD-40, the hammer and the tire iron. It didn't seem like a good idea to leave that stuff behind. Even if we don't need it ourselves, we shouldn't let our two friends get their hands on it. I'd hate the irony of being nailed with our own stuff.'

'You think they'll come after us?' I asked.

'What do you think?'

'Well, I guess Peggy probably laid into Donny the minute we were gone.'

'Unless she wasn't as angry as she let on.'

'If she *didn't* kill him,' I said, 'I suppose they might team up again and come after us.'

Nodding, Cat said, 'We hurt them both pretty good. They're probably eager for some payback. Plus, we know too much. They might want to make *sure* we never tell on them.'

'And Donny's got the hots for you.'

'The horny little shit.'

'I'm sure he'd like nothing better in the world than to get his hands on you.'

'And more,' Cat said.

'Exactly.'

'And Peggy'd be glad to kill me *because* of that.'

'Because of Donny?' I asked.

'Yeah. I think she's in love with the little rat, don't you?'

'Probably.'

'And jealous as a yellow dog. Look what she did to White. She'll do the same to me if she gets half a chance. And to you.'

'Why would she be jealous of me?' I asked.

'That won't be jealousy. That'll be sheer hatred. Remember the trade? White wanted to trade Peggy for me? And you wouldn't let me go.'

362

'Of course I wouldn't.'

'Well, he said he'd kill Donny if the trade didn't go through. Cut the kid's head off.'

'Or his ear.'

'Either way, Peggy really believed he meant to do it. She begged you to let me go. I think she's hated your guts ever since then. And everything after that has made it worse. I think she'd *love* to rip your throat open.'

'You're making me wish we'd gone ahead and killed them back at the mine.'

'Aaah, we could never do that. Kill them in cold blood? Anyway, there's always a chance they won't have the guts to attack us ... no matter how badly they might want to.'

'What do you think the odds are?' I asked.

Cat laughed. 'That they won't?'

'That they will.'

'A damn sight higher than the odds of being attacked by Elliot, that's for sure.'

I smiled at her. 'You don't really think Elliot's going to rise, do you?'

'I bet he doesn't.'

'He looked pretty dead, didn't he?'

'Sure did,' she said. 'And he'll probably stay dead. But I'd like to get there before sundown, just in case.'

57

First we got to Snow White.

As we approached his carcass, some horrible birds cawed and flapped away.

Careful not to look at him closely, I set down the pick and shovel, stepped over to the rope and started working it into a coil.

Cat set down her bag, then went to the area a few yards away where Peggy had stripped beside the van and changed into clean clothes. The towel she'd used to wipe the blood off her body was nowhere in sight. Neither were any of the wet wipes. Her dress was still on the ground, though. It looked like a twisted rag of black filth. Cat crouched over it and searched for her shoe laces. The dress was stiff with dried blood.

When she found the laces, she took the steak knife out of her pocket and cut them off. Then she sat on the ground. Knees up, she threaded them into the eyelets of her shoes.

I stood motionless and watched her.

Watched her sitting there in the ruddy light of the summer evening, lacing up her shoes. Her short, boyish hair shone like gold. Her shirt tail hung out. Her arms and legs looked smooth and tawny. She might've been a kid sitting on the sidewalk in front of her house after supper, putting on rollerskates.

I felt entranced.

And I realized it wasn't just the magic of the sunlight.

It was the magic of Cat.

And it didn't go away when she finished tying her shoes, turned her head, and smiled up at me. 'All done,' she said. Then she asked, 'What? You all right?'

'I'm great,' I said.

Grinning, she held out both her hands and said, 'Get a load of the mitts.'

They were stained red.

'The dress *felt* dry,' she said. 'Dry, but sticky.' She got to her feet and started rubbing her hands up and down against the front of her cut-offs. When she finished, her hands still looked as if she'd been playing with a rusty pipe.

'Oh, well,' I said. 'It's only blood.'

'But White's. I wish it wasn't White's. If it was yours, I'd lick it off.'

I let go of the rope as she came over to me.

With her stained hands, she clutched the edges of my torn, open shirt and pulled me against her. She mashed her mouth against mine. Then she murmured into my mouth, 'I love you so much, Sammy. God. If only . . . I wasted so much of my life. We could've been together all those years. It would've been so great.'

'We're together now,' I told her, my eyes going blurry, a tightness in my throat.

'And we'll always be together from now on, won't we?'

'If I have anything to say about it.'

''Till death do us part?'

'At the very least,' I said.

'Promise?'

'I promise.'

She squeezed me hard against her, as if her life depended on it.

58

We were about fifty feet away from the broad, dark split in the wall when Cat said, 'Oh, no. Look.'

I turned my head and looked.

The bottom edge of the sun touched the summit of the basin's western ridge.

I said, 'Shit.'

Cat said, 'We'd better hurry.'

We quickened our pace.

'I don't think this counts as sunset,' I said as we rushed toward the gap. 'It's going below a mountain ridge, not the real horizon.'

'It's *our* horizon. Maybe it's his.'

'Not that it matters,' I said.

'I know. He's dead. He's not getting up.'

'Right.'

'Right.'

We hurried into the deep gloom of the pass. The pick and shovel bounced on my shoulder. The coil of rope, draped over my other shoulder, flopped against my side.

'Why don't I run on ahead and put the stake into him?' I said.

'No, don't do that.'

'Are you sure?'

'Pretty sure. Let's just stay together.'

Maybe she simply didn't want to be left alone. I didn't want to be alone, either. But I don't think that was the main reason she told me to stay.

Running on ahead would be an admission of belief.

Apparently, we *did* believe. Cat had pulled out the stake on purpose to activate him so that maybe he would save us from

White. And now we intended to put the stake back into him – to defuse him before he went off. So we did believe he might rise after sundown. We partly believed, anyway. We just didn't exactly want to admit it.

We didn't want to make it more real.

If I'd run ahead to shove the stake back into Elliot, things would've seemed *very* real.

So I stayed by Cat's side.

We walked faster and faster through the narrow, twisting lane. Light came in from the strip of sky high above us, but it grayed as it descended the chasm. By the time it got down to us, it was a heavy gloom.

It allowed us to see, vaguely, where we were going. It kept us from bumping into the rock walls.

We walked quickly side by side.

We didn't talk.

Though we heard the wind, it couldn't get to us through the narrow, twisting gap. The still air felt heavy and hot. Sweat poured off me, drenching my clothes. The shovel and pick were slippery in my wet hands. I had to keep blinking sweat out of my eyes.

The wind, high above us, sounded like the surf of a far-off ocean. I heard Cat panting for air. I heard myself panting, and heard my heart pounding wildly. With every stride, the Pepsi cans made sloshing sounds in my pockets. Our shoes scuffed and crunched along.

'How you doing?' I asked.

'Okay,' she said.

'We'll get to him pretty soon.'

'Hope so.'

'Can't be much farther,' I told her.

'God, it's stifling in here.'

'Things'll probably cool off after dark.'

We didn't say anything for a while. Then Cat said, 'Maybe we oughta run.'

'Okay.'

So we ran. I was glad to be running.

We planned to stake the bastard – might as well get there in time to do it, even if we *do* both know he's dead as hell and will never get up again.

We ran side by side at a pace faster than a jog, slower than a sprint.

We would have sprinted, I think, in spite of the heat and our exhaustion and the burdens we carried – but the light was too poor. We would've stumbled on the rough floor or crashed into a wall.

The light was too lousy for running at all.

But we did it.

We had to reach him in time.

Earlier, the chance of Elliot rising had seemed incredibly remote. Virtually impossible. But it had come to seem less impossible as the sun had descended. By the time we'd watched the sun touch the ridge, Elliot coming to life had seemed almost possible to me. By the time we started running, it seemed *completely* possible. As we ran through the near dark of the gap, it began to look like a certainty. I was scared half to death.

And yet, in the back of my mind, I realized this was silliness. We were scaring ourselves, that was all. We'd let our imaginations get away from us.

But we had to reach him in time.

The running hurt. My lungs burned. Every muscle felt hot and achy. My head throbbed. All my wounds felt like fire. The shovel and pick, propped against my shoulder, bounced and pounded me. The dangling coils of rope swatted my side.

But I kept going and didn't slow down.

I told myself that we would get to Elliot soon. We'd put the stake into him. Then there would be no more need for running.

Cat suddenly cried out, '*Yaaah!*' She flung an arm out across my chest. '*Is it him?*'

As we staggered to a halt, I saw a dim, pale figure sprawled on the ground a few strides ahead of us. He looked pale in the near dark because he was naked.

'It's gotta be him,' I gasped.

Cat let go of her overnight bag and gasped, 'He's still down.'

'Yep.'

She flung her arms up, arched her back, tilted her head toward the dim strip of sky high above us, and whispered, 'Thank you, God. Thank you.'

'I'll second that,' I said. Bending over, I set down the pick and shovel. I let the coils of rope fall to the ground. Then I pulled the Pepsi cans out of my pockets and set them down. 'Before we break out the ... champagne,' I gasped, 'let's get the stake into him.'

'Hope we can find it,' Cat said.

'What did you ... do with it when you ... took it out of him?'

'Threw it.'

'Far?'

'Just gave it a toss. I'll try to find it. Why don't you take the hammer ... out of my bag?'

I dropped to my knees beside her overnight bag. While I opened it and reached inside, Cat wandered over to the body. She dug the lighter out of her pocket and ignited it. A spurt of flame rose above her hand.

She looked down at Elliot.

In the fluttery yellow glow, I could see where she'd torn apart the silvery tape on his back to get at the blunt end of the stake.

She crouched beside him and frowned. I don't think she was studying the body, though. I think she was doing a mental reenactment of tugging the stake out and giving it a toss.

She turned to her right, stood up, and started walking slowly toward the wall, her head down.

My hand, deep in her overnight bag, fumbled among the can of lighter fluid, some soft clothes and the tire iron before it found the hammer. I pulled the hammer out.

'*Voila!*' Cat yelled.

Startled, I looked up in time to watch her swoop down and snatch up the wooden stake. She whirled around, raising the stake in one hand, her lighter in the other. She was grinning. She was gasping for breath. Her checkered shirt hung wide open. Her left breast was entirely uncovered, gleaming with sweat, her nipple sticking out rigid. Her flat belly rose and fell as she panted. Her cut-offs drooped low on her hips as if ready to fall off.

She looked like a strange, lewd version of the Statue of Liberty. A savage. A tomboy. A vampire-killer.

'Good going, Cat!'

'Let's do it!' she cried.

With her stake and blazing lighter, she rushed toward Elliot's body. I hurried over to him with the hammer.

Side by side, we stood above him.

She tilted back her head. So did I. We both gazed up between the towering walls of stone. The strip of sky far above us was a rich, deep blue color.

'I wonder how much time we had to spare,' I said.

'Not much,' Cat said.

'We'd better do it.'

In a hushed voice, Cat asked, 'Wanta wait and see what happens?'

'You've got to be kidding.'

'Aren't you curious?'

'Sure,' I said. 'But curiosity...' I stopped my words. She looked at me. I met her eyes.

'Killed the cat,' she finished for me.

'We can't let that happen,' I told her.

'Want me to do the honors? I'm the idiot who pulled it out.'

'Sure. Either way. I can do it...'

'No, that's all right. But why don't you hold the light?'

'I'll get mine.' I switched the hammer to my left hand, went into my jeans pocket with my right, and found my own lighter. I thumbed it to life. Cat shut hers off. We both knelt beside Elliot's body.

I detected no odor of corruption.

I saw no ants crawling on his back. I heard no flies.

I figured there were probably scientific reasons for that. Maybe it had to do with where we'd left him. Something to do with being in deep shadows all afternoon. Maybe something about the nature of the rocky ground.

I've heard stories about certain saints who stayed fresh after death.

And vampires.

But there was nothing supernatural about the look of the wound in Elliot's back: a nasty, raw, pulpy hole.

Cat eased the point of the stake into it.

Slipped it in a little deeper.

Pushed it in an inch.

Then she clutched the top of the stake with both hands and

leaned forward, shoving down, thrusting it in hard and deep. The hole made a *squelch* sound.

We didn't need the hammer.

59

It shook Cat up. After shoving the stake into him, she turned toward me on her knees. I raised my arms to keep the lighter away from her. She put her hands inside my open shirt and wrapped them around my back and hugged me.

She was bare and hot and wet against me to the waist.

I could feel her trembling.

Letting my light go out, I whispered, 'It's all right now. It's all right. Everything's fine.'

But it wasn't.

The attack came about five minutes later.

60

We wanted to bury Elliot for only one reason: we thought he might be an actual vampire. We were afraid of the stake coming out.

Afraid of re-activation.

Resurrection.

Otherwise, we would've left him where he lay and gotten the hell out of there.

But we stayed to bury him.

The last of the light seemed to be gone, so Cat took the lighter fluid and a small bunch of the clothing out of her overnight bag. I hefted the pick.

We found a place near the body where the ground didn't seem to be solid rock.

Cat doused a sock and a pair of panties with lighter fluid, then set them ablaze.

They surrounded us with firelight and shadows.

I swung the pick-ax. Its blade bit into the hard dirt and

gravel. I pried a bunch loose, hoisted the pick, and swung again. This time it sank in only about half an inch, then struck rock with a noisy clang. A shiver rushed up the wooden handle, hurting my hands.

'Is there anything I can do to help?' Cat asked.

'Call the whole thing off?'

'I suppose we don't *have* to bury him.'

'No, we should. If we can.'

She put another sock on the fire. I raised the pick for another blow.

Then I got clobbered in the head.

I saw it an instant before it hit me – a chunk of something pale flying at my face. I didn't get a good look at it, didn't know what it was. But when it crashed against my forehead, I knew it had to be a rock.

It hammered me.

It made a *conk* noise.

A blast of light blinded me. My head seemed to explode with pain.

I stumbled backward, dropping the pick-ax. I heard it clank behind me. Then I tripped over it and went down. My back slammed the ground. But I kept my head up.

Kept it up and stayed conscious and saw Donny, completely naked, race out of the darkness. Cat, crouching by her small fire, turned her head and gasped. Donny dived at her.

As he took her down, Peggy rushed me, shrieking.

She was naked, too. Her sweaty skin gleamed in the firelight. Her face, streaked with shadows, looked hideous and mad. She clutched a big rock in one hand.

I reached for the knife in my belt, but my arm moved too slowly.

She hurled herself down on me, landing with a smack of bare skin. Her weight knocked my breath out and trapped my right hand against my belly. With my left hand, I caught hold of her wrist before she could bash my head in with the rock.

Her other hand clamped my face and jerked my head sideways.

Her head darted down.

Her breath gusted against the side of my neck. Before she got a chance to bite, I rammed a knee up. The top of my thigh

371

punched her between the legs. She grunted. The blow scooted her up my body. Her lower teeth jammed the edge of my jaw. I slammed my leg up again. She gasped, '*Ooomp!*' Her mouth made a quick, slobbery path up the side of my face. With the third blow of my leg, I twisted and flung her off.

She still clutched the rock, so I kept a tight grip on her right wrist as I tumbled her onto her back.

Somewhere nearby, Cat cried out, '*No!*'

I suddenly didn't care about the rock in Peggy's hand. I didn't give a damn about whether she hit me with it or how badly I might get hurt. I let go of her wrist and went a little nuts. She slammed me in the jaw with the rock, but only once.

Perched on her chest, I punched her in the face, gave her a right and a left and a right and a left, knocking her head back and forth. With each blow, a spray of sweat and spit and blood flew from her open mouth.

I hit her hard and fast about eight or ten times in the face, then leaped off her and whirled around to help Cat.

In the glow of the dying fire, I saw her sprawled under Donny. He had her arms pinned down. She was gasping for breath, whimpering, writhing.

I grabbed him by the hair.

I tore him off Cat and threw him down and kicked and stomped him until Cat clutched my arm with one hand and pulled me away from him. She didn't have her shirt on. Her cut-offs were unzipped and hung crooked. She held them up with her other hand.

Sobbing, she let go of them. As they fell, she hugged me.

'What did he do to you?' I blurted.

'Nothing.'

'*Nothing?*'

'I'm okay. I'll live. Okay? How are you? Did she hurt you?'

'I'm fine,' I said. 'Did he rape you?'

'He tried. Had trouble with my cut-offs.'

'I heard you yell.'

'The little shit bit me.'

'Where?'

Releasing her tight embrace on me, Cat stepped backward. The fire had gone out. She took the lighter out of her pocket and thumbed it to life. She held it close to her left breast.

I stared at the row of dents in the gleaming skin above her nipple.

'Donny did that?' I asked.

'Yeah.'

'Must've hurt like hell.'

'It did. But I've been bitten before. You know?'

'I know.'

'I've been bitten a lot worse. And better. That little asshole didn't even draw blood.'

'Does it still hurt?' I asked.

'Yeah. It does.' With her empty hand, she reached up and caressed the side of my face. 'Will you kiss it and make it better?' she asked.

I did.

She also had teeth marks on the underside of her breast, and I had to kiss those, too.

Then she held my face between her hands and guided my mouth to her other breast.

'Did he bite this one?' I asked.

'No, but it wouldn't mind being kissed.'

It took a while.

After that, Cat kissed the big, new lump in the middle of my forehead.

Then the swollen side of my jaw.

Then my mouth.

61

While Cat and I were making love, nobody else moved.

Nobody moved afterwards while we lay on our backs, worn out and breathless, holding hands.

But we knew that Donny and Peggy were alive.

A couple of times, we heard them moan.

After we'd rested for a while, we got dressed. Then Cat used the lighter fluid and started some clothes on fire. I bent down, groaning, and lifted the pick.

'Forget about that,' Cat told me.

'Huh?'

'We aren't going to bury Elliot.'

'Why not?'

'I've got a better plan.'

'Such as?' I asked.

She told me.

I gaped at her. 'Are you kidding?' I asked.

'Don't you think it's a good plan?'

'It's a great plan. Sick, but great.'

So we did it.

Together, we stripped the silver tape off Elliot – unbinding his hands, releasing his feet, unwrapping his chest and back. It was awful, touching him. But we had to touch him a lot: hanging onto him, rolling him this way and that, lifting his feet, his head, his back.

His skin felt warm and sticky.

He was fairly stiff, as if his muscles were hardening up. I don't know if it was rigor mortis. Cat and I didn't say anything about it.

We didn't say anything about his erection, either.

Maybe *that* was rigor mortis. I don't know.

But it made me think that maybe he *was* a vampire, and only sleeping, and having a hot dream.

It gave me the creeps.

I tried not to think about it. Soon, we finished peeling all the tape off his body.

Cat fed the tape to the fire.

I went for the rope.

Then we dragged Peggy over to Elliot. She didn't struggle. She hardly seemed to be conscious at all.

When we dragged Donny over, he whimpered and fought us. He didn't put up much of a fight, though, and it stopped altogether when Cat punched him in the nose.

We tied Donny and Elliot together, face to face. We lashed Peggy to Elliot's back.

Made a sandwich with the tall, skinny vampire as the meat in the middle.

I know.

It was a terrible thing to do.

Hideous.

But what the hell, we did it anyway.

Sometimes, while we worked, a groan escaped from me or from Cat. Sometimes, a giggle.

When we were done, I went to get the Pepsis. Cat disappeared into the darkness for a few minutes and returned with the tube top, denim skirt and socks that Donny and Peggy had discarded before attacking us.

She used them to keep the fire going.

We sat by it and drank the Pepsis and stared at our captives.

They lay together on their sides like a trio of lovers. Peggy and Donny, who seemed barely conscious, moaned and squirmed against Elliot as if they couldn't get enough of him.

62

We tossed our hammer and knives into Cat's overnight bag, where they clanked against the tire iron, the cans of lighter fluid and WD-40. I pulled the church key out of my sock and tossed it in. I'd never had a chance to use it. We'd never ended up using several of our weapons. I was glad we'd had them, though. They might've come in handy if things had gone differently.

In the interest of traveling light, we decided to leave the pick and shovel behind.

I took Cat's bag.

We walked over to our trio.

The bundle of naked limbs and torsos seemed to be swaying and writhing languidly.

Donny lay cheek to cheek with Elliot.

'How's everybody doing?' Cat asked. 'All comfy and cozy?'

'You've gotta let us go,' Donny said in a trembling, high-pitched voice. 'You've *gotta!*'

'Do we?' I asked.

'As a matter of fact,' Cat said, 'we just stopped in to say so long, farewell, toot-toot, good-bye.'

'You've gotta give us another chance.'

'No, we don't,' I said.

'We aren't killing you,' Cat explained. 'Maybe we *ought* to, but we're just going to leave you here, instead. You'll probably get loose in a few hours and come out of this ordeal in fine shape.'

'*Please!*' Donny whined.

'You two blew every chance you ever had,' Cat said.

'Fuck you both,' Peggy muttered. 'We get out of this, we'll come after you and nail your sorry asses.'

'That's no way to talk,' I told her.

'Certainly not a *smart* way,' Cat added. 'Someone in your position.'

Then Cat jammed her hand in between Peggy's chest and Elliot's back. The two bodies were bound tightly together. Cat had a difficult time. Peggy had a worse one; the way she cried out and squirmed, I think the stake must've torn up her chest a little on its way out of Elliot.

I opened Cat's overnight bag.

Cat tossed the stake in.

Then we walked away fast.

63

A few minutes later, we were still hurrying through the curves of the mountain pass when screams came.

Cat was holding my hand. Her grip tightened.

She muttered, 'Jesus.'

I said, 'I'd scream, too, if somebody left me tied to a corpse.'

'You don't think Elliot . . . ?'

'Nah.'

We walked faster.

The screams ended pretty soon. Or at least we could no longer hear them.

When we came out the other end of the gap, the slope below us was pale in the moonlight. We made our way down slowly to the floor of the desert, then walked for hours through the night and early morning. We found a paved road just a little before sunrise.

64

It's September now. The summer is coming to an end.

The past few weeks have been more wonderful than anything I ever could've hoped for.

I'm living in Cat's home. We're almost never apart, and we like it that way. I probably won't go back to teaching. There's no need for money; Cat's husband, Bill, had been a horrible man but extremely wealthy. I'm working on a novel. I've also gone back to writing poetry. The poetry is nearly always about Cat. She seems to like it.

I didn't know before, but she is an artist. She does incredibly bright, vibrant oil paintings. I love her work. Especially her self-portraits. Especially, of course, her nudes. Lately, she's been working on a portrait of me. We call it Big Chief Running Scared – but that's sort of a joke. I look a bit like Tarzan, wild and fierce and fearless. It's going slowly, though. Whenever I'm posing for it, things start to happen.

As for the other stuff...

The day after we got back to her house, Cat had the bedroom carpet removed. Then she called the police and reported her car stolen. A pleasant, polite officer came out the next day and wrote up a theft report.

There have been no police since then.

There have been no visits at all from Elliot, Peggy, or Donny.

We were both a little nervous about them at first. For a couple of weeks, we only slept during daylight hours. At night, we made love and had cocktails and ate great meals and read books and watched TV and talked and laughed a lot and made love and kept hammers and sharp-pointed stakes within easy reach.

Nobody showed up.

So then we tried sleeping at night. It was hard to do. I would lie awake for hours, staring into the darkness, listening. And I could tell by the sounds of her breathing that Cat was awake, too.

Elliot didn't show up.

Neither did Peggy or Donny.

They probably never will.

We don't have much trouble sleeping anymore.

Sometimes, we talk about hopping into our new Range Rover and driving out to the desert – up the steep slope and into the pass where we left the three of them.

We haven't done it yet though.

I don't think we'll ever get around to it.

We won't admit it to each other, but I guess we're both a little nervous about what we might find up there.

Or not find.